The Accidental Duchess

JESSICA BENSON

The Accidental Duchess

POCKET BOOKS

New York   London   Toronto   Sydney

An *Original* Publication of POCKET BOOKS

 POCKET BOOKS, a division of Simon & Schuster, Inc.
1230 Avenue of the Americas, New York, NY 10020

ISBN: 0-7394-4082-9

Designed by Melissa Isriprashad

Front cover illustration by Tsukushi

Manufactured in the United States of America

To Vanessa,
who made it possible on a daily basis

Acknowledgments

I would like to thank my amazing agent Laura Langlie, without whom everything I've ever written would be gathering dust on a shelf somewhere, and who routinely goes above and beyond the call of duty; and, equally, my editor, Amy Pierpont, without whose wisdom and guidance it would all be gathering dust on a shelf at 300,000 words with no plot.

In addition, my deepest thanks to Eloisa James, Frances Lynch (who would like all letters about historical inaccuracies sent directly to her), Megan Frampton, and my husband—who did lots of weekend duty.

1

In which I accidentally marry and am very nearly seduced by the wrong man

I married the wrong man.

And by this I do not mean, as people so often do, any of the more cryptic things that you might imagine: That I awoke one morning to the realization that my husband and I had grown apart. That I discovered something about my spouse that caused me to doubt that we were well-suited. Nor, even, that I had met by chance an old love in Bond Street. And as I shopped for reticules and he carried an armload of packages for his wife, our eyes met and it was as though the intervening years in which we had both found others had never been.

What I do mean is that yesterday I stood up in St. George's, Hanover Square, and before some three hundred witnesses promised to love, honor, and obey the *wrong* man.

Put that way, even I must confess that it contrives to

make me sound rather, well, like a fool. A complete and utter idiot. It is not as simple a case as it appears at first glance, however, and I would beg that you bear with me while I explain. I will also say that simply marrying him was not the worst of it, that before the day was done, things had got much, much worse, indeed.

I'd been at the time in the suite bespoke by my new husband at the Clarendon Hotel. We had made our arrival a short time previous, and in a rush of high spirits had laughingly discarded bonnets, hats, and gloves, and I with a great deal of relief, my new slippers, which I had been duly assured looked stunning, but pinched rather horribly. We were awaiting the light supper that Milburn had ordered. The table in front of the fire in the sitting room sparkled with crystal and white linen. We were awkwardly silent at the moment, the reprieve offered by the nervous giddiness of our arrival having faded.

Milburn had drawn back the heavy silk draperies. He stood now in his shirtsleeves, looking out into the falling darkness, his face reflected in the window. And, he was of a sudden looking alarmingly pensive. I stood some distance behind him. The carpet felt almost wickedly plush through my stockings, and as I wiggled my newly liberated toes, I debated whether to speak, or approach him, or simply leave him to his thoughts. As I looked at his reflection, it hit me suddenly, and with particular force, that I had married an uncommonly beautiful man. And with that thought came the considerably less welcome one that, in truth, I barely knew him.

Just as I was deciding to leave him to his thoughts, he looked up and caught sight in the glass, of me, standing irresolute behind him. He turned and smiled at me then, and held out his hand, saying simply, "Gwen."

I went to him, almost without thought, and he took my hand. "Forgive me," he said, "for abandoning you for my thoughts. It was ill-done of me."

"Yes. Now that you are leg-shackled you shall never again have license to be alone in your thoughts." I was attempting to lighten the moment. But oddly, as I stood beside him and looked out at the street, I felt I could sense something of his mood of a moment ago. Darkness was falling over the busy streets. It was that time of early evening when the sky is dark blue and the lamps are being lit, both inside and out, which can bring on that curious melancholy of a dying day. Behind us, the fire crackled, pleasantly emphasizing the contrast between the peacefulness of our luxurious rooms with the bustle of Mayfair outside.

The atmosphere of intimacy in the room made me very much aware that I had never been so *alone* with him before, even when I had been alone with him. And the feel of his hand on mine—ungloved—was sparking the oddest sensations. It was the first time in my adult life that my hand had touched a man's without at least one pair of gloves between us, and I was entranced by the way his felt. It was firm and warm and pleasantly rough against my palm and around my fingers. He moved his thumb, slightly, and something flickered inside me. Not unlike the way the wick of a candle sputters momentarily before it lights fully.

"Odd, is it not?" Milburn said at last, still looking out the window.

It seemed we were of one mind on that, at least. "Prodigiously," I replied, distracted from contemplation of his hand. My gaze sliding to him, I watched a dimple appear in his left cheek.

He turned toward me then, and smiled, but still with a somber, reflective air. "But not bad, I would hope?"

"No," I said, also quite seriously. "Only strange. After all this time to be . . . here . . ." I trailed off with a little lift of my shoulders.

He put his hands on my shoulders then, very lightly, but still I could feel the warmth of his skin through the fabric of my gown, and said, "I know. S'truth, Gwendolyn. I never thought to be standing here with you. On our wedding day."

Which I took to be a reference to war and its vagaries. And I was struck yet again by how different he was now as a man than the boy I remembered. By how much more gravity he possessed. Before I could summon a suitable reply, though, he took me by surprise, lowering his head to mine, and very slowly brushing his thumb over my lower lip. And then, without leaving me a moment to examine the startling effects of that action, he kissed me. Actually, he didn't so much kiss me as brush his closed lips across my mouth before lifting his head from mine. I looked up at him.

"Gwen," he said, a slow smile beginning.

My toes seemed to curl deeper into the carpet and my stays, to tighten. I nodded awkwardly, uncertain what he was expecting of me.

He was still smiling, looking somewhat rueful as he repeated my name. "Gwen." His voice sounded rough, not smooth and mellow as it had, and something almost like fear, and yet pleasurably not quite like fear, shot through me. His gaze was locked on my face. "You are so beautiful," he said.

Now, I had heard that from many gentlemen in my life. My friend Cecy and I even had a joke between us that the phrase was actually a botched translation from ancient Greek, meaning, "I do believe I am in love with your dowry. I have heard it's enormous." But Milburn, as of this morning, already had possession of my dowry, and had no need to flatter me.

While I have never precisely shuddered at my own appearance, it is hardly remarkable. My hair is dark, and so straight and slippery that I had long ago given up trying to get it to agree to conform to the current fashion of ringlets. My eyes are dark, too, and sort of almond-shaped. My nose is straight and neither too large nor too small, and my mouth is generous, but nothing out of the ordinary way. My teeth are rather fine—I have always considered them one of my better attributes—straight and white, my neck is graceful enough to show to advantage in the current fashions. And I have that typically English fairness that shows to advantage when I am in high spirits and good health.

But never before had a husband told me I was beautiful. And suddenly, I wanted, in an unaccountably desperate fashion, to believe that he meant his words. "I am?" I said.

He smiled. "Yes," he said, leaning closer. He brushed his lips over my cheekbone. And then he pulled me to him and kissed me. Really kissed me this time, with an unhurried thoroughness. My body, of its own volition, seemed to sway toward him. And, as though in response, he took my lower lip and teased it lightly between his teeth for the barest instant. The flicker jolted into a flame. And then, he stopped.

"I go too fast," he said. "And surely the food must be here at any moment."

He was waiting—for a reply?—an encouraging smile on his face. But my knees were shaky, my stomach felt odd, and my mind was decidedly sluggish. I looked at him again, and his brow was slightly raised. He had said *something,* I knew. But what, exactly? Food! He had said the food must be here at any moment. "I should think," I managed to say, sounding credibly clearheaded.

"A pity," he said. But I must still have been looking blank, because he added, as he took my hand, "About the imminent arrival. Of the food."

"Er, yes," I managed. "I suppose." I tried not to look down at our hands joined together.

"Of course," he said, stepping closer again, taking my other hand, and lacing his fingers through mine, "we *could* send the supper away. Tell them to bring it back later."

I swallowed. This was my chance. I could say no, that I was hungry, and I would have the reprieve I *should* want. "Yes," I said, without any cooperation from my mind. "We could."

"But then"—he leaned closer still, his voice pitched low—"perhaps we should simply seize the moment." He pulled me nearer and, despite my nerves, I felt not one iota of desire to push him away.

Words seemed to have deserted me entirely, as did any part of me that didn't want this. I nodded, unable to tear my gaze from his hypnotic eyes.

He took me in his arms then, and I was startled by the sensation of a man's body actually against my own; it certainly surpassed an ungloved hand, which I had thought pretty marvelous just a few moments ago. He was firm and warm through the linen of his shirt. Heat seemed to radiate from his body. And his pulse, to my surprise, matched my own. Without thinking, I put my hand between us, resting it over his heart. "It's beating so fast," I said, after a moment.

He laughed. "I'm nervous as hell, Gwen," he said, flatly.

"You?" I declined to take him to task for his language, instead looking up and watching with fascination as the dimple reappeared. "*You* are nervous?"

"You have no idea," he said, pulling me closer to his body. And this time, as his lips met mine, there was no hesitation there. We had tacitly agreed, and now there was something heated and dangerous openly flaming between us. But he didn't hurry, instead lingering, prolonging the moment. His lips traveled down my jaw, his motions surprisingly deliberate for a man with shaking hands. "It's my first wedding night, too," he said, his mouth finally against mine, the movement of his lips increasing the pleasurable sensation.

His breath was warm against my skin. My body, already against his, was straining to get closer. Still unhurried, he traced the top of my upper lip with the tip of his tongue, which should have been entirely shocking. I *was* shocked. And more than anything, I wanted him to do it again. But his lips had wandered to my earlobe, and his teeth nipped at it. *Oh,* I thought, as the flaming sensation took up residence in my midriff.

And then he stopped, and I almost cried out with disappointment. I desperately wanted him to continue those wondrous kisses. And, well, the nibbling, I suppose. But I was unresisting, as he turned me again to face the window.

It was darker now, and our reflections were more clearly pronounced. He stood behind me and our gazes met in the window glass. Still watching our reflection, he began, slowly, pulling the pins from my hair. Which, being my hair, was already doing its best to slip out of them of its own volition. Milburn had touched my hair before, but that was seven-and-ten years ago, and at the time he and his equally odious brother were attempting to plant a garden snail in it. Certainly I had not guessed that having his hands on me would someday be the most consuming sensation I had ever experienced. As he continued, carefully holding the pins in one hand, I was seized by the simultaneous, and conflicting, desires both to lie down and drowse, and to turn and press myself back up against the warmth of him, even closer than before. Which I found most confusing.

My hair was completely unpinned now. It fell heavily to my shoulders as I had, in a disastrously misguided move, cut it short two years ago and only now was it growing long again.

"It used to be longer, as I recall," he said, as he placed the pins on the windowsill next to us. "And, as I also recall, frequently had mud or some even less salubrious substance in it."

"I cut it," I told him, striving to find some corner of my mind that had not given in entirely to the languorous feeling that was stealing over my body, and could still converse. I should have been terrified by what was about to happen. I knew that. Instead it seemed that I was possessed of a hitherto unsuspected wanton streak, because I quite simply, shockingly, just wanted more. I only wished that I wasn't too shy to touch him as I ached to. "Two years back," I managed to say. "Because it was . . . ah, the fashion."

"I see," he said gravely. He pushed his hands into my hair and, starting with his fingers at the base of my scalp, lifted it onto the top of my head. He let go, slowly, and it felt as if I could feel each and every strand of hair fall. I wanted to moan aloud. And I was starting to become obsessed by the desire to touch him in return, to feel his body up against mine. He moved my hair so it hung over one shoulder, his fingers brushing the top of my spine as he did so. I shivered.

"But it's not seen mud intimately in many a year," I felt compelled to remind him. "And you, sir, are most unkind to recall it."

"I like it just this length," he said, as he bent so his lips were at the base of my neck. "Just exactly as it is. Unfashionable. With or without the mud." His breath was warm, feather-light, on the back of my neck.

My eyes were closed now. "Thank you," I managed, on a sigh.

"My pleasure." His lips moved over the place where my neck met my collarbone.

I was beginning to worry in some corner of my mind, that far from being an appropriately blushing maiden, stricken by bride nerves, I was going to prove a shockingly willing wife. Possibly, even scandalously so.

His hand strayed to my top button, at the nape of my neck. With the barest movement of his fingers, the little pearl fastening slipped free. My breath caught. He was undressing me!

I should speak. Object. This was not at all the way it should be done! Not here, like this, *standing* in the sitting room. Surely the supper would be here soon! But no words came. And when he ran his finger lightly up and down the half inch of skin that his action had bared, I had to forcibly restrain myself from purring like a cat. I was holding my breath, halfway between fearing and anticipating the release of the next button.

"Are you afraid, Gwen?" he murmured, his lips warm against my skin.

Since my eagerness to find out what would come next was positively unseemly, *afraid* somehow didn't seem quite the right word. My gaze met his in the window once again, and I found I could not dissemble. "Not half so afraid as I should be," I said.

He laughed aloud. "Good," he said. "A terrified bride would doubtless be the undoing of me." His lips again brushed the back of my neck, making my knees soft, as his hand came to rest on my waist. He held it there for a moment, and as I watched, he moved it slowly and deliberately upward until he was just barely touching my breast. I felt the contact with a jolt through the silk of my gown. I could see his hand, reflected in the window, big and sure over the fabric, and knowing that if I were to look down I could see the same thing in reality made my breath come faster.

His fingers moved, and when the fire crackled in the grate behind us, I felt the resulting shower of sparks in my stomach. An odd, strangled little noise came out of my throat. Our gazes met again. His eyes were dark and wild; my own looked oddly unfocused. His hair was falling over his forehead. And he was watching me watch him.

His hand cupped my breast, and this time, I moaned. He closed his eyes for a second, and I could feel him draw in a long breath. I knew it wasn't ladylike, or anything that was proper, but I was helpless not to; I leaned back against him, and let my head fall back on his chest. He shuddered, behind me.

I was behaving like the veriest wanton—pushing my body against him, watching his hand on my breast. And I simply didn't care. I pressed back harder. He held my gaze and that hand hardly moved as we both watched it, yet its very presence seemed to make me boneless.

He turned me around then, and pulled me roughly into his arms so I was up against the heavenly, terrifying, length of him. "Oh God, Gwen," he said, and the timbre, the roughness of his voice, seemed to actually *touch* my skin. He covered my mouth with his, hard this time.

"Bertie," I said, against his mouth, and I could hear that my voice held the same urgency as his had.

And then he let go of me and abruptly took a step back.

I blinked, wanting to say, *No! Please! Don't stop now.* My arms went out instinctively, to pull him back, but something in his face made my hands fall to my sides as well.

"What did you say?" His face was taut.

I tried not to let my puzzlement show as I reached around in the recesses of my drugged mind, trying to figure out what had upset him, and to recall what I had said, even. What on *earth* had I said? "Bertie?" I ventured, frowning up at him. "Bertie?" Not the most original thing to say in the situation, I supposed, but it had at the time seemed a fitting enough response to *Oh God, Gwen.*

I tried to read the expression in his eyes. Could it be that I had been too seduced by the surprising ease between us, and by the . . . well, seduction? Did he prefer that I address him by his title even when we were private? That would be the usual way of things, it was true, but still, it rankled me that I had been in his arms losing myself in the most shocking manner, and he was quibbling over forms of address. The silence stretched on between us. "Do you prefer Milburn?" I asked, finally. "Or Lord Bertie?"

"Not when we are private," he said. "Of course not."

I hoped I didn't look as befuddled as I felt. Not Bertie, not Milburn. What, then? I'd had a few nicknames for him in our youth, but in our current circumstances, both

Puddle-Drawers and Spawn of Satan seemed singularly unsuitable.

He took my hand, and answered my unvoiced question. "When it's us, just us—" he gestured around at the intimate room—"do you think you could call me Harry, or Cambourne at the least?"

Which was, well, to put it bluntly, one of the most—no, *the* most—bizarre request I'd ever heard. I disengaged my hand from his. "You would like to be called Harry," I said. "I see"—although I did *not* see. "But why?"

"Gwen," he said in reasonable enough tones, "surely *no* man wants to be called by his brother's name in an . . . intimate situation?"

I took a step back as I began to absorb what he had said.

"It is necessary elsewhere, but surely not here, like this—"

I simply could not believe what I was hearing. "You," I managed to say. "You are . . ." And that was as much as my mind seemed able to come up with.

"Gwen?" He looked confused as he took a step toward me.

I took a corresponding step back. "You—You're *Cambourne?*" I was finally able to articulate.

He looked wary. "Yes."

"But you *can't* be Cambourne. I would have—" And then I stopped, and stared at him. He was watching me carefully. Would I really have known? And then, just like that, with an almost audible click of my brain, everything, the entire day, slid into place and I understood.

And I could see, reflected on his face, the exact moment that he read my thoughts. "Oh my Lord," he said, bleakly. "You didn't know! They didn't tell you."

I just stared. "No."

"You thought I was Milburn! You *really* thought I was Milburn?" There was something in his tone that made me understand that he thought if he said it enough times, he might believe it. One of us might believe it.

I nodded as I looked, despite myself, at the pile of discarded hairpins on the windowsill. I had behaved like a light-skirt with Milburn's *brother!* I closed my eyes for a moment.

And I suspect he was having much the same thought, because when I opened my eyes, he took a step back. "All this time," he said, sounding stricken, "all this time you thought I was Milburn? *Bertie?* When we——"

He dropped to a chair and put his head in his hands. I stood, still rooted to the spot by the window. "I thought you knew," he said, looking down at the carpet. "I thought you had agreed."

He looked so utterly miserable that I almost felt sorry for him. Almost. But somehow the fact that I had been more or less panting in his arms a few moments ago was adding an edge of an entirely different emotion. "Agreed? Knew? That you——that you are *Cambourne?*" I said.

He nodded. "That I was only pretending to be Milburn."

"But why would I—— And you believed that I would allow——" I closed my eyes again. First of all, I was not entirely certain that I wanted to know what he believed. And quite honestly, I suppose I was hoping that when I opened them again this would turn out to be some type of delusion. He stayed silent while I tried to sort my words and wished he'd disappear. A fresh wave of humiliation washed over me. There was simply no getting around it: I had behaved like a common whore in his arms. "You certainly weren't *pretending* to seduce me," I said, at last.

"No." His voice was quiet. He was extremely still. "Forgive me. At the time it had not occurred to me that you were unwilling."

I laughed. I was bordering on hysterics, and I knew it. "Yes, I can see that," I said, disliking the way my own voice was rising. "Because under the impression that you were my *husband* and this was my wedding night, I behaved far too willingly?" And then, I started to cry. I wiped the tears away on the back of my hand.

He stood, and put out a hand. "Gwen," he said, in let's-be-reasonable tones, but I was having none of it. I was starting to sob in earnest.

I could see my reflection mirrored in the window. Tears were running unchecked down my face. My skin was blotchy. My eyes were red, my nose, redder. I turned and faced him. His dark hair was still disarranged, falling across his arrogant forehead. His improbably blue eyes were dark under straight brows, and his jaw was very square at the moment. He looked every inch the duke that he would some day be. And it hit me with the force of a blow: How on earth had I *ever* thought he was Milburn? How stupid could a person be?

I suppose it would be reasonable, at this point, were you to wonder how I could have ended up being quite so stupid. But understanding the situation requires going back a little way.

This was never, you must know, a love match. Milburn and I had been promised to each other likely since the week I was born. Milburn, who is Lord Bertie, and Harry, who is, as I have mentioned, the Earl of Cambourne and future Duke of Winfell, grew up at Marshfields, principal seat to the Dukes of Winfell since the days of Queen

Elizabeth. Give or take a year. And I was raised next door at Hildcote.

As my hapless brothers, Richard and James, ran tame with Milburn and Cambourne, so did I. Lord knows, over the years I'd seen a vast succession of nursemaids and governesses, and then later tutors and schoolmasters bamboozled by their tricks—among which, switching identities held pride of place. But for most of my life, I had possessed the unfailing ability to tell them apart. A lot of good this lifelong ability had done me, however, since it had obviously failed me at that crucial moment when I had stood at the altar and sworn faithfully in front of God and some three hundred witnesses to love, honor, and obey *the wrong man.*

And now, a new, even worse thought hit me. "Does Milburn *know* about this?" I demanded.

He moved a step closer, almost as you would approach a horse you were trying to gentle.

"Don't touch me! This is a joke, isn't it? One of your vile little twin practical jokes. Seduce your brother's wife? Oh God."

"Gwen," he said, very quietly, "I realize that you've had a shock, but surely you cannot believe what you just said?"

"I don't know what to believe," I whispered.

"Perhaps, then, I can enlighten you."

"No!" It might have been childish, but I had no desire to hear him. "Please leave me."

"I can't do that."

"Oh yes, you can."

"I see." He studied me unhurriedly. "I had thought better of you," he said lightly, and I was stung.

"But . . . Milburn . . ." *Does he care?* was what I badly

wanted to ask, but was afraid to hear the answer. At the thought that he very well might not, my tears started afresh. "Where *is* he?"

He stood for a moment, his back still to me, and took a breath. "I do not know," he said, as he turned to me. His face was carefully neutral.

I eyed him. How could he not know? "But we—us—I am truly married to *you?*"

"Yes," he said, with no trace of hesitation.

"Not to Milburn."

"No."

"But how could that be? It is not as though you have the same name, after all, for all that they are similar. . . ." I stared at him, and he was silent, I suppose allowing me to work it out. "It was *your* name!" I said, almost lost in wonder at my own stupidity. "Reverend Twigge said your name and I never even noticed?"

He nodded.

"Edmund Harold Bertram is you," I said, more to myself than to him. "And Edward Henry Bernard is Milburn, and still, they called him Bertie. I knew that, of course. But somehow I just . . ." I trailed off and looked at him. "Didn't notice, I suppose. And you thought—you thought I had *agreed* to this?"

He nodded. "I'm afraid so, Gwen," he said, very quietly.

"We can have it annulled, though?" I asked, and understood all too well the meaning when he hesitated. "Leave," I said to him. "I only want you to leave."

Don't misunderstand. I knew I was being unreasonable. I also knew that I had larger problems, but at the moment I simply could not get over my humiliation, both at his deception and my own behavior. My practically flinging myself at a man might have been excusable, if slightly overwarm, for my wedding night. My doing the same with the *wrong* man, was not.

"Gwen——" he began, and I cut him off.

"Not tonight. Just leave."

"Are you certain that's what you want?"

I nodded, despite the fact that I wasn't.

He looked at me, and I was uncomfortably aware of a hard-edged will beneath the surface. He seemed to me, though, to have decided to keep it submerged, because he took a deep breath and capitulated. "Right," he said, beginning to move toward the door with obvious reluctance.

And now, here we are, at my lowest moment: As he started to walk away, it occurred to me. My dress was unbuttoned. I had no maid and there was no question of me being able to button it myself. I had no choice. "Cambourne?"

"Yes?" He turned from the door.

"My, um . . ." I gestured at my back. "I cannot."

He crossed back to me. I could not for the life of me understand why the Earl of Cambourne, future Duke of Winfell, would have married me under false pretenses. But I also was too humiliated and too stubborn to allow him to explain himself. Unattractive, I know, but regrettably true. As his nimble fingers closed my buttons, I began to sob again. "Were you *pretending* to want me, too?" I shouldn't have asked, but I couldn't stop myself.

His hands still lingered on the last button as he turned me toward him. "No," he said, and then he kissed me. Hard.

There was no question at this point but that I was not going to be seduced by his kiss. Not even a little. But— and here is the absolute nadir of the humiliation part—my body wanted him still. And enough, even, to overrule my mind. As his mouth closed on mine, my knees seemed to disintegrate along with my will, and that hot, shaking excitement in my stomach that had so recently been stirred within me for the first time, started again. My arms, of their own volition, went to him.

After a moment, though, he lifted his head and stood looking down at me. I thought he might say something.

I waited a moment and hoped I wasn't panting. He didn't speak. But then, he hardly needed to. My response to his kiss had said plenty. "How could you?" I asked, trying to banish the light-headedness in favor of righteous indignation.

But his tone was equable. "Perhaps you'd best ask your parents. In the meantime, I'll have a maid sent up to help you." And then he left, striding out of our suite and closing the door very deliberately behind him in a manner that led me to believe that he was restraining himself from giving it a really good, satisfying kick.

2

In which I was married

I *dare say, I know precisely what you are thinking:*

How could this have happened? How on earth could she have ended up in that suite and almost in the bed of the wrong man? *Is* she the idiot she claims not to be, after all?

Well, *this* is how.

Two years of soldiering had changed Milburn was my perfectly reasonable thought upon sighting him. I was, at the time, standing in the vestibule of the church looking down the aisle, and he was standing straight and tall and surprisingly solemn in front of the altar.

It had not been my intention, certainly, not to lay eyes upon Milburn until the ceremony. But then, it had not been my intention to be marrying him this year at all. I mean, I always knew I would be marrying him some day. But the moment, to my mind, had not yet arrived. He was off soldiering (which seemed a fairly unlikely career for him, but never mind) and I was spending some time in London enjoying myself. Or, at least, I had been, right up until the Unfortunate Incident on the Stainsteads' terrace six months previous.

It was a lazy June evening, and their ballroom, lit with what seemed like a thousand tapers, was sweltering. There was a crush of overperfumed, underbathed bodies, and so, when Lord Trafford offered to take me out to the terrace for some air, in place of the quadrille I had promised him, I accepted. I should have known better.

I was three-and-twenty, and had strolled my share of secluded gardens and terraces. And even been kissed a few times. Rather sweetly once or twice by Milburn, in fact. But that's neither here nor there. In Trafford's case, when he launched himself upon me, pressing his wet mouth over mine, I was taken aback enough to sag against the wall, which is when we were spotted by Mother's mortal enemy, Mrs. Haworth.

Despite her dislike for my mother, the old harridan promised not to breathe a word. A promise she adhered to most firmly, except for the two or three hundred of her closest friends to whom she happened to *accidentally* impart the news. Needless to say, next thing I knew, the wedding was being planned. We had to wait six months (but not a day more), Mother had decreed, to prove to Society that it was not a *necessary* wedding, and then do the thing with great pomp and circumstance. To that end, Father bade Milburn return from wherever he was in time for the nuptials, and Milburn sent a return missive agreeing.

I was not unduly alarmed by the fact that this was followed neither by further correspondence nor an immediate appearance. I knew Milburn well enough to know that he would cut his arrival as close as possible. I was also enough of a realist to anticipate that his first days at home would be entirely occupied with heartfelt reunions with his tailor, haberdasher, bootmaker, pomade merchant, vintner, snuff blender, club members, and racing cronies.

But I was hardly looking for loverlike devotion from him. Milburn, I had long accepted, was Milburn. And what lay between us was indisputably quiet rather than passionate. While I never had difficulty accepting that we would wed, my pulse had never exactly quickened at the thought of him. I wasn't much bothered by that fact, though. I mean, I hadn't much experience at pulse quickening—except courtesy of the odd Minerva Press volume, and it was *comfortable,* being promised to him.

Other girls I knew dreamed of grand passions, and a few did make love matches. An awful lot, though, seemed to end up shackled to some horrible old man or some young care-for-naught in order to shore up their fathers' pockets. Seen from that perspective, marriage to Milburn didn't seem undesirable in the least.

He was a trifle lazy, perhaps, in his conversation and his demeanor. And it was true that he could always be relied upon to be not quite on time. If a really good lark was thought up, for example, or some splendid waistcoat fabric arrived at his tailor's, he might decide it imperative that he attend to that exigency, possibly forgetting to cancel previously made plans. But that was just Milburn, and I had no difficulty accepting that he would be my husband. And as my days before the wedding were well occupied, I hardly had time to refine upon his continued absence.

So there I stood, on my wedding day, clutching my father's arm. My eyes fixed on Milburn, and my breath unaccountably seemed to stick behind my ribs. "Are we *going,* Gwendolyn?" Father had asked gruffly at the very moment I was realizing that I was having difficulty exhaling. "Today?"

There was a sea of expectant faces turned toward me. My dearest friends, Cecy, Lady Barings, and Myrtia Conyngham had taken up their places, and my brothers stood next to Milburn. I wondered for the merest fragment of a second where Cambourne was. Alas, how easy it is to see irony in hindsight. At the time, however, this did not so much as touch off the slightest frisson of alarm.

And, anyway, I was far too busy being terrified to be alarmed. My knees were literally knocking. Milburn, there was no getting around it, just seemed indefinably different, from his clothing to his bearing. I'm not sure what exactly I'd been expecting. That he'd be rigged out in his finest, I suppose—something in a bottle green, perhaps, or a nice primrose brocade, topped off by a work of art of a cravat. But not this grown-up Milburn in a sober rigout and austerely perfect linen. Too, he seemed more substantial somehow.

Oh, he was the same height that I recalled, a shade over six feet, and had the same dark hair, which, I noted, was straight and falling across his forehead instead of fashionably tousled and curled as had been his wont. His mouth, well, I suppose I'd never really thought about it, because surely it was much more finely shaped than it had been before—fuller and firmer. I was suddenly, oddly, aware of a pang of anticipation at the thought that he would soon be my husband. That he would kiss me to seal the ceremony. And with that awareness came a little catch in my breathing, as though I had slid down a banister with my eyes shut, as I used to when I was little.

Milburn's eyes were still that bright shade of blue that I

remembered, but instead of his usual open expression, one brow was lifted just a little, as if our wedding was a shared private joke between us. And the glint in them was positively wicked. I wondered, for a moment, whether he was also thinking about the moment when he would kiss me. Perhaps, I thought, as his gaze seemed to tip off a sudden lurch of excitement, this is how all bridegrooms look at their brides.

Mother, to be sure, had not mentioned anything about sudden lurches of excitement in her talk with me last night. "Have you any questions, Gwendolyn?" she asked, from my bedchamber door, in a manner brisk enough so as to completely discourage any. "About the *proceedings?*"

It was not that I knew *nothing*. I had, after all, been at school, and there, the topic of what went on between men and their wives had been the subject of numerous fascinating conversations. And, come to think of it, many subsequent, but no less fascinating conversations, with Cecy.

"Actually," I began, "I do have—"

Mother sighed. "I've several cabinet ministers coming to dine, and have only a few moments to spare, so please do listen carefully the first time as I've no intention of repeating myself. Now: There are two pertinent things you need to know," she said. "*One* is: do not allow your night rail to get crumpled, no matter what, Gwendolyn. As then the servants might think you are quite common and look at you with impertinence."

"But what I—"

She held up her hand. "Please, allow me to finish. *Two,* is far more pertinent. It is to bear in mind that wanton feelings have no place in what will happen. This is a matter of authority to be established at the first, for it sets the tone for your entire marriage. It is a favor that you shall grant, and in so doing, establish your sovereignty in your marriage. Now. One assumes that your husband knows what he is about, but goodness knows, your father didn't and still doesn't and we have survived these many years." She turned. "To think! Your wedding! I vow, I am feeling most sentimental," she said as she sailed down the stairs without a backward glance.

No, not even so much as a word on little tingles of anticipation.

I tried to remember whether Barings had looked thusly at my best friend, Cecy. But then, I'd been preoccupied at the time with fulfilling my duties as bridesmaid: keeping Cecy's mother in hand. Which office, I am pleased to say, I fulfilled in a wildly successful manner, until she hiked up her skirts and sang a rousing refrain of "Pretty Peggy of Derby," from atop a table.

There was, to return to the subject of *my* wedding, something about Milburn's gaze that suddenly made me feel older, surer, as though I were suddenly possessed of a new, secret piece of knowledge that I had not held yesterday. In retrospect, this, of course, is a great joke on me.

I took up my place next to him, and I struggled to keep my breathing normal as my chest seemed to be constricting inward. For one horrifying second I worried that my odd physical state was apparent to everyone, that my breath might be ratcheting as audibly through the church as it was to my own ears. Then I realized that the sound was only the Reverend Mr. Twigge engaging in a lengthy bout of throat-clearing in preparation for a lecture on the sanctity of humility within the sacred bond of matrimony. And then, to my surprise, Milburn reached out and took my hand in his clasp. A gesture that he needn't have made, but one that I much appreciated. His hand, even through his glove, and my glove, felt sure and strong. It managed somehow to help settle the churning in my stomach and accelerate my heart at the same time.

As Mr. Twigge started on the ceremony, Milburn looked down at me for a long moment, holding my gaze, and still, my hand. And I had a quick flash of wonderment that in the future I would sit through many Sunday sermons at this man's side. I smiled tentatively at him, feeling unaccountably shy. Surely I had never felt shy with him before? He smiled back, the smile suddenly lighting his face. His hand tightened on mine, and everything seemed to blur.

"Wilt thou have this Woman to thy wedded Wife, to live together after God's ordinance in the holy estate of Matrimony? Wilt thou love her, comfort her, honor, and keep her in sickness and in health; forsaking all others, keep thee only unto her, so long as ye both shall live?" Mr. Twigge asked.

Milburn looked into my eyes and said, very clearly and seriously, holding my gaze all the while, "I will."

And God help me, he seemed to mean it. I'd more expected a quick smirk and a, *Right ho. So long as she doesn't run to fat or become a shrew like her mother, I will,* than this dead serious vow.

Then I spoke my words, and it seemed only a moment later that Reverend Twigge said that we were married. And, no, in case you are wondering, I noticed absolutely nothing amiss. But I was caught in the moment, and truthfully, in Milburn's eyes, which were having a very odd effect on me. So when he said, as he must have done, Edmund Harold Bertram Milburn instead of Edwin Henry Bernard Milburn, it didn't raise any feeling of alarm. I do know, for a fact, though, that Mr. Twigge did ask the congregation whether any man could show just cause as to why we might not be lawfully joined together in Matrimony. And if so, *let him now speak, or else hereafter forever hold his peace.* And no one, not one person, so much as squeaked, let alone said, *he's the wrong bridegroom.*

So there you have it. I am not a *complete* idiot. Or at least not as much as it appears at first glance. And besides, in my own defense, there were *Circumstances.*

Or at least, there were according to Mother's bosom bow, Violetta Egglesham, Lady Worth: *"Circumstances,"* she said, both darkly and knowingly, but that is for later. For the moment, I shall tell you what happened next.

3

In which we have a very odd wedding breakfast

As we walked back up the aisle to sign the register, Milburn looked down at me, his eyes alight. "Hullo, Gwen," he said.

"Hullo, Milburn," I replied.

Our first unscripted words as man and wife. Not exactly romantic, and yet, somehow suitable. In all our years apart I have had precisely three letters from Milburn, none longer than a paragraph, one of which stands out in my mind as being the very essence of him. It said: *What hey, the weather is foul, the wine is bordering on passable, and there is not so much as a drop of decent boot-blacking to be found. Vastly muddy country, this. Regards to your brothers and, should you bump into him, Stinker Boxhurst. Yrs, Milburn.*

And that, sadly, constitutes both the sum of my love letters, and of Milburn's profound correspondence about the bleak realities of war and the anguish of our separation.

Yes, all things considered, *Hullo, Gwen,* seemed about
right.

We signed the register. My neat hand above his scrawl,
and then no sooner had we put the quills down, but
Milburn bent to me. "Shall we take our leave?" he said,
very close to my ear.

I looked at him. "You don't mean now?"

"I do mean now," he replied, with something in his
voice, an undertone that made my pulse jump.

"But the . . . our guests—" I began to object, recalling
how many hours Mama and Violetta had spent debating
the size of the lobster patties, the flavors of the ices, and
the best sources of smuggled champagne.

Milburn, however, wasn't listening. He was smiling,
glinting some kind of wickedness at me, and suddenly I
knew I would not refuse him. "Forget our guests," he said.
"Come, Gwen, don't you think we can be excused from
doing the proper?"

He came a little closer. "No one will remark it. They
will simply think us . . . eager," he said in my ear, and
again my pulse seemed to skitter. Milburn raised my hand,
and turning it over, kissed my palm through the glove, his
gaze never leaving mine as he did so.

"Oh!" I said, startled, and pulled my hand back.

He smiled and said, "You prefer, then, to attend the
breakfast?"

The truth is, it was a token objection and I had known,
even as I protested, that I would prefer to be alone with
him. I could hardly say that, however, so, instead, I said,
"Er, well, of course not. Not, in fact, that I'm hungry, particularly, at all, of course, and in truth, I've never cared
overmuch for lobster patties—" before bringing myself to
a halt. Really, I was almost cross. Since when had Milburn

had the ability to put me out of countenance? Never. And yet, from the first moment I had laid eyes on him this morning, I had been a wreck.

"No lobster patties, then," he said, softly. "Unless you are concerned that I shall neglect to feed you?"

And suddenly I was fairly certain that we were not talking about lobster patties, after all. "Well, in that case," I replied, my mouth suddenly dry, "I should apprise Mama of our plans. She, you must know," I could not resist adding, "will be most put out with us."

He paused for a second, I assumed at the prospect of Mama's wrath, but only said, "I shall take the blame." His hand rested, warm on my back, and exerted a gentle pressure. "Consider it the first benefit of having a husband."

"Oh, but surely you cannot!" Mama exclaimed in her usual must-be-obeyed tones when we had detached her from Mrs. Foster-Morton and informed her of our plans to depart.

Milburn raised a brow.

"I meant, cannot *wish* to do that," she amended hastily.

And I was pleased to note that it was not just me—that Milburn was clearly having an odd effect on her also. My mother, you must know, is *never* out of countenance.

He flashed her a most engaging smile and I could see her unbend slightly. "W-e-ll," she said, patting her hair and peeping at him from beneath her lashes in what I deemed a most revolting manner. "I suppose you *are* newlyweds, after all. And no sort of mama-in-law would I be, were I to say *no* to your pretty request, my lord."

Then Violetta—who I believe I mentioned previously,

as Mama's constant companion—approached, making no bones about having eavesdropped. "Leaving already, are you?" she said, looking me up and down. "That eager, I suppose." She shook her head.

I blushed and looked down at my slippers poking out from beneath the hem of my gown.

"Yes, well," Milburn said in a completely unruffled manner that I could not help but admire. "We shall be off." He looked at Mother. "Will you send Gwen's things to the Clarendon?"

"The Clarendon?" Violetta said, raising a brow. "Not at home, then?"

It occurred to me to wonder at her surprise, but I dismissed it before it was even a fully formed thought.

"Not at the moment," Milburn replied.

And then, having apparently spotted someone judged in need of haranguing more than we were, Mama and Violetta left us. Milburn took the opportunity afforded by their departure to lean down and whisper into my ear, "Just us tonight."

I managed a smile, but suddenly having acquired a husband seemed more unnerving than one might have supposed it would be. "Am I to bring Larsen?" I asked him. "She was to remove to Milburn House with me as without a maid I shan't be able, you know, I cannot unbutton—" I stopped, aware that my face was flaming.

"I promise, Gwen. I will take care of your every need," he murmured, softly, which did nothing to soothe my blush as we made our exit. No sooner had we reached the bottom of the cathedral steps, however, but a boy came rushing up and said, looking directly at Milburn, "Are you Milburn, sir?"

And Milburn looked at him blankly for a moment,

before replying in a tone that sounded surprised—although, as with so many other things that day, I did not fully remark the significance of that until later—"Ah, yes. Yes, I am!"

"Message for you, sir," the boy said, holding out a document.

Milburn looked at it for a moment, frowning, before he reached over and took it. "Excuse me a moment, my love," he said to me, and moved a few steps away.

That quick, unthinking, *my love* had made my breath catch. Whatever was wrong with me?

Milburn was still frowning, and had not yet unsealed the missive. The boy stood, rocking on his heels, waiting for either a vail or a reply. Suddenly, Milburn seemed to become aware of both of us, me and the boy, watching him. "I beg your pardon," he said, and reached into the pocket of his greatcoat, and then stood, apparently finding nothing there.

And this gesture was just so . . . *Milburn,* that for the first time all day, I felt the comfortable relief of familiarity. I started to open my reticule. Of course Milburn would need me to tip the postboy! I relaxed a bit at this dependably Bertie-ish behavior. Just then, though, he located a guinea in his pocket and handed it to the postboy, who looked as though he could scarce believe his good fortune and took himself off before it could change.

As I stood feeling disgruntled by his lapse once again into adulthood and by my, well, not-neededness, I suppose, he tipped me an apologetic smile before unfolding the letter.

And then, not only was the smile gone as though it had never been, but I could have sworn I heard him mutter an oath under his breath. "I'm sorry, Gwendolyn," he said abruptly. "Something urgent has come up, I'm afraid."

"I'm sorry," I said, since I could think of nothing else. Since when, I wondered, had Milburn had any business at all to attend to? Let alone that of the urgent variety? I was finding this new husband most confusing. It would have been just like him, this change of plans, had he not seemed so very *serious* about it.

"Perhaps you should go on to the breakfast for a time, after all?" he said, his voice gentle. "And I will come and rescue you as soon as I can."

"Do you mean without you?" I asked, wishing my voice didn't sound so plaintive. "By myself?"

He smiled. "Well, hardly by yourself, since I'd numbered your two best friends, most of our relatives, and at least two hundred old tabbies in there. But without me, yes."

I laughed then, despite my discomfort. "Well, when you say it like that, it *does* sound like so attractive a prospect that it is rather difficult to refuse. You *are* certain you've been summoned on urgent business, sir?"

"Never tell me that you have become a cynic!" He looked injured.

"I most certainly have not! Very well, Milburn, I shall just have to trust you for now," I said. And then added, "I warn you, however, that should I learn that the urgent business is a prime blood at Tatt's, or a length of silk at your tailor's, I shall be *most* put out with you."

His eyes crinkled with amusement, but his tone was solemn. "I can assure you," he said, as, his eyes never leaving mine, he picked up my hand, and my skin seemed to come aware of itself beneath the glove, "that I can say with complete honesty that I am compelled to leave for a time." He turned so he was facing me, and slid his hands up the length of my French kid gloves. And for just a moment, his gloved hands brushed over the skin, above where my gloves ended and my sleeves began. "Lady Worth had it exactly—albeit somewhat crudely—correct, Gwen: I'm that eager," he said, looking down into my eyes with a rather astonishing intensity.

I was completely unable to tear my gaze from his. At his words, an alien heat had washed over me, and I rather wished I'd had a fan as part of my wedding ensemble.

"Can you truly believe that anything frivolous could summon me away at this moment?"

I blinked. "I suppose not."

"And mine?" he whispered, the words flowing over me like silk.

"Ah, your what?" I replied, thinking that I could hardly fail to impress with my intelligent conversation. Although, honestly, intelligent conversation had never exactly been Milburn's forte.

"My side," he said, leaning in, slightly closer and offering me a slow smile. "Tell me," he suggested, something in those words making my face grow even hotter, and I was suddenly much alarmed these little lurches of excitement might after all be those wanton feelings that Mama had warned me against, "what it would take to drag you from my side at this moment."

"Um, urgent business on your part. Apparently," I said, recovering something of my wits. "Or possibly a new length of silk."

At this he laughed. A real laugh, and I flushed, with the pleasure of having elicited it.

"It would have to be a truly *excellent* silk, though," I added.

"Ah," he said, drily, "Now you threaten to unman me."

And then he leaned over and kissed me, briefly. More of a brush across my lips with his, really, that left me breathless in its wake. "And surely no man can expect to rate over and above a truly *excellent* silk!"

I laughed. "Well, the excellent stuff, you must know, is quite scarce."

I expected him to laugh also, but he surprised me. His expression was serious as he said, just out of nowhere, "You bring me to my knees, Gwen."

And my stomach seemed to plummet in a way that squeezed my midriff even more. Surely I had never brought Milburn, or anyone, come to think of it, to his knees before? "I do?" I managed to croak. And then I frowned. "Is that a good thing?"

"Oh yes," he said leaning in a little closer, and I was conscious of how wonderful he smelled, all of clean linen, and once again of the odd sensation in my stomach. "An excellent thing. Regretfully, though, I really must go. And . . . Gwen?"

"Yes?" I looked up at him.

"This shall be quick, I'll make sure of it."

And with that, he brought me back up the steps and, with a few words of explanation to Mother, kissed my hand, and was gone. Just like that. Leaving me feeling foggy and perhaps a little resentful. This grown-up Milburn seemed to evoke in me an unsettling mixture of fear, anticipation, and confusion. And oddly, I wanted more of him.

Papa dozed, and Mama and Violetta ignored me entirely as I joined them in the family carriage for the ride back to Axton House and the wedding breakfast. At home we were greeted with a sumptuous repast, of which I could eat nothing, but I smiled, and smiled, and smiled.

And then smiled some more, as I endured both good wishes and what was surely an unnecessary number of jokes on the subject of hastily abandoned brides.

Myrtia and Cecy and her husband, Simon Hounslow, Lord Barings, stayed nearby, and I was grateful for what they did not ask. My brothers were, of course, odious, James saying, "Scared 'im off already, have you, Gwen?" And Richard suggesting that what Milburn deserved was a good pummeling: "Abominable to ill-use you so on your wedding day," he said, with a heartening amount of indignation.

James nodded. "Pity Cambourne's not here. Always was about the only person who could knock some sense of responsible behavior into Milburn."

"Where is he, anyway?" Richard asked, looking around as though expecting Cambourne to pop out of the champagne fountain. They both looked at me.

"I don't know," I replied. His absence was odd, certainly, but hardly seemed my most pressing concern at the moment.

"He must have been needed elsewhere," suggested Barings. "Crucial vote or something."

"Should think it's something like that. Ain't as though he despises you, after all," Richard added, unhelpfully, in my opinion, since he managed to sound surprised that someone might not.

"Don't be ridiculous," I replied. "Cambourne and I get on very well." And then I wondered if I had spoken the entire truth. We *did* get on well on the face of it, but it was indisputable that we had never been as easy together as Milburn and I were.

When our paths crossed in town, as they inevitably did, he always danced with me or brought me lemonade—in short, did the proper. But it was easy to see that

his heart wasn't truly in it. And that I could well understand. I mean, why spend time dancing attendance on a
girl you have known since childhood—who is your
brother's fiancée, to boot—when every gathering is
inevitably filled with much more intriguing women tripping over themselves for an introduction?

"I don't know," Richard mused. "Fellow gets spliced,
his brother should be there. Giving him courage in his
final moments. I'd do it for you," he said to James.

I disregarded my brothers entirely in favor of continuing my musings on my relationship with my new husband's brother. Naturally, there were rumors where he was
concerned. Everywhere Cambourne went, gossip seemed
to eddy in his wake: He was paying marked attention to
this eligible young lady, or had been most flirtatious with
that dashing young widow, or was said to be wooing the
ravishing new opera dancer. It's true that he *was* a favorite
with women. Handsome young earls are not exactly found
under every rock, and everywhere that he went, any number of women made it only too clear that they were happy
to be accommodating.

But if even half of it were true, he would have had to be
the busiest man in England. And since I knew that he
spent a good deal of time seeing to his holdings outside of
London, and an awful lot of time in Parliament when he
was *in* London, I always suspected the rumors of being a
tad overblown.

Oddly, Cambourne was a reliable correspondent. *Much*
better than Milburn, and I had more than the occasional
letter from him. And *that* Cambourne, I was comfortable
with. The one who wrote to me that Mrs. Endicott and
Lady Halstead were feuding again, this time because the
vicar preferred Mrs. Endicott's flowers for church of a

Sunday. Lady Halstead was furious because her younger son was taking orders to become a vicar, and she would think that *she* knew a pious flower when she saw one! Thank you very much!

He wrote when Bertie's favorite mare had birthed a promising foal, or to tell me that the weather was uncommonly fine this spring or that Mrs. Odderly's second daughter up Sussex-way had, finally, after six years of marriage, given her a vigorous grandson. When I put down a sheet of vellum, crossed by his bold but orderly handwriting, I could almost smell the familiar church, or the spring rain at Hildcote, and often was assailed by a quiver of homesickness.

I was recalled to my surroundings by James, saying, "But it's a pity all the same. Doubt Milburn would've managed to slope off that way if Cambourne were here."

"Milburn had urgent business," I reminded them both, coldly. "He did not *slope off.*"

And don't think for a moment that I missed the concerned glance that Cecy and Myrtia exchanged, supposing it to be behind my back. "Of course," Cecy said in soothing tones.

"Hah. He sloped off all right. Since when does Milburn have any business at all, let alone urgent?" Richard scowled. "Trust me. It will turn out to have been a race or a mill or some such. Don't get me wrong," he added. "Excellent fellow. Just not much in the husband line."

"Well, he is now," I said coldly.

Richard raised a skeptical brow.

"Before he left, he told me that I bring him to his knees," I could not resist adding. I did, though, restrain myself saying, *so there!* Why is it that brothers manage to reduce you instantly to your schoolroom days?

"He said that?" said Myrtia. "Milburn said *that?*"

Did she have to sound quite so surprised? "Is it that shocking then?" I asked, surveying their faces, "that I could have that effect on my husband?"

"Dashed right it is," Richard replied, as Myrtia hastened to say, in a kindly way, "Of course not. It's just that it's a bit, well, rather not *like* Milburn. But a man can change a great deal in two years, I daresay," she hastened to add.

"Milburn ain't changed. Mark my words," Richard said, most unhelpfully. "Likely too polite to mention where he really felt knocked." He smirked. "And it ain't got much to do with knees."

"You odious little—" I began, but James put a restraining hand on my arm. "There is no accounting for taste," he said to Richard. And then to me, "Milburn said that? Really, Gwen?" Our eyes met in shared understanding of how uncharacteristic it was.

I nodded. "Yes." And then, before we could explore the subject further, Mother came and dragged me away, scolding me for the shameful way in which I was neglecting my guests.

"I know it for a fact that you have yet to greet the Hampshire cousins. And, moreover, Violetta assures me that you have all but ignored the Countess Esterhazy, which I cannot like, and my goodness, *where* is your father?" She frowned and then steered me firmly in the direction of the Hampshire cousins.

And so it went for no small amount of time. I did the polite, wondering all the while where Milburn had gone, until, able to bear it no longer, I slipped out for a moment of solitude. I was stealthily crossing the front hall when I saw a footman swing the door open. I stepped back into the shadows, my heart quickening. Surely this must be

Milburn? And surprisingly—as these things so rarely turn out as one hopes—it was. As I watched him step inside, I was struck again by how intriguing he had become. He had always been handsome, but his face was more interesting than it had been before. There were hollows and shadows and lines that made one want to look at him more intently.

He handed his hat to the footman and pushed his hair off his forehead. He looked somber. Thoughtful. And, trust me, thoughtful is something that Milburn is not and never has been, so my curiosity increased. I was also very glad to see him.

Just then, he looked in my direction and saw me. He smiled and his thoughtful air evaporated. "Hello," he said, walking toward me. "Why are you skulking out here?" He stopped. "Are you well?"

I tried for a smile. "Only tired, I think. Is your business dispensed with successfully?"

He looked at me for a moment before replying. "I devoutly hope so," he said, and he sounded tired, also. "But perhaps you need to tell me: am I forgiven?"

And to my surprise, he truly seemed to be waiting for an answer. Forgiveness I had always assumed would be an oft-needed commodity for one married to Milburn. "Of course," I replied automatically.

"In that case, shall we steal away after all?" he asked. "Or would that be unforgivable, do you think?"

"Unforgivable," I replied, with a smile to show him that I was not serious. "At least until *you* have stood in there for hours smiling and enduring jokes on the defects in personality that could cause a new bridegroom to be abandoned by his bride at the wedding breakfast."

But he didn't laugh and tell me that it was no more than

a shrew such as myself deserved. Instead he tipped up my face with his gloved hand, and said, "My poor love. You do know that I would not have abandoned you, despite the defects in personality, had there been any choice?"

"Er, of course," I managed, even more perplexed by this odd new Milburn.

"Let us go, then," he said, sounding more lighthearted as he took my arm. "And since you have been so abominably ill-used by the guests, we shall do it without so much as taking our leave."

I allowed myself to lean against the warmth of his arm for just a moment. I felt unaccountably better. Less weary, and immeasurably attracted by the idea of slipping out with no farewells. "Mama, I should warn you, is already in something of a taking as, among my sins, I have sadly neglected not only the Hampshire cousins, but also the Countess Esterhazy."

"Ah well, as she is already distressed," he said, and I looked up at him, fascinated, as his beautiful lips formed the words, "we may as well make it worth her while." I tore my gaze away from those mesmerizing lips and met his eyes. They were full of devilment now, and it occurred to me that he was likely aware that I was, of a sudden, fascinated by his mouth. "Shall I go in after all and give the cut direct to a few cabinet ministers?" he added, pulling me a little closer.

His eyes were wicked and his bantering, lighthearted, but there was indisputably some kind of current between us that felt hazardous. And at the same time, sort of intoxicating. I boldly leaned even a tiny bit nearer, which he seemed to like, as he bent to me. "As long as you are set on observing the social niceties, I'd suggest you not neglect the Hampshire cousins," I advised him.

"Oh, but you are wrong," he said, his voice low and intimate for my ears alone. "I am not at all set on observing the social niceties." And there was something about the way he said it that made me even more aware of him, of the fact that he was so close that all I would have to do was sway the tiniest bit more toward him, and our bodies would be touching. *Merciful heavens!* What was I thinking? He let go of my arm to retrieve his hat and my wrap and bonnet from the footman, and broke the spell.

A moment later we were settled in his trim little curricle. Truly, I was almost feeling comfortable with him. Or would have been, if not for the oddly heightened awareness of his physical self that I seemed to have developed. The way he looked, the clean way he smelled, the heat from his body, the amount of space he took up, all occupied my mind at various moments in a rather worrying fashion.

I was tying on my bonnet with the smart little demi-veil, and he was taking up the reins, when a crowd began to gather at the door. Apparently word had got about that we were departing, and so we drove away into the cool, unusually clear January afternoon, much like any other couple: amidst a hail of cheering and good wishes.

Conversation was desultory as we traversed the crowded streets. Milburn was, for once, concentrating on his driving. For which I could not help but be grateful, as I still carried, with a great deal of clarity, the memories of previous driving expeditions over the years with him. He had always been an enthusiastic driver, but at times that enthusiasm had overreached his skill, resulting in some hair-raising moments.

"You are driving very well," I said, trying to radiate approval as he neatly, with apparently little effort, avoided a milk cart to the left and a pair of mettlesome bays to the right.

He slanted me an amused look from beneath his hat. "Thank you," he said, gravely. "I think."

I was casting about for conversation, trying to reestablish the ease between us and banish the unease over what was soon to come, and that gambit had certainly not got me far. "Did you, er, drive much on the Continent?"

"No," he said.

Hmm. "It's a pity that your father's leg injury was so severe as to keep him from traveling," I tried. "Although he is fortunate that it was not more serious. Don't you think?"

"Yes," he said. "To both."

"I think he would have enjoyed the wedding."

"Indeed."

"And your mama, too. She—"

"—would have enjoyed the wedding," he finished for me.

"Yes." I was starting to feel a little cross with him. But I was determined all the same to make polite conversation. "We are fortunate to have such a lovely day. I did think yesterday that rain looked—"

But then I stopped short as Milburn said, "Ah hell." And, suddenly, he drew the curricle to a halt so we came to rest right there in the middle of South Audley Street. Fortunately, there was a lull in traffic, or we without a doubt should have had some extra horses and some irate people planted in the back of the curricle.

There were any number of sharp remarks on the tip of my tongue, but they all seemed to slip away as he, at that moment, was rather expertly untying the ribbons of the aforementioned smart little bonnet. "It is true," he said, "that my mother would have enjoyed the wedding. She was planning to wear her new primrose silk. And it is a pity she did not have the opportunity as primrose, she informed me, looks most becoming on her. The day was lovely, it did look like to rain yesterday, and we are fortunate indeed that it did not. There." He took a breath.

I sat, silently, a little insulted. *Someone* had to bear responsibility for not letting us lapse into dead silence.

He flashed that wicked smile that I had never before realized he possessed. He leaned closer and said, as he removed the untied bonnet, "And I cannot kiss you with this fetching, yet entirely ridiculous, thing on your head."

Oh. He was going to kiss me! He had said so. Was I supposed to *do* something? I waited, hoping I didn't look as stupefied—or as eager—as I felt.

And then he laughed and dropped the bonnet to the floor. With one hand still on the reins, he tipped my chin up with the back of the other. I sat, waiting, for his lips to come down on mine. But for a long, aching moment, they didn't. "Gwen," he whispered, and I felt the soft brush of his warm breath, and then his lips moved briefly over my eyelids and skimmed down my cheekbone, unhurried, as though we had hours. Heat seemed to roll through me at his touch, and he trailed his lips along my jaw, and then, finally, brushed them over the corner of my mouth.

I could scarcely breathe from the heat of what he was doing. "I knew it would be like this between us," he said, roughly, and I understood that what I was feeling was there for him to see.

He bent his head again, and this time, his lips brushed

mine. I gave a little squeak of surprise. And he laughed against my mouth, and said, his lips still on mine, "Kiss me back, Gwen," as his one available hand cupped the side of my face.

And what can I say? He was my husband. The kiss was long and slow, and the tip of his tongue moved lazily across my lips, making me gasp into his mouth. And then, in the next instant, his mouth was feather-light again, teasing, making me lean into him to keep the contact. And then the kiss turned hot, and thorough, and I began to understand why I'd been so captivated by his lips all day. He threaded his hand through my hair at the nape of my neck and levered me closer, and, slowly and deliberately, opened his lips over mine. Heat swirled through my dazed body.

I was pulled out of the moment when a cheer went up from the crowd that had gathered. Milburn slowly lifted his mouth from mine. His breathing was rapid and his eyes were the darkest I had ever seen them. He rested his forehead against mine for the barest moment as we both struggled to catch our breath. I glimpsed the crowd, over his shoulder, and flushed, but he only laughed. Digging into his pocket, he produced a handful of coins, which he tossed into the air.

Another cheer went up. "Now," Milburn said, "that we have that out of the way, I can think again. And am entirely at your disposal to engage in frivolous conversation. As I believe I had already responded to all of your sallies, shall I throw out the first pleasantry?"

The problem, though, was that *he* might now have been able to converse with equanimity, but I was not certain I could. That kiss had left me shaken to my bones. Never in my wildest imaginings had I supposed, one, that there was such a kiss, two, that if such a thing existed, Milburn would know how to do it, or, three, that I would have reacted to him this way.

I shivered. He had kissed me on a curricle in the middle of Mayfair, with one hand on the reins, and I was almost a puddle at his feet. I had been perilously close to shamelessly begging for more. But somewhere in the recesses of my mind, I knew that it would simply never do to let Milburn—Bertie, who had once put frog spawn in my tea!—know that he suddenly had that kind of effect on me. *He* might have known it would be like this, but quite honestly, the thought had never before occurred to me. Of course, to be fair, I had not known that *like this* even existed.

"Do you offer because you are concerned that were I to begin the conversation, it would not be with a pleasantry at this moment?" I said, pleased with the tart note of my voice.

His gaze skated lazily over me, and he smiled with entirely too much complacency for my liking. "No," he said. "Not at all. I only offer to be polite, you understand."

"One would hardly have guessed politesse to be in your nature, sir, considering your conduct of a moment ago!" I said. (I did not really mean this, of course, but it *seemed* like something I should be taking him to task for.) "Which, incidentally, was entirely reprehensible."

"That is just the thing," he agreed. "I was attempting to make amends for my reprehensible conduct—"

I nodded with, I thought, a credible show of righteous indignation.

His lazy grin widened. "—before I do it again," he finished, and my throat tightened.

"Oh." I swallowed, and then pulled myself together.

"Reverend Twigge!" I said, brightly. "Did you not think him in fine form?"

He nodded. "I particularly enjoyed the bit in the homily about the necessity of a wife's humility and docility of opinion in marriage."

"Did you?" I said. "I must have missed that part."

"Pity," he replied. "Shall I invite the gentleman to tea so he can refresh you on it?"

"I do believe it is coming back, now that you mention it," I said, unable to completely repress a smile. "I am glad you enjoyed it. I, myself, thought it a little . . . lack-luster."

"Did you! And your brother Richard's coat was exquisite." And with that pronouncement, he leaned closer and brushed his gloved finger slowly down the side of my face, which action did not contribute to either my mental acuity or the steadiness of my heartbeat.

And now I *was* having trouble keeping the thread of the conversation, so I just nodded.

And the blasted man had the audacity to laugh as he straightened and, once again holding the reins in both hands, maneuvered us back into traffic. "It would be Weston, of course," he said.

"No doubt," I said, vaguely, still reliving in delicious confusion how his tongue had caressed my upper lip. Bertie's *tongue* had touched my lip! And I had liked it. The very idea made me want to die. Or perhaps what I really wanted was for him to do it again.

He leveled a smile at me that left me in no doubt as to exactly how well he understood my turmoil, and leaned a little closer, his eyes still on the road. "Later. I promise," he said very low, and I felt a tremor all the way down my spine. "But for the moment, perhaps we should dispense with trying to do the civil," he suggested.

To which I gratefully agreed. And so we lapsed into our mutually agreed upon silence until, a short time later, we pulled up in front of the Clarendon, which is where my story began.

4

In which my mother and Lady Worth set me straight

*B*ut that was yesterday.

Today, it was the morning following my disastrous wedding night, and the three of us—my mother, Violetta, and myself—were tête-à-tête in my mother's drawing room. The atmosphere was, to be blunt, somewhat hostile from the start. My mother does not receive before noon. Ever. (Except for Violetta, of course, but that is usually *en boudoir*.) That she had made an exception this morning was being pointedly conveyed.

"You *do* realize that your eyes are puffy and quite frankly, *red,* do you not, Gwendolyn?" After which opening sally, Mother had reclined in her chair, sipped her tea, and eyed me in a manner that made me certain that I also had something atrocious plastered to a front tooth. "That you are a trifle put out, one can certainly understand. But really," she had continued, as I ran a surreptitious tongue over my teeth. "I fail to see that the situation can call for such dramatics. I mean, Cambourne, Milburn, Bernie, Bertie," here she had given a languid wave of her hand. "Ask yourself: Can it really signify all that much?"

And before I could get so much as a word in edgewise: "Far be it from me to say so, as one, of course, cannot like to meddle, and while I personally never, but never, criticize—" Violetta had begun.

And that, anyway, was an utter lie. Even my mother, who had been Lady Worth's closest friend at least since time began, if not previous to that event, had looked surprised at the blatant untruth of this statement.

Lady Worth, with a minor adjustment to her purple turban, had continued, "—but it seems to me, that all things considered, what we have here is simply a question of *circumstances.*"

My mother nodded her agreement. "Brought about in part, I should hardly need remind you, Gwendolyn, by the Infamous Incident at the Stainsteads' ball!"

Now, while I was willing to accept full culpability for the rush surrounding the wedding, I was *not* willing to allow that my behavior had in some way rendered me deserving of having married the wrong man. *"Circumstances?"* I asked, coolly. "That could possibly account for this?"

"But it also seems to me, Almeria," Violetta replied over my head, "that the true *crux* of the problem, if you will, is that you have allowed the gel an excess of sensibility!" She nodded self-righteously and continued, with an accusing glance in my direction, "I mean, in my day, *our* day, I should say, Almeria, a husband was a husband and a properly raised chit did not refine on who that husband might be!" She paused to inspect the ginger biscuit she held, took a large bite, and very ladylike, without so much as tilting her regally covered head, brushed the crumbs off her whiskers.

"Violetta *does* have a point, darling," my mother said in what was clearly intended to be a bracing tone. "You are making rather much of this, don't you think?"

"I do not—" I began heatedly, only to be cut off by Mother.

"Because it seems to me," she said, "that it all comes down to a question of disciplining the mind!"

Violetta nodded her vigorous agreement, and then snaked her tea spoon beneath her turban to scratch her head.

"So," Mama continued in firm tones, "as such, it—marrying the wrong man—can hardly constitute a reason for such a fuss, really!" And then she leaned back, looking very pleased with this pronouncement.

Violetta nodded her agreement as she added more sugar to her tea with that very same spoon, ignoring the silver tongs that had been provided for just that purpose. "The difference is entirely in your head," she said.

"How can you say that?" I demanded.

Mother gave vent to a long-suffering sigh. "I suppose you are quite certain that you *do* have the wrong one, darling?" she asked, smoothing her already perfectly smoothed morning dress. "Well, what I mean is, their names are awfully similar, and if you are mistaken, after all—"

"Both the same enough in the dark, you may trust me on that, my gel," Violetta said bluntly, taking up a ginger biscuit. "Enough kerfuffle. Cambourne's the earl, ain't he? No need to be missish," she said in response to my mother's pained expression. "Once Winfell has the sense to stick his spoon in the wall, Cambourne'll be a duke."

"Perhaps. But the fact remains that he's not Bertie—Milburn," I pointed out.

"No he ain't," Violetta said, before adding, succinctly, "Head over arse in love with Milburn, who you hadn't laid eyes on in donkey's years, then, were you, gel?"

I had to admit she had me there. I was *fond* of him, of course. But was I in love with him? Certainly not.

And well Violetta knew it. "Didn't think so," she boomed, pointing the infamous spoon at me once again. "Only think! You'll be a duchess!"

I closed my eyes. "But I don't want to be a duchess," I replied heatedly, and then, stopped. Well, truth to tell, I didn't have any *particular* objection to being a duchess, in and of itself. And it would serve to take the wind out of Priscilla Fanshaw's sails. She's been babbling on practically our entire lives about being promised to a marquis and the *difficulties faced by one with such a weighty position to uphold* (and that is an exact quote). Hah! Let her *Your Grace* me a few times.

"What you want is entirely beside the point, darling," my mother said, sipping her tea. "You have been raised to be a lady. And a true lady, you can be sure, when faced with a small spot of discomfiture, such as having *accidentally* wed the wrong man, simply picks herself up, dusts herself off, and goes on."

That accidentally had enough emphasis to have tipped over her chair. I was about to point this out, but Violetta inserted herself.

"If only Ursula was not such a pea-wit, she would have had those twins marked," was her contribution. "An infant, you can be certain, barely notices a quick branding. Anyway, she likely mixed them up on the first day, and one shudders to imagine how many times hence, and no one knows who's who anymore, least of all them, so there's absolutely no point in your raising a fuss,

Gwendolyn. And that," she added darkly, and very much
as though the blame for this lay at the twins' door, "is what
you get for having a French mama!"

I declined to pursue this. "I know which one is which,
and I'm married to Cambourne," I said. "Although," I
reminded them, "it seems he's very much intent on being
Milburn for the moment."

They both stared at me as if I had mentioned that I was
thinking about performing at Astley's Amphitheatre.
"What I mean is that in public he wants to be his brother.
Not to say that he actually wants to *be* his brother, of
course. Who would want to be Milburn who actually
wasn't? Nobody." I knew I was babbling, but continued
anyway. "Still and all he's insistent upon *pretending* to be
Bertie. Er, Milburn. But I don't know why," I wound up.
"What I want to know is, why?"

Violetta chewed noisily. I forged ahead. "When I asked
him how I could have come to have married him, he
said— Do you know what he said?" I waited, feeling that
the answer to this question would have more effect were it
not taken as rhetorical.

"No, darling, but I am assuming you are determined to
tell us, so if I may speak for both of us, we are simply agog
to find out," Mother said, sounding completely uninter-
ested.

"He said," I paused for maximum effect before repeating the incendiary phrase, *"Perhaps you'd best ask your parents."*

"Did he?" Mother sounded even less interested than she
had a moment ago.

"Yes," I managed to say before being interrupted by
Violetta.

"You are a married woman now, Gwendolyn," she said.

"You've lessons to learn. And the first is: *You* make the decisions."

Mother nodded. "It's time to shorten the leading rein is what Violetta means."

"Tighten the girth," Violetta said.

"Hold the leash," Mother supplied gaily.

As I looked back and forth between the two of them, Violetta guffawed and then added, "Truss the chicken."

I really had to interrupt before there was even a possibility of there being another suggestion added to this list. "But I don't want to do any of those things. I just—"

"Don't be obtuse, dear," Mother said. "It doesn't matter what he wants. It's only what he *thinks* he wants, anyway. He wants to be called Cambourne in private and Milburn in public?"

I nodded.

"Well, surely you do see that that will never do? And that is where the wife comes in. You have to *tell* him what he wants, but without actually *telling* him, if you understand me."

This seemed a rather lengthy digression from the real topic. "Indeed I do not."

Mother sighed. "It's quite simple, really. You say, *yes dear,* and go right ahead doing as you please—address him in whatever manner you see fit."

I raised a brow. "Such as brother-in-law, perhaps? Because that's what I see fit."

"No, darling," Mother said in her most patient tones. "Such as Cambourne."

"Ah yes." I nodded. "You meant how *you* see fit. Well, when I do find Milburn—" I started to say, but Violetta piped up.

"Think he's going to ride to your rescue, do you, gel?

Not likely when you could be pregnant with his very own nephew as we speak." She looked quite taken with this thought. "You always have been a demmed stubborn little chit, Gwendolyn," she continued. "But hear this: On the topic of this marriage, your mama shall brook none of your recalcitrant ways."

"Ah, but you see," I said with, I admit, a degree of relish, "I cannot possibly be pregnant with my own, er, I mean, Milburn's nephew, as we speak, because we did not, ah, well . . ."

My ploy to embarrass them failed miserably. "No need for missishness here. Plainspeaking is best, I always say. He didn't bed you? Is that what you mean?" Violetta demanded.

My face flamed. "Er—"

"Well? Did he, gel? Speak up! Because if he did, the question of whether he's the right one or not is moot. No point in going mealymouthed now." She pinned me with her basilisk glare.

"No," I mumbled to the rug.

"Oh dear," Mother said, then, "Do you mean to say that that lovely trousseau has gone to waste? Those fabulous night rails of Madame Suzette's?" *Now* she sounded distraught.

"Suzette does do an exquisite night rail," Violetta said to her.

"Would it be considered forward of me to suggest that we perhaps return to enlightening me as to exactly how I came to be married to the wrong man?" I inquired.

Mother said to Violetta, "Did you see that jonquil silk she got in last week? It was—"

I tapped my foot.

"Suzette's night rails cost a packet, you ungrateful gel.

Now," Violetta said, eyes narrowed, "do you mean to say that Cambourne, or whatever he's calling himself at the moment, who stood up there at the altar looking as though he'd just as soon devour you on the spot as say a civil 'I do,'—*and* who rushed you out of the wedding breakfast like his breeches was on fire—*failed* to get the job done?" she demanded.

"Well he—I—*we,* were hardly disposed to—"

"In my day," Violetta said, ominously, "men did not choose to refine upon female sensibilities to such a high degree. They were *not,* I assure you, subject to such a soft-ness of character so as not to bed their wife because of a little skittishness on the girl's part! No, indeed! They were *men.* And a good thing it was, too."

And I was suddenly beset by the most awful vision of Violetta's husband, Rodney, the Marquess of Worth, who was approximately half her girth and a good six inches shorter, throwing her down on their Egyptian settee, pur-ple turban and all, and having his way with her.

"So you *do* mean that you are not really . . . That you did not . . ." Mother trailed off.

"No," I said, staring boldly back at her. "We did not. So I think an annulment—"

"An annulment?" Mama squeaked.

"An annulment!" Violetta boomed. "No. That, I can assure you, is quite, *entirely,* out of the question."

I was about to ask exactly who *she* was to make that decision, when Mama said, "Absolutely. There can be no question of that."

"How can that be?" I demanded.

"Well, to begin with," Violetta replied, "there is no way for anyone to be certain that you're not pregnant with that nephew. We've only your word to go on."

"But Cambourne—" I started to say.

"He ain't going to apply for an annulment," Violetta said. "You do know the necessary grounds for that? Do you not?"

"That the marriage is unconsummated," I said with confidence, only to have it shattered.

"Oh no," Violetta said with relish. "That he could not. Not *did* not, mind you. *Could* not. You do understand the difference, Gwendolyn?" And then she smiled. "Now, can you truly imagine Cambourne standing up and explaining to Parliament that he couldn't get the job done?"

And the answer was no, to be honest. I closed my eyes as, for just a second, I recalled, against my better judgment, just exactly how very adeptly he had begun the job—a job, I reminded myself firmly, that he had absolutely no business having undertaken in the first place. Nonetheless, the memory of his hands on my body and his voice in my ear made my toes curl in my boots and I could feel the heat flood into my face. When I forced my eyes open they were both staring at me.

"You are quite certain he didn't bed you?" Violetta said, directing a suspicious look at me, which had the effect of snapping me out of my reverie.

"Of course," I said briskly. "It hardly seems to be the type of thing one would forget."

"So one would hope," Violetta said, still staring assessingly at me. "Although one, quite frankly, does not know what to think about a chit foolish enough to have stepped out for a breath of air with that loose fish, Trafford."

I glared at her and then said to my mother, "Very well. If you are not disposed to help, I shall simply have to seek out Father."

"Well, I can hardly stop you if you insist upon such a

selfish course of action," Mother said, sounding exasperated. "But I shouldn't advise taking it up with him today.
We've thirty expected to dine this evening. *And* your father
has an important speech to deliver before the Board of
Control tomorrow, which Violetta and I have not finished
writing as we have not yet completely formulated his
opinions. Which task we had *planned* to undertake this
morning, you see."

Yes, I did see, indeed. But I was determined to try,
nonetheless. Just as I was about to rise, declare my intention, and bid them what I deemed a suitably chilly
farewell, however, I heard a voice emanating from the
front hall. An earnest voice. A reedy, long-winded voice.
And one that I had, as it turned out, rather ill-advisedly
summoned with my hastily scrawled note sent posthaste
this morning.

The voice of the very man who had conducted my farce
of a marriage ceremony.

5

In which we take tea with the Reverend Mr. Twigge and I learn some most surprising things

"*Oh dear me! I quite understand that Her Ladyship* is not receiving this morning. Most understandable, indeed! But I, you may rest assured, my dear fellow, can only be a desired visitor, coming as I do to offer spiritual consolation in this, what must be her hour of blackness—"

"If you could just allow me a moment, sir," Ladimer, my mother's butler, suggested pointedly to the Reverend Mr. Twigge from what sounded to be very nearly outside the door, "I shall ascertain whether Her Ladyship is able to receive."

"Be certain to tell her, though, that it is *I*, come to call upon her. Come to offer, yes, if I may be so bold, not only comfort, but guidance, in this, her hour of distress and despair, of dark and drear—"

"Oh, lud, how does that windbag know anything is

amiss?" Violetta hissed in the moment before Ladimer's tap sounded on the door.

"En-ter," Mama singsonged cheerfully before dropping her voice to a furious whisper. "Indeed. How does he? Gwendolyn?"

It took everything I had left not to cringe. "I might have sent a note round."

Silence greeted this announcement. Hostile, accusing, questioning silence.

"He did marry me to the wrong man," I pointed out, reminding myself that I was in the right of things. "And so, I believed, should be a participant in this little *discussion.*"

The tips of Ladimer's ears were flushed and his eyes were fixed on Mama's lacquered Chinese console, but his voice was impassive. "Madam. The Reverend Twigge is with us at present, wishing to offer, if he may be so bold, not only comfort, but guidance, in your, er . . . *hour.*"

"Loves the sound of his own voice, Twigge. Never uses two words when two thousand can say the same," Violetta said as Ladimer exited. I directed a significant look in her direction, to see whether she was able to recognize anyone else with that tendency. She, however, appeared undeterred by introspection.

Mama said, "And now we have a *real* problem."

Summoning the Reverend Twigge had *seemed* like the correct course of action earlier this morning. I mean, it seems to me that when a man of God marries you to the wrong man, he should have something to say for himself.

"It shall, I suppose," Violetta said as though such a burden fell to her lot daily, "be up to us, Almeria, to right the situation."

My mother nodded just as Ladimer ushered our visitor

in. "Ah, *dear* Reverend Twigge," she said so brightly I could hardly credit it. "How lovely to see you once again. And so soon!"

"My lady!" he said fervently as he bowed over her hand. Mama smiled benignly at him.

"Macaroon, Mr. Twigge?" Violetta inquired as he seated himself.

"Why, no, thank you. I could not possibly. Why, when I think—"

"Ginger biscuit, then, perhaps?" Violetta suggested, and then, when he shook his head, cried, "A meringue, then!" as she all but thrust the plate into his hands.

He looked down at it with a frown. "I am afraid that I am left quite without appetite by the thought of what has transpired," he replied.

"Transpired? What has transpired?" asked Mama, sounding artfully surprised.

"Why the, er, *marital* disaster, of course," Mr. Twigge replied, looking so distressed that I almost felt sorry for him. "Why, I am completely done up. I thought Lady Gwen was *supposed* to marry the Earl of Cambourne, even though everyone was to believe him to be Milburn! Which seemed easy enough to accomplish, what with the similarity of names and their identical appearances and the special license—"

I decided that the time had come for me to insert myself into the conversation. "What special license?" I asked.

He looked surprised. "Well, the one necessary so you could be married in the parish without having had the banns called for three Sundays before the wedding. It is a requirement, you know, which we were quite unable to fulfill due to the, er, supposed bridegroom being away at the time."

I nodded. "Yes. But—"

"Quite convenient, as it turned out," Mr. Twigge continued, "since the last thing we wanted people to be aware of was the change in bridegroom, which, of course, would have been difficult with the banns. I was quite proud that when I read the name during the ceremony no one remarked anything amiss. But I now greatly fear that I must have misunderstood the instructions given me by you, dear Lady Axton, and the earl was only meant to be a proxy groom." He leaned forward confidingly. "Although I realize we are forbidden to speak of it."

"Well, Mr. Twigge," said Violetta cheerfully, "what's done is done, as the saying goes. Lovely day, is it not?"

I had clearly been lagging a conversational footstep behind since entering the room that morning, but now I could not help but feel that I had missed the path completely.

"For this time of year the day is fine, indeed," he allowed, as Mama passed him tea. "Thank you, my lady," he continued. "I always say there is *no* restorative for the nerves quite like a cup of tea. And you always do a fine blend!"

I watched him sip his tea. "Ah." He sighed. "Do I detect a hint of oolong, Lady Worth? The merest *dash* mixed with your usual exceptional hyson?"

Mother nodded, looking modest.

"A bold move!" he said, his nose in his cup. He was rolling the tea around his mouth. "Am I not correct, my lady, in surmising that there is just a *soupçon* of lapsang in here?" he said.

"I look forward to a long coze, Mr. Twigge," said Mother. "My daughter," she said firmly, "is just leaving. She is positively bursting with impatience to return to her new husband!"

"Whoever he may be," I said, darkly.

But she only laughed gaily. "We elders shall simply have to endeavor to take my mind off how bereft I am at the loss of my baby, my only daughter, the last fledgling in the nest."

Since I had more or less been tossed out of the nest, and without any instruction at flying, this seemed a little much. When I had come to my mother this morning, I had hardly expected that she would throw consoling arms about me. It was not that she was not *fond* of me, precisely, but more that she was not overly concerned by my happiness or lack thereof, shall we say. All the same, I had never, in my wildest imaginings, thought that she would either ignore my plight so entirely, or possibly have conspired to bring it about. But she was, and it seemed she had, and I would have had to be an imbecile not to realize that I was being firmly dismissed. Her words, at least, seemed to have the effect of rousing Mr. Twigge.

"But—but—" the poor, confused man spluttered as he jumped to his feet, slopping some of the prized blend into his saucer. He looked pleadingly at me. "Your note, Lady Gwen, it said—"

Mother looked at me pointedly. *"Au revoir,* darling," she said, firmly cutting him off. "We shan't dream of keeping you a moment longer. Sit, Mr. Twigge!"

He immediately dropped back to his seat as bidden, and began mopping tea off his trousers.

Violetta affixed me with her gimlet eye. "Run along, gel. You've chickens to truss, in case you've forgot."

"Cookery!" said Mr. Twigge.

"Not at all," Violetta returned.

"Oh," he said, looking confused, as well he might.

"Now, Mr. Twigge," my mother said, "I am so glad you

called this morning, as my husband said to me only last night that he cannot help but feel that we have been lax in our patronage of your fine old cathedral. I am aware, however, that this is the sort of dull conversation that a new bride will not want to burden herself with. *Gwendolyn!*"

Most impressive in its subtlety. But I stood, nonetheless. And so did Mr. Twigge, this time having the foresight to place his cup and saucer on the table. He shot me a helpless glance, as though apologizing for my forced departure. I had to admit that I could hardly blame the man for crumbling in the immutable face of the Mama/Violetta united front.

Glaring, I headed for the door. Truly unable to legitimately linger any longer, I closed it behind me with a somewhat less than completely ladylike thump.

"Naturally, it *was* Cambourne's name on the special license," I heard Mother say.

Her tones had been unsatisfyingly muffled, so I bent down and applied my ear to the keyhole, and heard Mother say, very clearly, "I just *knew* we could rely on you, Mr. Twigge!" Her best laugh tinkled out. "Now, as I was saying, Axton said to me just last night that we should very much like to make a substantial donation to . . ."

I had to face it. There was something going on that I did not understand. My parents knew it, Mr. Twigge knew it—or some of it, anyway, Violetta knew it, and Cambourne knew it. In fact, I was apparently the only one of us whose mind was not burdened by any understanding whatsoever of what had taken place, since I could not for the life of me understand why on earth would the wrong brother—particularly *this* wrong brother, who could arguably have had any woman in England—want to wed, and almost bed me.

And now, it appeared my mother was buying Mr. Twigge's silence. "You are most generous. Exceedingly, my lady, but Lady Gwen was most insistent—"

"You would do well to disregard her behavior entirely," Violetta recommended.

"I trust I may indulge in speaking plainly with a man of such excellent sense as yourself, Mr. Twigge?" Mama added, and then continued, in a whisper, "Bridal nerves! My daughter has been prey to the most dreadful case of maidenly fear. Why, she has been in an alarmingly precarious state for some weeks now."

"In fact," Violetta piped in, "I should not, were I you, give credence to a word she says, at the moment. Dismiss them as the ravings that they are!"

Ravings! I gritted my teeth against the desire to march back in there, as Mr. Twigge said, pithily, "I did not like to say anything, but now that you mention it, I thought I did detect a nervous inattention and what I greatly feared was an incipient hysteria during the homily."

"Precisely," Mama agreed. "Now, let us move on to more pleasant topics. Such as the belfry. I understand that you have long desired to rebuild the belfry, Mr. Twigge?"

"The Axton Belfry," he tried, sounding delighted, now that they had disposed of me and my petty problems (not to mention ravings). "I *do* so like the sound of that. And do you know, my lady, I daresay, a macaroon or two should not go amiss after all. . . ."

And then, to my surprise, the door was flung open. "Aha!" Violetta crowed as she towered over me, her purple turban dangerously askew. "Precisely what I thought we'd find."

Had it been someone else caught in the act, I might have thought the situation amusing. As things stood, I was guessing that it would be quite some time before I saw the humor in it.

Before I could utter a word in my own defense, Violetta spoke up again, which I should have expected as at least ten seconds had elapsed since her last words. "Duchesses," she said, "may listen at doors with impunity. A countess can get away with the odd door on occasion. Clumsy virgin chits without a grain of sense to their names, who don't know any better than to get caught, have not got a prayer of carrying it off."

"Well then," I said, giving her a very hard stare, "I suppose that's reason enough to aspire to snaring a duke." I turned to Ladimer, who had appeared on silent feet. "Is my father at home?"

To which he replied, "I believe he is to be found in the library at the moment." I lifted my head another notch and glided gracefully from the room. And the effect of my dignified departure, I told myself, had not been the least bit spoilt by the remark I heard in my wake.

"A good toss between the sheets is what that gel needs," said Violetta in bracing tones. "And, mark my words, if that husband of hers had been just a trifle faster off the mark, she'd be right as rain today!"

6

In which my father reluctantly sheds a fraction more light on matters

As *I stood at the foot of my parents' Adam staircase* pondering the dimensions of my problem, I looked round at the familiar marble statues in their niches, and struggled to hold back tears. What I really wanted was to run to my best friend Cecy's cozy little house. She would summon Myrtia, away from whatever cause, society, or good work was consuming her today, and the three of us could sit in front of the fire and have a little tribunal. They would be powerless to *do* anything, of course, but just a little sympathy—just one person saying, *Oh my goodness, how dreadful!* would be awfully comforting.

I knew my father was unlikely to say anything even approaching that, and, since he never acted without Mother's approval, it was equally unlikely that he would offer any actual assistance, but I could see no alternative but to try. I poked my head into the library where he was asleep with the paper over his face. "Father?"

At my voice, he snatched the newspaper away and shot to his feet. "Eh? What? Gwendolyn?" He squinted down at me. "Just doing a little thinking about, er, Abernathy's proposal!" he assured me.

At the sight of him, something inside me burst. "Papa," I sobbed, giving way to my more dramatic instincts and casting myself into his arms.

He moved me away just a little so he could peer into my face. "Something amiss, m'dear?" He patted my shoulder ineffectually.

I managed a watery sniffle. "I should say so."

At this, he put me a little farther away, straightening his waistcoat as he did so. "You are overset and will be wanting your mother, I'm certain," he said, with an air of profound relief as he fished in his pocket and handed me a handkerchief.

I accepted it and sat in one of the well-worn leather chairs. "Actually, no," I said, dabbing at my eyes. "I have already seen Mother. It is your counsel I seek."

"Indeed!" He sounded surprised, and not, I must admit, particularly pleased, as he once again settled into his chair. "Me! Really? I suppose you'd best tell me what all this is about then."

I frowned at him, willing him at least to feel a shred of shame over his, *their,* duplicity. "Oddly enough, as it turns out, I am married to the wrong man!"

"You don't say?"

"Indeed," I replied through tight lips. "It came as something of a surprise to learn of that small switch at the altar—Cambourne for Milburn!—which, one hesitates to point out, no one deemed worthy of mention."

"Well!" he said, as he walked to the decanter and poured out two sherries. "Cambourne." He poured a third glass, this one of brandy, and lost not a minute in tossing it back. Having done so, he handed me the smaller of the two sherries and seated himself with the larger. He sipped, and I followed suit, waiting to see what he would say next. And then rather wished I hadn't.

Since, "Good man on Corn, Cambourne," was what he eventually did say. "Until recently at least. Does seem to have gone off course a bit in recent weeks, but—"

"Father!" I said, striving to keep my voice steady. "While I could not be more pleased that you approve of his stance on Corn Laws, that hardly addresses my problem."

"Right. S'posed to get sprogged to Milburn, were you?" he said as though I were quibbling over a triviality.

Since it had been his idea in the first place for me to get sprogged to Milburn, as he so delicately put it (it was undeniable: the man *did* have a way with words), this seemed a somewhat disingenuous question. "Yes," I replied, frowning darkly at him. "I was."

He shook his head. "I don't s'pose Milburn cares much one way or t'other—"

"How can you possibly say that?" I sputtered.

"—on Corn, I was about to say."

"Possibly not," I said through gritted teeth. "Milburn might, however, care quite a bit, one way or t'other," I parroted, "about his brother marrying his intended bride."

"Said so, has he?" asked Father blandly.

"No, but—"

"Well, then," he said, "p'raps not. If so, fellow needs must step up and say so, make himself heard, etcetera. Which, to be brutally honest, I ain't seen 'im doing. And we *were* rather in need of a bridegroom, as you might recall." He glared at me.

"Where is Milburn?" I demanded. "Does he even know?"

Father crossed his legs and eyed the decanter wistfully. "Not s'posed to let on that Cambourne ain't Milburn," he said as though that explained everything.

I closed my eyes against the headache that was beginning to steal up the back of my neck. "*Who* is not supposed to let on that he's not Milburn?" I asked.

"All of us. Shouldn't really be having this conversation a'tall, actually. One of the reasons we didn't mention any of it to you." He gave me a hard look. "Not sure if you could be trusted."

"With the identity of my own husband?" I asked, acidly.

"Listen," he said. "There we was, all sitting around here waiting for Milburn to turn up for the wedding, see? And as you might recall, he was taking his sweet time about it."

I nodded.

"Fellow always was a dashed loose screw," he muttered, I thought as much to himself as to me. "Two days before the wedding, still no Milburn. Went to Cambourne, I did—man to man. Said, 'Where's your leaky-brained coxcomb of a brother?' He said, 'Delayed, I'm afraid.' I said, 'How delayed?' He said, 'Apparently, quite.' I said, 'Quite as for a week? Or quite as for a year?' He said, 'I'm not certain.'"

Unfortunately, I could picture my father's half of the conversation all too clearly.

"I think you can understand, Gwendolyn"—he gave me quite a hard glare—"that we was in a very difficult position, particularly on account of the splash we was making because of the Trafford business. So that was when

I told 'im," he continued. "Said that the prospect of the wedding not coming off was a sure bet to drive your mama over the edge. Y'see?"

"I can well imagine," I said, drily.

"I hardly dared come home of an evening." He shuddered then, and stared into the fire as though reliving dark days indeed.

I gave him a level look. "And then what transpired?"

He shrugged. "Well, your mama and the Worth creature sat about whipping themselves into a frenzy of hysteria." He shuddered again. "Finally, she insisted that I go back to Cambourne and insist that he stand in for a proxy wedding."

"Was she not concerned that a proxy wedding was like to cause quite a stir on its own?"

He shot me a surprisingly astute look. "Not half so concerned as she was about no wedding and you ending up ruined, apparently," he said, and then added, "Only see, it was brilliant: She thought because they was twins it would work not to let it out a'tall that it was a proxy marriage. Wanted me to threaten breach of promise if he balked!"

"And Cambourne *agreed* to this?" I had to struggle to keep the disbelief out of my tones.

"But that's the beauty of it!" My father was positively beaming with delight. "I never had to propose it, thank the Lord! Because Cambourne came to *me! Offered* to stand in for Milburn! I tell you, never had such amazing luck b'fore in m'life! Not at cards. Not at horses. Not at anything."

"I see," I replied, slowly, trying to sort this out. "But did he mean to stand in as a proxy? Or as himself?" I asked, finally.

"I don't know, actually. But then, I cannot be held

accountable for everything, Gwendolyn." Father sounded huffy. "Thing is, with Milburn's return so unpredictable, we could hardly have the banns called, so we needed a special license. And I can hardly be expected to have noticed the fact that the bishop made an error and accidentally dispensed the thing with Cambourne's name on it, instead of Milburn's—what with the names being so similar and all."

"An error?" I said, quirking an eyebrow. "Accidentally? I am supposed to believe that?"

Father waved a dismissive hand. "Believe what you like. But you may certainly dispense with any pretty notions you might have about him being tricked at the altar, Gwendolyn. The fellow saw the license beforehand. Not only saw it, but said the vows, and signed the register, and you can believe that even if no one else does, he dashed well knows his own name and dashed well knew what he was doing."

Which was perfectly clear, and yet, went no distance at all in explaining things further. "But why?" I asked, finally. "Why would he want to do that?"

"I don't know, Gwen," he said, with finality. "Not my business."

I frowned. "You don't consider it your business?"

"No. Of course not."

"Did you even ask him?" I demanded. Father just shook his head in response, so I continued, "But why didn't anybody even tell me that Milburn had been delayed?"

"Didn't want you distressed," he said. "Your mama was nattering incessantly about blotchy complexions, etcetera." He eyed me.

"You married me off to someone else? So my complexion wouldn't be blotchy?"

"Well, that and to save you from ruin," he said, heavily, and I flushed.

"So where is Bertie—Milburn—now?"

"Larking around the Continent like the care-for-naught that he is, no doubt. He skipped. Or, more likely," he added darkly, "forgot until it was too late. Now *that*'d be just like the fellow."

"But, Father, suppose he is hurt, or injured, or—" I stopped. "Or worse!" I closed my eyes against the knowledge that in some dark corner of my soul, I actually hoped he was in peril enough to absolve him of his behavior.

"Nonsense," Father said firmly. "Fellow ain't seen a day of real war. Carrying supplies ain't war. Mark my words: He's right as rain. The family would've heard otherwise."

"So thinking he'd *skipped,* or possibly, ah, *forgot,* you decided to marry me off to his brother without mentioning it?" I frowned at him. Surely there was more here? Because none of this—nothing—accounted for Cambourne's apparent willing participation.

"Personally, I'd suggest you stop refining on that particular point and concentrate on the good of the situation." Father nodded encouragingly. "Like I said, he's—"

"I know," I replied glumly. "A good man on Corn. That does promise to bear me comfort in my darkest hours. And anyway, perhaps Milburn is equally good," I said with exasperation.

The look my father cast me was disgusted. "No use to me," he said, shortly. "Frippery fellow wouldn't recognize a parliamentary debate if it took place in his bedchamber."

"Surely you don't expect me to stay married to Cambourne?" I said, getting to the heart of the matter. "Since obviously the marriage was fraudulent?"

"Really, Gwendolyn," he responded in bracing tones, and I was momentarily surprised by how much he sounded like my mother. It was not as though the two of them spent any time together. "Quite certainly we do—" he broke off. "Look," he said, after a moment, "may I offer you a piece of advice?"

"I suppose so," I said, with some trepidation.

"If you pursue this avenue, of the marriage being fraudulent, you're just a foolish, ruined chit. If you don't, you're wife to one of the most powerful men in the country. He wants to pretend to be Milburn for a spell? I say, let 'im. It'll pass eventually. Bound to."

"But why," I asked, trying in my desperation for one last valiant grab at enlightenment, "does he want to do that? Pass himself off as Milburn?"

"Don't know, Gwendolyn. Again, not my business. What I do know is that, why, were things left to Abernathy, every child and tenant farmer could sell corn for whatever price they wished. Cattle'd practically eat for free!" he said heatedly.

"How tragic," I murmured. "But to return to the topic at hand: When were you going to tell me?" I don't know why, but I really wanted to know that.

"Well," he said, studying the fine, if somewhat risqué, Laguerre mural on the wall behind me. "Wanted to, of course, but, well, things got a bit hectic at the last minute. Saw no need to distress you with petty details. Meant to have when he had to leave the wedding breakfast, but"— he shrugged—"never quite got round to it."

"I see," I said slowly, much afraid that I did. "Wanted to save my complexion and all that?"

"Precisely." He nodded, looking very pleased by my grasp of the situation.

"But he just might have been under the impression that you had told me?"

"Possibly," my father allowed.

I studied his face. "You are advising me not to dispute the legality of this marriage?" I thought at this point we might as well dispense with the niceties. "Is that correct?"

"Doubt you could," he mumbled.

"Well, the marriage has not been consummated," I said, resolutely refusing to lower my gaze.

He, however, did not quail. "Zounds! Then I'd advise you to take care of *that* as soon as possible. Sooner! Lud, don't want your mama getting wind of that! She and the Worth woman'll no doubt want to preside over the event!" he said as he leaned over, took my sherry out of my hand, and drained the remainder. "They want consummation. And when your mama wants something, it's well nigh inevitable. Now is there more?" he wanted to know. "Because I really could do with a spot of a nap."

7

In which Cambourne returns

I more or less stormed out of the interview with my father. My marriage was a complete sham, and were that not bad enough, I had nowhere to go. Neither of my parents had explicitly said that I was unwelcome to return to their bosom, but then the actual words were hardly necessary.

It was clear now—even if nothing else was—that Cambourne knew. Not only knew, but was willing. And the one thing that kept going through my mind was, why? Why, why, why, on this earth would the Earl of Cambourne, future Duke of Winfell, willingly marry me? Step in to save me from disgrace, yes. I could see that very easily. But actually marry me, as in do it under his own name and then try to consummate it? Not at all. As I stood, debating this question, Ladimer appeared, followed by Cambourne himself.

The traitorous twin.

My husband.

At the sight of him, the memory of last night, my stomach plummeted to my knees. I steadied myself against the wall and forced my lungs to pull in a deep breath. And then a new thought hit me. I *assumed* him to be Cambourne, but given the events of yesterday, I was taking nothing for granted. I narrowed my eyes at him.

He smiled easily and said, "I *am* Cambourne."

"I suppose you are certain of that?" I replied, snappishly.

But he only glanced down at his flawlessly shined Hessians, and when he looked up again there was a glint in his eyes. "Quite certain," he said. "My feet are bigger."

"They are?" I was not entirely sure whether he was teasing me. "Than Milburn's?"

He nodded. "Yes. They always have been."

"Oh," I said. I studied his face for some indication of what he was thinking. His expression was pleasant, but he did not, I noted, look particularly rested. Where had he spent the night?

"I took another room at the Clarendon," Cambourne said, and I almost flinched at how easily he had read me.

"I see."

"It wasn't difficult, you know—"

What wasn't? Why was *I* always the one a step behind?

"—to guess what you were thinking." He glanced at Ladimer, who was busily straightening an already perfectly aligned portrait of Grandmama's favorite lapdog, and then at me.

"And yet, I'd hazard a guess that you've no idea what I'm thinking now," I said. "If you did, you'd likely be running for the door."

Behind us, Ladimer apparently lost his grip on the

painting. It hit the marble floor, the ornate frame causing an echoing crash.

Cambourne smiled at me. "Do you think?"

"Oh, I do," I assured him.

"Gwen," he said, almost tenderly, as he put his hand on the side of my face, just as the door to the library flew open.

Father hurtled through the door. "Ladimer! What the deuce is—Cambourne!" he said, coming to a precipitous halt. "Beg pardon. I meant, *Milburn*, of course." He laughed, heartily. "You and your brother, *Cambourne*, look so dashed alike, it's deuced difficult to tell you apart."

Cambourne dropped his hand from my face. "Good morning, sir," he said.

"Not particularly," Father said. "Devil of a morning, if you ask me."

Cambourne looked at me. It was back, that glint of amusement. "I don't suppose you shall have any disagreement from me on that," he said.

Ladimer was engaged in supervising as two footmen hefted the portrait back on the wall. "Please tell me that Gascon's likeness was not harmed," Father begged.

"No, my lord, Gascon is quite well," Ladimer replied.

My father sighed his relief. "Lady Axton would have an apoplexy if anything happened to that demmed picture of that demmed dog of her dem—of her esteemed mama's, and thankfully, I mean, *regrettably*, yes, regrettably, the foul thing is dead and can't sit for another. Come along, Cambourne." He glanced at Ladimer, and added, "I mean, come along, *Milburn*."

I slewed my glance to Ladimer, who of course knew everything. Well, if not everything, a darn sight more than my father, as a general rule.

78 *Jessica Benson*

"Come along. We've *things* to discuss, *Milburn,*" Father said, practically dragging Cambourne into his study. Cambourne's eyes caught mine in the instant before the door clicked shut. He looked so determinedly pleasant that I presumed him to be absolutely furious. Some of my irritation with him dissipated at the notion that he was about to endure an extremely unpleasant interlude likely revolving around the subject of the lack of consummation of our marriage.

After a moment, I dismissed Ladimer and the footmen, too. No sooner had they departed, but I went about my newfound means of eliciting information: applying my ear to the door. The problem, though, was that the men's voices lacked the carrying quality of Mama's and Violetta's.

"—mumble mumble the very devil to pay, should mumble Lady Axton mumble business accomplished mumble soon as possible," was what I heard my father say.

Cambourne must have been nearer the door, because his tones were clearer when he said, "Are you suggesting that I force myself on your daughter, sir?" His tones were equable.

"Of course mumble. No such thing. Mumble mumble."

I pressed my ear closer, wishing they'd left the door open just a crack.

". . . relieved to hear it, sir . . . fact remains . . . unwilling . . . discovered . . . was not Milburn." Cambourne must have been really angry, because his voice was at a level that I could hear clearly now. "*Which* information, by the by, I was under the mistaken impression you had already imparted to her. Had you done so as you led me to believe, I might have salvaged the situation. As things stand, what would you have me do, sir?"

"Convince 'er." Father was growing louder. "Shouldn't

be beyond your abilities to seduce your own wife. Least, not to judge by the tales of your exploits—"

"While your confidence in my abilities is gratifying," I heard Cambourne say in dry tones, "the fact remains that forcing myself on an unwilling bride is not to my taste."

"Which is why you need to see that she is willing," Father informed him. "Hear me, son," he began, "and hear me well—"

I almost recoiled from the door in surprise. Whatever the impetus that had brought Cambourne to this marriage, it must have been strong indeed: It quite simply was not done to speak thusly to the future Duke of Winfell.

He was silent, though, and my father continued, "—I only care about one thing. Lady Axton wants Gwendolyn married. To you. If Lady Axton wants a thing, I want it. I shan't know a moment free of torment until she gets it. Believe me, son, you'd do demmed well to turn this into a marriage in fact as well as name. Bugger your overnice scruples; just get the job done. I trust you take my meaning?"

"Allow me clarification on one point, sir: You are willing to sacrifice your daughter's happiness for your own comfort?"

"Yes," was my father's unfortunately succinct reply.

"I see," was Cambourne's chilly one. With that last, his voice was becoming more distinct, so I sprang away from the door. When he exited a moment later, I was busily browsing through the calling cards on the tray on the piecrust table in the entry.

"Hullo, Cambourne," I replied, with a deal of sangfroid. "Did you realize that Walter Arbuckle was in Town? I vow, I have not seen his face in—"

He smiled at me, looking completely unruffled by the

interview. "Listening at the door, were you?" he asked, lightly.

"—oh, a year, at least." I debated lying. "Yes," I said. "I was. You would be quite surprised by the amount of intelligence to be gained that way," I informed him. "I've only just discovered it as a technique today, and yet, I am already positively *swimming* in information."

"Swimming," he said, with a raised brow. "Are you really?"

I nodded. "Oh yes," I said, airily. "Let me see. I know that *you* knew what you were doing. I know that my parents bribed the Reverend Twigge to do the thing, and now I know that my mother wants this consummated, and now. In fact, I've had numerous conversations this morning, and yet, the only *real* information I've had has come from listening at doors."

He folded his arms, and leaned against the doorframe. "In that case, I suppose I shall leave you to it. Since you've found it so fruitful, of course."

"Perhaps we should talk," I allowed. "Provided, of course, that it would not be keeping you from any of those exploits my father was so keen on discussing?"

"Actually, I had quite cleared my schedule for this morning." He smiled, quickly, and God help me, my stomach lurched. Why, despite everything, did I feel such a strong pull to him? "On account of having assumed I would be occupied."

"We all make miscalculations at times," I said. "You likely forgot to include an unwilling and duped bride in yours."

"Apparently," he replied. "Amazing, is it not, how the smallest thing can throw off the equation?"

"Are you living at Milburn's house?" I asked, to change

the topic, and when he nodded, added, "The staff all believe you to be Milburn?"

"Although I'm having a deuced hard time keeping Sever, his valet, from becoming suspicious. It's the size of the feet, you see."

And that was when my attention went fully to his clothing, for the first time. I let my eyes roam over his heavily embroidered waistcoat and bottle-green jacket. I lingered at the spectacular falls of lace at his throat and wrists. "Oh, my," I said. "Those garments belong to Milburn?"

"You don't know the half of it," he said, darkly, taking a step closer. He should have looked a ridiculous fop in the outfit. But instead, the contrast seemed to make him more intriguing—there was nothing of the dandy about Cambourne.

"Are you concerned," he asked, looking down at me, intently, "that you endanger your reputation as a woman of good sense by being seen with me in this getup?"

I eyed him. "Certainly my judgment will be called into question."

He tilted my chin up. "Perhaps you can take comfort in the knowledge that it is widely known not to be a love match," he suggested drily.

My laugh died on my lips as I looked at him, feeling unaccountably deflated by his reminder. "You are right, of course," I said, turning my chin out of his hand.

He bent closer, and I held my breath. Surely he was not about to kiss me? I would not allow that, of course! I went up on my toes, closing the slight distance between us further. He straightened and I let the breath out.

"Perhaps returning to the Clarendon would be preferable to Milburn House for the moment. Because, then," he said, dropping his voice, and I found myself leaning slightly toward him, again, wondering what was to come, "I could at least divest myself of this jacket."

I hesitated. "You shall not," I began, and could think of no way to finish delicately, so decided to be out with it, "be pressing to, ah, *get the job done? As* my father put it?"

"I can assure you that I am fully able to master any baser impulses," he said drily, and I knew a moment of flaring disappointment. "Can you say the same?"

"Of course," I said repressively. "And gently bred females do not have baser impulses."

"Oh?" he said lightly, and I nodded.

He took a step closer. Just one step, but he suddenly seemed to fill my vision. His eyes glittered above his ridiculous frills, and he looked almost angry. My back was against the wall and the floor seemed to tilt under me. I let my fingertips brush against the rough silk fabric covering the wall to remind myself that I was in the safety of my parents' entry hall. He reached out and traced his finger down my jaw, letting it slide down to my neck. Heat flashed through me, catching me by surprise, and I sucked in my breath. He dropped his hand, but his eyes held mine.

"Make no mistake, Gwen," he said, his voice low, "if I weren't determined to act the gentleman, I could have you quivering with desire in ten seconds."

It was a challenge, and I knew it. He wanted me to acknowledge these disturbing sensations, that something indisputable lay between us. He looked dangerous, and arrogant, and challenging. How, I wondered again, had I ever thought he was Milburn? Easy, familiar Bertie?

I felt my spine stiffen and then I straightened so that the wall was no longer supporting me. *You already do,* I thought.

"We know your mother wants consummation. But what about you, Gwen? Do you?" He stepped even closer, so his body was almost touching mine. I scarce knew whether to suck in my breath to create more space between us, or to sway just the barest inch toward him, closing the distance. I looked into his deep, blue gaze, and could not lie.

"Too much." My voice was still a whisper.

"Just so we both know it," he said, low. Then a quick smile flashed across his face, and his eyes were sunny again. He took a step back. "But for now your virtue is safe," he said lightly.

"Thank you," I said, wondering if I meant it.

"Of course, having known your parents for some time, I have to take issue with whether or not you do in fact qualify as gently bred, Gwen," he said, as he offered me his arm.

I took it. "Having known them longer, I am in complete agreement," I assured him as we stepped out into the cool sunlit day.

So it transpired that we were, once again, laughing as we set out to the Clarendon, although this time, beneath the laughter lay the certainty that we would be having a very difficult interlude, indeed, before much time had passed.

8

In which we arrive at the Clarendon for the second
time and I get foxed

*O*ur arrival, this second time around, was less auspicious. True, it had started out as companionably as could be expected, given the circumstances, but somewhere on the journey that mood had faded, and was replaced by silence, each of us lost in our own thoughts.

Once there, Cambourne wasted no time in making good on his promise to divest himself of Milburn's garments. Within moments of entering the rooms we had almost shared last night, he had shrugged off his jacket, unwound his elaborate neckcloth, and removed his waistcoat. This was the second time in as many days that Cambourne had stripped off his jacket in front of me, and this time the gesture had left me strangely unsettled.

This undoubtedly sounds odd, so let me see if I can explain: To see a gentleman without the trappings he would ordinarily present to the outside world speaks of intimacy. The first time he had done it, then, on our wedding night, it had seemed an appropriate enough familiarity. But today, it only served to remind me that I'd been laboring under, shall we say, a rather large misapprehension at the time. And so, it seemed, perhaps more importantly, had he.

I gathered myself. "Cambourne?"

"Yes, Gwen?" he said, turning back toward me, as he loosened his cuffs.

I blinked, suddenly nervous. "Why?" I asked.

He straightened, his hands going still, but didn't pretend to misunderstand. "Ah," he said lightly. "I'd been about to offer you the proverbial penny for your thoughts. I see I needn't bother."

"No," I said. I still stood, just inside the door. "You needn't. Just tell me, why did you do this? Why would you?"

He didn't answer either question, but instead walked over to the little table that held a decanter and several glasses. "Brandy?" he asked. "It's French and it's smuggled."

"Perhaps spirits are not the thing, at the moment," I said, very repressively. "Is there ratafia?"

"Almost certainly," he said, picking up two glasses, and apparently completely missing—or more likely, ignoring—my intent. "But it's vile stuff."

"I rather like it." I smiled up at him, innocently. "But you've not answered my questions."

"No," he said, easily. "I haven't. But surely you cannot like ratafia? It's *sweet*," he said.

"Precisely," I told him. "That's *why* I like it. And besides, I have never had brandy. It is one of those things not generally considered suitable for green girls."

"Perhaps, then," he said, with a long look, "you are ready to try it. Or should be."

I gave him a long look back. "Not without being told why, I'm not," I said, firmly.

He unstoppered the decanter. "Well," he said, "it has a complexity on the tongue that is sweet and, yet, underneath, not sweet at all. With a subtlety that, I can assure you, could never be mistaken for the cloying simplicity of ratafia. It starts with a burn and then subtlely changes to something entirely . . . different."

I held my ground. *"Ratafia,"* I said, most sternly, "is appropriate."

"Yes," he said, lightly. "But entirely without any interesting, let alone unexpected, depths." And before I could object, he continued. "Of course, I am happy to send down for some if you are not prepared to try something new, Gwen."

I looked at him. He was perfectly amiable, but his eyes glinted, and I knew he was waiting for my reply. I opened my mouth to say that that would be accommodating indeed of him. "It is not that I'm not ready," I heard myself say.

He did not reply, but raised a brow. An arrogant brow.

"I am just not sure that I . . . want it," I finished, weakly. After a moment, I held out my hand, and he handed me a glass. I hesitated, though, looking at it. I both wanted to try it and didn't. "And, anyway, it seems foolish to be talking of beverages when we have other things to discuss."

"Were we talking of beverages?" he said, as he seated himself across from me.

"Yes, I—Oh," I said, feeling suddenly rather stupid as color flooded my face.

He raised his glass. "Think of it as medicinal," he suggested. "I know I am."

I laughed, despite myself, and took an experimental sip. It *was* rather nice, actually, and I could not help but think that his description had been fair. I liked the way I could feel it spreading through me.

"This is good," I said, as I took another, larger, sip. "Very comforting. I understand why they give it to people who have had a shock. Like me." I looked up and caught his gaze. "Us."

He lifted his glass to me. "Us, yes," he said wryly, before we both drank.

"May I have more?" I held out my empty glass.

His eyebrow went up, but he leaned forward and refilled it. I drank, deeply, again. I was convinced that its warmth would give me the courage not only to repeat my questions, but to be able to hear the answers. But somehow, before I knew it, my glass was empty again, and still I had not asked him. Wordlessly, I held my glass out again.

He looked at me. "As much as I'm encouraging you to get stuck into the stuff, I should warn you that it is a bit stronger than what you are used to," he said. "And I'd wager that you've not had much to eat since sometime yesterday."

I thought about it as I tipped my glass up, again, so that the last few drops slid into my mouth. When *had* I last eaten? I had only picked at my tray before the wedding yesterday, too nervous to eat. Then I hadn't been hungry at the wedding breakfast and by the time last night's supper had finally arrived, I, not surprisingly, had no appetite. And, now that I think on it, I had felt the same way about my breakfast tray this morning. "The day before, actually," I told him, and he looked surprised. "But I'm not hungry. Are you concerned I'll get foxed?"

"Yes," he said, succinctly, as he put down his glass and rose. He took mine and set it down. "Although," he said, with that quick, disarming grin that made those improbable dimples come up, "admittedly, that was more or less the point."

I giggled. "So I wouldn't be in any fit state to ask you questions, do you mean?"

"Yes," he said, which I thought very amusing of him.

"Do you truly mean that you've had nothing at all today?" he asked. "To eat?"

"A cup of tea," I told him, and then giggled again.

He looked at me, one eyebrow raised, as though waiting for more.

So, "A daring little oolong," I told him. "Oh, and a *small* sherry. With Father."

"I would never," he said, frowning, "have given you that second glass had I realized you hadn't eaten at all." I could almost *feel* his impatience as he said, "It will take too long if I ring. I'll go down and order food. Wait here." And then he strode out of the room, and I heard the outer door of the suite close.

Where would I go, I wondered idly, even had I been so inclined? I leaned back in my chair, now, unconcerned about my inelegant sprawl. I felt warm and relaxed, and I could not understand in the least what had him so worried. Silly to imagine that I would get drunk from a few tiny glasses of brandy! It was not as though I was not used to champagne, and spirits were spirits, after all. Exactly how different could brandy be?

I looked around the suite, and decided I might as well be really comfortable, so I took off my shoes and, putting aside all thoughts of ladylike decorum, put my feet up on the arm of the chair to better contemplate my situation.

Actually, seeing the world through a brandy-induced haze was not entirely unpleasant, I thought. Of course my problems were still the same, but somehow that didn't feel nearly so serious as it had a few hours ago. And I felt very sure that I would be able to get more information from Cambourne later. When I felt less . . . relaxed.

If not for the one moment in which I'd breathed that fateful, "Oh, Bertie," the entire thing would have been determined for us. I would be Cambourne's wife in every sense of the word right now, and quite possibly none the wiser. And the very devil of it was, that in some very small part of me, I was not entirely certain that that might not have been the most desirable outcome: to simply have been carried along a little further by events, not to have to make any decisions.

And even my feelings toward Cambourne were confused. I did know that I had to acknowledge that despite everything, my disappointment, my anger, my frustration, I felt an almightily powerful pull to him. That Milburn seemed to somehow slip further from me with each second that ticked by.

I let my head fall back against the Clarendon's exceedingly comfortable chair and thought back over my morning. Of my mother and Violetta, and poor, foolish Reverend Twigge, and my beleaguered father and his Corn, and started to laugh. From this perspective, the situation was vastly amusing, actually. I was still laughing when Cambourne returned.

"I've ordered us some food," he said, eyeing me worriedly, for which, really, there was no reason at all.

"It's very funny, actually," I gasped, not bothering to sit up. "You. Me. My parents— You're a good man on Corn, y'know," I explained.

"Naturally," he said, politely.

I nodded, ignoring the way the chair seemed to have begun to dip and sway in a most enjoyable manner. To be sure, it had seemed stable enough earlier. I closed my eyes, so as not to see the room whirling by, which felt like an exceptionally good idea. Why hadn't I done that sooner? The chair was still moving, though. "Funny chairs they have here," I giggled, before continuing. "Trussing chickens and whatnot. The Axton belfry. Violetta had crumbs on her whiskers," I explained merrily. "Violetta told Reverend Twigge that all I need is a good toss between the sheets," I told him. "Wasn't that an abominable thing to say?" I finally opened my eyes, and rather wished I hadn't. Because that was when I realized that it wasn't the chair that was dipping and swaying. It, in fact, was perfectly stationary. It was the *room* that was tilting and spinning. For some reason this felt much less pleasant.

"Yes," he agreed. "It was." His face was oddly out of focus. I quickly closed my eyes again. I really was sleepy, and the room seemed to have grown very hot.

"Thing of it is," I said, "that I always thought it would be Milburn. Tossing me, you know, between the sheets. Pardon my indelicacy."

"I'm nodding," he said, and I held up my hand in grateful acknowledgment of the fact that he'd spared me having to open my eyes, which suddenly seemed enormously difficult.

I let my hand fall. "Not that I ever particularly *wanted* him to, mind you. Just always thought that was how it would be. But he really didn't want to toss me, I suppose'," I said, suddenly feeling bereft. "He must have been desperate not to. So he never came back and you had to take responsibility for tossing me for him." Tears slid out from under my closed eyelids, and ran warm down my cheeks. "Milburn always did like to get someone else to do his dirty work for him."

I was dimly aware that Cambourne was kneeling in front of my chair and had taken my hands in his. "That's not precisely how it happened," he said. "And for what it's worth, I would be honored beyond words to toss you."

"Oh, how lovely," I said, sniffling. "Am I foxed, after all?"

He laughed. "I think a bit, yes," he said.

"But don't you see, Cambourne?" I said brokenly, aware that tears were still sliding down my cheeks. "As tempting as it is, I can't possibly let you toss me without telling me why you did this."

I felt awful. No. Awful implies that there is some chance that you might someday feel better. I felt far, far worse than that. My head ached abominably and my mouth felt as though I had been chewing paper. I wondered when, exactly, I had been put to bed.

Cambourne was sitting in a chair by the fire, a small book in his hand. A lamp was lit on the table next to him, but otherwise the room was in the encroaching darkness. He held a quill, but did not seem to be either reading or writing very prodigiously; but, rather, was staring into space. Careful not to open my eyes, I studied him from beneath my eyelids. On the surface he looked identical to Milburn, it was true. But he was so indefinably different that it made me feel like the veriest fool that I had not seen it instantly. *Even* taking into account that only approximately fifteen seconds had elapsed between my first glimpse of him and the commencement of the vows.

92 *Jessica Benson*

In childhood what I had always understood was that the secret to telling one from the other lay in understanding their dispositions. There was something in the way they held themselves; the way they moved set them apart. Milburn was a lounging kind of person. He had a go-with-whatever-the-outcome type of demeanor. Whereas Cambourne had a kind of intensity to him, as though he wanted to *determine* the outcome. While Milburn's movements were languid, Cambourne's were swift and decisive, with a quick kind of grace to them. His horses were always just a trifle faster, and their footing a tad more sure. His fish, bigger; his aim, truer. Milburn always played the prank gleefully, but Cambourne had usually been the one to think it through.

And, of course, always there was the fact that Cambourne *was* the heir. He, apparently more purposeful from the very start, had emerged first, and to hear the tale, did it in a very rapid and straightforward manner. Milburn had ambled out, backward, some quarter hour later. And for his pains, or more accurately, his mother's, ended up a second son, the simple Lord Edward, or as everyone referred to him, Lord Bertie.

A perfect match for me, it seemed, since the thing that no one had thus far mentioned, was that my birth, although perfectly acceptable, put me well below Cambourne's touch. It is true that my father is an earl, but he is not, you see, despite the vast quantities of blunt, a really old earl. The title of Axton goes back only a hundred years or so to a wealthy merchant ancestor who had the foresight to welcome the king with an open purse. We were respectable, by this point in time, certainly, but well below where Cambourne, as the future duke, would be expected to look for his bride.

But now, in this room, the lamplight spilled over Cambourne, burnishing his dark hair and edging into the hollows beneath his cheekbones, his dark eyelashes casting faint shadows above them. One booted leg rested on the other knee. Whatever turmoil he might be experiencing was certainly not visible on the exterior. I could not understand why he had such an unsettling effect on me. An effect that—if I were truthful I would have to acknowledge—Milburn did not, and never would. At this admission, the color flooded into my cheeks anew, and I was grateful for the darkness.

"Water?" Cambourne asked, his quiet words startling me. At my nod—which had a most infelicitous effect on the throbbing in my head—he stood to bring me some.

"How did you know I was awake?" I asked, when I could.

And could see his smile as he replied, "Because you stopped snoring."

I felt a rush of heat as more color flooded my face. I was profoundly grateful for the low lighting of the room. "I do not snore," I informed him with as much hauteur as I could muster, which, given my current woebegone state, was not all that much.

Not enough, anyway, to deter him. "Actually, it appears that you do. Or, at least, when you've shot the cat."

"Ladies," I said, making my tones icy, "do not shoot the cat."

"I see," he said, slowly. "Much, I suppose, as ladies do not have baser instincts?" His eyes held mine. Even in the semidarkness, I could see the intensity in his.

I dropped my gaze first. "I perhaps imbibed a tad unwisely," I admitted.

"No cause for alarm, though, your drunken snoring

was, in fact, most ladylike," he assured me. "And getting foxed seemed a perfectly sensible course of action under the circumstances."

"Don't tease me, Cambourne," I said. "I've a devil of a head." The angry throbbing of which, in fact, was entirely his fault, it was beginning to dawn on me. I sat up further, against the pillows, and allowed my gaze to sweep over him.

He had put down his journal, but held the quill between his fingers, still. He looked oh, so sure of himself, and suddenly I felt the anger curl through me. *He* hadn't gone two days without eating. *He* hadn't been tricked at the altar and almost seduced, or lied to, or not told the reasons for any of this. I doubted that *his* head felt as if it were about to burst. He looked like a man who is entirely sure of his place in the world. Too sure. "Cambourne," I said, firmly, feeling my hands curl into fists.

He met my gaze squarely. "Yes, Gwen?"

"You have to tell me," I said. "Why?"

He stood then, and walked to me, with that graceful economy of movement that I recognized now should have tipped me immediately that he wasn't Milburn. "I'm sorry," he said, not sounding it at all, to my mind. "But I can't." He sat down on the bed next to me, and I turned my head away as I felt the soft down of the mattress dip under him.

"I see," I said tightly. "You can't or you won't?"

He took my hand, and despite myself, my heart speeded up. He reached out and stroked my cheek, so that I turned toward him, almost involuntarily. "Gwen," he said, his voice rich and dark. "Does that really matter?"

I jerked my hand away and scrambled further upright on the bed. "How on earth can you say that?"

He looked almost impatient. "Because it's true. We are in the situation we are in."

"But, Cambourne," I said, very patiently and slowly, because I sensed it would irritate him. "You don't seem to realize that I hold all the cards. Let me get this right: You want me to pretend that you are your brother, stay married to you, and not ask any questions?"

"Yes," he agreed as though such a thing were entirely credible.

"But that's not reasonable of you," I pointed out.

He came closer. "In what way?" he asked, leaning down slightly, so I was backed against the pillows.

"All I have to do is tell everyone the truth," I pointed out.

"You won't do that," he replied with such an air of certainty that I wanted to hit him.

I settled, however, for raising a brow (much more ladylike). "And why not?"

He leaned over me in earnest then. "Because," he said, from very close, "you don't hold nearly so many cards as you seem to believe." He bent his head and his lips grazed past mine. "I hold just a few myself," he murmured against my cheek, as he laced our fingers together. His lips moved to my ear, and caressed it. I had a very difficult time not sighing in pleasure. "One or two," he murmured, the words vibrating against my skin.

My eyes fell closed. Although my anger was not in the least abated, I could see no reason to tell him to stop at this precise moment. Not just yet. And oddly, the urge to hit him seemed to have settled into something different. I was still agitated, vibrating almost, in fact, but it had an entirely different feel.

"Gwen," he breathed, as he pinned my hands on the

bed next to me. I looked down at the top of his head, as his lips brushed against my neck. Kissing the hollow there, and making me want to squirm with the warmth. The tip of his tongue traced the faintest pattern. The pain in my head was entirely forgotten. My limbs felt heavy and sort of tingling. "This could be so easy," he whispered seductively, as his warm mouth dipped lower, to the neckline of my gown. "So easy between us. If only you would let it."

Oh, don't get me wrong. More than half of me wanted to. Just one more minute I promised myself, but then his mouth grazed over my breast. Fully covered, by both gown and chemise, and still I could feel it with a shuddering jolt, his breath, warm and moist, and knew instinctively what I had to do.

"Touch me, Cambourne," I whispered. "Really touch me."

And when he freed my hands to do just that, I pushed him. As hard as I could, and he reeled back. "What on this earth," I demanded, scrambling to sit up against the pillows, "ever made you think I would go along with this in the first place?"

And despite what I had just done—what he had just been doing—he looked cool as a cucumber as he smiled down at me. "Because, Gwen," he said. "You *always* do what you're told."

9

In which Cecy and Myrtia give me food for thought

"*H*ow *insulting! What did you say?*" exclaimed Cecy, interrupting my recitation of events.

"What could I say? It is nothing but the truth," I admitted. "I *do* always do what I am told. So"—I shrugged—"I had some supper and took a hot bath."

Cecy brightened. "Please say he climbed right in with you!" Then, when I shook my head, offered, "I can tell you how to lure him in the next time, if you'd like."

"Cecy!" Myrtia said, with a warning in her tone.

Whatever Cecy would have replied was forestalled by the arrival of her husband. "Hello, Gwen, Myrtia, Cecy darling." Without removing his gaze from the book he carried, Barings bowed to us. "Did you know, my love," he continued conversationally, "that there are several dozen men about, hanging something apparently designed to make my study look like a madam's second-best bedchamber?"

"Do you mean you don't like the new wallcovering?" Cecy asked with a frown.

"Not at all," he replied equably. He still had not looked up from his book. How did the man avoid injury?

"Simon!" Cecy said. "How exactly do you know what a madam's second-best bedchamber looks like?"

"Hearsay only, my love." He dropped a kiss on her head and made to depart. "I was always in the best." Then he actually looked up at our faces. "Oh," he said. "That was a joke."

"It's not that, Simon," Cecy assured him, and he drifted out of the room, underlining something in his book.

"What else did Cambourne say, Gwen?" Myrtia asked when he had gone.

"Other than that I always do what I'm told? Let me see. Quite a few things, actually: that he couldn't tell me why, that we were where we were, and that I didn't hold all the cards," I said.

"And where precisely do you suppose his attempting to take you to bed fits in?" Cecy asked.

"It does beg the question: *Why?*" Myrtia said, and then looked at me. "Not, of course," she added, quickly, "that a man wouldn't have every reason to want to marry you, Gwen, but—"

"It's all right," I told her. "I agree completely; it makes no sense."

"And he absolutely knew what he was doing," said Cecy, decisively. "The question, as Myrtia so succinctly phrased it, is, why? *Why* did he do it?"

"Do you suppose something terrible might have befallen Milburn!" I asked them, and felt my voice catch in my throat at the thought of poor, hapless Bertie. "Suppose he, in his final hour, asked his brother to take care of me!"

Myrtia's eyes shimmered with tears of sympathy. "And he thought of *you* at the end!"

Cecy, though, looked less convinced. "It's not that I'm unfeeling, Gwen," she said, firmly, "but really, Milburn is like one of those cats, you know, who refuses to chase mice like all the other cats and sleeps in front of the fire all day, eating all the choicest morsels until he finally gets tossed out of the house for revolting behavior—like eating all the lobster patties and then being sick all over the clothespress. Then he turns up again months later, and everyone, despite themselves, welcomes him with open arms. And besides," she added for good measure, "if it had been the case, that something terrible had befallen him, Cambourne would have just told you."

Which, I had to concede, was true. "Milburn, then, is like a fat, lazy cat?" I said.

"Well, I didn't mean it in an *unkind* way," Cecy said. "And only think of those nine lives!"

"But, even putting the marriage aside," Myrtia said, wrinkling her forehead, "why would Cambourne ever conceivably want to continue to pass himself off as Milburn?"

I dropped my gaze. "That is what I am saying; none of this makes any sense whatsoever. And Cambourne is arrogant and irritating, and won't tell me anything. When I tried to insist, he—"

"What?" Cecy asked, with interest. "He what?"

"Kissed me," I admitted.

"And I collect you stopped asking questions at that point?" Cecy inquired.

I looked down, but forbore to answer. Which, of course, was as much answer as she needed. She smiled.

Myrtia squinted. No doubt this was the expression she

used to convey deep thought about weighty topics at Mrs. Robichon's Thursday At-Home Literary Salons, but she actually looked rather more charming than anything. "But what does he want you to do?"

Now *that* I could answer. "To live with him under the pretext that he is Milburn," I said. "To help him in his masquerade. And all without asking any questions."

"Do you know what I think?" Cecy asked.

"No, but somehow I am confident I will soon," I retorted.

Cecy smiled. "I think," she said, "that it must be something dire. Dire enough that he had no choice."

"Thank you," I said. "I could never have come up with that myself. And it's flattering, besides."

"Not flattering, perhaps, but pragmatic," Cecy said.

"Has he said what he expects—what he plans to do about, well—" Myrtia blushed.

"The marriage bed, do you mean, Myrtia?" asked Cecy, with a raised brow. "I think we know what he *expected* to do about it at the outset. But now . . . interesting question, indeed. What exactly *does* he expect, Gwen?"

I met Myrtia's gaze instead of Cecy's. "I don't know."

"But I suppose that being the ever moral and prudent girl that you are, you are determined to resist Cambourne's considerable charms and wait to see if Milburn comes back to lay his rightful claim to you?" Cecy asked.

"Yes," I said, raising my chin.

She laughed. "I'd lay a monkey on it that after once with Cambourne, going back to Milburn would be like, I don't know, going from riding a thoroughbred to a cart horse. But then," she added with a shrug, "I suppose under this arrangement you won't be riding Cambourne at all, so you'll likely never know what you're missing."

I looked at Cecy, with her modish outfit and glossy blond curls, sitting in her gracious morning room. "Really, Cecy, you might *look* every inch the proper lady, but you are absolutely appalling," I said.

She smiled. "It's only the truth," she insisted, and then became serious again. "And anyway, if Cambourne's half the man I credit him, he'll find a way to take what he wants."

I took a breath. "Well, *I* am in control of that," I said, taking some consolation from the fact that I could at least honestly say that *that* was true.

"How does he seem to *feel* about this . . . arrangement?" asked Myrtia.

"I honestly do not know," I said. "In fact, I've no idea how he feels about anything."

"That's not Cambourne, Gwen, that's men," Cecy said, with asperity. "Are you imagining that Milburn would be declaring his emotions at the drop of a hat?"

"Of course not," I said. "But Milburn, somehow, is more of an open book. He isn't overly complicated. Give him some decent food and drink, a few gaudy waistcoats, and a chair at his club, and he's happy. Cambourne is more like reading a book in a language you don't quite know—a few words here and there make sense, but that doesn't mean you understand it."

"Interesting analogy," Myrtia said. "Because many people find learning a foreign language, although difficult, is more rewarding. . . ."

My eyes filled. I was silent for a moment, gazing out at the trees in Berkeley Square, which blurred as I blinked the tears back.

"Gwen?" said Cecy, taking up my hand.

"You married for love," I said.

"Yes," she agreed. "I did. I married Barings because I love him. I also married him," she said, "for practical reasons. The two are not necessarily mutually exclusive, you know."

"You? Practical?" I teased, sniffing back my tears. "Tell me."

"Well—" Cecy took a deep breath—"it was also because he is good and honorable and *his* mother would not dream of singing bawdy songs from atop the pianoforte or publicly taking lovers young enough to be her sons. And it seemed unlikely in the extreme that Barings would end up the type of man who would gamble and whore his family into debt and disgrace," she finished bluntly.

Poor Cecy would forever be trying to live down her parents' antics. And it was true, Barings was such a stolid counterpoint to Cecy's sometimes outrageous spirits that it had often seemed something of a mystery that she loved him so steadfastly.

"Yes, there were wealthier, handsomer, more exciting men who offered for me," she continued. "But Barings is so very respectable—quite, quite, atrociously dull in his values, if not his birth, as my mother so despairingly put it. I do love him, yes, but I recognize that marriage is more than that, and I love him all the more for that realization." Cecy raised her chin. "And," she added, the glint coming back into her eyes, "he is the *most* astounding lover. The things that man can come up with—"

"You did not know that before you were married, however," Myrtia said firmly.

"Naturally not," agreed Cecy merrily. "And before you two poker up at me, let me assure you, men speak of these things all the time."

"This is very amusing," said Myrtia firmly, "if vastly improper, but it is not solving anything for Gwen."

"Ah, but it could. What I *was* getting at," Cecy said, "is that what you expect in a husband is not necessarily what you *need* in a husband when it comes down to it."

I frowned at her. "What are you really saying, Cecy?"

"What I am saying, is that perhaps you should try looking at it as a lucky escape. Regardless of why he did it, Cambourne is by far the better choice for you."

"The thing is," I said, wanting desperately to make some sense of this, "that all my life, I've seen Milburn from the perspective of being the man who would be my husband, and Cambourne as his brother. I never balked at doing what I was told—as Cambourne pointed out in so ungentlemanly a manner—even though I did not in all honesty love Milburn. But I don't know Cambourne in the same way, never saw him in that way. And, somehow, that *matters*. Do you understand?"

They both nodded, and then Cecy said, "Well, any number of women *have* seen him in that way, and should you decide not to *keep* him—"she grinned wickedly —"they will be only too happy to step into your place."

"Yes," I said, using my foot to smooth a pattern across the thick nap of the Turkey carpet. "I've heard things to that effect." I looked up at Cecy. "Tell me."

She shrugged. "He's almost shockingly handsome, Gwen; he's wealthy beyond imagining; he's heir to a dukedom. Surely opportunity must cross his path daily. And, on occasion, I would imagine he avails himself of what is so freely offered."

"Who?" I asked her, wondering, as I did, why I wanted to know so very badly.

"Who what?" Myrtia asked.

But Cecy understood me well enough. "Last I heard? Mathilde Claussen," she said, so promptly that I knew this liaison must have been the topic of some considerable discussion. I knew Mathilde Claussen. Unfortunately. She was a ravishing young widow with such a charming manner that even all the women liked her. I did, myself.

I shut my eyes for a second, against the sudden image of Cambourne letting *her* hair down, and watching himself unwrap her body in front of a darkened window. Whispering words of desire into *her* ear.

I opened my eyes and gave Cecy a questioning look. "I see. And are there others?"

"Not that I know of, at the moment," she said. "But I would say without question that there *have* been."

"And is Mrs. Claussen still, well, *present?*"

She hesitated, just a moment too long. "Cecy?"

"Honestly, I don't know, Gwen," she said. "The rumor mill has it that he has seemed unusually besotted by her."

"I see," I said. "Although it is of no concern to me, of course." Which was *entirely* true.

Cecy said, "Look, Gwen, you do need bear in mind that it *is* only rumor. In truth, I am not certain of how things stand between them—he is not a man to parade his indiscretions."

"No, but the fact remains that he is still a man who has them," I said.

Cecy gave me a good, long, look. "You would prefer to marry a man of no experience in the world, then? Because if that is your point, I can assure you that Milburn is hardly the one."

I was about to say something cutting (although I hadn't exactly figured it out yet), when Myrtia joined in. "In all fairness," she said, "considering the circumstances, you can hardly hold Cambourne's past against him."

"She's right," Cecy said. "And now that he's done it, and

married you, the question is not so much why, because that is out of your hands, but, what are you going to *do* about this?"

"Oh no," said Myrtia, with real trepidation. "You are not going to interfere!"

"I shouldn't dream of interfering," Cecy lied promptly. "I was merely thinking that perhaps we should assist Gwen by helping her discover what has transpired."

I looked at her. "What do you have in mind, Cecy?"

"Yes, what, precisely?" Myrtia added.

Cecy waved away our objections. "You two have no spirit of adventure," she said.

"No, we two have a modicum of intelligence and common sense," Myrtia said.

"Seems to me if you had that much of either, Gwen, you wouldn't have ended up married to the wrong man," Cecy pointed out.

"Well, Cecy," I said, "I think we've both learned our lessons about your schemes the hard way. Be warned: I've no intention of disguising myself as a coachman, this time."

"That Bow Street runner was very nice, actually," Cecy said coldly. "Once you returned the pocket watch. And Lord Smythe-Tobias was most understanding about the wrecked coach."

I opened my mouth, but Myrtia, for once, cut me off rudely. "And *I* have not yet fully lived down the humiliation of being caught at going through Lady Chelmesley's underthings!"

"She never knew that you weren't truly a thieving scullery maid!" Cecy replied, gaily. "And anyway, I was merely going to suggest that you have two options, Gwen. Or would that be too alarming of me?"

I sighed. "And the first is?"

"We attempt to learn what has happened to Milburn." Cecy sounded a little huffy. "You do, after all, through your family, have access to the highest diplomatic circles."

"I suppose that couldn't hurt anything," I said. Actually, it was surprisingly sensible, if one were to consider the source. "Oh, but that won't work as I'm not supposed to tell anyone that Cambourne's Cambourne."

Cecy lifted a brow. "And you have followed that request precisely to the letter."

I flushed. "Well, I cannot imagine he meant *you,*" I said, realizing, as I did, that he no doubt had. I looked at her still-raised brow. "Oh," I said.

"Who else knows?" asked Myrtia.

"Well, Mother and, of course, Violetta. And Father, and the two of you, and Milburn's valet, I think, and Ladimer, and Reverend Twigge."

"He has not got the slightest chance of keeping this quiet," Cecy said with conviction. "And," she mused, "he must know that."

"But surely none of us will tell," I objected.

Cecy looked at me as though I had grown a second head. "I suppose allowances must be made for the shock having addled your wits," she said. "Don't be ridiculous. Your mother would publish it in the *Times,* or possibly hand out leaflets herself in St. James Street, if she thought it would keep Cambourne married to you."

"But she hasn't breathed a word," I pointed out. "In fact, she blackmailed Reverend Twigge not to."

"She's choosing her moment," said Myrtia, slowly. "Waiting until she thinks it's the right time to make it public in a way that would ensure neither of you can live it down. Is that what you think, Cecy?"

Cecy nodded. "I'd go odds that's precisely what she's doing and Cambourne knows it."

I looked at both of them. This was my *mother* they were talking about. The woman who bore me and raised me and . . . "Oh, dear," I said, dully.

Cecy leaned over. "But all this is diverting us from the plan. And, of course, crucial to the plan of finding Milburn succeeding is that you manage to keep Cambourne out of your bed, Gwen. Because once he so much as sets foot in it, it doesn't matter if Milburn is dead or alive, there is no going back."

I nodded. I knew that much, at least. "What is my other option?" I asked.

Cecy smiled. "The one that is the complete opposite of the first, and the one you'll choose if you're smart: You go home, put on one of those night rails of Suzette's and lure him into your chamber without further ado."

I turned to Myrtia. "Do you agree with that?" I demanded.

She was silent for a moment, choosing her words, I knew. Myrtia always spoke carefully. "I think that you have to understand what he has done, and why he has done it, first."

"And, trust me, the night rail is precisely the way to go about it," Cecy said. My complete incomprehension must have shown on my face, because she continued. "There are some things that a man will do anything for. You want information. A beautiful woman in a flimsy night rail is a time-honored means of eliciting just that. Empires have fallen on less. And may I remind you, he wasn't above trying to silence *you* with a kiss. Turn the tables on him."

"Next you'll be suggesting I truss him like a chicken," I muttered, under my breath.

Her eyebrow went up. "Hardly for a beginner, I shouldn't think. I'd start with the flimsy night rail."

"Cecy was right," I said to Myrtia, the following day, and then added, quickly, "Not about the night rail. I think we should try to find out what has become of Milburn."

"Oh?" she said, very cautiously.

"I am not suggesting," I told her with asperity, "that we look to her for our methods. Only that she had the correct idea. But how to do it?"

"Your brother," she said, promptly. "James."

"James?" I asked, frowning at her. "Why on earth would I go to James?"

"James," she said, "has been noted with favor at a number of Ladies' Reform and Rescue Committee meetings, for his efforts in the War Office. He is held to be quite a rising force there."

And so it transpired that a short time later the two of us were ushered into his chambers.

"Hallo, Gwen," he said, rising to greet us from behind an impressive mahogany desk piled high with charts and papers. I eyed them. They certainly did at least give the *illusion* that he was working. He bowed over Myrtia's hand. "Miss Conyngham. What brings you two ladies— lovely surprise though it is—to a place like this?" he asked.

I looked at him with suspicion. He was being entirely too polite. I seated myself. "Milburn," I said, with, I admit, some sense of drama, "has disappeared!"

James, though, had *no* sense of drama. Never has. He leaned back in his chair. "You are confusing me," he said bluntly, with a frown.

"I mean," I said, "Cambourne replaced Milburn at the wedding and is impersonating him."

"Yes," he said, at length.

"Yes?" I said. "Yes, as in, you already knew that?"

He nodded.

"Fine," I said. "This is all fine and good that even you knew about this when I did not—I suppose the maids who clean the cathedral knew. But now I want you to find Milburn for me and bring him back."

"It seems to me I have two choices now, Gwen."

"There is a lot of that going around, apparently," I muttered.

He gave me a strange look and continued. "I can obfuscate or I can simply tell you the truth. Shall I be honest with you?" he asked.

"By all means. It promises to be a novel experience," I told him.

"As far as bringing Milburn home goes? Can't do it," he said.

"Why not?" I asked. "I don't understand. Are you saying it can't be *done*? Or that *you* can't do it? Or that he won't come? Does he want to?"

He didn't answer, saying, instead, "Cambourne, I take it, does not know you are here?"

"Of course not," I told him. "He wants me not to ask questions."

"Perhaps you should not," James said. "Go home, Gwen. This will take care of itself."

I clenched my teeth together to stop the fury boiling up in me. "Home?" I said. "And that would be where, precisely, James? To the house where I was supposed to live with the man who I was supposed to marry, but in actual fact contains the one who married me under false pretenses and won't say why? To Mother and Father? Why is everyone treating me like this?" I demanded. "Like I'm just some foolish little chit who has no idea what is good for me?"

"Is Cambourne treating you that way?" he asked, with a keen look.

"Yes," I said. "And Mother certainly is."

"Mother," he said, "treats everyone that way. Including the prince regent, the prime minister, Father, and myself. I shouldn't read too much into it. Infinitely more worthwhile to put your resources into convincing Cambourne that you're more than that."

"Are you saying, then, that I have to prove something to him?"

"It can't hurt," he replied, placidly.

"You won't help me?" I demanded. "Because I am not without resources, you know."

"Gwen," he said, leaning across the desk. "I *am* your resources. At least where the War Office is concerned. And, no, I am sorry, but I think you need to do as Cambourne asks. I know it won't be easy," he said calmly, as he turned an unused quill over in his fingers. "But I suspect if you act reasonably, you'll get some answers. And Mother, you should know, is going around saying you are off your oats," he said. "No doubt laying the groundwork for, I don't know what, but some plot. If you are smart, you won't make her sound in the right of things."

"*Off my oats?*" I demanded. "Like a horse off his feed?"

"That would be the general idea," he said. "Something about bride nerves."

I dropped my eyes down to my lap, trying to regain some degree of control over my temper, and as I looked up, I saw him wink at Myrtia. "What are you saying,

James?" I asked, mulling that wink. "And this time, say it as though you believe I'm clever enough to follow you."

"Very well, Gwen," he said. "Not to put too fine a point on it, I am saying, *go home.* Do as Cambourne asks. He has his reasons; they're good ones. Meantime, be patient. If you racket about complaining, you'll only provide Mother with more fuel for her fire *and you stand the chance of further endangering the person you would most like not to.*" He smiled, tightly. "There. Was that specific and yet cryptic enough for you?"

"Yes," I said, as I stood to gather my things. It cost me no effort at all to make my tone acid. "Very cryptic, indeed. Thank you for your help." And then I swept out of his office, with Myrtia in my wake. I managed to refrain from demanding an accounting of her until we were outside, waiting for John Coachman to put down the steps to the carriage. "What was that about?" I asked, watching her carefully. "The winking. He winked at you when he said that very odd thing about endangering Milburn."

Color washed over her as she turned away to climb the steps. "I don't know what you're talking about," she said.

"Yes, you do," I told her as I ascended behind her. "I saw."

"I don't know," she said, as she took her seat. "I am assuming he was saying to trust him. To trust them both."

"It's a bit like being told it's safe to put your head in the crocodile's mouth, being told to trust one of my brothers, don't you think?" I said, sitting down opposite.

"Oh, I don't know," she said, blushing again. "I think he's quite trustworthy."

"That," I told her, "is because you don't know him, really."

"Perhaps," she said. "But from a strictly pragmatic viewpoint, it doesn't seem to me that you've much choice."

Which sentiments I did not much like, but was forced to agree with. For the moment, anyway. "No, I suppose not," I said, crossing my arms and staring out the window. "Do you suppose Milburn is really in danger? James's hint was tantalizing, but hardly conclusive."

"Well, Gwen—" Myrtia sounded hesitant.

I turned and looked at her. "Well what?"

"As much as I hate to suggest it, you *could* always try Cecy's second plan."

10

In which we remove to Milburn House and my
mother and Lady Worth pay us a visit

Goodness knows, I had opportunity.

Cambourne and I removed together into Milburn's snug
little house in Mayfair, which I quickly came to love. Cozy
and informal, and presided over by a friendly and efficient
staff, it was altogether much less intimidating than the vast,
echoing rooms of Cambourne House.

At Mother's insistence, I had a new maid named
Crewes. Crewes was exceedingly grand. She garbed herself entirely in black bombazine. She was a genius with
hair, and ruthless with freckles, and had come to me from
the employ of the Countess of Amblesmere, and was wont
to tell me, at the least provocation—or even in the absence
of such—how the countess had done things. She was particularly fond of relaying the countess's little maxims for
everyday living.

"The countess, you must know, my lady, deems it

acceptable to embroider after dinner only if the light is adequate." (That was one of my particular favorites, as if we lesser mortals would be gauche enough to prefer going blind from squinting at a tiny needle in the dark.)

And, "On Fridays, from ten of the clock until half past, the countess, without fail, practices her handshake so as to have it perfect for church on Sunday: two fingers only. Never too firm, never too friendly, always with the proper air of kindly condescension!"

When I offered to eschew the handshake entirely in favor of licking people's hands like a small dog, she was unamused. "The countess, my lady, if I may be so bold as to point out, has said on numerous occasions that it is hoydenish to engage in levity with one's social inferiors!"

"Hello, darling," said Cambourne, appearing at that moment in the door to my bedchamber, where I was seated in front of the mirror, while Crewes finished dressing my hair. He looked amused by the scolding, but only smiled dotingly (entirely for Crewes's benefit, I assumed) at me in the mirror as he lifted my hand to kiss it.

At the touch of his lips, my heart did that ridiculous little trip-hammer thing it seemed to have deemed necessary whenever he appeared, let alone had the audacity to smile at me. Which meant it was happening quite a bit, living together as we were, and at the oddest times in the oddest places: on the second-floor landing. Over the breakfast sideboard. Once, even in the linen cupboard. It was all most disconcerting. And I was compelled to tell myself, quite firmly, on a frequent basis that I missed the safe, comforting presence of Milburn and would gladly consign his infuriating and unsettling brother to the devil to get him back.

Crewes sniffed, bobbed a curtsey, saying, "M'lord," and then departed.

"She has a warm and cheerful way about her," he noted.

"And to what do I owe the pleasure of your presence in my bedchamber?" I said, to cover the color that always came into my face concurrent with the trip-hammer thing.

He raised a brow at that. "Cannot a man pay his own wife a visit?"

"An ordinary man and his ordinary wife, perhaps," I replied. "But we are hardly on such easy terms."

He smiled. "Ah, but I must present the *appearance* of a doting husband, all the same."

I turned on my chair and looked him in the eye. He did not need to come to my bedchamber to dote, I reminded myself, removing my hand from his, he could have done it just as well in any of the more public rooms. "What do you want, Cambourne?" I asked. "It's hardly the correct time of day if you are trying to convey the impression that this is a . . . conjugal visit."

One eyebrow went up. "One would be naïve, indeed, to believe that such things were regulated by the hour."

I looked at him for a moment, his lean face at odds with the frivolous canary waistcoat he wore, and recalled with a flash of warmth how it had been when his hands had held mine, pinned to the bed, at the Clarendon. Indeed, I could well imagine that the time of day would not matter in the least to him.

He sat down on the settee in the corner. He looked so ridiculously large there, and the settee so feminine, that I wondered for a moment whether Milburn had had this chamber decorated with me in mind, thinking ahead to the day he would bring me home as a bride. The idea brought a little pang to my throat as I recalled James's words. Was he really in danger? And had *I* unwittingly endangered him further?

"I had assumed that a visit to your chamber at the, ah, correct time of day for appearances would leave me fearing for my life," Cambourne said. I raised a brow at this, and he went on. "So it is self-preservation, rather than inclination, that has kept me away."

I licked my bottom lip, and then realizing what I had done, closed my parted mouth. "I see." I busied myself with fiddling with the bottles on my dressing table.

He stilled my hand, taking it in his. His thumb moved across my palm and I felt myself being pulled back into that wild vortex of heat. For an infinitesimal amount of time, with his thumb stroking over my palm and his gaze holding mine, there seemed no reason not to do what Cecy had advised with the flimsy night rail. Or if there was, I surely couldn't remember it. Then, the miniature of Milburn that I kept on my dressing table caught my eye, and a thousand reasons came rushing back. Not the least of which was that, according to James, he was in danger.

And, I was forced to concede, my own motives were perhaps a shade murky, shall we say? Because while I wanted information—and I really *did* want information— there was perhaps a part of me that wanted the seduction almost as much. And I could very well end up losing at that game. I was not precisely a skilled seductress, and when it came to matching skills with Cambourne, I was not necessarily convinced I would come off the victor. And if he bested me, it meant that not only would I have no further information, I would end up in over my head— well and truly married to him, with no hope left of securing the annulment I knew I should want. That *both* of us should want.

At this sobering realization, I collected myself and my hand and sat up. "How lovely of you to visit!" I said politely, as I would have to an unexpected guest for tea.

His eyes were cool and unreadable as he replied, "How kind of you to invite me."

"I did not invite you," I reminded him, and he smiled.

"You will," he said.

"How is it that no one seems to notice that you and Milburn are never in the same place together?" I asked, always the one to add a repressive note.

"People are accustomed to both of us having prolonged absences from London," he said, as if thinking about it. And after a moment, he shrugged. "And somehow they don't seem to remark it, as long as they see one or the other of us from time to time."

I stared at him, something he had said clanging in my mind. "Has he been back during the last two years?" I demanded, well aware of how sharp my voice sounded.

"Yes," he said quietly.

"But I haven't seen him in two years," I said, dumbly.

"Actually, I'm certain you have." His tone was tight. "Sometimes he was me."

"And he—both of you—let me believe he was soldiering? That every day his life was in danger?"

"It likely was," was Cambourne's reply. "What would you have us do?"

"Tell me the truth is what," I said. "Were you him, then, there—wherever *there* is—when he was here, being you?"

"Mostly," he said, still quietly.

"But isn't traveling back and forth on the Continent impossible?" I asked, conscious that I was getting a headache. "Mama is forever moaning about not being able to get good silk or champagne or the latest fashions."

"It is difficult, yes, but not impossible given the right motivation," he replied.

"I see," I said. "The question—the question I am not allowed to ask—being, *what is the right motivation?*"

He did not reply.

"So you two have just been switching whenever the mood took you? When I thought I was dancing with *you,* it could have been him?" I was not certain, even as I asked it, why I so wanted to know. And his continued silence answered for him. "The letters from *you,* from home," I demanded. "Were those written by you or Milburn?"

"Me," he said, quietly. "Unless there were some I don't know about."

"Unlikely," I said. "And the one from the Continent with regards to Stinker Boxhurst?"

"Me," he said again.

"I see." My only love letter, as unsatisfactory as it had been, had been fraudulent. I had consoled myself over the content, at the time, by telling myself that Milburn had gone to a great deal of trouble to get it to me at all, since getting mail dispatched from the Continent to England was no easy feat. I looked at him. "Did you actually go to the trouble of disguising your handwriting, then?"

"Yes," he said. "I'm afraid I did."

"What about the time last year that I danced with you at the Rostons'?"

"Still me."

"The time Larsen and I met you in the rain on South Audley Street and you gave us a ride home in your carriage and careened into a milk cart?"

"Not me," he said, instantly, and then, tentatively, "Gwen? May I ask you something?"

I looked at him. He had thus far refused me complete

honesty, but would my doing the same gain me anything? Perhaps I could even inspire him with my dedication to revealing the truth and our relationship could proceed hence on honest terms. I squared my shoulders. "Yes, you may, Cambourne," I said with, I thought, impressive grace.

"That day? Was he driving the grays?" He closed his eyes. "Tell me that he wasn't driving the grays."

Despite the fact that I could cheerfully have throttled him at the moment, I had to laugh at his expression. "He was driving the grays," I said.

He shuddered. "He knows he's not *supposed* to drive the grays."

I couldn't seem to shake the feeling that it wasn't the earth tilting under my feet, after all: it was that it had been a different shape than I had believed all along. I wondered suddenly whether *anything* I had taken as truth about my world was accurate. "Milburn *is* alive?" I asked, sharply.

"As far as I know, Gwen. I fully believe he is." But it did not escape my notice that he did not look altogether comfortable.

"This list," I said, looking at him intently, "of the times I thought it was one of you and it was really the other could go on and on. Am I correct?"

Cambourne rubbed a hand across his forehead, in a gesture that I was coming to know represented weariness. "I realize this has all been an awful shock, Gwen," he said, not answering my question, but then, he didn't really need to. "With one thing piling up on top of another."

"I always thought I could tell the difference," I said. "Always."

"You really were very good," he said, gently. "Although perhaps not as good as we allowed you to believe."

"I see," I said stiffly.

"You are angry," he said, very quietly.

"Yes. And you are annoyingly cryptic—" I stopped. "It is all the deceptions. Not knowing really if Milburn is the man I believed him to be. Or even if my past really belongs to me. Does that sound ridiculous?"

"No," he said, taking my hand between his. I hadn't realized how cold mine had grown until it was ensconced between his two warm ones. "It doesn't. And I very much wish I didn't need to play out these games any further. They seemed worth it at one time, but I have lost my taste for them."

"Unaccountably," I said.

He slid his hand along my cheek. "Not unaccountably at all," he said, low, bending closer.

And, oh Lord, the awful part is that I wanted his hand to keep on moving on me. But I almost hated myself for that. "But what the games are, or why they are being played, or why I am a part of them, are yet more questions I'm not allowed to ask?"

He raised one of those arrogant brows and I could see it as the barriers fell once again into place. "Oh, you're allowed to ask them, all right, Gwen. God knows you keep doing it and I have not stopped you—" he paused and I knew we were both recalling that kiss—"or not for long, anyway," he amended. "I just can't answer."

"I see." I eyed him. "You are allowed to marry me, and try to bed me, then, but not to tell me anything?"

He bent very close. So close that it was almost as if he were touching me. "I didn't try to bed you, Gwen," he said. "If I'd tried, we wouldn't be sitting here talking right now."

I raised a brow back at him. "You're awfully certain of

yourself, aren't you, Cambourne? For a man married to a woman who is waiting for your brother?" I knew I was sticking my hand dangerously close to the fire, but I was suddenly so angry I didn't care.

He held my wrist, not hard, but firmly. "Fifteen minutes in my bed and you'd be lucky to remember my brother's existence, let alone his name."

"Don't you mean in your brother's bed?" I asked, as nastily as I could, which was quite.

He laughed. "It's the fifteen minutes that matters, not the location."

"So that's the way of it? Is it?" I asked, leaning toward him. "You think you can quiet me by seducing me, do you, Cambourne?" I was working up a fairly good steam, having conveniently not forgot—but well, shall we say, put aside?—the knowledge that I had been sizing up my odds of managing to seduce him for information just a few short minutes ago.

And he leaned closer, too. So close that I could see the beginning of lines bracketing his mouth, his perfect mouth, as he smiled slowly at me. "They do say the end justifies the means," he said, low. And then a look of astonishment crossed his face and he let go of my wrist.

"Now *that* is one of the most—" I started to say, and then I heard it, also. Unmistakably: my mother's voice. And right there, on the landing, too, from the sound of things. "Gwen? Oh, Gwennie! Darling!"

Cambourne got to his feet just as she fairly blew into the room. He bowed to her, and I blinked, my mind moving slowly from the intensity and unreality of the conversation we had just been having to the very real presence of my mother, once again out of her bed well before noon. I could still feel the pressure of his hand on my wrist and his eyes still looked almost black, but with what emotion I could not have said.

"It is hideous out there. Not at all the sort of day *I* would have chosen! *Most* inconvenient," Mother said, sounding annoyed at her lack of control over the weather. "We were in the area, darlings, at this atrocious hour—as we were on our way to the meeting of the Greater London Suffrage and Reform Society—and thought we would call in." She managed simultaneously to shoot me a quelling glare and smile at Cambourne. "How lovely to find you *à deux!*"

"I shouldn't read too much into it," I muttered under my breath. Who *was* this person masquerading as my mother? And where on earth was the butler, Giddings? "Er, never mind. Was there no one to announce you?" I inquired. "Giddings—"

She gave me a look to let me know that no mere butler was a match for *her*. "Giddings is otherwise occupied at the moment. Now, then—"

"Hul-loo-oo, Almeria!" cried a voice from the foot of the stairs, and I closed my eyes.

Mother held up a finger to tell us to wait, and then strode out into the corridor. Cambourne's gaze met mine. "Up here, Vi," she bellowed. "In Gwennie's chamber. Do join us!"

"Perhaps we should adjourn to the drawing room," Cambourne suggested, when she returned. "We can ring for some tea."

"No need," Mother said, arranging herself to best advantage on the tapestried Adam chair. "We shan't stay above a moment. Don't want to discommode you newly-weds," she said archly.

"Lud!" gasped Violetta, collapsing on the bed. "What a

trudge! Why would anyone put their bedchamber up so deuced high?" She glared at me, and then sat, panting, as she recovered from her exertions.

"Had the designer of the house envisioned it as a public receiving room, he would no doubt have placed it on the ground floor," I said, pointedly.

"Good morning, Lady Worth." Cambourne bowed again.

"Morning, *Milburn,*" she said, as coyly as is possible for an overweight woman in a green turban, who is perspiring copiously. She fluttered her eyelashes at him and then reached out, took my half-finished cup of morning chocolate (quite cold by now) from the nightstand and drained it in a gulp. "Ugh," she said, wiping her mouth on her sleeve. "Vile." She transferred her glare to me. "Small wonder you're such a bony chit. A real man likes to be able to grab a nice handful of bottom come a cold night, I can tell you!"

I was much afraid that she not only could, but would.

"Well," Mother said into the uneasy silence. "We came to see how you two go on."

"Indeed," Cambourne replied. His tone was courteous, but something in it sent Violetta's brow arching toward her turban.

"And how do you?" she asked.

"Very well, thank you," he replied, taking up the seat next to mine, and languidly picking up my hand.

I resisted the urge to cling to his as though it was a lifeline.

"*How* well?" Violetta asked him pointedly.

"Quite," he replied, blandly.

"Well, we really must fly," Mother said hastily. "And your father has stood outside long enough."

"You left Father in the rain?" I asked.

"Well I *instructed* him to stand in the drip from the overhang of the roof. The butler is watching to ensure that he does. Your father *will* ignore my strictures when one gives him the latitude. He is to address the gathering this morning, and we have decided it will garner him a more sympathetic audience if he appears wet and bedraggled. Makes one look more common, you know, and this Society, while influential, is simply packed with people of Whiggish leanings."

"Oh," I said. "I see."

"But I hesitate to leave him too long, as it would be inconvenient were he to take a true inflammation of the lungs, as Lord Colchester is coming to dine a week Tuesday. I trust you received my note saying that I am assuming you two shall attend?"

"Er—" I managed, before Mother continued briskly. "It is high time that you were out and about," she said. "There is talk already. To be blunt, word that you spent your wedding night apart has got out, and it ill behooves you to have tongues wagging." And here, it did not escape my notice that she gave Cambourne a *significant* glance.

What was afoot between these two? They seemed unlikely allies, to say the least.

"I think the wisest thing is to scotch any talk by being seen together," she continued.

"Thank you for your advice," Cambourne said, courteously but firmly. "We shall certainly take it into account." He rose and opened the door.

Mother stood. "We shall expect you on Tuesday, then," she said. *"Au revoir,* darlings."

"Still puffed from the way up," Violetta complained, heaving herself off the bed.

We listened to them descend the stairs. After a moment, when it seemed safe to assume that they had actually gone, and were not in fact likely to return, we both let out sighs of relief.

Cambourne turned to me. "Did that really happen? Perhaps we should agree that it did not."

"Did what really happen?" I asked.

He smiled. "I don't know," he said. "I seem to have forgot already." And for a moment it seemed we were in light-hearted agreement, but then he turned serious. "Or I wish I could."

I frowned at him. "What do you mean, Cambourne?"

"Well—" at least he had the good grace to look uncomfortable. "I'd been planning to take you away to Huntsdon for a few weeks—"

I frowned at him. "Huntsdon?"

"It's one of my properties, Gwen," he said. "In Gloucestershire. I'm overdue for a visit and I thought you'd like it; it's quite lovely. I thought that we could put it about that Cambourne had lent it to us for a wedding trip."

The impact ran through me like a dash of cold water. Gloucestershire. Away from London, away from Cecy and Myrtia, away from the possibility of snooping for more information about Milburn. "Absolutely not," I told him, crossing my arms. "No Huntsdon. No wedding trip."

That eyebrow flew up. "I see," he said, but I was not convinced that he did.

"Do you remember that thing you said to me the other night, Cambourne?" I asked. "The one about how I always do what I'm told?"

"Yes," he said.

I crossed my arms. "As of this moment, I no longer do."

"You are refusing to come, then, do I take it?" he asked lightly.

"Yes." I pulled my arms tighter. "I am."

He stood up and walked across the room so that his back was to me. He examined a little clock on the mantel for a moment, and then turned. "Very well," he said, equably. "I suppose I could insist, but arguing is so tedious. We will stay in London and make our public appearance, then. I suppose that suits my purpose just as well anyway."

I frowned. The last thing I had intended was to fall further in line with his plans. Whatever they might be.

"It's been permissible for us to have spent this last week more or less in seclusion," he said. "But your mother is right; now we need to start accepting invitations again if we are to give the appearance of a normal marriage."

"But why has the last week of seclusion been acceptable?" I asked, looking at him.

"A new bride is generally allowed some time to, ah, accustom herself to the . . . demands of the married state," he said stiffly.

"Would it really have taken me a week to recover?" I blurted out, horrified at the notion.

"No doubt," he said, his gaze meeting mine. And then he gave me one of those slow smiles of his.

This time the color flooded my face with such force I almost gasped. Heaven help me, I believed him. "Yes, well, thus far there has been little to recover from," I said, tartly. "So for now I am to sit, morning after morning, in the drawing room, smiling and greeting guests? In aid of some scheme of yours in which you don't even have the decency to include me?"

"Yes," he said, in cool tones. "Exactly right. You do have

a way with words, darling." And then he walked to the fireplace and drew a stack of invitations off the mantel. He flipped through them for a minute. "We have our choice for our debut, it seems. Is Caro Arbuthnot's premiere performance of her newly composed masque to your taste?"

As much as I adored Caro Arbuthnot, it must be clearly stated that in matters musical, her enthusiasm far surpassed her ability. I shuddered. "What else?"

"We're not lacking for choices," he said. "A rout, two balls, a drum, two literary salons, a dinner, a luncheon. Only imagine if it were the Season! Or would you prefer the theater?"

"The Arbuthnots," I said with reluctance. At least there would be some entertainment, which would lessen the need to converse with people.

"Very well. Tomorrow night. I shall plan on it. But for now I am afraid I have some business to attend to." And then he bowed and left.

11

In which we make a list

"Can you be there?" I asked Cecy and Myrtia later that afternoon. I felt in desperate need of knowing there would be some friendly faces there.

"Sorry," said Cecy, sounding glum. "My mother arrives tomorrow for a visit and it seems I must await her and learn what the latest calamity is. One can only hope it is short in duration, and preferably of a fiscal nature, since that is easily enough solved. Barings is optimistic that if we have on hand a big enough pile of blunt, she might not even stay the night! Have you decided what you will wear tomorrow, Gwen?" She tilted her head. "The shot-green silk evening frock, I think, would be perfect."

"Surely you are not serious!" I said, but she looked at me sagely. "Don't look at me sagely, Cecy," I said. "I dislike it."

She was quiet.

I was not going to ask her to tell me.

Definitely not. If she wanted to, she could just come out with it. I would not beg.

Why, why, *why* was silence so effective on me?

"What!?" I burst out. "What is it?"

Cecy smiled. "It is only that you are no longer *supposed* to be a virginal young girl," she said. "You are supposed to know secrets you had not even dreamt of previously. You may now adopt a knowing manner, wear bold colors should you so desire, and flaunt your décolleté. Now, tell us, *do* you know any secrets you had not even dreamt of previously?"

"No," I said, glumly. "Not of *any* sort. We talked— argued, really—and then my mother and Violetta burst into my bedchamber—"

"Oh my," Cecy interrupted. "Did they see anything shocking?"

"No," I said, "and, anyway, can you imagine what it would take to shock them?"

"No." She shuddered. "I am sorry, Gwen. There is simply nothing for it except to seduce him, preferably allowing him to believe all the while that *he* is seducing *you.*"

"I don't know," I said doubtfully.

"Nothing to it," she assured me. "All you have to do is to get him gibbering with lust, neatly extract your information, and then brush him aside. I'd suggest you start with the shot-green silk. He'll stare down at the enticing expanse of your bosom all night until he can stand it no longer and has to rush you home and ravish you. A few judiciously asked questions, and trust me, by the end of the night, you'll know everything you need to."

"I know it is not much," I said, "but I stood up to him yesterday. He admitted that he was planning to take me to the country and I refused."

"Good for you, Gwen," said Myrtia, staunchly.

"And look where that's got you! To Caro Arbuthnot's masque," Cecy said. "Possibly only the most dreaded social event of the year!"

What could I say? She had a point.

"What, if I may ask, is stopping you, Gwen, from *trying* to extract information from Cambourne the way I have suggested?" she asked.

I looked down at the carpet for a long heartbeat. "Well," I admitted. "Several things."

"Yes?" Cecy looked expectant.

"First, it seems wrong somehow. Disloyal to Milburn. Particularly when it seems that he's in danger." They were both looking at me with encouraging expressions, so I continued. "Second, I don't know anything about seduction. And, third, to be honest, Cambourne has a very . . . unsettling effect on me." I had to gather my thoughts before I could continue. "He makes me furious and at the same time, he makes me, I don't know, all melted, and I *know* it's improper."

"I thought as much," said Cecy.

"So the thing is—" Having started, I was having trouble stopping. "I'm not precisely certain that I'd be able to extract my information and then stop him from . . . you know, progressing with, ah, things."

"And would that be so bad?" That question came from Myrtia, of all people!

"Of course it would," I told her. "Because then I'd be really and truly married to him, possibly based on nothing except that he melts me. And what a ridiculous word for it, anyway."

"I don't know," said Cecy. "It seems as good as any to me. But I think what you need here, Gwen, is to really think about Milburn and Cambourne and your loyalties."

"What do you mean?"

"What I think," Cecy said, "is that you are holding out for Milburn because he's easy. Easy to read, easy to be with, easy to control. You'll never control Cambourne. He's got a mind of his own. The two of you will always have to struggle for mutual agreement."

"That hardly sounds a recipe for marital bliss," I retorted.

"But perhaps the ultimate result is more satisfying," Myrtia suggested.

"Milburn, though—"Cecy lifted her shoulders and let them fall—"you'll have him on a leash from the first day and you'll both be bored to tears by the second. Or *you* will, anyway."

"You really think this is about which one I can control?" I demanded.

"Yes," Cecy replied, not sounding in the least apologetic. "Not completely, but to some extent. Just like your mother controls your father."

"My mother does *not* control my father!" I said, heatedly.

They both looked at me. Neither saying a word.

"Well, this is different," I said, with less heat, recalling that the man *had* stood in the drip from the roof this very morning. "Much different." I clenched my teeth. "Perhaps the answer is to leave them both," I mused.

"But what would you do?" Myrtia asked. "Your parents would hardly welcome you home."

"No. Not if it means giving up hope of an advantageous marriage," I agreed.

"Far, *far*, more advantageous than they'd ever dared hope for," Cecy reminded us.

"The truth of the matter is that females like us, well, we don't have a lot of choices open to us other than marriage," Myrtia said, looking sad.

"And I don't imagine you'd much care for the ones that are," was Cecy's dry contribution. "Face it, Gwen, you're not governess material, and even if you were, no one would hire you. You're far too young and leagues too beautiful. You're not a bluestocking, you're an unlikely opera dancer or actress, as you possess neither the talent nor the inclination. What else is there?"

"I don't know," I said. "It never occurred to me that I'd need a choice other than marriage." I thought for a moment. "Ludmilla, in *Ludmilla and the Dastardly Duke,* became a sheepherder," I said, getting into the spirit of the thing. "Remember? She stole the shepherd's outfit from the—"

"There's such a sad shortage of sheep in London," Cecy reminded me dampeningly. "And correspondingly, of sheepherders."

"I could go back to Hildcote," I said. "Plenty of sheep there."

"Ludmilla ended up married to the duke anyway," Myrtia pointed out. "It turned out he wasn't so dastardly after all. But, Gwen!" she exclaimed, her eyes lighting. "I know what we need. A list! To help you understand what attributes Cambourne and Milburn possess, to help you make a rational decision."

I would have demurred, but Cecy immediately jumped up. "You're absolutely right, Myrtia! I'll just fetch something to write with," she exclaimed, before crossing to the writing desk and returning with some sheets of foolscap and a sharpened quill. "Now," she said, dipping it in the ink and looking up brightly, "where shall we begin? This promises quite the most entertainment I've had all day, what with Barings sulking at his club over Mother's impending arrival, and Mother's arrival impending."

"Shall we make two columns?" Myrtia suggested. "One of Things to Recommend Cambourne, and one of, let's see . . . Things to, well, *Not* Recommend Cambourne?"

"Perhaps one of Things to Recommend Milburn, would also be appropriate," I suggested.

"Absolutely not," Cecy said emphatically. "That is an entirely different list."

"You can hardly separate these into discrete categories," I argued.

"Perhaps a third column, sort of an addendum to note these observations as they relate to Milburn," Myrtia suggested. "Gwen's correct, Cecy, there must be some junction of ideas."

"Very well," Cecy agreed grudgingly. "I shall add a third column entitled, The Observations as They Relate to Milburn."

"Perhaps to start off, under Things to *Not* Recommend Cambourne we could put, 'Not supposed to be married to him,' and under the Milburn column, 'Supposed to be married to him by long-standing arrangement,'" I suggested.

They ignored me. "I know!" Cecy smiled, bending again. "Cambourne's shoulders!"

"Mmm. His legs," said Myrtia. "The way they fill out his trousers." And then she blushed.

"It's all those masculine pursuits," said Cecy knowledgeably. "And we really should not forget the way he moves," she said to Myrtia over my head.

Myrtia nodded. "Yes, powerful, and yet, graceful," she agreed.

"His eyes," I said, sounding dreamy to my own ears, recalling suddenly the way they changed colors from that clear blue to dark and smoky when— "Wait," I said. "This shall not be a list of his physical characteristics. Besides, Milburn has all the same ones."

"Yes, but somehow they are not the same," sighed Cecy. "I shall simply put in the Recommend column, 'Physique,' shall I? Or do you think, 'Physical Attributes' is better?"

"If you are including the way he moves, I think 'Physical Attributes,' " said Myrtia, seriously. "Although it would be more precise to use, 'Physique,' and then to have a separate entry of 'Grace and Athleticism.' "

"You're absolutely right, of course," Cecy agreed, scratching away with the quill.

"This list is already becoming positively lopsided," I said drily. "And I must insist that for 'Physique,' you note in the Observations column that Milburn's is the same."

"Very well." Cecy sounded grudging. "I shall, but I shall phrase it: 'Has same, but is somehow *not* the same.' "

I would have argued, but decided to be grateful I had had any say at all, when Myrtia said, " 'Responsible' for Cambourne, I should think."

Cecy nodded, head bent. "And I shall add . . . um, 'Imprudent' and 'Neglectful' in the Observations column for Milburn."

"Milburn is not neglectful," I protested. "He is simply carefree. A little . . . feckless, perhaps, but not neglectful!"

"Mmm. Neglectful, yes," said Cecy, ignoring me. "But we shall certainly save feckless as I shouldn't be surprised if we have a place for it later. Now, I do think that next should be, 'Deliciously Experienced but Not Rakish or Dissolute' for Cambourne!"

"Perfect," said Myrtia. "You have captured precisely the

right phrasing. Then perhaps, let me see . . . 'Indiscriminate,' under Observations for Milburn."

"Prudent" (Cambourne) and "Imprudent" (Milburn) was next.

Followed by, "Thoughtful" (Cambourne) and "Distinctly Thoughtless" (Milburn).

Then, "Perceptive and Discerning" (Cambourne) were paired with "Insensible and Care for Naught" (Milburn).

Cambourne's dancing was judged "Divine," while Milburn's was "Acceptable," and his conversation deemed, "Intelligent and Witty" to Milburn's "Passable But Hardly Scintillating."

The above were rapidly joined by "Loyal and Steadfast" (Cambourne, naturally), and "Feckless," for poor Milburn. ("See! We did use it after all, Gwen!")

"Charismatic" in Cambourne's Recommend column was thankfully left unpaired in Milburn's Observations. "Respected" in Cambourne's was, after some debate, answered by "Liked," in Milburn's, but then Myrtia and Cecy both insisted on adding "Well-Liked" to Cambourne's.

"Top of the Trees Wardrobe" was, naturally, matched with "Foppish Fribble." There, I could hardly argue, although I was highly tempted to point out that, ironically enough, Cambourne was the one sleeping in curl papers at present, in his efforts to achieve that Milburn-like halo.

"Drives to an Inch" was met by "Terrifying with the Ribbons."

"Future Duke" naturally enough paired with "Second Son." Although as I pointed out, Milburn could hardly be held accountable for that. Not only was my reasonable point ignored, it resulted in a "Frequently Late for Engagements" entry in his column.

"Rich as Croesus" and "Comfortably Heeled" came next.

And so it went on, until I finally interrupted. "You do realize," I said, pointedly, "that you have yet to enter so much as a single item in the Things *Not* to Recommend Cambourne column? You know, perhaps something like, 'Married and Almost Seduced Gwen Under False Pretenses'?"

"Also possibly translated as, 'Honored Family Responsibilities When His Brother Did Not'!" Myrtia said, nodding to Cecy to write it down.

"Did you have more suggestions, though, Gwen?" Myrtia looked at me encouragingly.

"Yes. How about 'Hiding Something,'" I said, aware that I was sounding plaintive.

"I have it," Cecy crowed to Myrtia, " 'Stands Firm Behind His Reasons.' "

"Well said." Myrtia smiled and I seethed. "Perhaps concurrent with that we should add 'Trustworthy' and 'Discreet'?"

My suggestion of, "Stubborn" somehow, in translation, ended up as: "Has the Courage to Stand By His Convictions and Up to Gwen," with poor Milburn receiving a corresponding "Weakness of Character."

I had had enough. More than enough, in fact, so I stood up and smoothed my skirts. "I understand that this has all been most diverting," I said stiffly. "And while I am exceedingly happy that the circumstances of my life were able to provide entertainment for you both on what might have otherwise been a dull afternoon, I do believe I should point out that my reluctance to accept Cambourne is not based upon some misguided belief that I prefer Milburn. It is based on the fact that Cambourne married me out of hand, tried to seduce me, and now refuses to tell me why. Would you jump into bed with that man?" I glared at them both.

Myrtia dropped her eyes, but Cecy smiled at me. "Absolutely," she said, irrepressible as ever. "But not until I'd taught him a dashed good lesson first, you can be sure."

"I do believe I shall take my leave now." I stalked toward the door, until Cecy's voice stopped me in my tracks.

"Gwen?" she said, and I turned.

"Yes?" I said, still coldly.

She waved the sheets at me. "You've forgot your list."

12

In which I stoop to a disgracefully low piece of behavior

I returned home, debating what precisely teaching Cambourne that dashed good lesson might entail, only to find a missive from him on the hall table. He had, it seemed, been unavoidably called away from London, and would be unable to attend the Arbuthnots' tomorrow, after all. He looked forward to seeing me shortly. Yours, etc.

I put the page down. Well, there was no question of me attending the masque without him, so that was that. It was three of the clock on a winter afternoon, and I had nothing planned for the rest of the day. Visiting any member of my family was not an option I cared to consider. Since the rain was bucketing down, going walking or riding were not possibilities. I was too restless to read. The menus for the next week were all planned, the linens inventoried, the accounts balanced. And the fact that this state of affairs was all due to the housekeeper, Mrs. Harbison's, efficiency rather than anything I had done was not lost on me. I tried, but could not settle to my embroidery, and then played the pianoforte in a desultory fashion for a few minutes.

I wished that I had someone to play chess with, or talk with. I would have been able to tease my old maid, Larsen, into a game of *vingt-et-un* or a gossip, but somehow I could not see myself in such cozy circumstances with Crewes. I prowled around the house, and stood for a while in the back drawing room, looking out at the garden, watching the rain fall in the drear that was rapidly becoming darkness, and fuming about my current situation.

I had been married and almost seduced under false pretenses and now, it seemed, abandoned on top of it. And as far as I could tell, I had no immediate way of figuring out more about what had happened to Milburn. I was as good as a prisoner. It was fortunate that Cambourne was not about, as, had he walked through the door at this moment, I would likely have strangled him. By the time I had finished with this rather pleasurable fantasy, it was all of half past four.

Still prowling, I went back into the library and, after a moment of standing inside the door, sat down in a leather armchair. After a few moments, I sat up straight as I caught sight of something on the table next to the chair. Cambourne's little journal! The one he'd been scribbling away in the night I got foxed at the Clarendon.

It drew my gaze, as though it held sirenlike powers. But my will was stronger. I would *not* stoop to reading it. No matter how curious I might be, it was not a fair way to gain information—not as, say, seducing him would be. I would not! I resolutely turned my head and studied the portrait over the fireplace. A Romney, not one of his best, but not bad. After a few moments of this, I reasoned that it could not harm anything so very much were I to just *look* in the direction of the journal again. And possibly to pick it up. I would not, of course, read it.

The outside was of dark, mellowed leather, worn smooth, I thought, by his hands. I ran mine over it, taking some pleasure in the certain knowledge that his had recently been in the exact same place. Holding it was surprisingly comforting—as though even in his absence, a part of him was here with me after all—and I realized how much I had come to look forward to his presence. Having made this admission, I leaned my head back against the chair again, and made the further admission that the house was too quiet without him. I let the book fall open in my lap, and smiled as I recognized his bold hand from my letters.

Monday, 16 December, I read, against my better judgment. This entry was written very nearly four weeks previous to our wedding, I realized. It was more or less the type of thing I had imagined he wrote in it.

> *Took a seat in the Speakers' gallery today, this being the fixed day for the discussion of Glenbray's scheme of commercial policy. Before debate commenced heard Arnold make credible speech. v. good for maiden speech, well received. Graham and six more spoke in favor and Sir Wm. Granger against. Then busied myself at my desk with various matters, rode out despite rain, conferred with D. who came to call, went a few rounds at Jackson's, dined at Lord R's.*

Was there anything to be found in here, I could not help but wonder, of a more personal nature? Not, of course, that I would look for it. But then, if everything was like the entry I had just read, what could be the harm in reading just a little further? Then a moment later: What I was doing was wrong, I told myself, as I flipped pages back, wrong, wrong, wrong. I kept going, however, skimming over more entries, much of a piece with the first two, until:

> *Friday, 3 January.*
> *Closeted at Whitehall with F. for most of the morning. Lunched with Atherton most congenially—he will depart tomorrow for Northumberland. Beat Hugo most handily at Jackson's Rooms. Dined with Vesper. Very interesting visit from Axton.*

That, at least coincided with my father's version of events. I started, thinking I had heard a noise, and quickly put the book down on the table. I sat very still, waiting for someone to appear. After a few minutes, in which I remained very much alone, I dared let out my breath, and my hand, as if of its own accord, crept back out for the journal.

> *Saturday, 11 January*
> *Dined with M.*

I stared at the wall, unseeing, as the blood pounded against my ears. That *M* could signify any number of people, I reminded myself—Michaels and Moncton, to name just two of his cronies. But it could also mean Milburn! Was Milburn back on 11 January? If so it would have been less than a week before our wedding, but eight days *after*

my father had apparently visited Cambourne. What could
that mean? M could also, I realized with a sinking heart,
represent Mathilde Claussen. Would I find out if I kept up
my snooping—sorry—reading? I had begun the undertaking with the idea of perhaps finding some information
about Bertie, or that would help me understand what
Cambourne had done, but now I was looking for something else entirely. Would Mathilde appear after the wedding? Would I? Would his feelings on our marriage be
recorded here?

I was half afraid to know, but at the same time, I had to.

Saturday, 17 January
Was wed this morning.

That was it? From a man who had recorded such
details as that he had partaken of midmorning coffee with
Atherton? I wanted to die from irritation. I also desperately wanted to read further, but I didn't dare. I closed the
book and put it back on the table. And not a moment too
soon, for no sooner had I done so, but Mrs. Harbison
tapped on the door to inquire as to whether I would be
taking supper at home this evening.

After she had gone, I took a deep, shaking breath, and
stood. My heart was pounding now as I went out to the
stairs and hurried up them. At the top, I stood irresolute
for a moment, before heading for Cambourne's bedchamber. Once inside, I closed the door softly behind myself
and thought to thank some unseen force that no servants
were there, going about their business.

The fire had been lit; a lamp burned low beside the
enormous bed. The covers had been turned down, but
showed no signs of having been occupied; the bed curtains

of ivory damask stood open. A couple of comfortable-looking chairs sat facing the fire, and a table between them held a pile of books and a decanter. It was the first time I had ever been in his bedchamber. It felt calm, and peaceful and masculine. I leaned against the door that I had pulled shut behind me, and again breathed deeply. At last I was rewarded. This room smelled like him: clean linen with just a trace of Mrs. Harbison's soap.

And the longing was so fierce that I drew in a very long breath, as I stood, trying to understand the way I was feeling.

He was inscrutable and secretive and arrogant and demanding and beautiful, and his journal was possibly the most frustrating item I had ever come across, for any number of reasons, and I was completely turned upside down as to what I wanted. I wanted Milburn to come back. Certainly I wanted him to be safe, and yet, I was beginning to entertain an almost frightening desire for his brother. And I well understood the underlying point of Cecy and Myrtia's little list-making exercise; there is more than one way to look at any situation. For example, what I had seen as stubborn, they had seen as having the courage to stand up for his convictions. And, yes, up to me.

And the very devil of it was that here I was. Cambourne was mine for the taking, but they were right; it would never be a comfortable marriage. In fact, were his brother to walk through the door this very instant, it would still be much the easiest thing to go to him. To the undemanding, quiet marriage I had always thought to have. And were I to do that, would I be giving up something precious? Or saving myself?

I walked to the window to peer at the sodden street below. Where was Cambourne? The treacherous thought that came to mind, of course, was: tucked up in another cozy bedchamber driving Mathilde and himself delirious with pleasure. Unfortunately, the picture of this possibility was all too clear in my mind. And, I told myself brutally, he had every right to be there, doing that.

Which was quite reasonable of me, considering that the very idea of it made me burn with fury. Could I really, I wondered, considering the idea seriously for the first time, seduce him? Or partially seduce him, anyway? And if I did, would it really be for information, or would there be another motive?

What I had said to Myrtia earlier about never having thought about what choices might be open to me other than marriage was true. Marriage—marriage to Milburn, anyway—was what I had been brought up for and what I knew how to do. At any gathering I could tell you the precedence of who should lead whom to table. I could arrange the seating at the trickiest supper. I could assess the household books and the quality of the linens. I could plan a menu. I could arrange a country house party with my eyes closed. I could organize a ball or a charity fête with equal ease. I could dance, converse in French, arrange flowers, play the piano, embroider, and watercolor. Not, in short, accomplishments that added up to anything more than *wife*. But was that it? All I was?

For one wild moment I debated undressing and crawling between the sheets to wait for Cambourne. Logic, though, made an appearance and pointed out that one, he had said he would not be back until the day after tomorrow, which would be quite a long wait, and two, if he was in fact coming from the arms of another woman, he might not be precisely overjoyed to see me there.

And anyway, offering myself up for the taking hardly

seemed to go toward teaching him that dashed good lesson that Cecy had recommended. I perched on the edge and thought about this. After a minute or two, I could not resist stretching out and burying my face in his pillows. Which, as it turned out, was my lucky—or unlucky, I suppose, depending on your viewpoint—moment. For there, on the night table, was the note in a very florid feminine hand.

> *I very much look forward to seeing you at the Arbuthnots', although I cannot plead equal enthusiasm for the music. M.*

So he *is* playing this at both ends, I realized with a flash of outrage. Sending out seductive little signals here at home, to get me to play his game, and consorting with his mistress on the side.

I sat up. It looked like I would be going to hear Caro sing tomorrow night, after all.

And, just perhaps, I'd be teaching Cambourne that dashed good lesson at the same time.

13

The best laid plans and all that, part one—
In which I attend a party after all

*C*ambourne *did not return home that night. The next* morning, I went shopping for a few things with Myrtia, and then, when she went home to ready herself for her weekly afternoon at the Soldiers' Hospital, went round to Cecy's. I knew her mother's visit was weighing heavily on her. And I thought to offer her whatever support could be had from my presence.

I found her in situ, taking tea with her mama. Rather to my surprise, Barings was absent. It is true that he often resorted to burying his nose in some musty book when one of Cecy's parents descended, but he knew how trying they were for her, and generally tried to help head off some of the worst skirmishes.

"Gwen!" exclaimed Lady Wainwright upon my arrival. "How lovely to see you! Your parents are well?"

"Yes, thank you," I replied.

Her eyes had a hectic glitter to them. "Perhaps you can join me in convincing my shockingly staid daughter that no harm can come from a little libation of a slightly stronger nature than this pap." She waved her teacup gaily at me.

I took in her high color—I thought it quite likely she had already partaken of something stronger—and Cecy's contrasting pallor, and regretted my decision to call. I was just now recalling how very much Lady Wainwright seemed to thrive on an audience. "I'm sure Cecy is only—" I said, sounding awkward to my own ears.

"Nonsense!" Lady Wainwright interrupted, her voice rising. "Cecy is not *only* anything. She is bound and determined to ensure that all those around her are as miserable as she is—"

She rose, along with the timbre of her voice, and my eyebrows almost followed suit at the transparency of her gown. One had to admit that Lady Wainwright was still possessed of an admirable figure, and was clearly determined that all should be aware of that fact.

"—in her prudish existence." Cecy looked alarmingly closer to tears with each word. "With her prudish husband who—" Lady Wainwright paused and her eyes gleamed as she said, triumphantly—"does not even share her bed!"

"Not now that you're here," said Cecy in a low voice.

Her mother arched a brow. "If he really wanted you, surely you don't think a paltry little thing like my arrival would send him scurrying, do you, my little innocent?"

I took Cecy's cold hand in mine. "And what do you plan to do during your visit, Lady Wainwright?" I asked, attempting to put things onto a footing more appropriate for a social call.

"Not have much fun, apparently," she said, coldly. "As I

am, thanks to my husband's both profligate and penurious ways—and the frightful old letch, by the by, is currently too busy bedding the downstairs parlormaid to notice I'm gone—insolvent at the current moment. And my *Methodist* daughter has told me that I am not welcome to stay."

"I am *not* a Methodist," Cecy said through tight lips, and I squeezed her hand in encouragement. She continued, sounding firmer, "*And* I offered you money."

"Ah, but I do not want only money," her mother said with all the grace of a three-year-old denied an ice. "I want a visit to London."

"But you have been here only one night!" Cecy cried. "And already you have upset my household beyond recognition: Barings has removed to his club *and* the butler and housekeeper are both furious and threatening to resign because you attempted to seduce a footman."

"An overwhelming need for a well-ordered household, Cecily," said Lady Wainwright, airily, "is a sign of a small mind. Were you open to the world around you—" she spread her arms—"to love, to gaiety, to *ideas* (ah yes, ideas: the true food of the soul); you would not care so about such a paltry thing as order."

"I do not understand," Cecy said bluntly, "how this sudden passion of yours for ideas translates into seducing the footman."

"That is because you do not understand the first thing about *embracing* life," said her mother. "And furthermore," she continued in considerably less lofty tones, "if the old goat can sport with parlormaids, I can do the same with your footman."

Cecy closed her eyes for a moment and then sat up straighter. "Fine," she said, disengaging her hand from mine and folding her arms across her chest. "Dally all you want. Embrace life. But not with *my* footmen, and not in *my* house."

"Are you jealous, darling?" asked Lady Wainwright in dulcet tones. "Did you want Thomas for yourself? I daresay you might now that Barings has abandoned the conjugal bed. And I dare you, Cecily, I *dare* you to throw me out. We both know you have not got the backbone." And then, smiling, Lady Wainwright drank her tea after all.

Her brief flare of spirits seemed to have passed, and Cecy deflated against the sofa. I hated to see her this way. "Is that what you think, Lady Wainwright?" I asked, "that Cecy doesn't have the backbone to throw you out?" I was aware that they were both looking at me in surprise. I thought of Cambourne's words. *Because you always do what you're told.* Hah!

"Because I can assure you she does," I continued. "And if she won't, and you continue to make her unhappy . . . well, *I* will. And now, if you will excuse me—" I stood. "I must be on my way to . . . to catch my husband out at meeting his mistress. I will call on you tomorrow, Cecily."

And then I left.

I was feeling nearly fond of *my* mother as I returned home in the carriage. By the time I arrived, however, I had progressed to recalling a few of her choicest sayings, and my warm feelings of familial affection had faded.

Cambourne, as it transpired, had still not returned. Feeling rather heady over having rebuked Lady Wainwright, I contemplated paying a visit to Mathilde Claussen. I am pleased to be able to say, however, that I had enough sense to discard this idea promptly, recognizing it as a very poor one. I would wait until tonight.

I once again prowled around the house for a while. By the time I had envisioned, for about the thousandth time, my infuriating husband tumbling a laughing Mathilde onto a soft, warm bed, I suppose it would be fair to say that I was working myself into something approaching a lather. I then went upstairs to rest and tell Crewes to please ready a bath and my shot-green silk evening frock. Cecy was correct; if that gown, with its slender column and shoulder-baring décolleté didn't raise my spirits, nothing would, and that was a fact.

Some hours later, I stood in front of the mirror, and was forced to acknowledge that it was almost worth putting up with Crewes's disposition: She *was,* as Mother had insisted, a genius with hair. I went down the stairs, feeling the brush of a loose tendril against my bared shoulders. I was also realizing that I was not entirely certain of what was required of me as a married woman. As an unwed girl, it was taken as fact that I would never set out for an evening of this nature on my own. I would have been with my parents, or friends, or, at the very least, a maid.

I was conscious, though, that there were very few rules of etiquette to guide one in my position: a woman, publicly married to one man, living with another, truly married to neither, and about to confront one of those men consorting publicly with his mistress while pretending to be his own brother. How, I wondered, idly, had he explained to Mathilde that he was now Milburn?

However he had chosen to approach it, I only hoped that my appearance would shock that damned (and I told myself with great pleasure that I could use that word, even if only in my own mind, since I was now a married woman) inscrutable, self-possessed, expression right off Cambourne's arrogant face.

I took a deep breath and settled into the carriage across from Crewes. "It promises to be a frightful evening," I said, brightly, as the carriage pulled away from the house.

"If the company is refined, the evening can only be pleasing," she replied dampeningly.

"One can only assume that you have never before heard Caro Arbuthnot sing," I said.

"The countess," she replied, "finds it ill-bred to note flaws in those of gentle birth."

I mulled this for a moment, and then concluded that the countess also had obviously never heard Caro sing. After that, the rest of the short carriage ride passed in silence. I pressed my face against the window, and Crewes, thankfully, did not offer any opinions as to how the countess would have regarded such behavior. The rain still streaked down—I thought the odds were high that it would never end—and the lights of Mayfair were blurred. Looking at the warmly lit windows, I wondered how many of these people were truly happy in their great houses.

Surely not all of them had had their marriages and their lives turn out the way they had planned? Many must have suffered the losses and disappointments that are inevitable in a life: children who did not survive; financial reversals; loveless marriages; illness. Surely, at some point, these things touch almost everyone, but how rarely I had thought about it.

Even merry, irrepressible Cecy had clouds across her sun, it seemed. And Myrtia—who was perhaps one of the most serene persons I had ever known—was she happy? She had her causes and her societies, in short, the purpose that I so lacked. But had she wanted more? She and Mr. Robert Wickersham had looked to make a match a few years back. We had all assumed an announcement was forthcoming, but then, Mr. Wickersham had left for the Continent, where he was said to be acquitting himself remarkably as one of the officers in the Seventh Hussars. Myrtia had certainly not *appeared* heartbroken, and said, simply, that they were old and dear friends and she had never had any expectations in that direction. But now I wondered.

I truly was blue-deviled tonight, I decided, as we arrived at the Arbuthnots'. There was no other explanation for my melancholy turn of mind. Footmen were waiting on the steps, and two ran down with umbrellas to cover Crewes and myself.

"Lady Gwen!" Caro and her parents were greeting their guests. "Or"—Caro frowned—"are you going by Lady Bertie?"

"Any of them are fine, Caro," I said, hugging her with genuine warmth, for she really was a delightful girl, aside from her unfortunate propensity to believe she could sing. "How wonderful to see you. I can't tell you how I am look-ing forward to your masque!" Which, I told myself, was no lie, since indeed, I could *not* tell her.

Her parents also greeted me warmly as Caro looked behind me, with a slight frown. "And where is Milburn?" she wanted to know, naturally enough.

Swallowing, and thinking that I had best get used to it, I told them that he was at the moment entertaining an old friend from Cambridge who had stopped with us unex-pectedly, but that he might join me later.

So much for a sad turnout, I thought as I entered the ballroom. Despite all the snide comments about Caro's singing, the place was an absolute crush. I edged my way into the room, greeting acquaintances and, with increasing confidence, making Milburn's excuses. All things considered, I was almost relieved to be waved over by Priscilla Fanshaw. "Naturally, Ravenhurst would never do such a thing as to send me out on my own," she said, eyes as guileless as she could make them. "He sticks by my side like a limpet. But then, a marquis must be more concerned than another gentleman with what might befall his bride."

"Yes," I said, looking conspicuously about for Ravenhurst, who was nowhere to be seen. "I can see that. And you, particularly, are such a precious little thing." Which little piece of nastiness went unrewarded, because she missed my sarcasm entirely, and looked pleased.

"Thank you," she said. "Nevertheless, Gwen, you have done quite well for yourself. I shouldn't refine overly on Milburn's lack of a title, were I you."

"No," I said. "You would be surprised by how little I think of that."

Finally, I saw Myrtia across the room. Unfortunately, I also saw both Violetta and my brother Richard. And unlike Myrtia, they had spied me, and Richard was already making his way over. Violetta, I was relieved to note, did not follow suit. She was talking about me, though—every head in her little group suddenly swiveled in my direction. Mrs. Trompington even raised a pair of opera glasses and studied me through them.

I debated pretending that I hadn't seen Richard, though he knew I had, and anyway, the crush around me was too thick to allow for escape. "Gwen!" he bellowed, waving. "Was wondering if you two was ever going to show your faces again." He arrived at my side and looked around. "Where's Milburn?" and without waiting for an answer, rushed on: "Never mind that. You'll never guess who's here!"

"Likely not," I said drily. "Since everyone seems to be."

And then, contrary to Richard's assertion, I did know: Cambourne. As himself. And even though I had known that would be the case, the reality of it still managed to crash into me with a cold wave of shock. I could see him across the room, in his stark evening black-and-white, his hair gleaming in the candlelight, laughing at something. The room started to swim.

"Cambourne!" said Richard, a moment too late, as usual. "Your brother-in-law!"

"Indeed. I am aware of the relationship," I murmured as I took in the little tableau before me. And tried to clench my hands into fists to stop the shaking. My husband was rather cozily, as it turned out, engaged in falling down the excessively large cleavage of none other than Mathilde Claussen. How *intime* the two of them looked! As I watched, she laughed at something he said, and lazily waved her fan. One glossy copper ringlet hung over her smooth white shoulder. He was leaning awfully close. Any closer, in fact, and he might just fall right down into that valley and we'd have to send a rescue party. If, that is, he even wanted to be rescued, which I took leave to doubt.

Fury began to curl through me, joining the jealousy that was already there. I hated him, I decided. And her. *And,* come to think of it, Milburn, too. My gloved hands were still curled into tight little fists. I knew I should laugh and say something gay or witty to Richard, and pretend not to have noticed them, but I simply could not tear my eyes away.

Then Cambourne looked up, and our gazes collided

with what I thought might very well have been an audible
thump. I know the roar of conversation around me seemed
to fade to my ears. His lazy smile was gone, on the instant,
as though it had never been. He looked extremely grim, in
fact. My heart was thundering in my chest and I was simultaneously shivering and noticing that my palms were
sweating inside my gloves.

"Gwen! Gwen?" Richard was saying.

Cambourne had managed to tear himself away from
Mrs. Claussen and her bosom and was making his way
easily across the room toward us. Myrtia, too, had spied us
and no doubt having taken note of my distress, was heading in our direction. She was not having the same success
as Cambourne in parting the crowd, and people kept
stopping her to chat, so it seemed I would have to greet
Cambourne on my own. Or, well, with Richard, which I
considered pretty much on my own. I squared my shoulders and lifted my chin.

"Gwen!"

I looked at Richard, noticing him again. "Sorry," I said.
"What did you say?"

He rolled his eyes. "Talk about woolgathering! I said—
about ten minutes ago, by the way—'What friend from
Cambridge is Milburn entertaining?' And then, if one is to
be specific, I said, 'Not that I blame him, mind, for sloping
off from this particular gathering.' And you just stood
there, looking as though you ain't heard a word I said.
Whatever is wrong with you?"

"Nothing. Ah—" It had never occurred to me that I
would be asked to attach a name to this phantom guest of
Milburn's. "Esterbrook," I said, finally.

"Esterbrook!" said Richard, giving me an odd look.
"Esterbrook? Ain't he dead?"

"Oh. Right. I must have meant, um, Fairhurst," I tried to look abashed. "I always did get them confused."

If anything, Richard sounded even more surprised. "Bit difficult to confuse those two. And, anyway, didn't think Milburn and Fairhurst got on," he mused.

Past his shoulder, I noticed Cecy standing in the doorway now, accompanied by her mother. Richard was still looking puzzled. "Could've sworn they hated each other!"

I tore my gaze from Cecy's pale, set face as Cambourne arrived at my side in time to hear the last. "I think your sister means that Milburn is entertaining Sherbrooke," he said, handing me a glass of champagne, and bowing.

I took it and momentarily debated pouring it over his head. I suspect he guessed something of my thoughts, though, because he said with alacrity, "You are looking flushed, Lady Gwen." He smiled. "Quite beautiful, but flushed."

"Too dashed warm in here," Richard offered.

"Very warm, indeed," I agreed in frigid tones.

"Drink," Cambourne said, nodding to the glass he had just handed me.

I knew that he was trying to mitigate the shock by getting me to take a drink. "No, thank you, I don't care for any at the moment."

He repossessed it and lifted it to his lips, then handed it back to me.

"Are we sharing?" I asked. "I don't share well. Phoebe Arundel still dislikes me because I would not share my nursery toys with her when I was four."

He looked down at me. "Have your own, then. But it's for your own good, Gwen; it will cool you down."

"Oh, not anywhere near enough, I shouldn't think," I said, affixing a smile to my face, and not adding, as I would have liked, *you odious, lying, cheating, high-handed, arrogant bastard.*

His eyes narrowed. "Surely it won't do for you to become . . . overheated, Gwen," he said lazily, looking at me in a manner that was not particularly brotherly, as he took back the glass and held it to my lips.

I turned my head away. "Rather overfamiliar behavior from a brother-in-law, don't you think?" And now I really *did* want the champagne. I reached out and took it, ignoring the flash of his smile. "But then," I said, coldly, "you have likely been overfamiliar with a majority of the women in this room, so what is one more?"

Cambourne looked amused as he glanced around the room. "Really? A majority? Don't you think you might be somewhat overstating the case?" he drawled.

"Oops," I said, by way of reply, as the glass slid in my grasp and just *happened* to pour down the front of his pristine white satin waistcoat. I watched with satisfaction as the stain spread. "Now how could that have happened?"

"Think nothing of it." He extracted a handkerchief from his pocket and blotted the spill.

"Oh, I won't."

"It can be very difficult to overcome a natural tendency toward clumsiness," he allowed.

"True," I replied, tipping my head back and draining the very small amount that remained in the glass with pleasure. I smiled at him. "Pity this isn't just a *little* colder."

"Indeed," he said levelly, as he liberated another glass from the tray of a passing footman. "Try this one—"

But just as he said that, Richard—who I believed had been occupied for some time in attempting to count his own feet—stumbled when a young lady tripped against him, and banged heavily into Cambourne.

"Oops," Cambourne said as we both watched the contents of the glass he was holding slide down my front, soaking my gown.

I looked down at my drenched bodice where the delicate shot-green silk no longer hinted at my curves, but clung, revealing them more or less in entirety.

So did he.

I lifted my chin, he pulled his gaze up, and our eyes met. At the stark hunger I saw in his, I felt color flood like a tide into my cheeks. *Oh no,* I thought, lifting my chin another notch. You don't get to drool over Mathilde and then ogle me. I took his handkerchief.

"I beg your pardon," he said, clearly meaning no such thing. "But do tell me," he said, all innocence as a smile lurked, "was this one colder?"

"Actually, yes," I said through still gritted teeth. "It was, considerably. But you tell me: Was this one *smaller?*" I gave him my sweetest smile, to let him know that I knew exactly where his gaze had been riveted.

At this point Richard rejoined the conversation. "Did you say Milburn was with Sherbrooke? I wouldn't expect to see 'im home and sober for a few days if I was you. If he ain't turned up in a sennight, check the Blue Chamber at Madame—well . . . think it's dashed nice myself to see you returned, Cambourne," he finished in overly hearty tones, having apparently thought better of what he had been about to say. "Don't you think it's dashed nice to see him returned, Gwen?"

"Ah yes," I said. "Returned from, where was it, Cambourne?" And then I congratulated myself that it had just the right sound: cool and unruffled, not overly interested, and yet civil. "I can't recall your precise location, but I seem to recall that I had heard you'd been, oh yes, *called out of London,* I believe it was."

"Perhaps," he said lightly, "since my recent whereabouts are a topic of such consequence to you, Lady Gwen, we can talk of them while I escort you home."

"Home?" I said, raising a brow in inquiry.

"Home. To my brother's house, so you can change out of your wet gown before you contract influenza."

"Nonsense!" I said. "I've just arrived. I am not going anywhere. And Richard, too, is agog to hear about your travels."

"Actually, Gwen, and no offense intended here, Cambourne old man, but I ain't all that interested," Richard said, with an undertone of apology.

"I understand completely," Cambourne said, whilst I directed a glare at my brother.

The malignancy of which Richard was completely insensible to. "As long as you are escorting her home, ask Gwen to fill you in on Milburn's behavior," he recommended.

Cambourne turned to me, his brow raised. "Is there something I should know?" he inquired with every appearance of concern.

"He is not escorting me home," I said. "You are not escorting me home, Cambourne."

"Been tempted to go round and thump Milburn. Disappeared at his own wedding breakfast, y'know," Richard said darkly.

"Did he?" Cambourne sounded appropriately shocked. "Come away with me, then, Gwen," he said, a glint in his eye that I could not like. "And on the carriage ride, you can tell me firsthand the tale of your ill-usage."

"There won't be a carriage ride, as I am staying." I crossed my arms.

"What do you know!" said Richard. "I see just the person I have been looking for!"

"Who?" I said to him, my doubt heavy in my tone. And then was rewarded when he colored as he glanced wildly around. Unfortunately for him, his eye alit on Rodney, Lord Worth.

I smiled at his fate. Served him right.

"Worth," he said, as he ran a finger around his neckcloth.

"Oh well, in that case," I said. "I should not dream of standing in your way. Go."

"Let Cambourne bring you home to change," he said.

"No," I said.

"I understand completely," Cambourne replied, still with that odd light in his eyes. "You cannot bring yourself to miss so much as a moment of the performance."

"Quite right," I said. "It has already been impressive, and to think the music has not yet begun!"

"So lowering," he replied, lazily, as Richard beat his hasty retreat like the rat that he was, deserting the sinking ship that I was, "when the pretheater performance eclipses the actual event."

I looked up at him and gave him my most guileless smile. "Does that happen often?"

The smile he returned was not guileless at all. "I have heard it does . . . to some."

"Does Mrs. Claussen dislike that also?"

"Mrs. Claussen has yet to apprise me of any disappointments she may have suffered in that respect." He took my arm. "Allow me to at least escort you to the ladies' withdrawing room so you may repair yourself."

"No," I said.

"I fear that your mother would hold me accountable should you succumb to pneumonia from standing about in a wet gown," he said.

"My mama," I retorted, "would not hold you accountable for anything, Cambourne, and well you know it. She would find a way to blame me for my own death, should the choice be between the two of us."

He bent very close and smiled. My heart flipped and I hated him. "Touché," he said, offering his arm.

What could I do? I took it and allowed him to lead me from the room.

There was quite a bit that I would have liked to have said, but somehow, I felt it was incumbent upon him to offer the first explanation. The silence seemed to stretch between us, though, until after a few moments, I could stand it no more. "Bit surprised to see me here, were you?" I asked, in casual tones, once we had gained the relative quiet of the corridor.

"I am sorry this had to happen, Gwen," he said, his voice low.

"That I had to be dragged into this sorry mess? Or that I had to witness your courtship of Mathilde Claussen?" I asked, knowing that I was not being entirely reasonable. "*If* courtship can be considered the right word. It had not hitherto occurred to me, Cambourne, that playing the husband would interfere with your social . . . diversions," I added, pointedly, as I recalled the picture Mathilde Claussen had made, laughing up at him over her slowly moving fan.

I was disastrously inept at any such wiles, but I was not

precisely a stranger to the games of flirtation that went on between men and women. And there was something about the way he had leaned over her, the look she had been giving him, that made me burn with anger all over again, just thinking about it. Not with jealousy, but anger. And, well, perhaps a little jealousy.

"We cannot talk about this here," he said, smiling so it looked as though we were enjoying a pleasant conversation.

I smiled back, just as sincerely. "Should we, perhaps, save it for the marital bedchamber?"

"If you wish," he replied, equably. "You need only leave the connecting door unlocked." I spun away from him, and would have left, but he reached out and took my arm. "You can throw objects and accusations at my head later to your heart's content."

He steered me up the stairs. "After I escort you back down," he said in my ear in low tones, speaking quickly, "I shall leave for a time and then come back as Milburn so we can be seen together. Reserve a seat next to you for me. I know it was a shock," he said, pushing me through the door of the ladies' withdrawing room before I could ask any questions. "But you did well, Gwen."

"You will never be able to leave and come back as Milburn," I told him as I paused, turning in the door. "People have just seen you. Surely they will not be deceived?"

"Just watch," he said, sounding a little grim, as he turned to leave. "I think you will find that people generally see what they want or expect to, and not much beyond that."

14

The best laid plans, part two—
In which I very much regret attending Caro
Arbuthnot's operetta

"Your brother-in-law got himself a nice eyeful, did he?" Lady Wainwright asked with a perspicacity that surprised me, as she looked my wet dress up and down.

"He hardly noticed," I assured her as she raised her glass to her lips and drained it.

"Didn't look that way to me," she said. "Looked like he was noticing every inch, and to judge by his expression, a few more, besides. Be a good girl, Cecy," she added, without removing her eyes from me. "Run along and find me some liquid refreshment other than this pap. And do the thing quickly. Before I am reduced to sucking Lady Gwen's gown for traces of champagne. I should think with your highly refined sensibilities, you would find that most embarrassing."

"Come, Cecy, I shall help," I said, hoping to circumvent

this eventuality. I took up Cecy's arm and we left Lady Wainwright in Myrtia's capable hands as we went to fetch the requested libation.

There was much I wanted to ask Cecy, specifically about whether Barings was still sleeping at his club, but she forestalled me, holding up her hand. "Don't," she said.

And I nodded, to show that I understood. "I thought you were not attending tonight," I said, instead.

"Mother wanted a night on the town," she said, dully. "And with your little parting salvo this morning, I could hardly stay away. Besides," she added, optimistically, "surely she cannot get up to any trouble here!"

Ah, but how wrong she was.

Bells tinkled to forewarn us that the musical portion of the evening was to begin. Lady Wainwright had been imbibing the arrack punch we had procured with gusto, and with each passing moment she seemed to grow rosier in countenance. We divided as we entered the music room, Cecy whispering in my ear that she thought her mother would be better behaved were they to sit on their own.

Myrtia and I sat together. Caro, according to Myrtia, was rumored to have been working under the tutelage of a Signor Delfino, from a traveling Italian opera company, so the evening might not be as hopeless as one had assumed. I settled in to try to forget the early part of the evening and enjoy the music as best I could.

To say the music was good would have been an overstatement. Overall, it was more competent than arresting, but it was not nearly so unpleasant as I had feared. After a while, Cambourne returned and slid into the seat beside me. He was Milburn now, though; there was no doubt about it. He had somehow managed to crimp his hair into tousled curls, and had stuffed himself into a bottle-green brocaded ensemble with great falls of lace at the wrists and throat. And don't ask me how he did it—perhaps he was not so mistaken about people seeing what they expect to see—but he somehow seemed softer, less physically commanding.

"Hallo, darling." He languidly picked up my hand and made a display of kissing it. "Decided I couldn't bear to be parted from you for an entire evening," he added, loudly, lest anyone had missed his display. "Told Sherbrooke that, I did, and here I am." No one shushed him.

"Yes, here you are," I said, removing my hand from his grasp with an alacrity that did not much speak of spousal fondness. He seemed unperturbed, however, as he crossed his legs and in his best Milburn fashion slouched back in his chair.

Caro was singing in Italian, moderately credibly, of love and loss, when I was distracted by something of a commotion in front. My heart sank as I realized the source of this bustle of activity was none other than Lady Wainwright. She stood and swayed unsteadily, raising the specter that she would fall upon one of her neighbors in the closely packed rows. "I like to sh—sh—sing a bit myself!" she shouted, and, hoisting herself atop her chair, cleared her throat.

"Oh no," Myrtia breathed. I could see Cecy tugging at her mother's hand, to no avail.

"Thish melody ain't original," Lady Wainwright shouted, as she swayed. "Sho sh—sh—sing along if you know it. She took a breath, and clearing her throat, deepened her voice to a resonant contralto that quite put Caro's soprano to shame.

One morning in autumn by the dawn of the day
With my gun in good order I straight took my way
To hunt for some game to the woods I did steer
To see if I could find my bonnie black hare

"Make a distraction," Myrtia whispered to me.
"What?" I whispered back, as Lady Wainwright launched into the second verse.

I met a young damsel, her eyes black as sloes
Her teeth white as ivory, her cheeks like a rose

"Do something so people will notice you instead of her," Myrtia said.

Her hair hung in ringlets on her shoulders bare
Sweet maiden, I cried, Did you see my bonnie black
    hare?

"No," I said, furiously. "I understand what a distraction is. I mean 'what' should I do? And why me?"
Several masculine voices joined for the third verse.

This morning a-hunting I have been all around
But my bonnie black hare is not to be found—

Myrtia said, "Because you are known to be some-what—clumsy, on occasion."
"I am not."
"The rumor is that you spilled your drink down m'brother's waistcoat this very night, m'dear girl," Cambourne drawled, from next to me. "Shocking abuse of

a fine piece of tailoring, not to mention a fine glass of champagne."

"Well, he—" I began to retort, but Cambourne cut me off, his voice low, against my ear, and much more his own, now. "I know this song, Gwen, and we really do not want her getting to the third verse."

The baritone voices were swelling through the room, gaining strength by the instant. Apparently it was quite a popular little ditty. Poor Caro had stopped singing, tears running down her face.

> *My gun is in good order, my balls are also*
> *And under your smock I was told she did go*
> *So delay me no longer, I cannot stop here*
> *One shot I will fire at your bonnie black hare*

"Do something," Myrtia hissed, as Cambourne said, low in my ear, "Forgive me, Gwen." And then with an extraordinarily un-Milburn-like decisiveness, kicked the flimsy leg on my chair.

I heard it crack, and I felt him surreptitiously grab me so that I didn't land hard, but that didn't stop the shock as I fell, in slow time, the chorale thundering in my ears, as I hit the ground.

Myrtia did her part by screaming, and thus attracting attention to the fact that I was now lying, wedged into the space between our two seats.

The singers lost volume as heads swiveled with Myrtia's scream, then quiet fell as Cambourne jumped to his feet, drawling, "Good Lord, darling, are you all right?"

He did not, however, help me up, but instead stood, looking down at me, to give people plenty of time to transfer their attention to my predicament. "Chair broke! Don'cha know," he said, very loudly, to no one in particular. People were standing now to try to get a look at the situation, some craning around backward.

Only Lady Wainwright's voice was now left, and it was almost inaudible in the growing din as everyone pressed in to see whether I was injured.

"No, no," Cambourne drawled. "She's fine. Just give her a bit of air. Might want to cut back on those sweetmeats a bit, old girl," he said, lazily, studying me through the quizzing glass he had produced from some flounce or ruffle, and sounding exactly like Milburn. I glared at him as well as my position could allow. Having apparently decided that I had served my purpose, he extended a languid hand and helped me to my feet. "Ah, Hillerton," he said pointedly, more than a trace of Cambourne apparent in his voice, to the gentleman seated to Myrtia's right who was craning his neck over Myrtia and staring at my petticoats. "Are you acquainted with my wife?"

I was also aware of Mrs. Trompington, once again surveying me through her opera glasses, which seemed a wholly unnecessary affectation, since she was all of two seats behind me.

"Good to see the gel putting a little meat on the old bones," Violetta stage-whispered. "I told her, I did. Said, 'a man likes to grab a nice handful of bottom come a cold winter night!'"

"Excuse me," said Cambourne to the elderly gentleman on his left. "Could I trouble you to let us past once more? Need to escort the wife home. Dreadful mishap, don'cha know."

"Mishap!" the gentleman bellowed as I hobbled behind Cambourne, trying my best to smile. "T'whole sorry evening is a mishap as far as I'm concerned and now I can't even get a decent spot of sleep. M'wife said opera. M'expecting opera. I *heard* the deuced infernal caterwauling racket, right enough, but I ain't *seen* any dancers. Where's the opera dancers, I ask?" He glared at me, and then a hopeful note entered his eye. "I don't suppose you're one, are you?"

Cambourne grinned back at me, a quick flash of mischief in his eyes.

"No," I said, icily. "I am not."

"Saw quite a bit of leg, though," said the gentleman on Myrtia's other side. "When she fell. Just up to the knee, mind. Vastly disappointed, don'cha know."

"Disappointed!" said the elderly man, leaning toward him. "Was it plump? M'self, I like a plump knee with a few dimples. That I do."

I promised myself that Cecy would be in debt to me for the rest of our lives. And as for Cambourne, well, the rest of his life was looking to be short indeed.

Lady Wainwright, having apparently abandoned both her musical efforts and her chair, was advancing on us. She and the elderly gentleman must have been acquaintances, because she said, "Hello, Leonard."

"Evening, Lady Wainwright," he said.

"Like a plump knee, do you now, Leonard?" she asked flirtatiously.

He inclined his head. "That I do," he said, as Cambourne led me away.

15

In which my friends provide consolation in a time of distress

"No one remarked it," Myrtia assured me, next morning.

"It's true, Gwen," Cecy said, and I loved them both for their dishonesty.

"Everyone remarked it," I told her. "Some remarked it with opera glasses. *You* just didn't remark it because *you* didn't have a good view of things because *you* were sitting in front of me."

"Well, yes, that plus that fact that I had my face buried in my hands." Cecy managed a smile. "Please tell Cambourne that I am forever in his debt," she said.

"And mine," I reminded her, somewhat less than selflessly. "It was my derrière, remember?"

"Well, that goes without saying," she replied. "I wonder, though, and not that I'm not grateful, but"—she looked at me—"would you have done it on your own?"

"If he hadn't dumped me off my chair?" I asked, looking at her. "I like to think I would have created *some* distraction," I said, "but in all honesty, not that particular one, and probably not so quickly or with such presence of mind. I think he saved you from at least a verse or two."

She nodded. "What I really want to know is, what did Cambourne *say* when you got home, Gwen?"

"He said"—I made my voice deep—" 'You didn't injure your . . . posterior, did you?' "

And we all started laughing with a notable lack of decorum.

"And then?" Myrtia said.

"And then, I said, 'Not so you'd notice, and put away that ridiculous quizzing glass before I am tempted to injure *you*.' And he said, 'Well, I am only trying to behave as Milburn would.' 'Excellent,' I said, 'then I shall behave as I would were I truly married to Milburn and lock him—you—out of the house to sleep at the club for the next, oh, ten years.' "

They both laughed. "Was that it?" Cecy wanted to know. "Not so much as a word as to how he had come to tell you he had to leave town and then ended up falling down Mathilde Claussen's cleavage?"

"Well, no, actually we did get to that a bit later on."

What had happened was that I'd asked for a bath. Once the water was ready, Crewes had departed with a sniff (in a huff because I insisted on bathing myself). And I had crossed the room to the mirror. In the aftermath of seeing Cambourne with Mathilde, it was occurring to me for the first time to wonder how he saw me, what I looked like to him. At the edge of my mind, the notion, *why do I care so much?* brushed by, but I declined to examine it.

I peered at myself, looking for some enlightenment, but saw only the same face and figure that had looked back at me for as long as I could recall. How can anyone know precisely how others see them? While I have never shuddered at my own appearance, it is hardly remarkable—not much to attract a man used to such delectable delights as Cambourne, I decided gloomily.

I am not, and have never been, exotic. Mathilde is exotic, with flaming copper ringlets and smoky gray eyes, set deep above fragile cheekbones. And, I wondered, torturing myself just a little further, what else? Was she wittier than I? Cleverer? More sophisticated? Capable of coming up with incisive repartee instead of finding herself foolishly tongue-tied by Cambourne's presence? No doubt she was all of those things and more, I decided, glumly, as I turned away from the mirror.

I climbed into the bath, slid down in the blissfully warm water, and then stuck a leg out and rested it on the side of the deep copper tub. I was hard-pressed to find anything I actually disliked about my foot, but then, I reminded myself, I have never seen Mathilde's feet. Perhaps *they* possessed a mysterious ability to make grown men weep with awe. Not that I knew how that might be, but one never knew. Mine was acceptable. Slim and pale with a high arch. My legs were long and slender—but then, I was a bit on the tall side—and I had always secretly felt them rather elegant. Being tall had never before bothered me unduly. I was not precisely a giant and Milburn was tall enough that I had never worried that I would feel like an Amazon beside him.

That happy attitude, however, was before Mathilde. She was, in a word, tiny. And thus was able to do that looking up a vast distance over the fan thing, no doubt making Cambourne feel huge and masculine and protective. It was hard to imagine him pushing *her* off her chair, that much was certain. And if he had, she no doubt was possessed of those highly desirable dimpled legs of which gentlemen seemed so enamored. *Mathilde* wedged on her bottom between two chairs would likely have been quite the crowd pleaser. I lifted my leg higher and examined it as I slid farther down in the water. Not so much as a *hint* of a dimple. I sighed.

I ducked under the water to soap my hair. I had just finished pulling on my wrapper and coiling my wet hair on top of my head, when Cambourne himself scratched at the door that connected our two dressing rooms.

All I really wanted was to yell and scream at him for his odious behavior. For making me like him and want him, while at the same time driving me into a fury and keeping me in ignorance. Not to mention dumping me off my chair. *But,* I reminded myself, no matter how I felt, I needed to retain my dignity. A calm, ladylike—or better yet, countess-like—air of detachment was what I was striving for. Chilly. Cold, even. No, better yet, completely dispassionate, as though I did not even care enough to bother being cold.

"Yes?" I said, coolly, in keeping with this decision.

"Cambourne," he said, politely.

"Oh," I said, as though the identity of the person knocking had not previously occurred to me. Then I paused for effect, the implication being that I was thinking about whether I wanted to invite him in. "Come in, then," I said, adding, ungraciously, "if you want."

In his hand he held a heavy tumbler of something amber. And his hair, like mine, really did not hold a curl, because it had fallen straight again, over his forehead. I had the wayward thought that any children Cambourne and I might have together would have very straight hair indeed, which thought brought a blush at odds with the detached demeanor I was determined to present.

He had changed into his own fawn-colored breeches and white shirt, open at the neck, with no cravat, and pulled on a *robe de chambre* over the whole. I yawned, discreetly covering my mouth with my hand, to show my utter boredom with his presence.

"Would you like to rake me over the coals now?" he asked equably, taking a seat. "I do believe that I did agree earlier to appear in the marital bedchamber for precisely that."

"Why on earth would I?" I replied. I would have liked to have stretched and yawned again, to imply that I couldn't have been bothered to put myself out to such a degree on his account, but I was a bit concerned that my wrapper would not stay entirely closed. "Do be seated," I said, pointedly, since he was already ensconced.

He raised a brow. "Thank you, I will," he said. "You are angry with me?"

I raised a brow in return. "Angry with you? Why ever would you think that?"

"It's no matter," he replied, sounding most unruffled. "All that is important is that you are not." He stretched then, uncoiling his long, lean body in such a relaxed way that it made my teeth hurt with the effort of keeping them clenched in a smile. "And in that case it appears that we have nothing we need discuss."

"No," I said, through my still clenched teeth, attempting to sound as though the idea could not have been more foreign. "In fact, I find myself unable to think of a single thing that necessitates discussion." I forced a gritted smile.

"I think I shall retire, then. It has been a long day." He started to rise.

"Yes," I said, civilly, the fury starting to race through me to such an extent that I could almost *hear* it. Despite my best efforts, it began to leak out. "I can well imagine that it has, what with all of the various roles you have had to play today: yourself, your brother, the besotted lover, the caring husband, the gentlemanly rescuer. And all of them to different women! Why, you must be positively wilting with exhaustion!"

He sat back down. "And which, exactly, of that list has you so angry, Gwen?"

"Oh, you choose," I said.

"Very well." He looked at me assessingly. "I doubt it was the gentlemanly rescuer."

Actually, the gentlemanly rescuer role was the one I had least objected to, but, come to think of it, I did have a few questions on that front. "Would you have shoved Mathilde Claussen on the floor?" I asked, or, well, demanded. So much for my cool, uncaring demeanor. I knew it had deserted me, but at the moment I was too furious to care.

"I do not know," he said, after a moment. "It had not occurred to me before the fact that I would be shoving anyone onto the floor. It was a spur of the moment decision, you understand."

"I do understand that," I persisted. "But would you have?"

"Do you want the honest answer, Gwen?" he asked, slowly.

"Yes," I said, although that was likely a blatant untruth.

"No," he said. "Likely not. But, then, I thought you a loyal enough friend that you would not object to the affront to your self-respect if it meant sparing Cecy further embarrassment."

"I see," I replied, feeling slightly ashamed of myself.

"I'm not sure that you do," he said.

"But am I so devoid of sensibility—or is it that I am so clumsy that you believe me to be accustomed to showing my bottom in public?" I asked.

"Oh Gwen," he said, looking almost sad. "Is that what you believe of me?"

"I believe that you thought you could coerce me into an unwanted marriage because I always do what I'm told," I said. "And I believe it because you told me. Isn't that enough?"

He stood, then, and crossed to me, setting down his glass on the table next to me. "For what it's worth, you did not show your bottom."

"You think that only because you did not have opera glasses," I snapped.

"Actually, I had quite a good view." He smiled.

I stood, too, wanting to go, if not nose to nose, at least something closer to it. "I am sorry that you are so tired of this forced descent into dull domesticity that you felt the need to be out playing the bachelor. But the domesticity was not, as you might recall, my idea."

It did not escape me that his gaze had slipped to my clinging silk wrapper. "I'm more than aware that it was not your idea," he said, not lifting his eyes to my face. "And since you persist in reminding me at every opportunity, not likely to forget it any time soon."

"Oh?" I replied, crossing my arms, and waiting until he had raised his gaze.

"And," he said, letting his gaze fall again and roam over me, and despite myself I once again felt something shimmering between us, "are you implying that you expect domesticity? With me? Because that was not the impression I was under."

"I can well imagine that you would not have spared much thought for the subject, given your other . . . concerns," I said tartly.

He looked at my face then, for a long moment, and then shrugged off his robe. With our gazes locked together, he reached for me. We were so close I was able to feel his breath as he slid his robe up my arms and pulled it closed at the front. I sighed at the luxurious warmth of it. And the understanding that the warmth was *his,* from his skin, sent an involuntary shiver up my spine.

"Actually, I have given it a good deal of thought. And it seems to me," he said, quietly, as his nimble fingers tied the sash, "that you have made it extremely clear that you are marking time with me, waiting for Milburn."

"No, Cambourne," I said, in measured tones. "What I hope to have made clear is that I consider myself an honorable and loyal person who has been thrust without my consent into a most untenable situation and who is unable to get anyone to give me the answers I deserve."

"We all find ourselves at some point in an unfortunate situation, not of our own making," he replied in equally measured tones. "It is up to you to decide how you go from there."

"But don't you see? That is precisely what I am trying to do. And you, damn you, won't cooperate."

"Things are at stake that you know nothing about. That I am not at liberty to tell you." He shrugged. "I suppose making decisions requires a higher degree of maturity than simply going along telling oneself that one is a victim of circumstance."

"I *am* a victim of circumstance," I pointed out, in what I was pleased to note was a controlled voice, since I was as angry as I had ever been. "And making decisions based on incomplete information is *not* an indicator of maturity."

"You might want to consider the fact," he replied coolly, "that the alternative to the situation you are in would be for Milburn to have simply not arrived for the wedding. You would at this very moment be living in your parents' house waiting for him, likely with no more understanding of what had become of him than you possess right now. One hardly thinks that would be preferable."

I raised a brow. "Milburn would not have shown up even if you had not stepped in?"

He gave me a level look. "No," he said, finally, as though deciding that he could part with that much. "I think it is safe to say that he would not have."

"I see." I added that fact to my scant information.

"You are angry that I was with Mathilde tonight?" he said in tones that almost sounded conciliatory.

"No," I said, casting about for something that made me sound like a person who was not a complete stranger to logic. "Surprised, perhaps, that you are incapable of going even a short time without"—I forced myself not to blush—"female *companionship.*"

"Do let me understand then," he said, evenly. "You are asking me to forgo female companionship?"

"No," I said, attempting to find a way out that at the same time made me sound rational, spared me the sight of Cambourne romancing Mathilde, and allowed me to do it without needing to blurt out that I wanted to kill him for even *thinking* about another woman.

He looked interested. "Then what do you want, Gwen?"

"Discretion," I lied. "At the very least, I expect you to be discreet."

For the merest instant, I thought I might have seen a flicker of some strong emotion in his eyes, but when he replied, his tones were equable. "Of course. We are to spare your maidenly sensibilities! So, am I correct in assuming that were I to very *discreetly* bed anyone who took my fancy, that would be acceptable?"

Now what was I supposed to say? "No," I said. "Yes." Then, "I do not know."

He raised a brow. "How conclusive," he said. "Perhaps you would explain your reasoning to me, since it seems that I am having difficulty in deciphering it on my own."

"Well—" I began, feeling rather boxed into a corner. "I suppose we must both be sensible about this."

"Sensible," he said, "I see. I suppose it is fortunate that you feel this way, because I might as well tell you: Something has come up and I will need to appear to be myself some of the time. And if I am to be myself, then I must behave as people are accustomed to seeing me."

I stared at him. "Something has come up?" I said. "And by that, may I assume you do not refer to your manipulation of me into a sham of a marriage, but to something *important*?"

"In fact," he replied, crossing his arms, "you are right. I do refer to something *important*."

I raised a brow. "So *people,* am I to take it, then, must be *accustomed* to seeing you pant over Mathilde like an animal in heat? And what's come up is that you have to trot around town whoring so no one will think that the almighty Earl of Cambourne has fallen?"

"I had not realized that I was conducting myself with such unusual restraint," he said tightly. "I shall take pains to remedy that immediately, but then, that is of no great interest to you."

"You lied to me, telling me that you had business out of town," I accused, sounding very much the shrewish wife, compiling a litany of wrongs, but too angry to care.

"I did have business out of town," he said, evenly. "And then I learned that someone I needed to see was expected at the Arbuthnots', so I returned."

"And how nice of her to ensure that you could see so very much of her! I was momentarily alarmed that her dressmaker had forgot the bodice entirely! But, then, your reverting to playing Cambourne will likely afford you numerous such felicitous opportunities," I said.

"Oh, thousands," he said, airily. "If not hundreds of thousands."

"I see," I said.

"I'm not entirely certain that you do," he replied.

"Oh, but I do," I returned, sweetly.

"I think," he said, slowly, "that I shall avail myself of them all. Each and every one."

"How very fatiguing for you," I said, looking right up into his face.

"And how very nice of you to care," he replied, looking down into mine.

"I am concerned about your health, naturally," I told him.

"As a dutiful sister-in-law should be. But do let me understand: While concerned for my well-being in a completely dutiful way, you do not care *personally* if I bed those other women?" he asked.

"Of course not," I replied, striving for an air of careless insouciance. "Why on earth would I care about that?"

"You damned well do, and you know it," he said, his

face very close. "And you can damned well tell me why."

"You *swore,*" I said. "You swore at me *twice,* Cambourne."

"Yes," he said, taking a step nearer. His eyes glittered. "I did."

I backed up a corresponding step. It was not that I was afraid of him, precisely, but I was suddenly aware of something simmering beneath that cool surface, of the way his eyes were narrowed.

"In fact, I have never," he said, his tones still equable, "in all my life, met a female so readily capable of rendering me completely furious."

The funny thing was that although everything on the surface was calm, there was an almost palpable blaze of something strong in the air. He moved again, and I thought for a moment that he was going to back me against the wall. And then what would I do? What would *he* do? I wondered in a heady swirl of anticipation and terror. But, instead, he dropped his gaze and picked up his glass from the table and took a drink. His knuckles were white.

I had never before this moment, in all our years of knowing one another, seen him display even a hint of temper. "You lost your temper at me," I almost whispered.

"No," he said, over the rim of the glass. "*Most* people lose their tempers. I don't."

"But," I said, with a sudden flash of insight (of which I was quite proud). "Underneath that very heavy mantle of your titles, you are just a person. Not so different from *most* people."

He ran his hand through his hair and took a step back and the atmosphere lightened. "Tell me, Gwen," he said. "Are *most* people completely exasperated by you?"

"More than a few," I admitted. "You only need ask my brothers."

"Somehow," he said, "I suspect this is different. On the optimistic side, since it seems you are partial to a display of rage, there does seem to be every possibility that the more time I spend with you, the likelier you are to get one." He handed me the glass, then, wordlessly.

I wondered, as I drank, if my lips were touching the same place that his had.

"Just because I am not choleric, Gwen, do not mistake me for a man of lukewarm emotion," he said, very softly.

I swallowed, and nodded, my gaze still locked with his.

"And do not throw my faults in my face without acknowledging your own."

"Mine?" I looked at him. It was not that I did not recognize that I possess them, many and varied, but I had not realized them to be currently under discussion. I placed the glass down.

"Yes, Gwen," he said, still softly. "If you are honest, the reason you care about the possibility of my bedding others has nothing to do with discretion." He put his hand out and hooked a finger in the knot he had made in the sash of the robe. "Does it?"

He pulled me closer, so I had no choice but either to look up at him or straight ahead at his chest. I looked up, but found that view no less disturbing. "Our wedding night," he said from very close. "Do you know what I remember most?"

I shook my head.

"The way you seemed to burn, Gwen. The heat of you, against me, beneath my hands."

My stomach seemed to turn molten. All the reasons not to go where he was leading churned around in my head: *He has not been honest with me. He is using me for his own ends. Likely he was saying similarly heated words to Mathilde*

Claussen a few short hours ago. And I belong to Milburn, I reminded myself, *not to this man.* Although, were I to be honest with myself, I knew that the last was not what was holding me back.

He stroked a finger down my cheek. He had moved a step nearer so that he was not precisely pressed against me, but there was not a good deal of space between our bodies. "And you never would have burned like that had there been nothing between us."

Speak up again now, I told my brain, which had suddenly fallen into silence. When it didn't, I licked my lips, and to my surprise, noticed that he seemed fascinated by that action. I did it again. And again, he seemed unable to pull his gaze away. I may not have been diminutive, and gazing adoringly up at him over a fan, but nonetheless I was aware of something in the air between us, making my body grow heavier. I put my hand in his.

His robe was still wrapped around me, and I was pleasurably aware of it, lying heavy and warm over my body. He pulled me close, and bent his head to mine, and said, his words warming me, "You tempt me to go places I've never been, Gwen."

Then his hands skimmed up my arms, seemingly touching places on my body that they were nowhere near. My hands clenched in his shirtfront as he lowered his head, and then, very slowly, as though we had all the time in the world, he ran his tongue across my lip, following the same path mine had taken.

I sighed against the heat of his mouth. And then he did it again. "Gwen," he said, sounding unlike himself. His eyes were dark and heavy.

I pressed against him, made shockingly wanton by the need he was summoning in me. The silk of his robe seemed to slide between us. I could feel that my breasts had grown tight and were pressing into his chest. I moved again, boldly wanting to make certain he knew it. His hands came up my back, stilling me and yet pressing me closer still. I could not fathom that any sensation could feel so wicked, and yet so sweet, as his mouth on mine and the hard length of him against me. He was muscles and angles and planes, and we seemed to fit perfectly. I groaned.

"What?" he asked, roughly. "Tell me what." He looked hungry. Predatory.

"More," I whispered.

"Yes," he said in a rough voice, as his hand came up to close over my breast. "Everything you want."

My head fell back, as the sensation rippled through me. He bent and lowered his head to where the pulse beat in my throat. He kissed me there, and then ran the tip of his tongue up my neck. I shivered. His hand left my breast, and I would have protested had he not immediately begun to untie the sash of his robe. I let my arms fall to my side, and looked up at him, offering myself. Our eyes stayed locked, as the robe fell open, and then his hot gaze swept down over me.

I could hear his breathing quicken. I felt a surge of power that this was *me* having this effect on him. And despite the effect *he* was having on me, I forced myself to think, which wasn't easy, with his gaze burning into mine. Perhaps, just perhaps, I thought, I could *try* doing what Cecy had suggested, after all, and allow him to seduce me—not entirely, of course, since I would only be allowing him to *think* he was seducing me—in order to get information from him.

If I were going to, it was now or never. I took a deep

breath, and dropping his robe to the floor, stood before him in just my thin wrapper.

I forced myself to be still under his gaze, until he lifted his darkened eyes to mine once again. Without letting my gaze move away from him, I slowly reached up and took down the wet hair that I had coiled on top of my head. It fell, warm and damp and heavy to my shoulders. He was still watching as if he could not bring himself to tear his eyes away. Encouraged, I very deliberately licked my lips again, and untied the ribbons that closed my wrapper at the neck, relishing the slip of the silk as they slid free. He swallowed.

"Have you been thinking about this, Cambourne?" I asked, surprised by how husky my voice sounded to my own ears.

Instead of answering, he stepped even nearer, and pulled me to him.

"Wanting this?" I whispered.

"Constantly," he said against my ear, as he slid the palms of his hands down my silk-covered arms. "Without cease."

This was going much better than I had expected! I took a step back from him. "And this?" I asked, as I parted the very top of my wrapper. He was watching me now, with narrow-eyed intensity. Every inch of his body was taut, but *I* could still think, I realized with some satisfaction.

Now. I had to start the questioning innocuously, I knew. "Were you thinking about this before we were married?" I whispered, licking my lips. "When you decided to step in for Milburn?"

Then I almost gasped as the air hit my hardened nipples. And my firm grip on rationality seemed to tilt, when he made a sort of strangled noise and pulled me to him.

His hands slid to my hips, where they seemed to melt a path. Still gripping my hips, he lowered his head, and his lips sought mine. This time, his mouth seemed to whisper across mine for only a moment, before he turned the kiss deeper, his tongue swept across my lips. Our thighs were pressed together and his hands left my hips, one to trace the lightest caresses over my breasts, the other to stroke my bottom, pushing me harder against him. His strangled sound was mine now.

"Cambourne," I gasped as he rocked against me.

"Easy," he whispered, against the side of my neck. "Easy, Gwen," as his nimble fingers parted the wrapper further. His hands were almost touching bare skin!

And I confess, I realized then and there that I didn't have the stuff of which empire breakers are made. I no longer remembered what I wanted to know or why. I only wanted his hands on more of me.

"Come to my bed, Gwen," he whispered, as he moved his hand so that my breast filled his palm, his skin causing the most delightful friction against mine.

I gasped, and nodded, as I made the discovery that pushing myself back up against him made things all that much better.

He groaned. "Do you want this?" he whispered against my lips, as the flat of his hand pushed against the burning point that was my nipple.

"Oh God help me, but yes," I said, arching into his wicked hand.

"You'll be my wife," he said, keeping me tight to his body. "Come what may. No questions."

And that did it. I tore myself out of his hands and snatched frantically at both what remained of my wits and my wrapper, trying to reassemble both to the best of my ability. *He was seducing me for his own reasons just as I had started out seducing him for mine.*

I stood clutching my wrapper, panting and looking up at him. "You just want to bed me so I have no recourse to end this marriage," I accused.

He smiled, that look of absolute certainty back in his eye. "Not *just* because of that," he said, coolly. *He* certainly had managed to get himself under control quickly. "Do not try to beat me at my own game, Gwen. You don't stand a chance."

And then arrogant as ever, he turned and left. When he had gone (and my breathing had returned to something resembling normal) I had once again retrieved his robe. And I had sat, wrapped in the warmth of it, holding the glass we had shared, and stared into the dying fire for what seemed like hours—reliving that wild heat we had shared, fuming at his very unaffectedness, and planning many satisfactory ways to take revenge on Harry Cambourne.

By the end of my recitation of events, Cecy was looking thoughtful. "I can tell you a few tricks that will wipe Mathilde out of his mind. And," she continued, "it sounds like the situation has potential. You really should let him bed you, Gwen, and see if he does it differently as—"

Well, I have to admit it, my interest was piqued. But only by the larger intellectual ramifications of her point, mind. "Do you think it would be different?" I asked. "I mean, he's the same person regardless of which he's being."

Cecy looked at Myrtia. "This should be your forte," she said. "A nice, edifying theoretical debate!"

"No theory to debate," said Myrtia, promptly. "I posit that as Milburn it would be all flash and no substance. Cambourne knows how to get a thing done."

"This," I said, as repressively as I was able, still being rather preoccupied with Cecy's supposition, "is not aiding my case, Myrtia. I expect lewd suggestions from our friend here"—I inclined my head toward Cecy—"but you! You shock me!"

"Oh well. Console yourself with the thought that at least *you* aren't having to put up with my darling mama," Cecy said, sipping her tea. She sounded breezy enough, but there was no getting around the dark circles under her eyes.

"Cec?" Myrtia said, with some hesitation. "Is there any-thing—would you like to talk?"

"No," Cecy said, decisively, and then, "Well, perhaps." We waited.

Finally, she said, "It is her new, ah, *amour.* Oh God—" she stopped and put her head in her hands—"I don't know what to do."

I touched her shoulder hesitantly, and when she lifted her head, I thought the tilt of her chin was almost defiant. "She's . . . expecting a child," she said quietly. "My father has thrown her out. She says she *wants* him to sue her for a divorce. *Wants him to.*"

We were quiet. Myrtia, I suspect, was, like me, trying to imagine the enormity of the scandal that was sure to result.

Cecy, by this point, had regained her customary con-trol. "She wants to go live with him, the father of this child. She says that she has, finally, after all these years, 'discovered real, abiding, and true love.' 'If you have found real and abiding love,' I said, 'why were you trying to bed my footman?' And she said, 'Real and abiding love only opens one's eyes to the amount of love in the world and makes one want to experience more of it.' Oh, and it gets worse!"

That was hard to imagine. But if Cecy said it got worse, I would have to assume it did.

"He's a groom," she said, quickly. "Neither of them has a feather to fly with. Father has turned him off with no reference, of course. She wants to live with us until they can set up household." She dropped her head again to her hands. Her shoulders began to shake.

This time, Myrtia put a gentle hand on her, brushing back her hair. "Don't cry, Cec," she said, "like everything else, this too will pass."

Cecy lifted her head and it was impossible to tell whether she was laughing or crying. Tears were running down her face, but the shaking seemed more due to gasps of laughter than sobs. "So she will live with us, growing visibly more with child every day, while she waits to marry her lover who is, by the way, not yet two decades. *I'm older than he is!* And she thinks it would be lovely if I were to make her an allowance, to compensate her, as she puts it, for all the sacrifices she has made on my account."

We were silent.

"Well, what do you think?" she asked, finally.

"*I* think," I said, slowly, "that all things considered, my drawers through opera glasses don't sound all that bad."

"Somehow I thought you might see it that way," Cecy said.

"Oh, Cec, is there anything we can do?" I asked.

She shook her head. "Just promise that when I end up

cast off by Barings, living with my mother and her new husband, henceforth to be known as the child, and *their* child, you will still come visit me and bring me tales of the polite world."

"Not only will I visit, Cec," I promised, "I'll bring fruit."

And Myrtia nodded. "Any kind of fruit you want!"

16

In which Cambourne continues to be both brothers

I thought quite a bit over the next few days about some of the things that had been said to me. In particular, though, it was one thing that Cambourne had said that kept running through my head. It had been something to the effect of: Sooner or later we all find ourselves in an unfortunate situation not of our own making. And that it was up to me to decide how I wanted to go on.

The point being, I supposed, that regardless of why he had done what he had, the fact was that it *was* done, and now the responsibility for my own behavior was firmly on my shoulders. It was so like him. Direct, uncompromising, arrogant, and yet so frustratingly elusive that it made me want to shake him, to loosen something that would help me to *know* him. At least, I told myself, with his revelation that he thought himself in some way above losing his temper, I felt as though I had gained the tiniest foothold in understanding him.

"Am I a petted, cosseted, spoiled brat?" I asked Myrtia, as we sat in my drawing room.

She hesitated. "Why do you ask?"

"Is that your kind way of saying yes?"

"No," she said, smiling. "I just wondered. It always helps to know the context before one commits to answering a question like that."

"Oh Myrtia," I said, laughing, and then told her what Cambourne had said.

"You are no more petted, cosseted, or spoiled than the rest of us," she assured me.

"Truly?"

"Truly," she said, and I felt better. "But," she added, and my new sense of well-being faded abruptly, "that doesn't mean there is no room for improvement. We can all always improve."

Which gave me more to stew on. "How do you think *you* would react to finding yourself in my situation?" I asked.

"I don't know," she said.

"You would be more mature about it, wouldn't you?" I said darkly.

She laughed. "I honestly don't know."

But I *was* spoiled, I decided. All my life I had been surrounded by privilege without ever thinking about it. My parents, whilst not exactly doting, were hardly ogres. I had wonderful friends, and had been blessed with wealth, good health, the promise of an advantageous marriage, and healthy, if odious, brothers. And perhaps, most of all, I had always been able to drift along without having to make any decisions of more gravity than which new gowns to order and which balls to attend.

"What do you like about me?" I asked Cecy the next day.

She had bid me to come visit and take her mind off her problems with her mother, so of course I had headed straight round. I had found her slumped in the sitting room off her bedchamber. "Now," she had said, "entertain me with tales of life, chez Milburn. I declare, between our two households, one hardly needs go to the circulating library anymore!"

So I told her of the latest, how against all odds Cambourne and I seemed to have fallen into an armed détente. How he was going back and forth between his two identities with a speed that I found astonishing. How he was completely exhausted from spending long hours over estate business and in Parliament, and then coming home and assuming his Milburn mantle. Then I had asked her my question about what she liked about me.

In reply, she gave me a rather diabolical smile. "Well," she said, after a moment. "You are loyal, clearly—you did, after all, expose your derrière for me. And you're very amusing."

"Do you think so?" I said, pleased.

"Absolutely," she said, firmly. "Lively and witty and clever."

"But do you think I am immature?"

She waved a hand. "Maturity is greatly overrated," she said. "Plenty of odiously mature people about, and one hardly finds oneself seeking them out."

"Myrtia's mature," I pointed out.

"But not *odiously* mature," she said. "And, anyway," she added, "she's really more thoughtful and serious than mature. But what are you getting at, Gwen?"

"I suppose I am wondering what Cambourne sees when he looks at me," I said.

"I see," she replied, looking at me as if she were thinking hard. "I suppose that would depend on how he feels about you. Two different people would have two different visions of any one of us, I would guess.

"When I first met Barings," she continued, "I thought he was rather ordinary, both in looks and demeanor. Pleasant, but nothing much out of the common way. But, then, as I came to know him, he seemed to grow steadily more handsome and fascinating until I couldn't understand how I had ever seen him as ordinary." I would have asked her more, but she held up her hand. "Don't ask."

I opened my mouth to object, but she shot me a look that would have done Violetta proud, so I acquiesced. It was not as though I did not have my own fair share of problems to occupy myself with at the moment.

More days passed in which Cambourne kept up both sides of his deception. I thought a lot, shopped, saw Myrtia and Cecy almost every day, and entertained endless visitors to endless cups of tea.

One Tuesday, Cambourne/Milburn and I were entertaining an assortment of visitors. At some time nearing four of the clock, the room emptied, as people began to recollect that it was time to move on to their next call. Only Lord Trafford (yes, *the* Lord Trafford of the Stainsteads' terrace Incident) and the Honorable Mr. John Darleigh had overstayed their welcome. I was attempting to simulate rapt attention to Mr. Darleigh's accounting of a rather splendidly fascinating (his words, not necessarily my impression) curricle race in which he had recently participated, when Cambourne and Trafford, who had been seated across the room, made their way over to us.

"Afternoon, Darleigh," Cambourne said, making a

slight bow, and then turning to me. "My love." He fastid-
iously shook out his cuffs and sat down beside me, crossing one yellow pantaloon-clad leg over the other, pausing
momentarily to admire the shine of his Hessians as he
did so.

Trafford perched on a chair. "Gloomy day, ain't it?" he
observed, but before we could get far with this thrilling
line of conversation, two new arrivals were announced:
Lady Emily Arbuckle and Mrs. Fanny Toth to pay their
respects. Both were friends of my mother's, but I was fond
of them, nonetheless.

"You two *are* attending my ball?" demanded Lady
Arbuckle without much in the way of preamble. "For, I
warn you, I shall be most put out if you do not."

Cambourne, in best Milburn fashion, appeared preoccupied with Darleigh's cerulean waistcoat. He eyed it with
apparent disfavor. "I believe we are planning upon it," he
roused himself to say. "P'raps m'wife might even go so far
as to save me a dance."

"Bit in the wife's pocket, these days, aren't you, Milburn?"
observed Trafford.

"D'you know, p'raps I am," drawled Cambourne, reliev-
ing his sleeve of an invisible lint speck. "You have something to say to that, I collect?"

"Bad ton," observed Darleigh. "That's all."

"Quite true, young man," agreed Lady Arbuckle. "It is
not done for couples to appear overly fond of one another
these days."

"I blame," said Mrs. Toth, "this mania for fashionable
ennui. That was not the way of it in my youth!"

Lady Arbuckle nodded her agreement. "To be sure, one
does quite expect young couples to display a marked lack
of preference for one another, I'm afraid."

Cambourne crossed his legs, and leaned back, some- how managing to possess himself of my hand. "Far be it from me to step a foot from the realm of the fashionable," he drawled, pushing up the ruffle of my long sleeve, just enough to touch, for the merest instant, the sensitive skin on the inside of my wrist.

"Truly, Milburn. Never thought to see you take quite so strenuously to playing the devoted husband," observed Trafford.

"Did you not?" Cambourne said lightly, his glance brushing me. "It had never occurred to me that I would be anything other than an . . . affectionate spouse."

"Only be warned, they are saying that you are a sad case, indeed," said Trafford.

"They?" inquired Cambourne with a raised brow that, in my estimation, looked just a little too ducal to have come from Milburn.

"Y'know. They. At White's, etcetera," explained Dar- leigh.

"How lowering," replied Cambourne, not sounding in the least bit lowered. "To be thought a sad case! Am I to suppose we figure heavily in the betting books at the moment?"

"How vulgar!" said Lady Arbuckle. "One cannot like this deplorable tendency of the young men about town to bet on the least little thing!"

"I think it's rather exciting," said Mrs. Toth, merrily.

"The wags are giving it another week," Trafford assured him.

"A week for the charms of one as lovely as my wife to pall!" said Cambourne, as he slanted a laughing look at me. "I hardly know whether the slight is intended toward m'self or toward you, *wife.*"

"Oh, me, you may depend upon it, *husband,*" I assured him, returning his look. Surely Milburn's eyelashes were never that long and dark? "I am certain your reputation remains intact."

"Then I shall simply prove wrong all those who would doubt your attractions," Cambourne said, possessing himself once again of my hand and making a great show of turning it over and kissing the palm. When he raised his head, he directed a smile at me, so entirely different from Milburn's that I wondered if anyone else had observed it.

I tried to tear my eyes away from that smile, and the blood seemed to rush into my face. Cambourne, I realized, was flirting with me. Here. In front of a room full of people.

But, "Ain't like you, Milburn," was all Darleigh said.

I darted a look at Lady Arbuckle, but she, too, seemed to notice nothing amiss.

Cambourne raised a brow slightly, as if to let me know that *he* knew precisely how much he could get away with. "Sometimes, Darleigh, a man is simply not himself," he replied, with a hint of a smile, not looking at Darleigh, but at me instead.

I almost choked on a laugh. "So long as he recognizes it," I said.

"He would have to be a fool not to recognize it," he replied, not removing his gaze, and I felt my skin heat beneath the soft wool of my gown. "And no one who knows me," he said, with lazy assurance and a hint of steel, "would mistake me for that."

And I knew that this was Harry to Gwen, nothing at all to do with Milburn. "No," I almost whispered, my eyes caught with his.

"I find it quite touching," said Mrs. Toth. "That one so

fashionable as you are known to be, Lord Bertie, could be willing to be thought a fool for love."

"It seems to me," Cambourne said, still in that lazy Milburn-like way, "that a *foolish* man is one who leaves his wife open to any opportunist who might come along. Even one, say, inviting her to gaze at the sunset from the Stainsteads' terrace." Although Cambourne did not look his way, a slight color suffused Trafford's countenance.

"I don't know," mused Darleigh. "Are you implying that a man of wits would hang on his wife's sleeve, Milburn?"

"A man of wits, I think," said Cambourne, looking directly at me, "would make certain his wife was so happy with her current state of affairs that she would have no interest whatsoever in . . . observing sunsets." To me, his light tones conveyed a message not the least bit suited to the drawing room, but no one else seemed to have noticed.

"Clever boy," said Lady Arbuckle.

"But surely one cannot expect a woman to lose her interest in natural phenomena simply because she has become a bride, Milburn!" Darleigh said to him.

"Oh, I think one can," he said, low, and I recalled, for a fleeting instant, our wedding afternoon. How he had stood behind me at the window and I had watched our reflections against the deepening sky as his hands had moved knowingly over my body. I knew the sun must have been setting, because it had grown steadily darker, and our reflections more pronounced, accordingly, but could not for the life of me have recalled what colors had streaked the sky, or, in fact, whether there had been any.

Our gazes met, as the recollection heated my cheeks. I knew we were sharing the same thought. I let my glance fall away from his, and resisted the urge to open my fan and use it. Surely the room was not that warm?

Fortunately for my peace of mind, Mrs. Toth turned to me. "And what time does the sun go down, my dear?" she asked, with a twinkle in her eye.

I pulled myself together. "At forty-two minutes past three, yesterday," I replied promptly, which was greeted by much laughter.

"Now you shall have to redeem yourself, wife," said Cambourne, smiling at me. "By agreeing to save a dance for a mere husband at Lady Arbuckle's ball."

I dropped my gaze first. "A quadrille," I said.

"A waltz," he replied, low, and I could almost feel his hand, warm, at my waist.

I swallowed. "A quadrille. And that only if you are very well behaved between now and then."

"That's the way," said Lady Arbuckle, approvingly. "Keep him on a short string."

Everyone laughed further at this, but my mouth was dry as Cambourne's gaze held mine.

"He was *flirting* with me, I would swear it," I told Myrtia later the next morning when she came to call. "And he was doing it so that I knew, but no one else did."

Since my disastrous attempt at seduction, I had more or less decided to bide my time, while I figured out what to do. And so Cambourne and I went about our lives, venturing out into Society. Overall, he was so good at being Milburn that I was able to tell myself that I really could not be faulted for not having recognized the deception from the first. Yet, every once in a while, I would catch him out. He would be unable to resist adding something to a debate about parliamentary issues, or his eyes would glaze over during a discussion of the Season's colors, and he would give me that quick, secret smile of mutual understanding. And that, somehow, that growing connection, might have been the most troubling thing of all.

If he was escorting Mathilde Claussen on the evenings he went out by himself, well, neither of us made mention of it and I didn't witness it again. I had my dark moments of suspicion, of course, but refrained from confronting him with them. If anything, I was more aware now than before that as much as I might object to his seeing Mathilde, I hardly was in a position to tell him he couldn't.

At home, we managed, seemingly by mutual agreement, to keep a rather civilized distance. As companions, there was no question that we rubbed along well together, although with each of us so intentionally on our best behavior, things were not as easy between us as they had sometimes been. And with the slight distance, I kept thinking that I should be less physically affected by him. The problem, of course, was that this was in no way the case.

That traitorous trip-hammer-blush sequence seemed to happen quite a lot still. And I was no longer able to sit across from him at the table without recalling what it felt like to smooth my fingers through his hair, or press up against him, or be kissed by him, or, even, disgracefully, for him to have his hand on my breast. A little knowledge is indeed a dangerous thing, as the saying goes, and I often found myself wondering at odd moments if he would make that strangled kind of groaning noise deep in his throat were I to rise and press myself against him. Not thoughts particularly conducive to harmonious coexistence or restful nights of sleep.

I also discovered, quite by accident, that Cambourne played the cello every morning. It had been my custom to stay abed fairly late in the mornings, partly because, in truth, I didn't have all that much else to do. But then, early in the second week following the night at the Arbuthnots', Cambourne bought me a horse.

What happened was (all right, I admit it, despite my rational assurances that I understood I was hardly in a position to object to him seeing Mathilde, and rather rosy version of our life given above, the truth was that I had . . . objected) that we had argued. He had returned to Milburn House quite late one night, after having gone out as Cambourne. I was in the study reading (snooping for information), as I usually did when he went out. He had seen the lamp burning, and had come in.

"Evening, Gwen," he had said, leaning against the doorframe and crossing his arms. "You did not go out?"

He was indisputably himself. Lean and immaculately tailored and . . . drunk? I wondered, as I took in the glitter in his eyes. And likely fresh from Mathilde Claussen's arms, if not her bed.

"No," I said, sweetly, trying to discreetly close the drawer of his desk behind my back. "I did not want to interfere with your amorous activities by bumping into you anywhere. Since I do understand that it is of the utmost importance that you are able to be yourself with rakish impunity."

"Well then," he said, still leaning against the door. "Since one does so hate to reiterate the same tedious conversation over and over, I will simply say that your assistance and tact is much appreciated. Not to mention your rifling my desk. I should likely save you the trouble by telling you that you will not find what you are looking for there."

"Or anywhere, apparently. But thank you, all the same." I smiled, insincerely. "I trust that the evening's raking about helped keep your reputation intact?"

"Never better," he said, straightening and taking a step toward me. His hand closed about my wrist and he pulled, gently. I stood, and looked up to him. "Perhaps," he whispered, "you would care to assess my techniques?"

I went up on my toes. "You are not too tired?" I inquired. "I would have assumed you to have quite worn yourself out. Your stamina must be the envy of all of London."

He laughed. "And quite a bit of the countryside, beside," he said, pulling me roughly against him.

I almost sighed as the heat flashed as I was pulled up against his smooth, hard body, enveloped once again by the clean smell of him. He certainly was not . . . worn out. That much I could tell. And I knew, somehow, that whatever his faults, he would not have come to me like this from another woman's bed. I let him pull me closer, and watched his eyes fall closed as he bent his head to mine. I reached up, around his neck, heedless of his cravat, and he groaned as his lips found mine.

"Where have you been, Cambourne?" I asked, against his mouth.

"Nowhere that concerns you," he replied, dipping his head to nip at my ear.

"Oh!" I said, leaning my head, to give him better access to my neck. "But it does."

"No," he said, doing something to my neck with his teeth that made me want to squirm against him. "It doesn't."

"Damn you," I whispered, as his hands slid down my spine, to the small of my back, and pressed me against him. I was almost whimpering with the desire for them to stay there. "How could I have thought you were honorable."

His silky hair brushed my face as he moved his head to lick at the hollow of my throat. My head fell back. "And how could I have thought you were biddable?" he asked.

I jerked my head up and pushed him away. *Biddable!*

"I misjudged, apparently," he said, coolly, his eyes unreadable.

"Yes," I said, as I turned. "You did." And then I stalked from the room, churning with equal parts fury and frustration.

I avoided him the next morning, remaining in my chamber, seething and refusing to emerge until I had sent Crewes down to check that he was gone out for the foreseeable future. But that evening, he returned to the house in his Milburn garb, catching me unaware at tea, and announced, in his Milburn voice, "Dropped a packet o' blunt at Tatt's today on a real sweet goer, for you, a prime little chestnut." Then he changed to his own voice. "She's a beauty, Gwen. Even-tempered and yet not too biddable to be spirited. In short, perfect."

"Do I understand," I asked, "that the perfect horse is not *too* biddable?"

Our eyes met. "Yes," he said. "You do."

But I could not resist pushing just a little further. "And that her lack of biddableness is a *desirable* quality?"

His quick smile flashed and those dimples appeared. "Yes," he said, "it is."

And I had known it was a peace offering.

"I thought you might miss riding. I recall that you always enjoyed it at home. Come see her." And then he had extended his hand and I had taken it and we had walked together out to the little stable in the mews behind the house.

It had felt like just the smallest victory.

Her name was Dulcinea, Dulcie for short. The product of Moreford's prize thoroughbred and Glendavy's Irish mare, he told me, as she whickered, pushing her soft nose against my hand.

"Thank you," I said, almost in a whisper, and that something was there again, churning up the air between us. Our gazes caught and held until we both took a step back at the same time. We agreed to ride together, then, on Friday morning, two days hence. It was almost pitiful how much I was looking forward to it.

The next morning, though, I woke up early. I tried to will myself back to sleep, but was simply too restless. I drew the curtains to discover that it was one of those rare occurrences—a fine day in London in winter. Even though Cambourne and I weren't scheduled to ride together until tomorrow, I was anxious to test Dulcie's paces. I rang for Crewes and sent her to ask a groom to prepare to accompany me and then she hurried back with a tray and to help me dress. A short time later, I was quietly descending the stairs. I had assumed Cambourne was still abed, but as soon as I heard the music, the soft tones of someone playing a cello floating across the hall, I knew it had to be him.

I stood, on the steps, outside the closed door to the music room, and listened. I recognized the song as, "Lull Me Beyond Thee," and the music struck me as absolutely heartbreaking. To my admittedly imperfect ear, it sounded as though every note was just right, but also, somehow, deeply felt. I realized that I had never known he was musical, and wondered briefly what he had made of Caro

Arbuthnot's dreadful masque. On the one hand, I wanted to walk in and tell him how lovely it was, and ask him to play for me sometime in the evening, perhaps even offer to accompany him on the pianoforte. And on the other, I felt like an interloper. It seemed, somehow, like a private moment for him, and I was not certain that I should have been standing there.

I was having a hard time walking away, though. For some reason I could almost picture him. I knew, even, which chair he was sitting in. The carved mahogany Hepplewhite in the corner near the window. He would have his eyes closed; well, I amended, perhaps he would need to be reading the music. His hair would be straight. Cambourne hair. And no doubt, falling down over his forehead. He would have the slightest frown between his brows. And then, I really did feel like an interloper. So I straightened, brushed away my inexplicable tears, and continued on my way. I did not see him again that day.

In the days that followed, we fell into the habit of having an early ride together in the park every morning that weather permitted. It was interesting to me that the one place he seemed to have trouble adopting his Milburn mantle was on horseback. He would mount, fuss conspicuously with his various frills, and amble indolently out of the stable. But almost immediately after that, I could almost see the urge to ride neck or nothing steal over him. Once we had achieved the park, he invariably asked if I wanted to race. And even though he won handily every time, I always agreed. I suspect the reason I did had something to do with seeing him allow himself a few moments of genuine pleasure.

"I do not know why I agree to race you, you odious man," I said one morning. "The very least you could do is allow me to win just once! It's only gentlemanly, you know."

"It is gentlemanly for me to assume that you would be foolish enough to believe it were I to pretend that my horse is not faster and that riding sidesaddle is not to your disadvantage?"

"Absolutely," I replied.

"That," he said, looking at me with an odd intensity, "is how men behave with their bits of muslin, not with women whose intellect they respect and admire."

"Do you respect and admire me, Cambourne?" I asked, truly wanting to know.

"Are you begging for compliments?" he asked, with a smile.

"Yes," I said.

"Then, yes," he said, roughly. "More and more every day."

"Well, you are not supposed to make us respected and admired females feel inferior," I told him with severity. "Our intellects may be formidable, but our sensibilities are easily offended."

He laughed and I glared at him. "It's not fair, Cambourne. We shall have to match our abilities at something where I stand a chance of winning."

"Actually, I think we do. Every day," he said quietly, as he easily moved his horse closer. "You make me look at aspects of myself that I would prefer to ignore, Gwen," he said, bending slightly and brushing my cheek with his leather glove. "It may not be something one can measure in tangibles, but don't ever underestimate how important a gift that is."

And as my heart raced at his words, I reminded myself most firmly that I really must redouble my efforts to find out what had become of Milburn, because this simply would not do. That resolve, however, did not stop me from hugging those words to myself all that day, like a shawl. And it became something of an obsession for me to rise early enough to hear Cambourne at his music before we left for the park. I had got into the habit of sitting on the bottom step, outside the music room, and listening. I never mentioned it, though, and by the time he had emerged, I would be waiting for him, sipping coffee in the breakfast room, dressed and ready to go.

As Cambourne, he went to endless debates in Parliament. It seemed that things were particularly heating up over my father's pet cause, the Corn Laws. And two nights running Cambourne had left the parliamentary session and gone back to Cambourne House with several ministers, to continue to discuss into the night the proposed changes that seemed to have everyone up in arms. He slept there, both those nights, but returned in the morning.

After the second time, I said to him over breakfast, "All my life it seems, someone or other has been droning on about these Corn Laws. What are they, actually?"

He finished chewing his bite of beefsteak and put down his fork. He was dressed as Milburn, but his voice was pure Cambourne when he said, "Do you really not know?"

"No," I said, "I don't." I frowned. "Why would I?"

"It's just that your father, or perhaps your mother, actually, is at the forefront of the disagreement over them. I suppose I had simply assumed it would have been a commonplace topic of discussion in their household."

"They don't spend a great deal of time in conversation with each other." I took a careful bite of my egg. We had also fallen into the habit of taking our breakfast together after our ride. But for some reason, eating alone with him still made me uneasy; I was always waiting to spill something down my front or realize that I had something hideous stuck between my teeth.

"I don't suppose my parents do either." We were both silent for a moment, and then he said, idly, "Did you envision that you and Milburn would spend much time in conversation?"

I thought about this. "Beyond, 'the weather is very fine today!' 'True. And what do you think of this waistcoat?' 'Why it suits you to perfection.' 'But is it *au courant* enough?' 'Why yes, I do think so.' 'Excellent. Shall I see you tonight at the Billingsleys'?' do you mean?"

He smiled. "Yes. Beyond that is precisely what I mean."

"No, I don't suppose so," I said, spreading jam on my toast. "But in truth I'd never thought much about it. I doubt it's occurred to my parents, either, that they would want to converse more than that."

"But surely," he said, looking reflective, "your parents must discuss parliamentary issues? Your mama often seems to me to be the driving force behind your father's ambitions."

"Oh, she is." I put down my toast. "But Mama and Violetta write his opinions, you see, and then tell him what they are."

He looked amused. "It must be nice not to be obligated to waste time coming up with them on one's own," he said.

"That is what Father always says," I agreed. "But then I don't suppose with Mama it would make much difference if he wanted to. Likely a good thing for him that he doesn't."

A footman appeared with more coffee, and I added cream to mine. "Actually," I said, not looking at him, "it might be interesting to find out what this is all about, this Corn Laws business."

I suppose I had expected that he would laugh off my interest. I was not precisely known for my intellectual pursuits, after all. He seemed to be studying me, and then he said, "Would you like me to tell you about it? Or if you prefer, I can bring you something to read at your leisure. I can easily have my secretary at Cambourne House put together a packet for you."

"I'd like that," I said, wondering if I really would.

"Consider it done." He rose and dropped his serviette on the table. "And now I've an appointment with Milburn's tailor. I understand pomona green with silver embroidery is *de rigueur* this season if one is to be *comme il faut*," he said, in his Milburn drawl. "I shall see you this evening at eight of the clock for the theater?" Then he kissed my hand and left.

"Corn Laws!" said Myrtia as we strolled down Wigmore Street on our way to buy ribbons. Crewes and Myrtia's maid, Louise, followed at a discreet distance, carrying our packages.

Cecy had declined to accompany us, which was worrying. "Saving my shillings for my mother's allowance," she had announced gloomily.

The Honorable Mr. Theobald Newstrom and Lord Rothwell were tooling down the street in a phaeton perched so high it looked in danger of tumbling over on its side with every bump in the road it passed over. "Ladies," cried Rothwell, doffing his hat. "Good day, Miss Conyngham, Lady Bertie. You're both looking vastly fetching this morning."

We nodded a greeting to them. "Yes," I said to Myrtia as we turned into Clark and Denham of Cavendish House, Purveyors of Sarsenets, Satins, Millinery, and Pelisses. "I find I am developing quite an interest in the Corn Laws."

She was examining and discarding bonnet ribbons and trimmings in a very decisive way. "Is there anything to be done, do you think, about Cecy and Barings?" she asked. "I cannot credit that he is behaving this way when she so obviously needs him."

I looked at the pink ribbons she had put down. I quite liked them for my new bonnet. What I really wanted was to ask her about Mr. Wickersham, my curiosity roused, I suppose, by the odd turn my own life had taken. What had been between them? Was she waiting for him? Did she love him? But I didn't know how to start. "I agree," I said. "But it's so hard with Cecy to know how much help she wants, and when one is overstepping." Myrtia agreed with that, and then I went on, tentatively, "Myrsh?"

"Yes?"

"Ah, Mr. Wickersham—Am I overstepping my bounds with *you* if I ask?"

"Of course not," she said, just a little too quickly as she picked up some yellow ribbons and examined them with surely more interest than they deserved. "These are nice," she said, "don't you think?"

"No," I said. "I think they're perfectly repulsive."

She smiled and put them down. "You are right. The truth is that I do not love Mr. Wickersham," she said decisively. "I feel a great deal of . . . fondness for him."

"And is he aware of this lack of more heated emotions on your part?"

"Not precisely," she said, once again picking up the

loathsome yellow ribbons. "It hardly seems the type of thing one wants to send a soldier in a letter."

"No," I agreed.

Then she said, "But I beg of you, let us speak no more of it for the moment. I can hardly bear to think of it myself."

We then went on to spend a pleasant interlude at Hatchard's bookshop, after which I returned home, and Cambourne (as Milburn, naturally) and I went to the theater followed by a late supper at the Newsomes'.

It was all starting to feel almost dangerously cozy and domestic.

17

In which I read about the Corn Laws with a most surprising outcome

Which is why I didn't hesitate the next evening, when Cambourne suggested we take a night off from the social whirl. A quiet night at home, he had said, just like any other old married couple on a Tuesday night. And, he added, he had the packet on Corn Laws that I had requested.

I declined to think about the myriad ways in which we were emphatically not any other old married couple, Tuesday night or not. I also declined to tell him that my enthusiasm for furthering my education on the topic of the Corn Laws had dimmed a bit after listening to an extremely tedious exchange on the subject at the Newsomes' just last night. I had been seated between Mr. William Huskisson and Charles Spencer, Lord Althorp, and the two of them had shouted cholerically over me for what seemed like hours while Cambourne, as Milburn, had flirted outrageously first with the beauteous Lady Elizabeth Hounslow, to his left, and then the almost equally fetching Mrs. Alnwick, to his right.

Cambourne handed a packet to me. "As promised, a treatise on the Corn Laws, including but not limited to, the Reverend T. R. Malthus's essay."

"Oh. Thank you." It was just a trifle *thicker* than I had anticipated. "I'm looking forward to it. Enormously."

"Yes, well, you're bound to find it fascinating. I envy you, really. Quite a treat to be able to read it for the first time."

I looked sharply at his face to see whether he was having a laugh at my expense, but his expression gave nothing away. Before, well, all this, I would have taken his bland look at face value. But now, I knew, just somehow knew, that he was secretly amused. It took me by surprise, for a moment, this realization that I was moving toward being able to read him.

Fine. Let him be amused, I decided, vowing to stun him with the depth, insight, and understanding I was no doubt about to glean. "Yes, well, as I said, I'm looking forward to it."

"You did mention that," he agreed, still with the utmost gravity, and I had to restrain myself from glaring at him.

We sat down across from each other, in armchairs on opposite sides of the library fire. Cambourne crossed his booted foot over his knee and picked up his little leatherbound journal. I flipped over the tract he had handed me: 273 pages!

I began to read. It was fascinating. Really, it was.

"Who would have thought," I said, halfway done with the first page, "that the Corn Laws had been in effect in some form or other since 1361!"

After a few moments, the fire crackled, breaking the

silence, and I glanced up. Cambourne had the end of his quill held between his teeth, and he seemed to be staring intently at his journal. Then he looked up. "Enjoying your reading?" he asked, mildly.

"Absolutely." I turned my eyes back to the page in front of me. "To think! The bullion price of corn is now under sixty-three shillings!"

We went back to our reading, and after a few minutes Cambourne breathed out what sounded like a sigh, uncannily echoing my own feelings. I mean, I was beginning to think 269 more pages on Corn Laws was perhaps more joy than one person should be allowed to have.

As I looked up, he put his book and quill down onto the little table by his elbow. I watched him surreptitiously from under my lashes as he steepled his fingers together and stared into the fire. Despite his contemplative pose, I sensed a certain restlessness. After a moment, he picked up something from the table. I guiltily went back to my reading. Half a page further, in which I learned that the original intent of the laws was importation and exportation duties or tariffs on a sliding scale, I stole another glance at him. He was reading now, too. Although it appeared he'd got much the better end of the deal, as while I was wading through the minutiae of the Corn Laws over the last five hundred-odd years, *he* was perusing the latest issue of *La Belle Assemblée!* I scowled at him (to which he was oblivious), and then, once again, returned to my reading.

After a few minutes of this, he said, "Interesting riding habits this season, don't you think?"

"Hmm," I replied, trying to sound deeply involved in my reading. "I suppose they are," I murmured. Really, he was making it exceedingly difficult to concentrate!

"Although I do think this one would benefit from fewer epaulets."

"These laws could eventually lead to a depressed market for manufactured goods!" I said, and he nodded. "But that could lead to rioting, it says here!"

"I know that also and in fact, am becoming quickly convinced that such an outcome would be the likely result of the laws as they now stand, although your father . . . your mother . . ."—he smiled—"vociferously cannot agree. You really should consider having one of these made up." He looked at me appraisingly. "It'd be extremely fetching on you."

"Pardon?" I said, looking up. I did my best to give the appearance that I was positively reluctant to put my reading down, but was forcing myself nonetheless: I summoned a casual yawn, and placed the treatise on the floor next to my chair. "Which?" I asked.

He leaned closer and I reached out for the journal. Somehow, though, I did not end up, as expected, with it in my hand. As, instead of giving me the magazine, he grasped my hand in his, our eyes locked, and then suddenly, in the space of a second, I was propelled from my chair and ended up ensconced across his lap.

"This one," he said, very close to my ear. "Right there."

I was reeling from the suddenness, from his nearness, and from the shock of my scandalous position. His breath feathered down my neck. The atmosphere in the room had changed, from cozy and domestic to sort of thick and still.

"It is very nice," I said, through dry lips. "Perhaps I will."

We were silent for a moment, both looking at the picture. I could feel the rapid rise and fall of his breathing. "In blue, perhaps," I added.

"Red," he replied.

"D'you think?" I asked, intrigued. Surely red was for ladies much more exotic than myself?

"Absolutely," he said, and I was absurdly pleased.

We looked at one another until the air seemed to crackle between us, and then he very deliberately tossed the magazine over his shoulder. He put his hands into my hair. He wasn't precisely rough, but he wasn't particularly gentle, either. He pushed my hair down, not slowly and methodically like on our abortive wedding night, but quickly. Pins scattered wildly on the thick carpet.

He threaded his hands through my hair and slowly, very slowly, brought my face to his. I held my breath. Instead of touching my lips, though, he leaned his forehead against mine, and said, "God help me, but I don't think I can stand this any longer."

He hadn't asked anything, but there was a question there nonetheless. I met his eyes, through the curtain of my hair. "No," I agreed. My voice sounded odd to my own ears. I wanted desperately to give in to the pull, to allow him to lead me along just . . . because. Not in exchange for information or power or anything. Just for *him,* to be with him. But surely I couldn't agree so easily? It wasn't at all seemly! (Not that what I wanted him to do to me was either, mind you, but a lady really ought to at least object!) "I mean, no. I don't know, Cambourne."

"I had to do it, Gwen," he said carefully. "I hadn't any choice, but right now I don't give a damn about that. I want you."

The heat rose in my face. "But is there more?" I asked. "Or is it just in your bed that you want me? Because I won't deny it, the pull *is* strong, Cambourne. Strong enough, perhaps, to make me forget the things I should remember."

"There's more, Gwen, and we both know it."

"I see." I needed to think clearly, and couldn't do it with his hands in my hair and his words, and his breath so seductive against my skin, so I lifted my head and looked down at him. "You want this that badly, then? That you would be willing to go ahead and damn the consequences?"

His lips curved into a slow smile, the one that always seemed to tighten something corresponding in my stomach. "For this *and* conversation across the breakfast table?"

And then, he was kissing me, hard, soft, one kiss after another. And the idea that I would resist this slid out of my mind as if it had never been. I clung to him, returning each kiss. It was as though we could not get enough of each other. Our harsh breathing was audible in the quiet room. After a time, he tore his mouth from mine, and we both sat for a moment, catching our breath.

He leaned his head back against the chair. His eyes held mine. "This, between us, will never be easy," he said, his hands still cradling my jaw.

I nodded to show that I understood, that I was relinquishing my only chance at annulment. Just at that moment, I didn't care. I should have, but I didn't.

"Show me."

He was going to force me to accept responsibility, to be a willing participant. I debated how, exactly, to show him, for the space of a second. I leaned down and brushed my lips slowly across his.

"Gwen," he breathed. "I'm greedier than that. Touch me." His eyes were dark, almost black. His voice was level, but even in the firelight, I could see a wash of color in his cheeks.

Heat lurched through me. I slowly leaned forward and placed my palms very deliberately against his chest. His eyes fell closed. He was solid under my hands, and his heart thumped with a pleasingly rapid rhythm. Experimentally, I slid my hands up. He moaned softly, almost as though he were in pain. A quick shock of excitement coursed through me. *I* was doing this to him.

Encouraged by this success, I toyed with the ends of his neckcloth. "Yes," he said, his voice urgent now, "take it off me, Gwen."

And no sooner did he say it, but I realized that I wanted to do exactly that. And of course, the other part of my mind could not believe what I was doing. This, I knew with certainty, was not how well-brought-up ladies conducted themselves. They did not encourage gentlemen (particularly those who had married them under false pretenses) to relieve them of their virginity in the library. They did not sit on said gentleman's lap at seven of the clock on a Tuesday evening, unwrapping him as though he were a Christmas package. I knew this, of course, but I could not find it in myself to care: In truth, I had to resist the urge to tear the cravat off.

I began to unwind it, slowly, deliberately undoing his perfect waterfall. I took my time about it, enjoying both my own boldness, and the sharp intake of breath on his part that it had elicited. Until at last, when it was completely unknotted, I pulled the starched cloth off his neck and let it slip from my fingers. I swallowed as I turned my concentration to the column of bared neck rising out of his shirt. I was reaching out to touch his skin—even as I pushed down the thought that what I really wanted was to put my mouth on the pulse point at the base of his throat—when his hand came up and stilled mine.

"It's my turn," he said, his dark eyes holding mine. "Now I get to take something off you." More heat flooded through me and into my face at the thought, and he said: "You choose."

I pretended to think for a moment, enjoying the way the expression in his eyes belied the coolness of his tone, and even the way my own body seemed to vibrate in expectation of his touch. I shifted a little in his lap and he groaned. I moved again, to see if it elicited the same reaction, and this time he leaned forward, and, taking my face in his hands, said, "Have a care, my love. I shouldn't do that again, else I can promise it shall all come off you at once." Then he kissed me, slowly licking his way across my upper lip.

"My shoe," I said, breathless, against his mouth.

He lifted his head, his eyes glinting. "Very well," he said. "But I must insist on both together."

I pretended to give this due consideration. "I only took the one thing off you," I said, as he swung my hair out of the way to better run the tip of his tongue down the side of my neck. I shivered with the pleasure of it.

"I'll allow you two items the next time," he said. "Now give me your foot."

I was not sure of precisely what gentlemen wear beneath their garments, but I was guessing it was considerably less than we ladies do. I had a chemise, a corset, my newfangled underdrawers, and stockings beneath my wool gown, so I was assuming that he would be fully unclothed long before I was. Secure in my thinking, I bent my knee to give his hands access to my foot.

He unlaced the ribbons of the left slipper with a deftness that put Crewes's nimble fingers to shame, and slid it slowly off my foot. With our gazes locked, he dropped the shoe, and stroked his finger up my instep. I shuddered. His hand glided over the silk of my stocking, as he traced up the top of my foot to loosely circle my ankle. He trailed his hand up my calf to the back of my knee.

He whispered my name in a low voice, which seemed to add another layer of heat to the excitement lurching inside me, and stroked his hand, slowly, back down. "Say my name," he said, low, into my ear. "I want to hear it on your lips."

"Cambourne," I whispered.

"Harry," he said urgently. As he kept up the maddening stroking. "My name.".

"Harry," I managed to get out. I had truly never supposed my body capable of such feelings: the back of my knee had always been just that. I was beginning to understand exactly why the ankles were always kept hidden from gentlemen! I let my eyes drift closed, and my head fall back on his shoulder, giving in to the sensations that were licking at me, as he began the same process on my right foot. When he had finished, I forced myself to sit up—although I could have sworn I was boneless—and attempted not to eye him with unseemly relish.

He still had his boots on. I could certainly choose to remove them. But somehow the prospect of kneeling and pulling and tugging at them was not altogether appealing. His waistcoat—an elaborately brocaded item, since he was Milburn today—offered more intriguing possibilities. I wet my lip with the tip of my tongue while I debated.

"Never tell me that you are preoccupied with the bullion price of corn," he said softly.

I shook my head.

"What *are* you thinking?" he asked, looking hard into my eyes.

I looked hard back at him. "The truth?"

A trace of a smile crossed his face. "Unless it's something I'd prefer not to know."

I stiffened my resolve. "I was thinking about what to remove next. Your boots or your waistcoat."

"Waistcoat," he said.

He drew back to allow me access, and I parted the heavy fabric. He was very still, waiting, I thought, for me to touch him. When I did, sliding my palms up his chest, his breath hissed out between his teeth. I pushed the waistcoat the rest of the way off him, and it remained trapped behind his back and the back of the chair.

I was too busy, though, running my hands up his chest and arms, listening to his harsh breathing and marveling at the way his muscles seemed to jump and tense beneath my hands, to spare much concern for the fate of the garment. I moved my hands to his shoulders and ran them slowly down the muscles of his arms, paying strict attention to the way his hands clutched the arms of the chair. I was preparing to do it again, when one hand shot out, and grabbed both my wrists.

Still holding my wrists, he sat up straighter and kissed me again. His mouth closed hotly, hungrily, over mine. My eyes drifted shut. After a moment, he lifted his head. "Let me see." And even with my eyes closed, I could *feel* his gaze sweep my body. "I believe I was deciding whether or not to play by the rules."

I opened my eyes. "The rules?"

"Yes. You know, you remove an item, I remove an item?"

I nodded. Thus far it had been working rather well.

"Exactly how many layers do you have on under that gown, Gwen?" he asked, releasing my wrist. His gleaming hair fell over his forehead, and that elusive dimple came and went.

"Ah. A few, I suppose."

"A few dozen, more like," he said.

"Is there a problem with that?" I asked.

"Well, yes and no," he said, smiling, and I found myself unable to tear my gaze away from his lips and the faint brackets that surrounded them when he smiled.

"You *always* play by the rules, Cambourne," I reminded him, suddenly nervous.

He raised a brow. "Perhaps not so much as you think," he said. "It would surely be breaking them were I to tumble us both onto the carpet and tear your clothes off so I could feel your skin against mine this very instant."

"Oh!" I said, thinking that it sounded like an appallingly good idea, if a bit shocking.

He smiled. And then tipped us out of the chair, so we lay sprawled on the carpet.

I regret to say that I did not protest the indignity.

"It is only," he continued, moving over me and propping himself on his elbow, so he was looking down at me, "by dint of recalling word for word the salient points of Adam Smith's 'Digression Concerning the Corn Trade and Corn Laws,' that I have managed to wait this long."

I said. "And?"

He smiled, slowly, and heat seemed to lick up my legs. "It seems that Mr. Smith had fewer salient points than I had recalled."

"Oh," I said again, this time looking up into his eyes.

"I have come to the end of them, you see," he said.

"How disappointing."

"Or not," he said as he bent his head and kissed me fiercely. His tongue curled possessively over mine, and my head whirled with dizziness. He brought me closer and pulled me against him. I could feel him, hard against me. I knew both what it was, and that he had let me feel it on purpose.

I should have been shocked, recoiled in modest horror. Problem was that, in truth, it excited me even more. I pressed back against him and he moaned. I wanted to reach down and run my fingers along him, but didn't quite dare. So instead, I reached my arms around his neck and pulled his mouth to mine again, to let *my* tongue curl possessively around *his*.

He lowered himself to me, so I could feel his heartbeat thundering against mine. Neither of us said anything more for quite a long time, lost in a whirl of hands and mouths and the untucking of shirts, and undoing of buttons and laces. For a while the only sounds were some sighing and murmuring, the occasional gasp, and the crackling of the fire.

He had just managed to bare my breast, by dint of pushing my bodice down. After lifting his head and looking at what he had bared for a long moment, his eyes glittering, he had said, "Do you know what you're doing to me?"

And you to me, I thought, but didn't say, as I seemed to have lost all facility with words. I moved my head jerkily. Let him interpret that however he would.

"Let me show you," he said, running his finger down my neck, over my collarbone. I wanted to move, to thrust my breast in the path of that finger, but didn't dare. I held my breath, and waited and waited in an agony of anticipation until, at last, he circled the nipple and then touched it. I almost came up off the floor as I gasped. I arched my back, forcing my breast more fully into his hand.

He groaned and lowered his head, taking it into his mouth. I was on fire. I grabbed his head and held him there. His hand came up and cupped my other breast as he gently bit down on the nipple. "You're perfect," he said in a rough voice. "So absolutely perfect, I think I'm finding religion, here, Gwen."

My breath was coming in little pants. "That's blasphemy," I managed to say.

He laughed, his breath blowing cold air against my burning nipple. I gasped, as his hand moved upward, pushing my gown with it.

"No," I whispered.

"Yes," he said, as his lips met mine. His hand stilled for a moment, and then, when I was thoroughly lost in the kiss, began to move again.

I felt the cool air on my legs, as he pushed my gown over my thighs, but no longer cared. In fact, I let my legs fall apart like the complete wanton I had obviously become.

Even so, when he reached the edge of those newfangled underdrawers, and said, "I like these," and slid his hand inside, I had a moment of utter shock.

"Harry," I whispered, scandalized. "Don't! You can't!"

"It's all right, Gwen," he said, his voice strained. "It's all right."

I half wanted to restrain his hand, but then his fingers moved gently over me, touching places no lady even mentioned. My eyes fell closed, and I was as good as gone. His fingers seemed to skim and dance and then grow more purposeful. I almost screamed. His mouth moved over mine, and at the same time, the stroking went from gentle to sure. I could no longer breathe. I let my head fall back, away from his kiss, because I needed air.

"I can't breathe," I whispered.

"You're breathing," he whispered back, as his fingers stilled. "Open your eyes," he said. "I want you to see me."

Our gazes met. "Easy, love," he said, and, never taking his eyes from mine, slid a finger into me.

After a moment, when the shock of what he was doing subsided, I strained against the finger. I could not believe it. I was writhing half-naked on the floor with Cambourne. My breasts were rubbing against his shirtfront. I could not even allow my mind to contemplate what his hand was doing. I was sobbing. And yet, I was urging him to continue. I *knew* my behavior was utterly unacceptable, but my mind had no say over my body. I couldn't restrain myself any longer. I reached down and stroked the place I had wanted to touch all along.

"Oh God, yes!" he urged. He was lying half over me, and lowered his head and kissed me.

Needless to say, a little thing like the door opening did not register with either of us.

"Hallo, Cambourne," said a lazy voice from the doorway.

18

In which Milburn makes his return known

I was grateful for the fact that Cambourne was sprawled half on top of me, hiding me from view. I could feel him unhurriedly pull my bodice up and smooth my gown down over my legs. Slowly, he lifted his head.

"Bertie!" he said, drily. "How absolutely *delightful* to see you again!"

The horror of the moment had done something instantaneous to cool my body down, but my heart still thundered and raced and my breath was still coming fast.

"Yes, you *do* appear overjoyed, brother," Milburn drawled, from the door, where he was leaning against the frame, as his gaze swept slowly over us.

An entirely different heat washed over my face as shame swept through me.

"Indeed," Cambourne replied, still lying over me. "As anyone must be to see a brother after a prolonged and worrying absence."

"You are *me,* at the moment, I trust?" Milburn looked surprisingly hale; I registered somehow, amidst my shock, for a man who had recently been in grave danger. He was immaculately groomed and turned out, and even looked as though he had a touch of color from the sun. His sleek, well-fed air, in other words, was a far cry from the ragged, pale, half-starved prisoner of war I had envisioned a hundred times over in my mind.

"Well, this is quite simply one of the most shocking, no, disgraceful, things I've ever seen," Milburn said, stepping into the room. He eyed the tangled heap we made on the carpet.

I could only imagine what a man would feel to return from a harrowing campaign only to find his affianced wife scandalously entwined with his twin brother on the library floor.

"This is an outrage!" he continued. "Those trousers you are wearing are a disgrace, Cambourne! And this waistcoat!" He picked up the garment from the chair, where it had ended up pushed behind Cambourne's back before our precipitous descent. It dangled off one finger. "It's, it's . . . *crushed!*"

He seemed fully prepared to continue in this vein, but Cambourne said, in quite a dangerous sounding voice, actually, "Milburn!"

"Yes?" Milburn enquired, staring despondently at the waistcoat, hanging from his hand.

"As edifying as this conversation is promising to be, I think we should postpone it. Perhaps we could meet you in the drawing room shortly?"

"Very well," Milburn said. "But do bear in mind that I've an appointment at Hoby in an hour—m'boots are a wreck—so don't be too long about it. Hallo, Gwen," he added, as though noticing me for the first time, and then he left the room, still clutching the waistcoat, and rather rudely—if one were to take into account our state of dishabille—leaving the door wide open.

Cambourne swore as he jumped to his feet and then turned and extended a hand, helping me to mine. My legs were shaking like jelly. I could barely bring myself to look at him as I tried to straighten my bodice. "Gwen," he said, looking down at me, intently.

But I was staring at the door through which Milburn had so recently departed. "He saw," I said, stupidly. "Us. He saw us!"

"Yes," Cambourne agreed. He crossed the small room in two strides and kicked the door shut with a good deal of force. It did penetrate my foggy brain that he was angry. Really angry.

"He didn't care!" I said as he picked up his cravat.

Cambourne turned from the door and draped the cravat around the neck of his crumpled shirt, as he looked at me.

"But you, you—" I broke off, blushing "—had your hands—he didn't care!"

"And did *you* care that *he* didn't?" He looked at me intently.

"I—I—How could he not have cared?"

"I shouldn't be too certain that he didn't, anyway," Cambourne said, his fingers deftly tying the cravat.

"I was," I said, thinking aloud, "no *we,* were about to take an irrevocable step, and now suddenly, here he is. Milburn!" And he didn't care! I simply could not believe it. Did I say that already? It is just hard to convey the depths of my shock and disbelief at that moment. I looked down, ineffectually trying to smooth my hopelessly crumpled gown. Embarrassment heated my face. I cast about for words, but found none.

Cambourne studied my face, and spoke, after a moment. "I see," he said, slowly. I thought he was about to head to the door, but he surprised me, taking my shoulders and turning me roughly toward him, forcing me to look at him. "Is it your intention, then, to run to him?"

"I'm not—I don't know," I whispered. In truth, I was still too shocked to have thought about how I felt. I did know, though, that while I no longer particularly wanted to cling to the idea of my marriage to Milburn, Cambourne's words and tone were making that old, familiar contrariness rise. "Are you saying that I can?"

"Will I stop you, do you mean?"

I nodded. "Will you?"

"Are you asking if I will bind you in legalities?"

"No," I whispered.

"Well, I won't," he said. "If that's what you want."

"And will you bind me in other ways?" I asked in a whisper. "By telling me the truth?"

He hesitated. "I cannot, Gwen. I just, simply . . . can't."

"I see," I said. "Well, at least now I might be able to find out what has transpired."

"You think Milburn's going to tell you?" he asked, with a raised brow.

"Yes," I said. "Why wouldn't he?"

After a moment he bent down to pick up my slippers. As he handed them to me, I was startled by the realization that those were the only items I had actually shed during our interlude. His gaze met mine, and that slow smile spread across his face. "Let's go see, then, shall we?" he said.

As he knelt to help me lace my slippers, I looked down at the top of his head, and my throat tightened. "We'd best be quick about going to see him," I managed to say around the lump in my throat. "Lord knows, one doesn't want him to be late for—

"Hoby," we finished together.

19

In which Milburn is late for Hoby—
Very, very late, indeed

*S*o regrettably late, in fact, that I later heard he had suffered the fate of having been canceled in favor of Rowan Craddock—*quite* an insult, considering that Craddock's shine was widely known to be dubious, at best.

Once we had put ourselves as close to rights as we could, Cambourne, ever the gentleman, offered me his arm, and we headed together toward the drawing room. After the warmth of the library, the hall was chilly, but I doubted that accounted for why I was shaking so much. I would have been hard-pressed to say which was in more turmoil: my body or my mind.

I have often heard it said that worry assuaged turns quickly to anger, and looking at Milburn sitting in the drawing room, with his spectacularly unscathed boots stretched out before him, drinking brandy and looking so well, I was suddenly so angry that I would gladly have thrown something at him.

And then I realized he was not alone.

"Hard to say," he was saying. "Style is a fickle master, of course, but m'self, I always prefer an oxblood color for a boot—"

He glanced up as we entered and my eyes went to his companion. A woman. No. Not a woman, a vision. The vision, who was seated on the sofa beside Milburn, and appeared to be possessed of her own glass of brandy, had glossy black hair and cherry lips. Not to mention pale, flawless skin, beautifully arched dark brows, and smoky violet eyes. The woman actually had purple eyes! Who has purple eyes? She had décolletage impressive enough to completely eclipse Mathilde Claussen's, and had an air of self-assurance that I could feel from across the room. I highly doubted *she* had asked for ratafia.

While I was still attempting to make myself comprehend the situation, the vision rose in a rustle of silk skirts. With no regard for proper modes of introduction, she held out her hand to Cambourne and smiled. " 'Allo," she said in English with a charming French overlay. "You must be Ber-tee's brother, I think. I am his wife, the Countess of Cambourne, but you, please, must call me Thérèse."

It would be something of an understatement to call the silence that followed this stunned. Thérèse indeed looked nonplussed by the complete void that followed her pronouncement; just a tiny bit of her self-assurance seemed to fall away.

I blinked at Milburn, unable to fully comprehend his betrayal. He smiled and leaned back on the sofa.

"How lovely to meet you, Thérèse," Cambourne said in courteous tones, after a moment. His voice rang clear, but his gaze was also fixed on Milburn. "You must understand that this comes as something of a surprise, as I have long been accustomed to thinking myself the Earl of Cambourne." He paused. "And this is *my* wife, Gwen."

Well, not *exactly* his wife, I thought, but forgave him his presumption, under the circumstances.

Thérèse looked puzzled. "You must excuse me. It is my poor English, doubtless, but I think I do not perfectly understand you."

"*Your* wife?" Milburn said.

Cambourne bowed over Thérèse's hand. "I somehow doubt that the problem is your English, ma'am," he said, still looking hard at Milburn. "And, yes. My wife."

"Still I do not understand," Thérèse said, a slight frown edging between her perfect brows. She turned a questioning gaze on Milburn. "Ber-tee?"

"Perhaps," Cambourne suggested silkily, "Ber-tee could see his way clear to enlightening us all?"

"Indeed," I said. "Perhaps he could." And refrained from adding, and it had best be good.

"Glad to," replied Milburn. "Need a bit of sustenance first, though. Deuced peckish."

Cambourne nodded as he steered me toward a chair and I slid into it, grateful that I no longer had to concentrate on forcing my knees to hold me up. "I'll ring for something," he said.

"Don't bother," replied Milburn, rising to walk to the bell rope. "My house," he said, slowly. "My rope. My bell. My butler. Remember?"

I looked hard at Bertie. What on earth had happened to him? Instead of his usual lazy, amiable expression, his eyes were cold and surprisingly sharp.

Giddings arrived, and without so much as betraying a

flicker of surprise, took the request for refreshments and departed. And then—as bizarre as this sounds—we all sat and chatted of inconsequential subjects while we waited for it to arrive. Fortunately, their journey and *zee wezzair,* as Thérèse so charmingly called it, provided any number of conversational openings. Eventually, even these topics palled as fodder for witty repartee, and we all seemed mightily relieved when the trays arrived. I know I was.

"I was traveling to Toulouse," Milburn began, and his gaze met Cambourne's for a moment.

"Yes," Cambourne said, tightly. "I know that."

"Well, I did not," I said.

Milburn ignored me. "But of course you did, dear brother!" he said. "But then, it was at your behest. Almost got killed a few times, but, what hey, that's neither here nor there. Not like I'm the heir or anything."

If Cambourne flinched inwardly at that, it was not apparent to me.

"Anyway," Milburn continued, "as you know, I like to, you might say, *enjoy* the local color when I travel."

"You do?" I said, my surprise forcing me to find my voice. "With guidebooks to local flora and fauna and such?" It seemed inconsequential, but somehow it was so at odds with my picture of him that I could not leave it.

"Well, not guidebooks exactly."

"Then what?" I demanded.

"Perhaps you'd like to continue with your tale," Cambourne suggested, quickly.

Milburn shrugged. "Anyway, in this particular village there was quite a bit of local color to explore. And I had to spend some time there, as I had some business to undertake that entailed waiting. I was enjoying a bit of sightseeing with Thérèse—"

"It was my father's barn, that I was showing him," she said.

Cambourne raised a brow. "You have developed an interest in barns?" he said to Milburn.

"Some," Milburn said. "Particularly fascinating, this one."

Thérèse nodded. "And my father, he catch us."

"Touring the hayloft," Milburn contributed.

"He is something of a terrier, my father."

I stared at her. All things considered, it seemed highly unlikely that she had been sired by a small dog. "A terror?" I suggested.

She broke into a grateful smile. "Thank you," she said. "A terror, yes, of course he is. He insisted that Ber-tee and I become very quickly married."

"*Oui,* he insisted with a large gun to my head," Milburn said. "The man has a positive fondness for large firearms."

"You were *sightseeing* in Thérèse's father's barn when you were supposed to be on your way back to England to marry me?" I asked, as the fury rose in me.

"And you, I collect, were pining for me there, on the library floor?" he returned.

"That," I said, "is entirely beside the point!"

"How?" he demanded.

Cambourne's eyes were locked on Milburn's face. "Could I have a word?" he asked politely. "Outside the room?"

I was beginning to think that inside the room would have been much more appropriate.

"I s'pose," Milburn replied, taking his time about setting down his plate and standing. I guessed the hardships of travel to have taken their toll, because his hair was straight, his jaw was tight, and he looked remarkably like Cambourne.

"Do excuse us," Cambourne said, as they stepped from the room. He looked utterly calm, but I could tell by how carefully he closed the door that he was absolutely furious.

Me too, I thought.

I wished I was alone so I could listen against the door. I looked at Therèse; she looked at me. After a moment I raised an eyebrow. She nodded. As of one accord, we stood—some things transcend issues of national origin— and rushed for the door. Unfortunately, we couldn't hear a thing other than the low rumble of their voices. It was clear that they were disagreeing, but the content was a mystery. Therèse shrugged her frustration and we again took up our seats. Some time passed. We toyed with some biscuits and discussed fashion in a desultory sort of way. And then, finally, the gentlemen returned.

Cambourne was looking extremely still and composed, which, like the quiet closing of the door, I was coming to understand signified anger. Milburn was bright red in the face.

"Well—" said Cambourne when they had closed the door.

Milburn interrupted, turning, and tapping him on the chest. "Why do *you* always get to be in charge of every-thing," he demanded. "It's my house. It's my problem, too. *I* want to tell them."

I resisted the urge to shoot Cambourne a meaningful look. He *did* always get to be in charge of everything.

"Be my guest, brother." Cambourne sat down next to me, folded his arms across his chest, and looked expec-tantly at Milburn.

"Ber-tee! It is the truth, I think!" Therèse burst out. "You are truthfully not the earl?"

"I should say not," I replied, for him.

Milburn shrugged. "Missed it by about a quarter hour, I am given to understand."

"I see," she said, and then, "You will continue, please."

"Yes," I said, starting to feel some solidarity with her. "This promises to be *very* interesting."

The tips of Milburn's ears turned red. "Well, I couldn't marry her under my own name," he said, hotly. "Because I was *supposed* to come home and marry you, Gwen."

"You did it for me?" I demanded. "Is that what you are saying?"

"This situation, it is most interesting to me," Thérèse said, as she turned her head and looked Cambourne over. Very slowly, her eyes traveled the length of him, from the tips of his Hessians to the top of his head. Then her gaze made the return journey, equally slowly.

He returned her perusal; I could only assume he liked what he was seeing. *I* was seeing red. Did he truly think he could tumble me on the carpet and then an hour later be salivating over another woman? I gave them another moment to finish. "Enjoying the view, are you, Cambourne?" I said sweetly, when they had.

He tore his gaze from Thérèse and smiled at me. "The local color *is* quite spectacular," he said. "A man could surely be forgiven for wanting to linger in the barn."

"The native passion for firearms might prove somewhat dangerous to you," I said.

He aimed his smile at Thérèse, and, as that dimple came out in force, my heart plummeted. When he set out to charm, I knew better than anyone that he could be positively dangerous. "In that case, I should be forced to allow the women of the village to nurse me back to health," he said.

"I meant here," I said, thinking that if I'd had a gun to

hand at this moment I'd likely have shot him myself.

Thérèse returned his smile as the tip of her tongue darted out to wet her lips. That charm was obviously working.

"Ahem," I said.

"Then this is all right," Thérèse said decisively to Cambourne, after but a moment's consideration. "You will do very nicely, instead. Since you married Ber-tee's leetle Gwen—" (I ground my teeth at this) "—and Ber-tee married me, we can switch, no? Ber-tee, he is very sweet. But he is too meek. Myself, I like a stronger man."

"Exactly what are you suggesting?" I demanded loudly.

"Actually," Milburn said, "Thérèse has hit on the perfect solution! She and Cambourne move back to Cambourne House. You and I remain here."

I glared at him. "Now you want me?" I demanded. "After dawdling around Thérèse's father's barn? And missing our wedding? You just think you can show up here and have me?"

"You're missing the point, Gwen," Milburn replied. "It's not to do with what I want. It's to do with what I have coming to me."

I opened my mouth, but before I could respond, Cambourne spoke. He was looking at me very intently, having apparently managed to tear his gaze from Thérèse's many charms, but, as usual, it was impossible to tell what was going on in his head. "Do you have marriage lines with Thérèse?" he said to Milburn, although his gaze was still on me.

"Of course," Milburn replied, and then he smiled as he added, "Pack of French folderol, of course, but marriage lines all the same. They're in your name, and, don't worry, I made certain to sign them in a signature *precisely* like yours, brother."

"I see," Cambourne replied. "Then it seems we've a problem. Because I made very certain to sign *mine* precisely like mine, too."

"You put your own name on *my* marriage license?" said Milburn, looking almost as indignant as when he'd discovered the crushed waistcoat.

"Ignorant of your newly developed passion for pastoral architecture as I was, I *thought* I was doing what I needed to in order to help you. Not to mention quite possibly save your life," Cambourne said tightly, and my heart squeezed.

I had known, of course, that it had likely been something like that that had propelled him into marrying me, but it stabbed, nonetheless, to hear him say it.

"Did you know that you were marrying him and not me, Gwen?" Milburn demanded.

"No," I whispered. "Not at first."

"Well, well. This does indeed add a new dimension to our discussions. The earl is a bigamist, it would seem," said Milburn, his eyes sharpening further. "What do you know?"

"What do you want, Milburn?" Cambourne asked, quietly.

"Annul your marriage to Gwen," Milburn replied. "And take Thérèse. It shouldn't be difficult. Here on this sceptered isle, I would imagine fraudulent identity constitutes just cause."

Cambourne stood and walked to the mantel. I do not think I have ever done, or will ever do, anything more difficult than waiting out those few moments. My heart thundered so hard against my ribs, I had to glance surreptitiously about to see if anyone else could hear it, while I waited to see if Cambourne was going to give me up, just like that. Trade me for the beauteous Thérèse, like a horse.

But a small part of me was thinking, I don't have to simply wait for him.

"But how does that help anything?" Cambourne asked Milburn, at last.

"Because then I can marry Gwen," he replied. "Ain't as if I'm in a position to complain overmuch even if you did sample her. I certainly took care of things with Thérèse."

I am not helpless here, I reminded myself, and opened my mouth to issue a retort, but Cambourne spoke first. "I'd watch myself, were I you, Bertie," he said, "unless you're interested in finding yourself choosing seconds."

Milburn held up a placating hand. "No need for that, surely," he said. "And, anyway," he said, brightening, "I've a better idea."

I leaned forward, reminding myself that I was no longer, by any stretch of the imagination, biddable. As of today.

Cambourne raised a brow. "Yes?"

Milburn got up and paced to the window. "Annulling the marriage to Gwen would be a public disgrace, would it not? And correct me if I'm wrong, brother, but avoiding the blackening of the mighty names of Cambourne and Winfell has driven your entire life, has it not?"

Cambourne went pale, but inclined his head in a civil manner. "What are you saying, Milburn?"

"It's simple, really." Milburn looked very pleased with himself. "*I'll* become you, and then Gwen can just come along with me, no annulment necessary!"

"That makes no sense!" I burst out. "I might be legally married to him, but the entire world thinks I am married to *you*, Bertie. That's been half of this entire disastrous charade. Your brother has been mincing around town like a veritable macaroni in an effort to convince people that he's you."

"I am confident," Milburn replied, "that we can come up with something that will please the world at large. Or at least Cambourne can. He's quite the expert, you see, at finding ways to serve his own ends."

I would have issued a retort, but Cambourne spoke first, his level tones halting our exchange. "Do I understand, Bertie," he said, "that you are offering a deal? To put it bluntly: that you will refrain from publicly humiliating the family in exchange for the titles and Gwen?"

Oh, he can offer, I thought, but that does not mean it will happen.

"No need to make it sound so cold, brother," said Milburn, sounding offended. "You make me appear a blackmailer!"

"You are," I pointed out.

"I am only looking for some clarity," Cambourne said. He had recovered his sangfroid and, in that way of his, seemed completely at his ease. He sat down again and leaned back, his legs sprawled out in front of him. "That is what this comes to, then, that you want to be earl?"

"As I said before, I want what's mine. What I have coming to me," Milburn said.

I looked hard at him, thinking that he really had changed. The easygoing, lazy charm was gone, replaced by something hard and angry. And that's when I reached my breaking point.

"I am not yours!" I said, almost surprising myself with my own vehemence as I rose to my feet. "And I am not what you have coming to you. Not by any stretch of the imagination."

They all looked at me. Thérèse's coolly raised brow conveyed her doubt that it was normal to be victim to

242 Jessica Benson

such excess of emotion, but I didn't care. Once more I was not going to do as I was told.

My legs were surprisingly steady beneath me. "Oh no," I said. "I've been married and almost seduced once already in the middle of this business, and I am through, absolutely finished, with being a pawn."

Milburn sputtered, but Cambourne said, very coolly, "Do I take it you are placing a counterproposal to Milburn's little . . . offer on the table, Gwen?"

Despite his coolness, there was something almost encouraging in the way he was looking at me. "Yes," I said. "I am. And it's a demand, not a proposal." I tilted my chin up. "Whoever stays here, as Milburn, I stay too. Until you two figure out this business, whatever it might be, between you, I am not budging." And then I sat, and crossed my arms. "Not so much as an inch."

"I see," said Cambourne, his gaze on my face. "You seem most determined in that."

"I am," I said. "I've been pulled about enough. Now it's up to you two. Only you might, as I've already mentioned, want to bear in mind that as far as I know, the entire city of London believes me to be married to Milburn, and it might just cause the stir you are looking to avoid if I suddenly turn up married to Cambourne."

Milburn glowered at me, while Cambourne spoke again. "So all this," he said, turning to Milburn, "it's really about Winfell? About the dukedom?"

"Of course it's about Winfell," said Milburn, his tone sharpening. "Isn't everything always about Winfell?"

"I don't know," said Cambourne. "You tell me."

"Seems to me the answer is yes, always yes," said Milburn. "That we'd do anything to protect the hallowed names of Cambourne and Winfell. Marry someone under false pretenses. Risk lives, either our own or someone else's will do."

"Although, as it turns out," said Cambourne pointedly, "we'd also do that to *save* the lives of those nearest and dearest us if we believed them in danger."

"Cambourne?" I said.

"Yes, Gwen?"

"It's becoming downright unchivalrous, the way you keep reminding us all that you only married me to save Milburn's bacon. Also, all things considered, that fact might have been best brought up *before* you tried introducing me to the library rug."

And then, the mighty Earl of Cambourne blushed. Actually blushed! I tell you, the feeling of power was going to my head. "My apologies, of course," he said, but in a way that was not altogether convincing, and then ruined it (and my feeling of power) entirely, by adding, "And I will refrain from telling you that *that* piece of information is a veritable love poem compared with what I have not told you."

I was fairly certain my mouth was hanging open.

"It was you and your willingness to do anything to protect your damned name that put me in danger in the first place," Milburn said, "to move things away from the library rug, of course."

"I cannot give you the titles, Milburn." Cambourne's head was bowed now, so we could not see the expression on his face. "You know that I would do most anything for you, but I cannot do that."

"Oh," said Milburn, slowly and deliberately, "but I think you can, you see. And you will. Think hard, brother, very hard."

Cambourne raised his head and the two of them stared

at one another. "I see," Cambourne said, after a moment. There was a long silence, and then, finally he said, "Very well, then, take them."

I burst out, "You can't mean it, Cambourne!"

"I don't see that I've a choice," he said, tightly, still looking at Milburn.

"But it's not the way it works," I replied, which seemed inadequate. "You can't give up your titles for me!"

"Oh, it's not for you," he said easily. "It's for Bertie, here."

I stared at him.

He shrugged, and said, "He's intent on it, it seems. And, anyway, I actually *like* being him." A light came into his eyes. He had the almost frightening intensity of a long-imprisoned man glimpsing freedom. "No endless debates in Parliament," he said. "Just think: no hours spent discussing sheep, and breeding stock, and new roofs and drains. No interviewing candidates for the schoolmaster position. No females trying every conceivable tactic available to snare a future duke. No reading the lesson in church on Sunday, no tea with the vicar!"

"I am glad you can see the advantages, brother," Milburn said, not looking quite so pleased as he had a moment ago.

"Oh, I do!" Cambourne said to Milburn. "I, well, *you*, really have plenty of blunt. I *like* living in this house instead of that great rattling mausoleum—it's actually *warm*. I'll have a word with my men of business and the stewards, tell them to bring you current. No yellow trousers, though. No peacock brocade. No quizzing glasses, fobs, rings, or brooches."

"Very well, then." Milburn squared his shoulders. "I have what it takes, Cambourne, even if you don't." He took a manful breath. "I can give them up. But you—" he held up the crumpled waistcoat he had picked up from the floor of the library—"can you wear them like a man?"

"Watch me," Cambourne said, folding his arms.

Somehow, this scene was *not* unfolding the way I would have liked, which was, well . . . come to think of it, I was not entirely sure. Not this way, though!

"Curl papers," Milburn specified. "Every night. Even though—" his eyes raked over Cambourne with disdain— "your hair will *never* hold a decent curl."

"Every man must have his cross to bear," said Cambourne equably.

"Fobs, seals, rings, snuff boxes. Every time you go out."

"I'll be so heavily loaded with trinkets, I'll barely be able to stagger around town."

I could not believe he was doing this!

"Champagne in the boot blacking," Milburn pressed.

"Fine," said Cambourne, crossing his arms. "Call me Milburn. Again."

20

In which I attempt to break up an assignation

"*I* *shall tell you, I was waiting for them to simply drop* their breeches and compare the sizes right then and there in the drawing room, no?" Thérèse said.

We all laughed, and then Myrtia said, "And then what happened?"

It was the fifth day after the switch had occurred, and Cecy had called a Council of War. She said that it would take her mind off the problems in her own household. What the precise dimensions of these problems might be at the moment was anybody's guess, as the only fact Cecy had been willing to share was that Barings had returned, saying, "Either your mother goes or I go."

"But I cannot simply turn her out in a delicate condition," Cecy had argued.

"So do I understand that you are prepared to sit idly by and allow her to ruin your life completely this time?" Barings had said, after which he had thrown some books and a few clothes into a portmanteau and departed.

Cecy was now, as far as Myrtia and I could tell, throwing herself into discussing my problems with a feverish air of gaiety. She particularly seemed to be fascinated by Therèse, almost as if Therèse was a new device I had come up with solely to provide entertainment for her. And unlikely as it sounds, Therèse just seemed to fit in, and we three had become four. Don't misunderstand, I'd have greatly preferred it had she not so clearly had designs on *my* husband, but aside from that she was a highly enjoyable companion.

"Did you suggest it?" Cecy asked Therèse. "That they simply compare?"

Therèse shook her head. "I was afraid that they really would do so and that my leetle cousin, Gwen"—she patted my knee—"she would completely expire from the mortification."

Ah, yes, her leetle cousin, Gwen.

Somehow the outcome of the entire scene was that Milburn was off to become Cambourne. Cambourne was staying to be Milburn. I was staying put at Milburn's house with Cambourne, and yet *I* had gained temporary custodial responsibility over Therèse.

There had been some disagreement over this, but in the end it was decided, rather high-handedly by Cambourne, who was still behaving in a markedly future-dukelike fashion that Therèse would be introduced as a distant cousin on their mama's side (fortunately, their mother was the person least likely to grasp the fact that Therèse was not a relation of hers that she had simply forgot about).

When Milburn caviled, I did suggest that perhaps the

twins' great-aunt Laetitia could be tracked down somewhere and summoned as a chaperon. Since Great-Aunt
Laetitia was well into her eighth decade, and known for
three things—her fondness for weeklong hikes across bar-
ren moors, the more inclement the weather, the better; her
tendency to prod people with her walking stick if they
were judged to be too slow in their hiking or talking either
much or too little; and her habit of leaving her wooden
teeth about in some very unlikely places—Milburn did
not appear in any kind of hurry to accept this offer.

During the discussion, Thérèse had pouted a good
deal, which procedure I watched with fascination. She'd
pushed out her lower lip, but just enough to make it look
even more attractive. Her eyes had swum with just a *suggestion* of luminous, unshed tears, and her already impressive bosom had heaved with emotion. I admired this display greatly. I was not certain that I possessed the requisite
agility (or, for that matter, the bosom) to put all of this in
train at once, but resolved to try at least one or two of
these maneuvers in front of my mirror.

A very small corner of my mind began to wonder how
much of Cambourne's insistence that Thérèse remain with
us might be due to wanting to keep her in the same house
as he was. And he *was* very insistent on that point.

So Thérèse had said, with a knowing glance out of her
exotically tilted eyes, "I shall simply have to stay, I think,
with my leetle cousin, Gwen, and try to make my best of
it, then," and smiled, slowly, at Cambourne in such a way
as to make one think that her best would be very good
indeed. I had narrowed my eyes as he smiled at her in
return and told her that he admired her fortitude in the
face of such a trying situation.

How, I wondered gloomily, had I been reduced in the

blink of an eye from having the two brothers fighting over me to playing duenna to my husband and his sister-in-law? I decided then and there to be sure Mrs. Harbison assigned Thérèse a bedchamber close enough to mine that I would be aware of any nocturnal comings and goings. Unfortunately, I thought it might be considered a little off to suggest a large lock be installed on the outside of her door.

Which is all a rather long way of arriving at explaining how it was that I'd ended up sneaking into Cambourne's bedchamber last night.

I had come home yesterday from bringing Thérèse on a visit to Madame Suzette's establishment to find Cambourne, bedecked in regalia fit to make Milburn weep with envy. His hair was still holding a curl. Sparkling lace spilled over at his collar and cuffs, perfectly emphasizing the buttercup yellow of his waistcoat and the deep maroon velvet of his jacket. His stockinet breeches fit like a second skin, and one might have been forgiven for thinking his boots were liquid, so glossy was the shine.

" 'Allo, Milburn," Thérèse had said, flashing that smile of hers.

"Cousin Thérèse," he said, adopting that irritating Milburn drawl, and rising to bow over her hand. This accomplished, he paused, momentarily distracted, it seemed, by a wayward curl he had glimpsed in the mirror in the hall. He smoothed it back.

"I think I'll go and rest," I said, hastily. "I'm feeling a bit fatigued." (Translation: nauseated.)

"Y'do look a bit peaked," he said as he fished out his quizzing glass and surveyed me.

I sighed and said that surely a rest would be all that was needed to put me to rights, and headed up the stairs. I slept fitfully through the afternoon, finally waking into the blue dark of early evening. The fire had been lit, so I knew that Crewes must have checked in on me at some point. I sat up and drank some water from the jug by the side of the bed and then rang for her. I told her that my headache had grown worse, and begged off going to the Delameres' for supper, and to please tell Lord Milburn and Thérèse to go on without me.

"The countess," she told me, "has found that one can overcome the headache by simply *refusing* to countenance such a thing."

I felt too miserable even to try to annoy her over this, but asked her to see to the preparations for a hot bath. Afterward, I sat by the fire to dry my hair, and then picked at my supper on a tray, before once again retiring to my bed. I wondered, as I lay there, and not for the first time, whether sending Cambourne and Thérèse off together, on their own, was a particularly wise course of action. I had the idea that it was not, and resolved to avoid it in future. Eventually, my thoughts began to blur into nonsense and I fell back to sleep.

When next I awoke, the fire had gone out and my room was in complete darkness. I lay there, listening as Cambourne and Thérèse made their way up the stairs, laughing and talking companionably, no doubt about their evening, as Cambourne and I had many nights these past few months. I lay utterly still until I heard the sounds of two distinctly separate doors being closed. Thérèse's chamber was across the corridor from mine, as I had specified, and Cambourne's was on the same side, and down a bit, since our dressing rooms and the connecting sitting room lay between. Reassured that nothing untoward was occurring, I settled back into my pillows.

A little time later, though, I heard another door close. I sat straight up, my heart pounding, but then let out a breath when I realized by the purposeful footsteps that it was only Thérèse's maid leaving her room. This was followed shortly by a door closing that I took to be Milburn's valet leaving Cambourne's room. With everyone present and satisfactorily accounted for, sleep should have come again, but would not.

Perhaps it was because I had slept too much during the day, but it was clear that I was going to be awake for quite some time. I lit the candle by my bed, propped the pillows behind my back, and picked up Cambourne's Corn Law tract. I was deep into a digression concerning the practicability of effecting an independent supply, when I heard the sound I had been both dreading and anticipating: stealthy footfalls in the corridor.

The blood thundered in my ears as I sat, in suspended motion, holding the page I had been reading in midair, and trying my hardest not to breathe. But, alas, I could hear nothing further. After sitting for a while, debating, I came to the decision that I had been appointed chaperon, and as such, it was my job—no, my *obligation*—to ensure that nothing untoward was taking place. And, if it was? Well, I should have a thing or two indeed to say about it.

I was feeling very righteous as I pulled on my old green wrapper, picked up a lamp, and tiptoed to my dressing room. What could he be thinking to be conducting a dalliance right under my nose? I was never *that* biddable! I pulled open the door, and tiptoed in. Then crept stealthily through my dressing room, and, holding my breath, yet again, turned the knob to open the door into the sitting room.

I was holding the lamp with extreme care. My hands

were shaking badly, and I was certain that it would not be at all the thing were I to drop it, and set the house on fire. I lifted the lamp and stepped into Milburn's dressing room. Right, I told myself. There was business at hand: breaking up an illicit rendezvous between my husband (or possibly my brother-in-law) and his sister-in-law (or possibly his wife). Whoever they were, in relation to me or each other, I thought I could safely say it was time to forge ahead. How *dare* Cambourne dally with Thérèse under the circumstances? For that matter, how dare *she* dally with him (particularly after I had been so kind as to introduce her to the best modiste in London!)? They positively *deserved* to be caught!

I was almost looking forward to the opportunity, I told myself, of giving that arrogant, perfect, nonhusband of mine a piece of my mind. That thought whipped my fury to an even higher pitch (and if it also happened to fan the jealousy in me, well, I was not going to think about that). I put my hand on the knob that would open into Cambourne's chamber. I paused, listening for any gasps, or whispers, suddenly not so certain that I wanted to know. After a moment or two, I had heard, precisely, nothing. I took a deep breath, and in one motion flung the door open.

And *saw*, precisely, nothing.

His fire was lit, the covers on the enormous bed had been turned back but the curtains stood open, and the room was silent and empty. It occurred to me, in an excessively delayed rush of common sense, that the footsteps had likely been Cambourne going in search of a book or something equally innocuous. And with that came the thought that had they had an assignation, exactly *how* awful it would have been to have burst in.

Likely much more mortifying for me than for them.

And yet, even worse than having burst in on them in flagrante, would have been to find Cambourne sitting alone, watching me come flying out of his dressing room like an avenging Fury. Relief at being able to creep out, undiscovered, washed over me, as my gaze strayed to the bedside table.

I had been over every inch of this house in my search for clues as to why he had married me—I mean, I knew the gist of it certainly, but I also knew there had to be something specific. Every inch, in fact, except for that one. And feeling a perfect fool for not having done this sooner, I crossed to it, jerked the drawer open, and my breath caught. It looked remarkably similar to the letter that had pulled Cambourne away from our wedding breakfast.

Still holding my breath, I reached out, snatched it up, reclosed the drawer, and had taken one step toward the door, when I heard the unmistakable sound of someone approaching from the corridor. If I could only have compelled my feet to obey me, I probably could have escaped undetected. I did have the presence of mind to smooth the folds back into the letter and place it in that time-honored hiding place—the bosom of my night rail. Fortunately, the gathered empire waist just below my breasts ensured it was held securely. I was reclosing my wrapper as the door opened; I had already decided that the best thing to do was to throw myself on Cambourne's mercy and confess that I had been undertaking my chaperoning duties perhaps a tad overzealously. A little embarrassing, but, all things considered, better than admitting to my pilfering of his correspondence.

"I can exp—" I had started to say when Thérèse put one delicate, scandalously bare, foot through the door. I watched in horror as the rest of her equally elegant self followed.

We faced each other. "Oh dear," she said. "Gwen. This, it is a very awkward thing, *n'est-ce pas?*"

To say the least, is what I would have said, had I been able to articulate anything. "Gahrgh," is what I did say. Or something equally eloquent. I couldn't help myself: I stared. Thérèse *en déshabillé* was a sight to behold. Her hair had been brushed out so it hung loose in lustrous black waves of ringlets down her back. Her complexion looked positively translucent in the firelight, her lips just as cherry-red as in daylight, and those stunning eyes glowed.

The night rail in and of itself was a confection that I assumed would likely cause grown men to stutter with lust. It had filmy little straps that were sliding down her smooth shoulders, open work down around the scooped neckline over which her breasts seemed to be in grave and imminent danger of spilling, and slits up each side to the thigh. And the few parts of the garment that were actually sewn closed were so sheer as to make me doubt their existence. And she was planning to use all that on my husband!

I turned away, a furious blush racing up my skin. Not only was I embarrassed beyond description, and so angry I could hardly breathe, but on top of that I felt like a dowdy, English . . . *cabbage,* swathed in yards of crumpled fabric. My toes peeped out from beneath my hems, but not so much as a glimpse of ankle was to be had, not to mention a hint of shapely calf or so much as a suggestion of voluptuous thigh. My arms were covered by long sleeves, and while I suppose most people would have guessed there to be a bosom concealed beneath it, there was absolutely no creamy, spilling evidence of such to be seen. What man, I thought glumly, would possibly want cabbage for dinner when he had just been offered a ripe, succulent, smooth, sun-warmed peach for pudding.

"Gwen?" Thérèse had a little frown between her beautifully arched brows. "I say, 'This is a very awkward thing, no?' It is only the good manners, I think if you say, 'Yes, Thérèse, it is'!"

I knew she was correct on her point of etiquette, but I didn't much care, since it was *only the good manners* for her to keep her hands off my husband.

Questions rattled around in my head. They had an assignation. Was this the first? Where was Cambourne? Were they embarking on an *affaire?* Or were they planning a more permanent liaison? Where did that leave Milburn and me?

"You are dressed to . . . go out?" I said, with an extremely insincere smile.

"I am not," she replied, as she swept her gaze up the length of me. "I am dressed to—I think you would say it— *stay in."*

"Shall I tell my *husband* you called to see him?" I asked.

After a moment, Thérèse gave one of her little Gallic shrugs. I had to restrain myself from squeezing my eyes closed, horrified that her gesture might well send the night rail slithering to her waist. She smiled, and bent her head toward me, looking conspiratorial. "You have been very discreet. I will not say to you that I am not disappointed, but," she said, "you will have to tell me what this one likes. We shall compare the brothers, perhaps."

I gave her a long look while I thought. What right did she have to ask me that? None whatsoever. I was absolutely not compelled to answer. *But,* part of me was thinking, if I did . . . well, it could go a long way toward convincing her that Cambourne was not unclaimed property.

"He likes," I said, trying hard to marshal my nerve, *"things."*

"Things!" said Thérèse. "You intrigue me! What kind of things does he like?"

"Er," I said, looking around for inspiration, and unfortunately finding none. "Ah. Well . . . kissing," I suggested.

Thérèse looked amused. "How unusual," she said.

In desperation, I cast my mind back over any and all marital advice I had been given. "He likes being trussed like a chicken!" burst out of me. I clapped a hand over my mouth. Where had *that* come from?

"Yes, but of course he does," Thérèse purred.

"Absolutely, that's my favorite," agreed Cambourne, at just that moment stepping through the door. "Nothing, *nothing* sets a man's blood afire more than being compared to poultry."

And right there, right then, I thought death was undoubtedly a much better thing than staying where I was. Cambourne was very much Cambourne at the moment. His hair had slipped back into straightness and was falling across his forehead. And he was still wearing his stockinet breeches, but the waistcoat and foam of cravat had been dispensed with. He looked sleek and powerful and tired, I thought.

"You're early," he said to me, and I wondered why he was playing along with me.

"I, er, well, yes, I am." I hauled myself back from the brink of death by embarrassment and congratulated myself that I was growing more articulate by the moment. "I understand that you aren't ready for me. So I shall just, leave, shall I?"

"No," he said, reaching out and circling my wrist. He pulled me closer to his side. "I'm always ready for you, *darling*. What man would not be?"

I fluttered my eyelashes at him. "And what woman could let such a paltry thing as the time keep her from you?" I said, and then, recalling his last remark, added, *"Darling."*

His eyes went slowly from my head to my toes, as Thérèse's had, and I felt yet more color flood my face. He raised a brow. "And now that I've glimpsed you in your seductive glory, how can I let you go?"

"Yes," I said, glancing down at my enormous wrapper. "I wore it specially. I know it's your favorite, *dearest."*

"Are you feeling modest, *darling?"* Cambourne said, the glint really coming back in full. "I own myself a little surprised that a woman so obviously dressed for seduction, with such a bag of tricks up her sleeve, would be so shy." He looked around. "Where *is* your bag of tricks, by the way? I shall be vastly disappointed if you did not bring the feather duster as you promised."

I glared at him. "Yes, well, do you know, I was in such a rush I forgot to ask the chambermaid if I could borrow one."

He raised a brow. "You were planning to use a dirty feather duster?"

I glared at him.

"I can see we shall need to discuss this in private," he said, putting his hand on Thérèse's elbow and steering her toward the door.

She looked up at him through her long lashes. I've tried that a time or two, with no success. The only thing it does for me is to roll my eyes up into my head so only the whites are showing and I look demented. On Thérèse it worked, though, especially as her shoulder strap slipped just a tiny bit more. "Good night, Thérèse. Sweet dreams," he said, gently pushing her through the door. "What I plan to do calls for two, not three." Then he closed the door.

I had taken advantage of his back being to me, and had wasted no time in retreating. I was just about to close the door to his dressing room on my way out, when his voice halted me in my tracks. "Oh no, you don't," he said.

I came slowly out of the dressing room. "I was just—"

"Yes. I know what you were just."

"Perhaps you should be grateful that I appeared when I did. It would have been a bit awkward for you otherwise." I crossed my arms, hoping that the letter would not crackle.

He looked amused. "Do you think I would not have been able to take care of Thérèse?"

"Actually, I was more concerned that you would have been able to take care of her only too well," I told him. "That's why I am here, after all."

"Perhaps I should amend that, then," he said. "Do you think I would have had difficulty sending her away on my own?"

Difficulty in execution or inclination, I wanted to know, but only said, "Well, I'd best be getting back now." The letter was starting to become itchy.

"I do not think I can let you go, just yet," he said, and I looked up at him in surprise. "I suspect Thérèse would find it a bit odd if you were to hare out of here so quickly," he said. "Why don't we sit for a while until a decent interval has passed. Then you may retreat," he suggested.

I could not resist. I smiled at him. "Or an indecent interval, perhaps?"

"If you prefer," he said lightly, as he handed me into a chair and took one opposite me.

"Decent will be fine," I said hastily, although to be perfectly honest, the prospect of any interval was a little alarming. "Why do you want her to believe we are lovers?" I asked.

"Why do *you?*" he returned.

"I thought it would be unseemly of you to have an *affaire* with your purported cousin, who might or might not turn out to be your brother's wife."

"Ah, so your motives were completely selfless," he said, in a bland voice. "Saving me from myself, as it were."

"Yes," I said, righteously. "As it were. And your motives?"

"Mostly selfish," he replied. "It's not that she's not enough to tempt any man, but it's one too many complications at the moment, if she thinks I am, ah, interested."

Oh. Talk about a lowering response! "Cambourne?" I burst out, and when he looked at me, continued, "I could accompany you, when you play the cello, on the pianoforte. The Beethoven sonatas were written for accompaniment, I think."

He looked momentarily surprised. I would imagine he was wondering where that had come from, as I was myself. And then—sounding just as awkward as I felt—he said, "That would be very nice. Your headache is better?" he asked.

I nodded. "Yes, thank you. And how was your evening?" I inquired politely.

"Tolerable," he said with a notable lack of enthusiasm. He stood, again, and poured two glasses of brandy, and, wordlessly, handed me one. Then he sat back and sipped his drink with the air of a man completely comfortable with the silence. I thought of a few more remarks in the same light, desultory vein that had characterized our last attempts, but discarded them.

He broke the silence. "I trust that fetching confection was not part of your trousseau?"

I looked down and blushed. "No," I said.

"I am relieved," he said. "A man would need a great deal of fortitude to attempt to breach that fortress."

I was insulted. "*You* would not attempt it? I am asking only hypothetically, of course."

"You question my fortitude?" he said. "Even if only hypothetically?"

"Well, how much fortitude are we discussing precisely?"

He smiled as he eyed the wrapper, and then lifted his glass to me. "Not more than a bottle's worth. Maybe two."

"Shall I hide the rest of the decanter?" I asked.

"I shouldn't think it necessary. I'm barely one glass into this one."

"I had not thought that I would be creeping about when I retired," I said, coldly, stung by his attitude.

"I see," he said, with a sudden grin. "If you had, you would have worn something more . . . enticing?"

"Of course not," I said, severely. "But more attractive. Every woman has her vanities, after all and I—I look like a cabbage," I said, unsure why I felt compelled to continue with such honesty. "Thérèse looks like a peach."

"I've had a peach or two in my life," he said, lightly. "They can get cloying after a time. Good old, plain, English, boiled vegetables are more . . . sustaining."

"Truly?" I was aware that I was grinning like an idiot, which was odd, because I am not entirely certain that I even cared for his implication. Being likened to a boiled cabbage was really no cause for celebration, and who, really, wanted to be thought of as sustaining?

"Yes," he said, and then we fell again into silence. The quiet stretched on between us. Cambourne seemed to be regarding me with some secret amusement. "When you said you were tired of being a pawn in this?" he asked.

"Yes."

"I'm curious: What precisely did you mean? Were you actually implying that I possess the ability to move you at will?" he asked. "Or was it that I'm setting you up so as to defend myself? Or that I'm willing to sacrifice you to advance my position?"

"I don't know," I whispered, now truly unable to take my gaze from his face. And, then, to this day, I do not know what came over me, but I stood up and moved to his chair. I stood over him and he looked up at me, his expression unreadable. "But isn't that why you married me? Because you believed I would allow you to do any of those things?"

He looked at me oddly. "I wouldn't say that exactly, Gwen," he said, quietly.

I suddenly felt very bold. I reached out my hand and he took it and drew me onto his lap. I waited for his touch, feeling so tightly wound with expectancy that I almost felt as though I would snap if he did not put his hands on me.

"And? Are you willing to sacrifice me to advance your position?" I asked, finally, when he did not.

"You don't think I already have?"

I looked him straight in the eye. "Have you?"

And for just an instant a flicker of doubt actually crossed his face. "I don't know," he said, and I wondered just how close to the mark I was. "Why do you ask so many questions, Gwen?"

"And why do you answer so few?"

He smiled. "Because talking is so very overrated." And

then he shifted, so that I was still on his lap, my legs across his, but my back was against the back of his chair. "Don't you think?" he asked, as he bent to unfasten the wrapper at my neck.

I opened my mouth, but he forestalled me. "No," he said, taking both my wrists in one of his, "don't answer that, it would just be more talking, after all, and I need all my powers of concentration to breach this fortress."

"I thought," I said—despite his ban on talking—as my head fell against the back of the chair, "that this required a bottle's worth of fortitude, at the least."

"Sometimes a man has to summon all his courage in order to quiet the enemy," he replied, as his lips found the hollow of my throat.

"I'm the enemy?" I whispered, as my eyes fell closed. "And here, I thought we were, for the moment, a team."

"Jesus," he said. "How much do you have on under this tent?"

My eyes snapped open. "You are worried you won't know what to do?"

"I know what to do," he said, in a dark voice, turning toward me.

And he did, as it turned out, with both his hands and his mouth. His hair brushed over my face, as he put his lips to my neck. "Time to conquer the enemy," he said, with a laughing tone to his voice, as his lips slid down to my breast.

Liquid. My entire body was liquid as his lips grazed the very tip of my breast. His hands held me firmly against his lap. I twisted my torso to be closer to him and he swayed over me, sliding his hands along my sides, pushing the wrapper open further. I groaned as his hand cupped my breast, his thumb was so tantalizingly close—

I bolted upright in his lap. The letter! I had completely forgot about the letter and his fingertips had been a bare half-inch away. I scrambled off the chair. "This was very pleasant," I said, practically tripping over my own foot.

His eyebrow went up. "Pleasant!" he said.

"Oh, indeed. But I really must . . . go." I was half afraid (hoping) that he would try to restrain me, but he didn't.

"Apparently, you really must," he said, as the dark, heavy look in his eyes was replaced with something perilously close to amusement.

I didn't stay to watch, but rather fled toward his dressing room to return the way I had come. "Well, good night, Cambourne," I said.

"Good night, Gwen," he said, his voice heavy with amusement now. "Enjoy your letter."

I stopped and gaped at him.

"I always think," he said, "that the better part of chess is being willing to wait for your opponent to make a mistake. For what it's worth, I'm a patient man. I *always* win."

Which left me wondering as I made my way back, who, in this case, he was playing against: me or Milburn.

21

In which I am summoned to attend my mama

My Dear Fellow,

While it pains me no end to put pen to paper in this fashion,
I find myself at point non plus. As you know, I held reserva-
tions from the first on the notion that Milburn was suited to
the undertaking of our Task. And it seems that the worst of
these have been realized. I am informed that subsequent
to his safe arrival in Toulouse, he has disappeared. I am
assured by our numerous contacts in the area that there is no
question of harm having befallen him. As you know, a good
deal of the King's money is at stake. Should my men be successful in locating your brother, as I am certain they will be,
I will find myself with no other choice than to try him for
treason. At which time, regrettably, it is more than likely that
the Other Matter will become public. I am yours, most
regretfully.

I folded the letter, having read it for about the tenth time since the previous night, and stared unseeing at the wall. What I really wanted, of course, was to bring it round to Cecy's. But then Thérèse would no doubt want to accompany me, and since she believed Cambourne and I were lovers, I would be unable to speak freely. There was only one thing for it, I decided: I had to tell her that we were not.

I was only just managing to convince myself that telling her would not be as awful a prospect as it seemed, when Giddings, the butler, entered and handed me a missive. I recognized the handwriting instantly and opened it with a gloomy sense of foreboding. I had, it seemed, been peremptorily summoned to attend my mother's drawing room later this morning. Surely things could not get worse?

I made my confession to Thérèse on the way to Cecy's. "It is a very large shame—" she said as I lifted the knocker at Cecy's front door. Then we both fell silent as the butler relieved us of our outer garments and ushered us into the morning room, where Myrtia was already ensconced. The moment the butler had left Thérèse picked up the thread of her conversation precisely where she had left it "—that you are not sharing your Cambourne's bed, if it is him you want."

Cecy held up her hand, then. "Just a minute," she said. "This is completely unacceptable. You send urgent notes round to Myrtia and myself about having found *evidence,* and here we are, waiting, verily holding our breaths with anticipation, and now you two enter talking about something else altogether—something highly interesting to be sure, but something different! Oh, no, you will back up a few steps, please."

"Good morning to you also, Cecy," I said, kissing her on the cheek before sitting down and handing her the letter. "Behold the evidence."

"Just right there. In the drawer of his bedside table?" said Myrtia, her disbelief clear in her tone, when they had finished reading. "Not hidden? Not locked away?"

I shook my head.

"But what does it *mean?*" Cecy frowned, still holding it. "Other than that he was obviously being blackmailed."

"The letter?" Myrtia asked her. "Or the fact that he left it for Gwen to find just now?"

"He couldn't have known that she was going to sneak into his bedchamber and look in the drawer," Cecy objected.

"I suspect he had a good guess that it was a likelihood," I replied. "He certainly knew I'd been ransacking the house at every opportunity. He's probably wondering what took me so long."

And Cecy said, "The meaning of the letter is obvious enough in the basics, but what on earth do you suppose that *Other Matter* could be?"

"I don't know," I replied. "But whatever it was, it was enough for Cambourne to have sent Milburn into danger."

We were all silent again, staring into the fire for a few moments.

"Yes," Cecy said after a moment. "I don't think he'd do that lightly."

Myrtia looked at me intently. "Now that you know Cambourne, Gwen, what do you believe would be worth that risk to him?"

I thought about this. "I don't know," I replied. "Honor, I suppose."

Thérèse spoke up for the first time since we had seated

ourselves. "But perhaps more importantly, we must ask ourselves why it is if Cambourne wants Gwen to know what happened, that he tell her sideways."

I shouldn't have understood her, but I did. "Letting me find it instead of just *telling* me, you mean?"

She nodded.

"I agree," said Myrtia.

"I think, because that is his way of telling me in a neutral way, of getting *me* to come to him with what I want. That is the thing of it with him. He never tells me what to do, but always seems to be waiting to see what I will do," I said, getting up and beginning to pace as a sudden excitement came over me, as I realized that I, and I alone in the room, understood him. "And because there is something more that he doesn't want to tell me. He said the oddest thing the other day about what he *had* told me being a veritable love poem compared with what he had not."

Thérèse tilted her head, looking at me thoughtfully. "How interesting. You have not in all this time been to Cambourne's bed? You tell me the truth when you tell me that on the way here?"

I shook my head. "No," I said. "I have not. I did tell the truth, but what has this to do with the letter?"

Thérèse lifted her cup and sipped. "It seems to me that Cambourne, he has so far played along with what Bert-ee has asked, has he not? And I say to myself, and now to you, I do not understand it—"

"Well, it seems obvious that Milburn knows what the *Other Matter* is," I said, "and is using it to blackmail Cambourne. So whatever it is, it's serious enough for Cambourne to cede to his demand. It was clear that Milburn was threatening him."

Thérèse shook her head. "I do not know Cambourne so

well, but even I can see how important this title, it is to
him," she said. "And I think he play a leetle game with
Ber-tee, but he does not have the intention of really giving
up the titles. I make doubt that he would allow this to
continue if he thought there was a question of endangering the . . . succession, I think you call it?" At my nod, she
continued. "You English, you are very keen on the succession. That is why, after all, that Cambourne, he did not
allow me to go with Ber-tee."

I stared at her. "It is?"

"Of course," she said. "He was thinking that if I became
with a child, it would give him less of the control of the
situation. Now, he knows he can take time. So all you have
to do is become pregnant."

Become pregnant! I stared at her. "I don't know," I said.

"You need to learn to take what you want, Gwen," said
Thérèse gently. "I was beginning to think you are tired of
being the good girl. And Cambourne, I think, he think it
too, and that's why he leave you the letter now."

I sighed. "Old habits are hard to break," I added,
glumly. "And anyway, to do that I'd have to seduce him,
which I can't seem to manage. Believe me, I've tried the
thing."

Thérèse shook her head in apparent disbelief. "All this
time you are together, living alone in the house, the two of
you. And you have not managed a simple seduction! But
now," she said, briskly, "we shall apply some practicality to
the situation, *n'est-ce pas?* That is why we French are so
good at love! We understand that one must take a practical
approach to the matters of the heart."

"Rather like preparing for battle?" I asked her, trying for
a teasing tone.

But she was serious when she replied, "We French, we

prefer to be to the point, without this insistence had by you English to never do or say what one means."

"And it complicates the situation nicely," Myrtia said. "Since consummation makes this marriage to you much harder to dissolve. Perhaps," she said, looking up, "this is exactly what he wants you to do."

"He certainly hasn't behaved like it was all the times he tossed me out of his bedchamber," I said.

"It was the robe." Thérèse shuddered visibly.

"The robe?" Cecy asked with interest. "You must tell us all about it, Thérèse. But now, Gwen, is it not time for you to go pay that visit to your mama, as promised?"

I looked at the clock. "Unfortunately," I said. "I've been trying to forget."

Cecy waved gaily. "Don't blame you a bit," she said. "I'm trying to forget about mine, too. Now, go and do what you have to, and do not fret about a thing: the three of us will come up with a plan to get you pregnant."

Now why, I wondered all the way to my parents' town house, did that thought not bring me comfort?

When I arrived, my mother, my father, and Violetta were already assembled.

"This is simply unacceptable," my mother had said, right off, without so much as a greeting. "Tell her, Axton, that this is simply unacceptable."

"This is simply unacceptable," my father said, as directed.

"Do you mind if I sit before you roast me alive?" I asked.

"Forward, impudent chit!" snapped Violetta.

My mother looked to be considering whether or not to

grant my request, but I sat down anyway, before she could tell me not to. "I know *I* didn't raise you to be so disrespectful!" she said, eyeing me in such a way that would have reduced me to a puddle just a few short weeks ago.

"What the deuce is going on over there?" my father wanted to know.

"What do you mean?" I asked.

"Rumors are rife," my mother said.

"Loose Frenchwomen," Violetta said, darkly. "Running about Milburn House half-clothed."

My father brightened. "P'raps I should come assess the situation," he suggested.

"Oh, do be quiet, Axton," my mother suggested back.

"Just the one loose Frenchwoman," I said. "Fully clothed." And my father looked disappointed. "A cousin to the Duchess of Winfell," I added, and his face fell further.

"That silly ass Milburn's returned!" Violetta said, as though she were delivering news of the utmost import.

"Actually, I was aware of that," I replied. "As I happen to be living there and I'm not quite so stupid that I don't know who's under my own roof."

"Oh, but don't you see? This ruins everything," my mother almost wailed. "I was certain he was dead. Why, *why*, could he not have been dead?"

"*Excuse* me?" My voice was positively dripping with frost.

"Milburn is back. Cambourne has taken up his rightful place, and now you're living with that ridiculous man milliner, and his French trollop, while legally married to his brother," she said.

"And I'd lay a pile of blunt on it that you were far too namby-pamby to have let Cambourne bed you while you *were* still living together!" Violetta crowed.

I stared at them. Now, it is true that my intellect was not precisely in top form at the moment. It *had*, after all, been a trying few days, but I was alert enough to distill the fact that they apparently believed Cambourne had gone back to being himself. I'm not certain why this surprised me, but it did. I decided, just for the moment, that nothing in particular was to be gained by enlightening any of them as to the actual composition of the two households.

"I—" I began, but my mother spoke, her voice almost rising to a shriek. "Cambourne never consummated that marriage?" she wailed.

"No," I said, very precisely. And then I smiled sweetly at her, enjoying the way she went pale.

"Only disaster can come of having someone with French blood under your roof," Violetta said. "If I've said that once, I've said it a hundred times."

I believed her. "A hundred at the very least, I should think," I said.

"None of this would have mattered had you taken my advice and treated him with a firmer hand," Violetta said pointedly. "How do you think I brought Worth to heel?" she demanded, and then went on. "A fine piece of man like Worth doesn't just *fall* into step, y'know!"

"Had to be beaten into it, as I recall," my father said.

"Oh, do be quiet, Axton," my mother said again. "The entire point was consummation. For Gwen and Cambourne to consummate the marriage so he couldn't cast her off when Milburn returned. Now there's nothing to stop his annulling and she'll be married to *Milburn!* Of all people."

"I thought that was the original idea," I said, looking from one to the other, "me being married to Milburn."

"Not my idea in the first place," my father said, holding up his hands.

"That would imply, by association, that you've had one, Axton!" my mother said.

"Demme, no!" my father replied. "Not much in the idea line," he explained, cheerfully.

"This should have been taken care of from the first," my mother said, giving my father a most unpleasant look. "And it would have been had you only done as I said and"—she glanced at me—"never mind."

I stared at her and yet barely saw her. *Honor,* I was thinking. Cambourne valued honor above all, and surely he must have known that he was risking his by marrying me.

"And at the very least you should have forced him to consummate it!" She was almost yelling, but I was uncertain whether it was directed at me or my father.

"Hey ho," my father said to my mother, rather rudely. "I defy even you, Almeria, to tell a man when to f—consummate his own marriage."

She glared at him. "I told *you,* Axton! And a good thing it was, too, as I doubt you'd have got around to figuring it out on your own. But never mind that. Now, we have to think about how to help Gwen."

I could hear Cambourne's voice in my head: *We all find ourselves at some point in an unfortunate situation not of our own making. It is up to you to decide how you go on from there.* I looked at my mother looking at me. She was going to tell me what to do.

"No," I said firmly, and then was heartened by the fact that they all gaped at me. "I think it's time to cut line. I want to know how you forced him to marry me."

"Are you defying me, Gwen?" my mother asked, with a lifted brow.

"Yes," I said.

"Odious, ungrateful gel!" Violetta said.

"Yes," I said, again. "Now tell me."

"You might as well, Almeria," Violetta said, her gaze still trained on me. "The silly chit's got the bit between her teeth and she's never going to let go of it now."

"Very well," my mother said.

I leaned forward in my chair, and removed my father's brandy glass from his hand. "Thank you," I said, taking a long swallow and leaning back with the air of one waiting for an excellent tale.

"Well, as you know, because Milburn was away," Father said, "we did not have the banns read—"

"Yes," I said. "I was in possession of that piece of the puzzle."

"We'd assumed all along that we would need a special license. The bishop knew, of course, that we would need one, and Milburn was going to take care of that upon his return. When he didn't return, however, and Cambourne offered to step in—" Mother broke off to glare at Father "—*we* offered to get the license."

"And *that*," Violetta said, "was when the unfortunate mix-up with the names occurred."

"Most unfortunate," I said. "So what you are saying is that you tricked him?"

"Not precisely," my father said. "I'll grant you, your mother changed the names—" he broke off to glare at her "—but Cambourne knew it before the ceremony and still agreed to go through with it."

"Agreed," I said. "An interesting choice of words. Does one suppose there was some, ah, impetus to his agreement?"

"Oh well," said Violetta. "As to that, who's to say? One man's agreement is another man's coercion. Semantics. I make it a point never to waste time on them."

"I see," I said, thinking that at last, I did. "And you somehow failed to, ah, find the correct time to mention all this to me?"

"You know how emotional you get about every little thing, Gwen," my mother said. "As I said at the time, Bernie, Bertie, what's the difference? Now, it is imperative that you do not do anything to imperil the validity of your marriage to Cambourne."

I stared at her, not certain I was comprehending. "Oh!" I said after a moment. "Have I let Milburn consummate, do you mean?"

Violetta nodded. "Not that that would help, of course, because Cambourne's name is still on that license. Bed Milburn and you're just an adulterous woman." She looked at my mother. "The gel needs our help, Almeria."

"No," I said. "I absolutely do not need your help."

"Of course you do!" my mother said.

"Actually," I said, wondering why I'd never before found the courage to stand up to her, "you've already helped quite a bit. And your help has been irrevocably damaging to my marriage and to my future happiness. I don't want any more."

"Don't be ridiculous," Violetta said.

"Let me put it this way," I said, leaning forward. "If you help me? Even once more? I'll go and bed whichever of them I come across first. And you'll never know which it is!"

There was silence. I could hear the faint noise of a door closing somewhere in the house, the fire hissed, and I stared at the bare branches of the plane trees outside.

"P'raps—" ventured my father, but got no further.

"Oh, do be quiet, Axton," Mother said. "I think she means it. Do you truly mean that?"

"Yes," I said. "I do." I stood and gathered my pelisse. "So only remember, one wrong footfall on your part and I'll have one of them in my bed before you can so much as blink. Could be Cambourne, but then, it could just as easily be Milburn. Do I make myself clear?"

And then I swept out the door.

22

In which Bertie pays me a visit

I was still shaking from the encounter when Giddings announced, "Lord Cambourne."

"It's exhausting." Milburn cast himself into a needle-point chair and tugged at his cravat with a most uncharacteristic disregard as to its appearance.

I raised my glass to him. I was on my second brandy of the day. Not bad for a girl who not too long ago had been afraid to try the stuff. "Good afternoon, er, Cambourne," I said, waving toward the decanter. "Help yourself to refreshment."

"Thank you, no," he said, glumly, and I eyed him. I wouldn't have called him mussed, precisely, but he was lacking a certain gloss that I had come to associate with him. And I had to admit: He seemed somehow diminished without the aureole of curls. Even his hair seemed dispirited. It fell straight, as Cambourne's did, but instead of having an appealing shine that made me want to run my fingers through it, it lay there, looking limp and dispirited. "Afternoon, is it? Feels like bloody midnight to me. I don't know how he—anyone—can stand it."

I raised a questioning brow. "Stand what?"

"This dashed miserable existence of his." He waved an arm. "All day, it's Corn Laws, Corn Laws, on and on, etcetera, ad nauseam. I mean, how is a fellow supposed to know what the deuced farmers are getting paid for their plaguey corn?"

"Actually," I said, "I believe it's seven shillings a bushel at the moment."

He gave me an odd look. "That's not the all of it." He looked about furtively once again, and lowered his voice still further. "That Mathilde Claussen is, well, *insatiable*. I'm exhausted. Cambourne, it appears, don't sleep. Me? I *need* my sleep." And then he slumped back dispiritedly into his chair.

I repressed a smile along with the delicious feeling that I really should not be participating in this conversation at all. "Perhaps she finds you more, er, pleasing," I suggested.

He looked taken with this suggestion, sat up straighter, and for a moment, his chest seemed to swell, but then deflated. "No. In fact—" He seemed suddenly to recall himself. "Never mind." He slumped back once again and studied his boot in gloomy silence.

I nodded sympathetically, since that seemed to be all that was required of me, and he continued.

"Haven't been to the club or out gaming since this started. Cambourne's time—" he looked around again, and dropped his voice—"is not his own. Every evening it's some insipid debutante's ball or some dull supper or wretched thing like that. And did you know, I don't—he don't—even decide which to attend! His secretary does that. I rise at the crack of dawn, and am expected to be clothed in a quarter hour! Then I'm s'posed to drag myself out for a ride or to Jackson's or some such. Finally return, throw down m'breakfast, already exhausted from rising at first light—digestion's a complete shambles!" Milburn closed his eyes.

He looked deeply pained, but once again, no response in particular seemed required of me.

"Then, no sooner are the covers taken away, but his secretary is waiting in the library to go over his demmed ledgers. He *was* used to going over it *at the table!"* His tones were indignant. "I soon put a stop to that, you can be sure! Why, it's positively *uncivilized."*

"I can see your point," I murmured soothingly, since I was beginning to fear he might have some kind of attack, so patent was his indignation.

"First we go over Cambourne's engagements for the evening: 'I have taken the liberty of accepting this one for you, my lord'—" Milburn did a credible imitation of an obsequious secretary—" 'It's for Lord Sheridan's daughter and that gentleman can be quite helpful in your attempts to introduce your motion to etcetera . . . ,' you know the type of thing." He shuddered. "Reason enough to stay away, if you ask me."

"I see your point," I said.

"But *that*—" he leaned closer and adopted a confiding tone—"is precisely the type of thing Cambourne does! Goes to an entertainment because it is *expected."* His revulsion was apparent. "And women positively *throw* themselves at my, his, head. D'you know how many carriages have broken down outside Cambourne House this week alone? There's quite the epidemic of poorly made carriage wheels in this town, I tell you that," he said darkly. "I'm actually expected to lead out whey-faced debutantes and fetch them lemonade and such, and then to stand in corners listening to old bores prose on about parliamentary matters. And last night even some dead bore Oxford chap, antiquarian cove, telling me about how I'm funding his excavation—digging up the ruins at St. Dunstan's, apparently! And moreover, I can't take advantage of any of the women who want to offer, well, *something else* to him—me—on account of having had to cater to Mathilde's every—er, sorry, Gwen."

I motioned to let him know that I was not offended, and to continue.

"I tell you, I'm beginning to understand why the fellow was so keen to keep you after all."

"You really must cut line on the excessive flattery, Milburn," I said.

But he was undaunted. "Then it is luncheon, perhaps at White's. And I assure you, there is no sleeping with a paper over my face there. No chance of that, oh no. No sooner do I step a barely shined boot through the door, but there's a gaggle of people wanting to discuss this blasted parliamentary strategy. Then I am supposed to take another ride or do something else sporting—the fellow is a fanatic for punishment! And sometimes Mathilde expects servicing midday, in which case I have to go round and perform. Seemed like a dream come true at first, but now it's like some kind of blasted nightmare. And then I go sit in the house, which drags on interminably, then some prosy old ass inevitably wants to discuss the day's developments there, as though I paid any attention! Then home to change, out for the evening to some poisonously dull entertainment, and then if I ain't visibly dead on my feet, it's back to Mathilde."

"Why are you telling me this?" I asked, when I could get a word in edgewise.

He had the grace to look embarrassed. "Thing is," he ran a finger about his cravat. "Don't know how much more of it I can take."

I considered this. "But you wanted it," I reminded him.

"Didn't know what I was letting m'self in for," he said, as though that explained all.

"Talk to him," I suggested.

"No," he said, and I waited for him to pout as he was used to when he was a child. "You talk to him for me."

"Me?" I said. "Why ever should I do that?"

"Because you're my wife," he said, sounding obstinate.

"Don't be ridiculous," I reminded him. "*You* chose to have your little idyll with Thérèse instead of coming home and marrying me."

"I consider my idyll with Thérèse, as you phrased it, entirely separate from my marrying you," he said bluntly.

"Well, it ought not be," I pointed out.

"Idylls and marriage are not mutually exclusive," he said. "Y'know."

"When the marriage concerns me, they are," I said, crossing my arms. "And anyway, I'm Cambourne's wife now."

"You are no such thing," Milburn said briskly.

"It's his name on the license," I said.

"It's his name on the other license, too."

"What do you want, Milburn?"

"I want to be m'self again." He pushed out his lower lip, and for a moment I saw the seven-year-old I had once known. "He can have the titles back, but he can't have you."

I leveled a long look at him. "Are you in love with me, then, Milburn?" I asked, finally.

He leveled an equally long look back at me. "Do you want the pretty answer to that, Gwen?"

"No," I said, "I want the truth."

"Of course not," he said. "And are you in love with me?"

I was tempted to toss back a flippant remark, but instead I took a moment to think about his question. "No," I said, slowly. "But I suppose I had a certain vision of marriage to you that seemed both easy and expected, somehow, and I've been reluctant to give it up. I am a little surprised, however," I continued, "that you are fighting for me like a spoiled child with a toy. And come to think of it, you are behaving the same way over the titles. Forcing him to give them up for you."

He laughed at this. "I didn't force him to give them up. You did."

"Me?" I demanded, my voice rising. "I wasn't the one blackmailing him. And he *said* he was doing it for you."

"Don't be ridiculous," he said, quietly. "It was so he could stay with you. He loves you Gwen, and I've always known it. I've watched him watch you since you were sixteen years old."

I stared at him. "Really?" I whispered. "Is that the truth?"

He nodded. "Doesn't matter, though," he said. "You were s'posed to be *my* wife. Not Cambourne's." He jutted out his chin.

"Do you love Thérèse?" I asked him.

"Not hardly," he said.

"Where did the old Bertie Milburn go? The pleasant easygoing companion I knew?"

"He disappeared somewhere about a year ago," he replied. "When he started risking his hide to protect his brother's ridiculous notions of honor. Meantime, I'd suggest you get one of your husbands to switch back with the other."

I eyed him. "And what would you do if I said no?"

"That would depend," he said, uncrossing his boot, and leaning toward me with his elbows on his knees. "I could just go right on being Cambourne. Thing is, it seems I ain't much in the way of an estate manager, so I wanted to offer him the opportunity to have his precious land back." He shrugged. "Plenty of blunt there, though, even if I completely ignore the estates. I could just enjoy m'self, let the estates go to hell, I s'pose, if he's intent on hanging about as me. Only thing is, I would need him to relinquish you—"

"But why?" I burst out. "You just admitted you don't love me."

"Because he wants you, Gwen," he said, leaning closer. "You're the only thing I've ever had that Cambourne wanted and couldn't take. Anyway, I can ruin Cambourne without even letting out his dirty little secret."

I suddenly felt very tired of this. "What are you saying, Bertie?"

"S'pose it all comes down to this, Gwen: I owe Cambourne. The way I see it, he has two choices. He can choose you, or he can choose his titles. Can't have both. If he tries, a few correctly placed words from me will put paid to that notion. Why don't you give it a shot? See what's worth more to 'im, you or his land."

"You can't mean that," I said.

Bertie rose and dusted off his immaculate jacket. " 'Course I do," he said. "I'm Cambourne now, for the moment, at least. I don't say things I don't mean. Believe me, when it comes right to it, you'll come a distant third to his land and his honor. *Those* are in his blood." Then he flicked the tails of his jacket and stood. "You, you are just in his life," he said, from the door. "Not his blood, not his bones, not even his bed."

We both fell silent for a moment, and then Milburn said, with a perceptiveness that surprised me, "Bad luck for you, old girl, that he didn't bed you before I came back. Because you can bet on it that the noble Harry Cambourne won't ruin you with the situation so unsettled. Tripped up by his own sense of honor, I'm afraid. You'll never get him to bed you now."

After he left, I stayed, curled in my chair. Bertie might be right about a lot of things—a surprising number in fact, but not that last. Because *that* was precisely what I was determined to change.

23

In which I seduce Cambourne

"*O*of, Ber-tee." *Therèse gave a languid wave when I* told her of his visit later that afternoon. "Pay no mind to him. He is like a little, annoying dog. One good kick and he shall come to heel, sure enough. One only has to decide wisely on when and where to administer it, the kick."

"But he's right," I said. "In that I have to get Cambourne to break this rigid sense of honor or nothing can change, I see that now. And if nothing does, we're all of us doomed to unhappiness."

At this, Cecy looked up from the letter she had just sanded.

"I tell you, honor and nobility I do not know about. I think it is all the fault of the robe"—Therèse shuddered—"Imagine attempting seduction garbed like *une grand-mère!*"

"*Une grand-mère?*" Cecy repeated, looking amused.

"I was not attempting seduction!" I felt compelled to point out. "I was breaking up an illicit rendezvous." I glared at her repressively.

She was unrepressed. "I would not be seen to flee a fire in a robe such as that! This time—" Therese waved a hand—"you will have Cambourne begging for the mercy!"

Which is how I came, some time later that evening, to find myself grabbing Thérèse by the elbow. To be sure, I had not intended to put our plan into action quite so soon. I had agreed to it in theory, but had somehow been under the happy, if false, impression that I would have a few days to work myself up to it in practice. But as it happened, that very evening found Thérèse going to the theater with Myrtia, and Cambourne announcing his intention to retire early. A heaven-sent opportunity, if there ever was one, at least according to Thérèse.

"I've changed my mind. I cannot do this," I whispered, as I grabbed her elbow.

I was freshly bathed, not to mention creamed, emolliated, and perfumed. I had even, as per her instructions, brushed my hair dry, leaning upside down in front of the fire. My neck was stiff, but my hair looked stunning.

"Yes," she replied, apparently unmoved. "You can." As though to emphasize her point, she liberated her arm and shook out the extraordinarily sheer night rail. "This is perfect. Your Madame Suzette is indeed the genius."

I eyed the tiny scrap of lace with disfavor. "It is simply not the type of thing I do," I attempted to explain.

"No," she agreed, turning the little slippers she had chosen this way and that as she examined them from every angle. "You are wrong. It is not the type of thing that you *did*. But before you have always been the good girl, and you are now trying to change that, no?"

I hesitated.

She sighed. "Look, Gwen," she said in patient tones, putting the slipper down. "I do not apologize for coming to your Cambourne's chamber to seduce him. At the time, I do not know that you want him, you see? And he is very . . . full of delights? Delightful! Yes, that is it. Delicious and delightful, I think, and perfectly beautiful in a way his twin, he is not. He is so very English and proper on the surface of things, but beneath, I think are unexpected depths. If you want him, you have to be brave enough to take him for yourself."

Thus far I had been reluctant to share what Bertie had told me about Cambourne being in love with me. I debated spilling it to Thérèse now, but did not. First of all, I was not entirely certain I could believe it. I mean, consider the source! And, too, if felt private, somehow, like something I wanted to hug to myself a while longer.

And besides, should this seduction fail, it would only serve to make the entire thing more humiliating. I had been unable to seduce a man rumored to be in love with me.

"But—what if it doesn't work?" I was almost bleating.

Thérèse held up the indecent scrap that passed as a garment again. "Look at this," she said.

I did.

"Look at you," she said.

I did. And hardly recognized myself in the flushed, wanton-looking creature whose gaze met mine in the mirror.

After a moment, she continued. "If this does not work, then, well . . . then, I know nothing of the men." Then she smiled, catlike, exuding confidence that she in fact knew everything about men. "And, also, I think you should remember that the garments—" she paused and shrugged—"well, they are not everything."

I stared at her. "But I thought you said they were."

"I lie," she said, sounding perfectly comfortable with that fact. "Because I think you are not ready for the real truth."

"Which is?" I was almost whispering.

"That you, you want him to give up something that is precious to him, his sense of his own honor. Now you must in return give to him something dear to you."

"My pride," I said, almost to myself. "But, Thérèse—" I was seized momentarily by guilt "—if this succeeds, I am consigning you to a life with Milburn."

She gave me a wry smile. "You think Ber-tee and I will not be suited, as you English like to say?"

"I am not entirely certain, at the moment, that Milburn and anyone would suit," I admitted.

She shrugged. "As I have said it before. He want someone to give him a little kick, and I will be the one to do it. Ber-tee, he will do fine, *n'est-ce pas?*"

"But what about love, Thérèse?"

"Gwen—" she looked exasperated "—you want love. Me, I want to be gone from my village, from my father. Love will come where I tell it," she said. "Now, stop wasting the time, and let us get you ready." She held out the night rail.

It was immodest. It was appalling. It was completely transparent. I leaned closer to the mirror. Good heavens! My eyes looked positively feverish, my lips, thanks to just a touch of some special salve from Thérèse, were almost as cherry-red as hers, and my hair fell in luxuriant shiny waves down my back. Not entirely convinced, I stuck out my tongue, and sure enough, the vision did also.

"See, it is you," Thérèse said, drily.

"Yes," I said. "I suppose it must be. Thérèse?" I turned toward her. "I—I need a moment . . . before I go. Alone."

"You will—how do you say it?—lose your nerve, then, I think."

"I won't," I said. "And you will be late for Myrtia if you do not go." She glanced at the clock. I could see her hesitate. "Traffic will be a terrible crush," I said, "and Crewes is bound to fuss you about whether you are properly attired for such inclement weather."

She smiled. "Do not think I do not know what you are doing, Gwen. But I know also that in the end you will have to walk in there by your own self." She paused by the door.

"Thank you, Thérèse," I said, quietly. "I don't deserve you."

"Oof, think nothing of it," she said, airily. "And I agree that it is too kind of me, since I think I am encouraging my husband to commit the bigamy."

I was laughing as she closed the door, but not for long. I think the only thing that propelled me toward the door that connected my rooms with Cambourne's, in the end, was the half-formed idea that anything was better than being alone with my thoughts.

I did pause, though, and cast a glance back over my chamber, where it fell on the cabbage wrapper draped across a chair. Suppose one of the servants was lurking about in the sitting room, tending to the fire or some such? Was it truly necessary to the success of this plan that they be made privy to the sight of me in a transparent night rail? I, for one, didn't think so. I swooped back into the room and shrugged the wrapper on. It went on like a breath of relief. I would discard it when I reached Cambourne's dressing room undetected, I assured myself as I set off through the connecting doors.

I took a deep breath to shore up my resolution, and lifted my hand to knock.

"Gwen?" he said, when I did.

I cracked the door open, and peered around it. "Hello! Cambourne!" I said in extremely hearty tones.

Perhaps too hearty, because he lifted a brow, and said, "Would you like to come in?" He was sitting on his bed, reading a book.

I was blushing as I stepped through the door and pulled it closed behind me. "Don't get up," I said, waving at him to sit back down, as he made to get to his feet.

A few hours ago, when last I had seen him, at supper, he had been in high Milburn alt. At some point since, he had returned to being himself. He was wearing plain buff breeches and a white shirt, the simplicity of the outfit setting off the lithe perfection of his body. His hair fell across his forehead, and he pushed it back as he looked up at me. He looked tired, I decided. In fact, I realized with some guilt, he seemed to look increasingly more tired each day that he lived with me. And the fact was that the shadows under his eyes, the slight hollows in his cheekbones, only made him more attractive.

"And to what do I owe the honor of this visit?" he asked.

"Well . . ." Blast! I had forgot in my nervousness to remove the cabbage wrapper. Which omission, I told myself, was entirely responsible for the friendly, but distinctly unsmoldering-with-passion expression in his eyes. My hand went to my throat where the garment was very efficiently closed. Absolutely no chance of it accidentally sliding open to reveal my barely concealed charms. I doubted even gale force winds would serve to part the neck. Here I was, in his bedroom, trying to seduce him, looking like the spinster of the parish. "I just came to, ah, *see* you," I managed.

"How nice," he said politely, and followed with a nice long silence.

As usual, this had the effect of making me want to babble like an idiot. "I haven't seen you in, well, quite a long while," I said.

"Yes, supper seems positively eons ago," he said, agreeably.

There was simply no possible scenario under which I could begin to imagine seducing this man at this point. In fact, were I to try at the moment, I was convinced he would likely have run screaming out of the room. Right. I took a breath.

And did not realize that I had spoken aloud, until he looked at me with a raised brow, and said, "Right?"

I looked at him. "Right what?"

"I don't know," he said, frowning. "You said, 'Right.'"

"Oh," I said. "I meant, Right! And you decided not to go out this evening?"

"Yes," he said, his frown deepening. "As I believe I mentioned quite specifically at supper."

"Your silences are more silent than most," I blurted out.

"Gwen," he said, sounding both weary and wary. "Would you like to sit instead of hovering inside the door?"

I nodded and he rose from the bed in a fluid motion and crossed to the armchairs by the fire. "I'll come sit with you by the fire. Now, tell me about my silences."

I sat opposite him. "They stretch. And you seem so comfortable in them that one—well, I, really—feel compelled to fill them. They make me babble like an idiot."

"I am sorry," he said. "They are certainly not intended that way. For what it is worth, I have never thought you an idiot."

"Thank you." I smiled at him. "It's always nice to know that there's someone who hasn't."

"And I am inordinately fond of babbling," he added, staunchly. "Always have been."

I directed a dark look in his direction.

"It's interesting, though," he said. "The idea of different people having different silences. I'd never thought of it. Tell me, what kind of silences does, say, your mother have?"

"Impatient," I replied, promptly.

"Your father?" he asked.

"Relieved," I told him, and he laughed.

"Cecy?"

"Provocative."

"Myrtia?"

"Attentive. Thoughtful. This would be an excellent parlor game," I said. "I can see whiling away a snowy afternoon at a house party with this."

"Milburn?"

"Selfish," I replied (a little snappishly, perhaps, as our recent encounter was still fresh in my mind).

Now he was really laughing, and he looked less tired. "Lady Worth?" he asked.

"No silences there," I assured him. "She, you see, does not ever need to draw breath. Your turn."

"Very well," he agreed.

"Umm. *Your* mother."

"Slow," he said. "As if she is trying to figure out what was just said."

Now I laughed. *"Your* father?"

"Well," he said, with an odd look, "it depends on his, ah, mood."

I wanted to ask about Mathilde, but I didn't dare. Likely he would have said something to cast me into the dismals, like *irresistible,* or *bewitching* or *smoldering.* "Me," I said, instead.

"You." He looked at me for a long moment. "I don't know, Gwen. They're just sort of . . . *you.* Unexpected, perhaps, in that I never exactly know how they are going to end."

I moved in my chair, which had the miraculous effect of parting my wrapper. I saw his gaze drop to the scrap of lace that almost covered my breasts. "Do you like that?" I asked.

He looked startled for the merest instant.

"I meant, the fact that you don't know how my silences are going to end," I said, leaning toward him, so that the wrapper opened further.

"Very much," he said, gently, as I took a deep breath and the scrap of lace threatened to shimmer down altogether.

His eyebrow went up, and he looked at me. I smiled, slowly, at him.

"I collect you are testing my fortitude again?" he asked, coolly. He leaned forward in his chair. "I am flattered."

"You are?" Flattered was not precisely the reaction I'd been hoping for.

"Of course." He smiled gently. The smile, I realized, of a man trying to let a lady down as politely as possible. What had happened to the Cambourne who had more or less threatened to tear my clothing off on the library floor? "What man would not be?" he finished.

I raised a brow at *him*. "A rather cool reaction, don't you think?" I said. "Although one might suppose this type of thing happens to you frequently."

"That females come tripping through the door into my bedchamber unannounced discussing silences and dressed for seduction?" He shook his head. "I can't think of the last time."

"I am glad you are finding this humorous," I replied, the heat of anger seeping through my blood. I stood slowly. "But let us see how funny you think this is." And then I untied my voluminous wrapper entirely and shrugged it off, letting it pool at my feet. I forced my chin high as I stood before him in that insubstantial bit of lace, and forced myself to meet his gaze.

He was smiling, but his hands, I noticed, were gripped tight on the arms of his chair. To a casual observer, he still would have appeared entirely relaxed in his chair.

"It's such a shame, really," I said. "That this will go to waste."

"Yes." He smiled, tightly. "But then, at least you may console yourself with the fact that not much fabric was wasted."

"No," I said, drawing my finger lightly but deliberately down my throat, to where the neck dipped. "Scarcely more than a few scraps, really, I suppose." His eyes, I noticed, followed the path taken by my finger, and he swallowed. "It's awfully flimsy," I said. "Look, one can see right through it." I slid my finger down toward my breast, molding the transparent fabric against my skin, as I felt the weight of my own breast in my hand. "It is quite shocking what a person can see."

"Perhaps you should complain to the modiste," he suggested. His tones were still measured, but his color, I noticed, was considerably higher.

I nodded. "It's not all that well-made, either. I'm a bit concerned, in fact," I said, taking a few steps closer, keeping my hand on my breast, since I had noticed that he did not seem at all inclined to remove his gaze, "that the entire thing might just *fall* off at the least provocation." I shrugged off a shoulder strap, just to demonstrate my point, and the sheer fabric slipped low.

His eyes seemed riveted to the skin I had just exposed. I was beginning to feel a burst of something like power. He wanted to resist me, I knew, but he was beginning to find it difficult. "Were I to sneeze, for example," I told him, "there is every possibility that the entire thing would be in tatters." I shrugged, just a bit, and the other strap slid dangerously close to the slope of my shoulder.

"Well, in that case, perhaps you should put your robe back on," he suggested drily. "We wouldn't want you to take a chill."

"I'm not worried about that." I moved closer to him. It meant I was giving up the light of the fire behind me, shining through the transparent gown, but I was gaining proximity. His hands were still gripping the arms of his chair, and his eyes were hooded. "In fact, I'm practically burning," I told him, fanning myself with my hand, which had a hazardous effect on the not-very-secure fastenings of my gown. "But then, perhaps you'd like to feel that for yourself, how warm I am." I reached for his hand.

But he pulled it away. "I'm just a little warm myself," he said.

I looked straight into his eyes. "But are you burning?" I asked.

"I think I can safely say, yes. I am," he replied, coolly, looking straight back into mine.

"Then why not, Harry?" I asked, thinking that perhaps the best approach was an honest one. "Since we both want to."

"Yes," he agreed. "I want to, all right. More than I can tell you. But it would be wrong."

"You sound like a man of the cloth," I said. "Perhaps if Milburn takes to being the earl, you will find you have the calling and take orders. Do I understand that you are a man of too much honor to accept what I have so freely offered? Or," I taunted, untying the ribbons at the front entirely, "is it that beneath it all the rakish Earl of Cambourne is nothing more than a prosy old bore? Next you'll be digging up St. Dunstan's!"

His lips tightened, as his eyes followed my hands. "For a blushing maiden you're awfully sure of yourself," he said.

"That," I said, "is because I understand you, Cambourne, enough anyway to know that you want me." I let the ribbons slip from my hands as the lacing fell open. I deliberately allowed my gaze to sweep over him and I smiled. "Those are some pretty tight breeches." I pulled my gaze up again, to his face. "And judging from what I see there, if you decline to take me, it will not be out of lack of desire."

His jaw tightened. "Do I understand, then," he said, furiously, "that if I try to conduct myself with some accounting of honor, I am to be accounted a martyr to myself?"

"Yes," I said, heedless, "yes, damn it, Cambourne, you *are* a martyr to yourself and your honor."

He stood and took a step nearer and raised a brow.

"Strong language from a girl who always does what she is told."

"Yes, well, marriage to you has changed that," I said, almost enjoying the danger of the fact that I was making him angry.

"This hasn't been marriage, Gwen," he said, his tones suddenly low and dangerous.

"Then show me, Cambourne," I said, unlacing the next set of ribbons, aware that I was barely covered. "What is marriage?"

His eyes narrowed. "I seem to recall obedience being mentioned."

"Would that have been along with love, honor, and cherish?" I replied. "And something about worshiping me with your body?"

He laughed. "God, you have a sharp tongue, Gwen," he said. "Am I to think that you invaded my bedchamber, dressed in virtually nothing, to demand an accounting of my sins?" And while he was saying that, he reached out and closed his hand around my wrist.

"No," I said, after a moment, "but I think you refuse to recognize your greatest sin."

He raised a brow, pulling me nearer. "Which is?"

I resisted his tug. "Your nobility."

"That's a sin?"

"Not in and of itself, perhaps, but it is if you delude yourself that your nobility is in the name of a greater good," I said.

"Jesus," he said.

"Cambourne," I said, softly. "Do you recall that morning that we were out riding, and you told me that I made you look at aspects of yourself that you'd rather ignore?"

He let out a long, frustrated breath. And then he added,

"Yes. Unfortunately." I could see that I was straining the edge of his patience, but I wanted him angry.

I took a deep breath and decided to take a risk. "I think you said it because you are yourself with me." I looked at him, daring him to tell me otherwise. "You're Harry rather than the Earl of Cambourne, future duke."

He took another step nearer.

"You forget your honor and all those cold rules of comportment and duty then."

His unfailing polish seemed to have deserted him. His hair was disheveled, and he looked truly, genuinely angry.

"And your land and your sheep and your tenants and your vicars," I added. "You can admit that you need something from someone."

"Oh, I've found that plenty of other places," he said, his gaze traveling up over what was so clearly on offer.

"It's more," I said, "and you know it. You play the cello," I said. "Even though there's nothing in it for you except pleasure. No duty, no tangible reward." There was a blaze of something in his eyes, and I would have looked down, so suddenly nervous was I, but he put a hand under my chin, denying me that possibility.

"Very well, Gwen. We'll talk about your faults, too. You, you are always after the easy way. And that, if you are honest, is why you were so reluctant from the first to acknowledge—really acknowledge, rather than just allow it to be there—what hangs between us, and that it will always be there. Two, five, twenty years from now, all I'll have to do is look at you over Christmas dinner. We'll be wed to other people, surrounded by our children, and it will still be there, burning, and we both know it."

I tried to look away, but he wouldn't allow it. "You don't love Milburn and he has never loved you. He's always seen you as the girl he was told to marry; as you were when you were two, or six, or ten. But still, you have been intent on clinging to the safety of that marriage, because I frighten you, Gwen. I see you as you *are.*"

"And how am I?" I whispered.

"A lot more like your mother than you'd like to believe, for one thing," he said, and I gasped.

"How can you say that?" I asked. "That's a terrible thing."

"But it's not," he said, quietly. "It's only a terrible thing because your father is not an equal. It could be a wonderful thing if he was. And I'm an equal, Gwen. Sometimes I think I see things in you that you don't even see in yourself."

"But do you like those things?" I asked him.

He smiled, slowly. "Often I do, sometimes I don't, but no more do you always like what you see in me, and it will always be that way with us: a push and pull of wills. Are you game for that challenge?"

My gaze never left his as I jerked my head in what I suppose must have passed for a nod. My heart was beating so hard that I could barely breathe.

"Come to bed, Gwen," he said, suddenly, pulling me toward him hard enough that I was powerless to resist.

I looked at him, at the narrowed eyes, and the intensity in his expression. "What are you doing?"

He pulled me hard against him. "Preparing to worship you with my body. Even though I know there's not a prayer you'll ever obey," he whispered, sliding his lips across my cheek. His lips grazed my earlobe. He licked my top lip.

I leaned into him and moaned as the heat unfurled over me.

"When I am near you, Gwen, I feel that I am standing in your light," he said, against my ear. "Always. Even when you are taking the easy way out."

There was nothing civilized about the way we came together. There was no gentleness between us. It was as if we were ravenous for each other. He pulled me against him, hard, so I could feel that he was fully aroused. I moved, as deliberately provocative as I knew how to be, and the sound he made in his throat was unrecognizable. His lips devoured me, and his hands were everywhere. Sliding up my night rail, stroking me with his fingertips, cupping my breasts, my bottom. He was whispering roughly in my ear about the things he was going to do to me. And how much I was going to like them. Each touch, each whisper, each sigh seemed to intensify the heaviness that had completely taken over my body.

This wasn't him seducing me as it had been that night in the library. This was us, both of us, desperate for each other.

I was tearing at his clothing, yanking his shirt out of his breeches, not caring if I tore the fine linen. Not caring that I should be a shrinking virgin. My shaking hands finally made contact with his skin, sliding up under the shirt, skating over the hard, smooth planes of his chest. He gasped. I lowered them, and brought them down over the flatness of his abdomen, and he swore under his breath. His palms came up, to slide over my nipples, and I bit his shoulder, actually *bit* him. To my surprise he laughed, and tripped backward over something on the floor, pulling me with him as we fell onto the bed so that I landed over him.

"I didn't break the skin, did I?" I asked, suddenly anxious, as we went down.

"I don't know. I don't care," he said, sliding his hands

up the backs of my thighs to my bottom and pressing me to him. I groaned. A most unladylike sound, I am ashamed to say.

He rolled us over, so that he was on top, and lay over me, his thigh between my legs. I could feel him, hard and pressing against just the right places. I would have rocked against him, but his hand came between us and skimmed over just the place that made me gasp. "That," I said, greedily. "Do that again."

I was moaning now, with absolutely no shame. I reached up to cup his face and pull it down toward mine and he did the thing with his hand again and I rocked my hips up against it. Then I licked my way across his lips. He shuddered, and started to pull away. "No." I grabbed at him, desperate for him not to go.

"Gwen," he said, smiling down, looking infinitely less tired than he had earlier. "To do this properly, I really have to undress."

"I'll undress you," I gasped. "Just don't go."

He looked like he wanted to laugh. "You are easily the most demanding virgin I've ever known," he said, but came back against me all the same.

I wrapped my arms around his neck, fitting myself to the length of him. He rocked his hips rhythmically against me. I was straining to get closer still and with every movement, a little mewing noise seemed to come out of my throat. "I'm sorry," I half whispered, half panted.

"About what?" he almost groaned, in my ear.

"I can't seem to stop making noise."

And then he did laugh. "If you'd let me get my clothes off," he whispered into my ear, his voice rough, "I'll make you scream." He rocked against me again and, God help me, I believed him. And even though he sounded awfully arrogant, I declined to take him to task.

I reluctantly let him go. "Hurry," I whispered.

He slanted a laughing look down at me as he stood. "I'm hardly inclined to dawdle," he said, reaching up to pull his shirt over his head, and then unfastening his breeches. He bent, then, and removed his smallclothes. I stared at his body. It had never before occurred to me that unclothed the male body would be a thing of beauty. But he looked like some kind of pagan, golden god with the mellow light from the fire playing over the planes of smooth skin and muscle.

I am deeply shamed to have to admit that I did not avert my eyes in maidenly confusion. Nor even close them. Instead, I leaned forward over the edge of the bed and ran my fingers along the part of him that should indeed have been eliciting the most maidenly blushes from me.

"Jesus." His breath hissed out from between his teeth as he lowered himself to me again. And then he *tore* my new night rail off me. Tore it!

But, in truth, I didn't care. Because his naked body was sliding over mine, hard and firm and warm and satiny, and his lips were against my ear. He settled his weight between my thighs. "I'll worship you later," he whispered. "Right now I just have to *have* you."

I moaned by way of answer.

"Open your eyes," he whispered.

I did, and found myself looking into his eyes, from very close. His lids looked heavy and his eyes were black.

"I want to see you," he said, bracing himself on his arms. "I've imagined this moment a thousand times, and in each of them, I've wanted to see your face."

I wanted to see him too.

And he bent his head to me, brushing his lips once over mine, before saying, "This might be painful—"

"Harry—" I grabbed his face in my palms, and pressed a kiss to his lips "—I don't care, *just do it.*" I lifted my hips to him, urging him on. I truly was wild for him.

And then—just then—someone knocked on the door.

24

In which I learn something I would rather have not

Cambourne *froze over me. "In the name of everything* that is holy," he whispered, hoarsely, "this cannot be happening *again.*"

"Perhaps whoever it is will go away," I whispered back.

"We can hope," he said, low, although I think he was not all that optimistic, because he did not continue with what he had been about to do. Instead he moved back slightly, and ran his thumb over that place again, the one that induced the mewing sounds. He must have seen my lips part, because he brought his other hand up over my mouth. "Ssshhh," he said, laughing, and then replaced his hand with his lips. "Because this is the only certain way of keeping you quiet," he said against my mouth.

"The door . . ." I managed.

"It's locked," he whispered, as I writhed against him.

"I learned a lesson I won't soon forget in the library."

"You in there, Cambourne?" called Milburn's voice from the other side.

"Oh," I breathed out. "It's him. Again. We should— God! What are you doing to me? Oh!"

"Not what I'd like to be," he replied tersely as the knock came again.

"Cambourne?"

"He's right out there," I summoned the presence of mind to articulate.

"I don't care if Wellington's regiment is out there," he said. "I'm not answering. He'll go away."

"Are you in there?" Milburn called. "I think you must be and I ain't going away!"

Cambourne's silky hair brushed against my face. "Damn and blast," he said.

I was getting very close to something, and was finding it increasingly difficult to speak, to control my voice. "Is that how you sweet talk all your women?" I managed to gasp.

"Ssshh. No. Only you, darling," he said, with a smile.

"Harry," I gasped. "Oh God!" Even though he had touched me like this once before, I still had the feeling that were I not so entirely lost to reason, I should have been shocked and horrified instead of urging him on.

"Cambourne!" Milburn again, and this time more insistent. "Giddings told us you had retired for the night. Well, or more precisely that I, Milburn, was in there, retired for the night—"

Cambourne was working some kind of dark magic on me. My drugged mind heard Milburn, registered that he was still outside the door, but I didn't care; like Cambourne, wouldn't have, had it been Wellington's regiment.

"—But, naturally, he meant you, as me, was in there. So I know I am. You are! Answer me, man! Open the door, Cambourne! P'raps I'll try coming through the dressing room!"

Then Cambourne really did swear, long and hard, under his breath before he raised his voice. "Bertie?" he called, doing a credible imitation, I thought, of someone being awakened from a deep sleep. "Is that you, Bert?" he asked, drowsily.

"Cambourne?" called Bertie. "Cambourne! Is that you?"

"Who the hell does he think it is? Boney?" Cambourne muttered before calling, "Yes, it is I. What is it? Quiet, you'll wake the household."

"What are you doing in there?" Bertie howled.

"Sleeping. Or rather, I was," Cambourne replied, as I traced a finger down his chest. He shuddered and caught his breath, and then my hand, to still it.

"Can I come in?" Milburn called.

"Ah—" In some far-off corner of my mind, I was vaguely aware of Cambourne glancing at me, writhing beneath him. "Not sure that's the best idea," he murmured, before raising his voice again. "I'll come down to the drawing room."

"Oh." Milburn sounded as though he was thinking about this. "I s'pose the drawing room is all right," he called, having apparently reached a decision. "But why can't I come in, anyway?" he wanted to know. "Dashed inconvenient, this shouting through the door!"

"Well, we can't have that," Cambourne murmured. "I'm not clothed," he called.

"Nothing I ain't seen before," Bertie shouted back. "Hey!" he shouted as though a new idea was occurring to him as he spoke. "You ain't got a female in there, have you? A high flyer or something?" Bertie called.

"In your bedroom, brother? I shouldn't dream of it," Cambourne replied. "Just go belowstairs and I will be down in a moment."

We heard him retreat. Despite my best efforts to keep myself still, I was writhing and panting against Cambourne now.

He kissed me, long and deep. "Let it happen, Gwen," he said against my lips. "I'm not going to be able to make love to you, but at least give me the pleasure of giving you pleasure." He moved his hand, with certainty, and lowered his head to my breast, to catch the very tip between his teeth.

And what could I do but oblige?

Fortunately, his lips were still over mine, swallowing the scream that he had, as promised, managed to elicit as I tumbled over into an abyss. An abyss so heavenly that I was not entirely certain I wanted to climb out of, it occurred to me, as he gathered me close against him. "I have to go," he said, eventually, into my hair.

"Oh Harry," I breathed, when I had regained my ability to form words. Which did not, I assure you, sound quite so trite at the moment as it no doubt does in the retelling.

As he smoothed the sweaty hair back from my face I heard the thump of heavy footsteps approaching and I rubbed my cheek over the silkiness of his shoulder, then the roughness of his chin.

"What now?" Cambourne sighed.

"What the deuce is taking you so long, brother?" Milburn yelled.

"I am . . . dressing," Cambourne replied, still holding me tight against him.

"No need to take an age about it, y'know. It's Mathilde. She's in a terrible taking. Said you was supposed to meet her, vastly important, etcetera. The woman's furious and she's waiting belowstairs, tapping her foot."

The blood that ran through my veins was like ice. "*That* explains why you were so conveniently at home this evening: you had an assignation planned for later. In *my* house?"

"Don't look at me like that. This is not what you are thinking. We did not have an assignation planned in your house."

"I don't give a damn whose house it was for. I give a damn that it *was.*" I jumped off the bed, vaguely aware that my legs were shaking beneath me. He handed me my wrapper and then, oh-so-politely turned his back. "You have finished *servicing* me, so now you may go on to your next appointment," I said, coldly.

And then a new, horrible thought struck me. "Mathilde," I whispered, so shocked I was simply standing and staring at him as he again turned to face me. "She *knows* that you are you. That you've switched places."

"Yes." He finished pulling his shirt over his head and then looked directly at me. "She does. She has since the very beginning."

And that, somehow, was the worst betrayal of all. "Exactly how close are you?" I asked.

"Honestly, Gwen?" he said, looking up at me. "We have been very close in the past."

"But what about now? Have you been carrying on your *affaire* under my nose?" I debated asking him if he knew that she and Bertie had become . . . intimate, but did not.

He shook his head, as he sat down to pull his boots on.

"I don't understand you," I whispered, wrapping my arms around myself for warmth. "Or myself, either, come to think of it. I want to give myself to you completely, and yet, I hate you."

"Sounds suspiciously like love," he said, drily.

"Why are you leaving, Cambourne?" I asked, no longer feeling I possessed the energy to be anything but blunt.

"I have no choice, Gwen," he said, as he began to close his shirt. "You think I do everything for honor? Well, the fact is that I have been dishonorable enough that I may have ruined everything these last few months."

"*You* have been dishonorable?" I asked. "In what way?"

He laughed, although without amusement, it seemed to me, and turned away to put a cravat around his neck. "I suppose I ought begin with the fact that I put myself into a corner where I had no choice but to give away titles that don't belong to me," he said.

I stared at him.

"I hold them for the next duke. If I am who I should be—who I have always strived to be—they will thrive and go forward to the next generation. I have always treated this as a trust. But it's not *mine* and I don't have the right to bestow it on anyone else."

"But you had no choice," I whispered. "Surely?"

"Oh, you're right," he said. "But I made sure of that by what I had already done."

I frowned, as his fingers began slipping the cravat into a knot. "What had you done?" I held my breath, while I waited for an answer.

He turned away from the mirror, so our gazes met. "I was weak," he said so softly that I could barely hear him.

"How?" I asked.

"I married you," he said, simply, and my heart dropped. "Your father's coming to me offered me a way to play for time for Milburn, by pretending to be him. But while your parents are telling you the truth—that I knew before I did it that they had changed those names, that it would be a legal marriage—they don't know the whole of it. They think they were manipulating *me,* but the truth is that I let them, because I wanted you and I took you."

I could not pull my eyes away from him.

"I, who have always prided myself on doing what is right—honor comes before all, you're right, Gwen—just took what I wanted, even though I knew it to be wrong. And now, it seems, we will all pay for it."

"And what is wrong with being a person, Harry?" I asked. Tears were running down my face. "With allowing yourself your humanity?"

"Oh, I'm human," he said. "Damnably human. Just as willing as the next fellow to throw away my beliefs to get what I want, it seems. And tonight, well"—he shrugged his sleeves into his jacket—"I chose to stay here and dally with you. And now, I have to go figure out how to pay the price."

"But why?" I asked, as I hugged my knees to my chest. "Why did you do it, Cambourne?"

He ran a hand through his hair. "Do you save your correspondence, Gwen?"

"Yes," I told him, not sure why he wanted to know.

"It is still in my chamber at my parents' house."

"Perhaps," he said, lightly, "you might try rereading some of your letters with the eyes of the woman you are becoming. And I am afraid that now I must ask you to excuse me, as it seems I've business to attend to below-stairs."

25

In which I search for Cambourne's letters and make
a most harrowing discovery

*I*mmediately the next morning, I hared over to my parents' house. I emerged from the carriage, if not at a run, at
a distinctly unseemly pace, and continued thus up the
front steps. I was through the door and headed up to my
old bedchamber before Ladimer had managed so much as
a greeting.

"Good morning, Ladimer," I had called over my shoulder. "Don't bother about me, I'm only here to retrieve
something from my old bedchamber. I'll be done in a
trice."

I burst through the door, hardly able to contain myself,
and then, as inelegantly as a team of horses with Milburn
at the reins, I skidded to a halt. It was gone. All of it. My
bed, my clothespress, my reclining sofa, my chairs, my
desk. The soft peach silk on the walls had been replaced
by stark white paint. Even the draperies were gone.

I looked around more carefully. Now that I was paying attention, there *was* a faint smell in the air, of . . . linseed oil? The rug was splotched with paint, and a pile of palettes and brushes stood on a rough wooden table. Standing against the far wall was a group of canvases. I walked over and looked at the first one. Not altogether horrible. It was a bowl of fruit and I was fairly certain I could identify cherries, either a peach or an apple, and that the fuzzy purple mass was intended to be a bunch of grapes. The signature in the corner was "A.E." My mother. I pulled that one away from the wall and tipped my head to look at the next. Primroses, I thought, growing in a garden, but she must have got some of the green of the grass mixed into her yellow, because the flowers were sort of a sickly color. The third was a huge naked woman in a purple turban—that is, the naked woman was huge, the canvas was the same size as all the rest.

I gasped in horror, and the canvases slipped out of my hand and banged back against the wall. It was Violetta! Naked! Reclining on purple cushions and eating grapes, no less. I covered my eyes, even though it was no longer visible. Naked! Not even Reubens's famed paintings were fully naked. I had seen Violetta unclothed! Argh! I was bound to have nightmares for years.

I backed out of the room, and, naturally, smack into my mother. She immediately launched into a diatribe. "Ladimer tells me that you barged past him with excessive speed, Gwendolyn, without so much as giving him time to announce you properly."

"My—my chamber!" I managed to stutter, my tongue still tied by the horror of what I had so recently seen.

"I have converted it," she said, airily, as she stepped past me and into the room. "To a studio. Ernesto—my art tutor—is convinced that I have *talent*. *Talent* like this, he says, must be carefully nurtured. Cared for. Fed. Sustained. Strengthened. Fostered. Cultivated. Call it what you will, I have quite come to dote on it. The talent, that is. Having perfected my natural objets—note, if you will, the astoundingly lifelike aspect to my pear—"

"I thought that was a peach," I could not resist saying. "Or possibly an apple."

"That," she said, "is because you do not have the *eye*. I have now moved on to the greatest challenge an artist can face: the human form. It is not generally *done,* of course, for the female to paint the unclothed human form. But I, as you know, have always prided myself on being an exceptional female! And Ernesto agrees—"

"What happened to my things, my furniture?" I asked, cutting her words off.

"Why?" she said, turning a gimlet eye on me.

"I am looking for something. Some papers that I kept in the escritoire."

She directed a keen glance at me. "Papers. Is that what you called that pile of junk cluttering up the drawers?"

"Where are they?" I persisted.

She shrugged. "I suppose they were thrown away. You know I cannot abide clutter."

"That clutter," I said, beginning to feel truly stricken, "was composed of my letters, all my documents. Everything that could someday prove I existed."

"Not your marriage lines," she said with asperity as she stepped into the corridor and turned away. "Some of it may be in the attics," she called over her shoulder. "Some was likely sent home to the country, and the gardener burned the rest. Now, I am off to don my smock. And by the way, I am having a dinner. To celebrate the return of your brother-in-law, Cambourne, and to give him a chance to fete you, the new addition to his family. He has already accepted and I fully expect you and Milburn to as well. Friday evening at seven of the clock. No excuses shall be entertained!"

I closed my eyes for a moment, wishing for a serenity I did not possess. Oh God, she must mean that Milburn had accepted as Cambourne. What on earth was that idiot thinking? I also seemed to have a vision of the reclining, unclothed, Violetta permanently imprinted on the inside of my lids. So much for serenity. I shuddered and snapped them open. "Did you forget what I said about inviting Milburn to my bed should you try to interfere?" I asked.

She stepped back into the room, and put her face very close to mine. "You may have changed, daughter," she said, pronouncing each word very distinctly, "but not so much that I can't still make your life a misery. If you want to tempt me to do so by inviting that miserable little fribble to your bed, you may certainly do so, but do bear in mind all the while that I want you to be a duchess and a duchess you will be." And then she tucked a paintbrush behind her ear and made her departure.

I set off for the attics, resolving to tackle the issues of my mother's dinner and Milburn's idiocy later. After an hour of poking about in the vast piles that seemed to fill the attic to overflowing, I had come up empty-handed. For a woman who professed to loathe clutter, my mother certainly seemed to have amassed a good deal of it.

Finally, as I was about to give up the search, I saw just

a corner of the light blue silk ribbon that had been around some of my letters from my school friends. I dove deeper into the pile, and scrabbled about, in the hope that something else of mine would have been unceremoniously dumped there. And there, finally, under my grammar composition book from the year I was seven were the letters. I grabbed the pile and headed for the stairs, running down the four flights at a trot, and out the door to the carriage.

It was an act of will, to sit in the carriage, watching the streets and houses pass by, and not so much as peek at a letter, but I forced myself to wait until I was alone in my bedchamber. I sank down in a chair and untied the ribbon with trembling hands. I could hardly even bring myself to read them in their entirety. Instead, little pieces seemed to jump out at me, from different letters, different seasons, different years.

> *. . . Perhaps it is this war, and Bertie being gone, but I find myself savoring the lengthening days here in a way I had not thought to. The light, the air, all seem somehow different here . . .*

> *. . . I read a book in your garden today,* The Dark Castle, or, Count Armando's Revenge. *Your name was scrawled in the flyleaf, and I felt your presence as I read. Goodness, you do read the most awful trash! I took it home with me to finish at my leisure, surely no rational person could sleep at night without having learned whether Count Armando was truly a werewolf . . .*

. . . Have you already torn the paper off the attached package, Gwen? Or are you being restrained and reading this first? In that unlikely event, I will tell you what it contains: The south meadow at Hildcote is so entirely covered in blue-bells this year it looks to be carpeted in blue. I have never seen it this way before and do not know whether it is the meadow or my vision that is different. It occurred to me, though, that as you are not to be here this spring, you will not see it. To that end, I engaged Mr. Thomas Wilkins to capture it on canvas for you. I think it a most credible effort . . .

I let the letters fall into my lap. Tears were running down my face, and I let them. How had I ever thought that these were only amiable letters from a childhood friend? There was nothing untoward in any of them. But suddenly shimmering clearly before my eyes was the fact that they spoke of love in ways that impassioned avowals never would. As I sat, staring ahead, the letters on my lap, it seemed inconceivable to me that I had been so blind. What Bertie had said was true: Cambourne *did* love me.

It is true that they were not filled with pretty, facile words, or avowals of undying passion. These were filled, instead, with *him,* with reminders of how deep our roots together went. With the man who, underneath a veneer of aloof sophistication, noticed the light and the bluebells. Who took home a book to finish because it was mine (and, believe me, having read that book, there was no reason having to do with literary merit).

And had chosen to share himself with me, to love *me* enough to trust me with his thoughts. And although I well understood that Cambourne had shared his body with any number of women over the years, I knew that this was a part of himself he had not.

Also, shimmering clearly before my eyes was the knowledge that I loved him, too. With all his faults, his arrogance, his secretiveness, and possibly even his mistress, I loved him, and likely had since the moment he had taken my hand in front of the altar.

Less pleasing, however, was my sudden understanding that he did love his birthright and his land, that it was too deeply a part of him for him to ever give up. And surely the people who depended on the estates that went with the titles deserved a better lord than Milburn? I stared at the little gilt framed picture of the bluebells that had hung on my bedchamber wall—wherever that bedchamber might be—since I had received it.

I admit, that for a few moments I indulged in some rather bleakly romantic fantasies of disappearing from London, never to be heard from again. Cambourne would be heartbroken, naturally, but eventually would return to his birthright, marry sensibly, and abide by his duty (pining for me, of course), while I, a study in self-lessness, lived quietly in a small town—perhaps a simple cottage by the sea? A garret?—doing good works and devoting myself to spinsterish pursuits. It occurred to me, though, that I did not precisely know what a garret was, or even whether I would find it comfortable, which, it seemed to me, was taking selflessness entirely too far.

No, I would simply have to find a way for Cambourne

to have his land, salvage his belief in his own honor, accept his frailties, and have me, too.

A small undertaking.

Particularly as I never would have imagined that someone living under the same roof could disappear so thoroughly as Cambourne did for the few days that followed. Discreet inquiries amongst the staff confirmed that he was still residing on the premises, although one would never have guessed it. I did hear him come in, the night after I had read the letters, and lay in agonies of hope that he would stop at my door. Alas, his light tread continued past without pause. By the time I arose the next morning, he was gone, and had been since before daybreak, my informant (well, all right, it was Mrs. Harbison, if you *insist* upon knowing) told me.

The next night, I heard him come in and make his way down the corridor. His tread was stealthier than usual, and I wondered whether he had guessed I was lying awake, waiting. I had planned to let him pass by, unaccosted, but my body sprang out of bed, without much cooperation from my mind. I grabbed the infamous cabbage wrapper and swung the door open. He was leaning against the wall opposite, staring at my door. His hair gleamed in the light of the sconces that had been left burning, and he looked . . . hungry. At my appearance, he smiled. "Hello, Gwen."

"Cambourne," I said. "What are you doing?"

"Leaning against the wall," he told me.

"Yes," I said. "I can see that. But why?"

"Because," he said, enunciating very precisely, "I am foxed thanks to your curst brother James and his liberal hand with the bottle. And, too," he added, "because I wanted to be."

I looked at him more closely. I would never have guessed it, but now that I knew, I could see that his color was high and that there was a hectic glitter in his eyes. "Oh," I said. "I see." And then, after a moment, I said, "Would you like to come in?"

He shook his head. "Actually," he said. "I think that would be inadvisable."

His hand, I noticed, was bandaged. "What happened?" He shrugged. "I punched a windowpane at White's."

"Are you all right?" I asked.

"Yes," he replied. "Only foxed, like a coward, and still hating myself, despite it."

Don't hate yourself because of me. I can't bear it, I wanted to say. "Oh, dear. Can I do anything?" is what I did say. I hoped that he would ask me to kiss his wounds, soothe his brow, or whatever it was that a gentleman needed at such a time.

But he only said, "Yes. Don't fuss."

"Very well, I won't. But may I ask you a question?"

He smiled crookedly. "Can I stop you?"

I shook my head. "I've been wondering this entire time, Cambourne. The whole of London and half the countryside knew I was promised to Milburn. When you decided to marry me, how," I asked, "did you plan to explain to the world at large that you had taken Milburn's place?"

He stopped smiling. "I don't know," he said.

I stared at him. "You don't know? Do you mean you had no plan? No way to save yourself from the scandal of having switched places at the altar and then hared around London having pretended to be your brother?"

"My plan, Gwen?" he said. "My only plan was this."

And then he moved toward me quickly, the drink having apparently not dulled his grace in any way. He pulled me tight against him. "This," he repeated as he touched his lips to mine. Falling into me, deepening the kiss, making me feel his hunger. His heartbeat pounded against mine. I opened my lips beneath his and he kissed me like he would never stop. Unlike our previous kisses, there was no teasing, no element of seduction to this, only need. It felt as though he were trying to memorize me. And I let him. Tried to memorize him back as I felt the dizziness overwhelm me, and the thundering of his heart against mine. I was completely lost in the moment, in the harsh rhythms of his breathing, and the need I could feel in his kiss. I would have liked to stay like that forever.

Eventually, though, he lifted his head, and I was startled to see tears in his eyes. "That was it," he said, brokenly, "and it failed. Because I wanted something so much that I let it overwhelm me. And all over a secret, Gwen. But a secret that's not mine to tell."

"Good night," I heard him say as he resumed his passage to his chamber.

My eyes were swollen almost shut the next morning from having spent more or less the entire night in tears. Cambourne's misery seemed to have crept inside me. But Cecy withheld comment until I had poured out the whole story.

"Lud. I'd be blubbing, too, if it had been me who had seen Violetta naked," she said.

"But he loves me," I sobbed. "Enough to have just married me with no plan, nothing. And I love him, too."

"Stop being such a widgeon," she said briskly. "We *must* decide what is to be done. Where is Myrtia?"

"She took Therèse with her to the Foundling Hospital."

Cecy raised a brow. "Do I understand that Therèse is taking up charity work?"

I sniffled into my handkerchief. "I suspect it was more the promise of bonnet shopping and a treat at Gunter's following that induced her to go."

"Well, that unfortunately leaves us without Myrtia, but fortunately without Therèse, who is lovely, but can be a distraction."

"But Cecy," I protested, "should we not be concerned with your problems for a change?"

She smiled tightly. "My problems, for the moment at least, can only be unraveled with the cooperation of those causing them. Yours somehow seem infinitely more likely to be solved with a little plotting and planning."

"Cec," I said. "Where *is* your mother?" I had not seen Lady Wainwright for quite some time.

"Oh," she said, airily. "She has taken herself off—temporarily only, unfortunately—with the new footman. Thomas's replacement."

"Cec—" I began.

She interrupted. "Gwen. Let us get you sorted. Then, I promise, we can turn our entire attention to dissecting every aspect of my life. Now, what do you want?"

"Cambourne. And I know what I *don't* want," I said. "To be married to Milburn. I never understood until now how important it is to be married to someone you truly want.

Oh, Cec," I said, the tears suddenly beginning again. "What am I going to do? Cambourne was utterly miserable, he seemed . . . defeated, almost. I've never even imagined him that way."

"I know you will think this suggestion revoltingly unworthy of me," she said, "but there is always honesty. Have you thought of that? Simply going to him and confessing that you are in love with him and trying together to find a way out of this mess?"

I shook my head.

"No, well, I thought not, of course." She sighed, theatrically. "Honesty so rarely accomplishes anything. Subterfuge is generally much more effective, although frequently so fatiguing to plan!"

"The thing is that he might well come up with something," I said. "But this is where *I* have to prove myself to him, I think. I already know he was willing to sacrifice for me. That he married me with no plan, but what about me?"

Cecy gave me a long look. "What about that party your mother is having to celebrate Cambourne's return?"

"What about it?" I asked. "Did she send you a card?"

"Yes," Cecy said. "She did, but I had to decline. One assumes that my mother will have tired of the footman by then and will be back. I am not bringing her to any more entertainments."

As much as I would have liked Cecy there, I could hardly quibble with that decision. "Understandable," I said. "But what about the party?"

"Do you think she has a plan?" she asked. "Something to force Cambourne's hand?"

"Does she breathe?" I replied. "Of course she does."

Cecy shrugged. "So let her."

I stared at her. "Let my mother force him into staying married to me?"

"Why not?" she asked. "You want it. He wants it. Let her do the work for you."

"I don't know," I said, thinking. "It seems the wrong way to go about it. If anyone is going to force Cambourne into having me, it should be me."

"But perhaps that's precisely the point. That is what you are willing to sacrifice to have him." And then, before I could reply, she continued, "Unless, of course, this has more to do with resisting your mother's wishes than with what you both want?"

I dropped my gaze. "It's not that precisely," I began. "It's—"

"Pride, Gwen," she reminded me. "And stubbornness. Your besetting sins."

"Are you implying that I would be telling Cambourne more about my feelings for him if I *allowed* my mother to strong-arm him into having me?"

She smiled. "Perhaps it would be a good bargaining tool. He can prove he wants you by telling you this great secret. You can prove you want him by hopelessly, and publicly, compromising him—and yourself—during your mother's dinner."

"Not bad," I had to admit. "But little does Mother know that she's going to be forcing Milburn's hand, because she really believes him to be Cambourne."

"And?"

"And," I said, sitting up straighter, "I'm thinking that to begin with, there's absolutely no reason I shouldn't stop by Cambourne House and convince Milburn to assist me."

"How?" she asked. "I thought he was set against it."

"Well," I replied, "I am thinking that it cannot harm anything if I give Milburn a little taste of what life with me would be like, can it, Cecy?"

"Oh," she said, looking pleased. "Now we are getting somewhere!"

26

In which I pay a visit to Bertie

"*H*allo, Cambourne," I said, after I had been announced and then ushered through the myriad corridors that led to the study where Milburn was sitting behind the huge mahogany desk that had no doubt belonged to his grandfather, and his grandfather, and *his* grandfather before him. It was a hideous behemoth of a thing, actually. One of the grandfathers definitely should have got rid of it years ago. I shivered and drew my shawl more tightly around me. God, but this house was miserable, almost miserable enough to make me falter in my determination to have its owner.

And it was not lost upon me that its ersatz owner did not look precisely overjoyed to see me at the moment. "Hallo, Gwen," he said, irritably. "Curst ledgers." He pushed them aside and shoved his hands through his hair, apparently oblivious to the damage he was doing to his coiffure. "To what do I owe the honor of this visit?" he asked before recalling his manners and standing.

I made my voice heavy with meaning. "I have come, Milburn," I said, "to take my rightful place by your side. Give Cambourne back his ledgers, his problems, and his mistress. You can have me, after all."

"Oh," he said, eyeing me warily.

"And don't worry, Milburn, I understand that you have been exhausted by Mathilde's . . . knowing ways. Rest assured that I have been well instructed by my mama as to how a good wife is expected to summon all her fortitude and composure during The Act, thus avoiding acknowledging the horrors that are being perpetrated upon her body in the name of conceiving an heir. I shall," I assured him, "have such perfect composure that you will barely know I'm there!"

His enthusiasm seemed somewhat tempered as he replied. "Oh. Good."

"Yes," I said, advancing a step on him. "I have come to see that you are correct. Cambourne needs his land, and you need me!"

"How so?" he asked.

"Look at you, Milburn," I said. "Going through life, making nothing of yourself. And do you know why I think that is?" And then, without letting him reply, I continued: "It's because you don't have the right woman behind you! Helping you, championing you, planning for you, pushing you ever forward."

"Oh," he said, eyeing me with even more disfavor than before.

"Sit down, Milburn." I placed a hand on his chest and more or less pushed him onto a miserably uncomfortable-looking chair. I stood over him. "First, you need a purpose. I have given this a great deal of thought, and I think Enclosures will do."

"Enclosures?" he asked, looking up at me.

"Yes. The Enclosure Acts. It's a fascinating area of agricultural legislation. Or so I think you will find when you are more conversant with the finer points. But the important thing is that we throw ourselves into this with devotion and vigor. I have taken the liberty of dashing off a letter to Mr. Stephen Fairfax-Lacy, a great crony of Cambourne's and one of the foremost authorities in the country on the subject!"

He squinted up at me from the chair. "What gives here, Gwen?" he asked.

"As I've already told you, I am here to offer myself to you."

"Believe it or not, I ain't that stupid, Gwen," he said. "What game are you playing at?"

Calling my bluff, was he? "You know, Milburn," I said, loudly, "I do think that before we tell Cambourne about my decision, we ought to ensure that everything is nicely . . . tied up by making certain that there could be at least a chance that I am increasing. Do you not?"

"Suppose so," he said, unenthusiastically.

"I do believe," I suggested, "that we ought to go above-stairs right now and get to seeing about that *before* we tell Cambourne. Just so he has no means of objection, you understand."

"Right now?" he asked.

"Yes, of course." I frowned at him to imply that there was no time like the present. "I would think you would want to get about this quickly. And I have heard that gentlemen are always enthusiastic for this activity. As for myself, I intend to inventory the household linens in my head as per Mama's recommendation."

"How enticing," he muttered gloomily.

"Mama is a great believer, you must know, in killing two birds with one stone." I started for the corridor. "Well, let's be quick about this. Efficiency! Which way is your bedchamber?"

He had yet, I noted, to stir from his chair. I turned around and put my hands on my hips. "Never tell me that you are lagging off the mark at this, too, Milburn?"

"All right, Gwen, sit down and cut line," he said, and I went back into the room and took a seat opposite his. "It's patently obvious that you are head over heels with Cambourne, and you no more want to run upstairs with me than I want to familiarize myself with the Enclosure Acts. Again, what game are you playing at?"

"I see we understand one another," I said.

"Perfectly, m'fraid," he replied. "So tell me what you're really doing here."

"Very well, Milburn. The thing of it is, that I've done a good deal of thinking over the last few weeks. Cambourne needs his birthright back. He can no more give it up than he can stop breathing, and he never truly intended to. And deep down, you know that, as does he. And besides," I pointed out. "You hate it." I motioned around. "This house"—I shuddered—"well, actually, who wouldn't hate this house? The responsibilities, the details, the tedium—"

"The clothing!" he interjected, a spark of the old Milburn in his eyes.

"The clothing," I agreed. "And I know that you'd dearly like nothing more than to give it up. But I also know that you're furious at Cambourne, and you don't want to do it without causing him distress."

"That is true enough," he replied steadily.

"Well, it seems that what I'm here to say is that either

you do it, let him have his birthright back *and* let him have me *and* do your best to make Therèse a good husband (when you marry her, legally, this time) or I will do it. I'll marry you, Milburn, and I'll become just that type of wife, Enclosure Acts and all. Because you're right, I do love your brother, and I'm fully prepared to walk away if he can only have one: me or his titles. That does not mean, however, that I won't devote myself to making the rest of your life a misery."

See? I had learned something from Mama!

"You really do mean that!" he sounded surprised. "His happiness is worth more to you than your own?"

"Absolutely," I said.

"But why should I care about that?" he asked.

"Because I know you, Bertie," I said. "I've known you for a long time, and this isn't like you. I understand that you are angry, but I don't truly believe that you want to do this to Cambourne. Particularly since it is obvious that this arrangement is not making you happy either."

"Well, I have said all along that I'm willing to take you and give him the titles."

"Look, Bertie," I said, leaning toward him. "We both love Cambourne. If you don't love him enough, I *will* marry you, but I can more or less guarantee that it won't be that easy, undemanding marriage you've always counted on."

"What do you mean by that, Gwen?" he asked.

"There's more out there and I know it now, Bertie. *I'm* not the same easy, undemanding person anymore. You know all that material on the Corn Laws that I read? I found it pretty interesting, actually. I wouldn't mind writing your speeches."

"Good Lord!" he said with real horror. "You are turning into your mother!"

"I think that's the point, Bertie," I said. "With you, that has the potential to happen because you're not interested in a challenging marriage. You want an easy marriage, and that's fine, but we'll never really be happy together. Cambourne and I will."

He looked at me very intently. "I'm not sure you'll feel that way when you know what propelled us all into this mess in the first place."

I crossed my arms. "I'm certain I will."

"There's no pretty way of putting it, I'm afraid, Gwen. He was blackmailed into it."

I frowned at him. "Marrying me?" I asked. "But I thought that he was protecting you . . . Oh!"

"What?" he squinted at me.

"I *am* a complete idiot for not having figured this out sooner! Of course! He was protecting you, but then my parents found out about the blackmail and used it to their own advantage by threatening to reveal it if he didn't marry me. Unless—" I looked up at him "—you don't think they're actually the ones *doing* it, do you?"

"I honestly do not know," he said. "But doesn't it bother you, Gwen? That he was forced to marry you?"

"Not particularly," I said. "Because he never would have allowed it if he hadn't wanted to. You said that yourself. They thought they were forcing him, but actually he was letting them." I started to laugh. "No wonder he said that odd thing about what he *had* told me being a veritable love poem, though. But, Bertie, what on earth is the secret that they're holding over him?"

"It's my father," he said, giving me an obstinate look. "He's sending money to Mother's relatives for that . . . Corsican monster, Boney, and someone's twigged and is blackmailing Cambourne. Using the threat of revealing that to force Cambourne and me to journey to the Continent."

"Your father supports him?" I asked, struggling to hide my surprise. "What he's doing?"

Bertie shrugged. "Hard to say whether it's really a philosophical decision," he said. "The old boy's half, if not completely, mad, but then, you know that. I think if it wasn't for that fact, Cambourne would probably feel obligated to turn him over to the authorities rather than protect him. I don't think any of the money has actually got to him, though, because as soon as Cambourne found out, he started arranging to have it intercepted. Still, even a rumor about this would be terribly damaging to that revered old family name."

"Yes," I said, as I stood and began gathering my things. "You are absolutely right, and we'll just have to ensure that not even a hint of a rumor gets out. Now, this is what to do: Come to my parents' tomorrow night fully prepared to admit in the end that you are Milburn, or else prepare yourself for becoming the country's new foremost expert in Enclosures."

"The frightening thing here, Gwen," he said, "is that I absolutely believe you."

"Good. Because it would be extremely foolish of you not to," I said.

27

In which my parents hold a dinner party and I am forced to compromise my husband in the second-floor drawing room

"Thank you, Crewes," I said, the next night, as I collected my shawl and reticule and headed for the stairs. I had prepared for my mother's dinner as if going into battle. At the foot of the stairs, I ventured to the pier glass to check that my hair was still wound into the silver ribbon that Crewes had placed there. I'd not laid eyes upon Cambourne since the night he'd been in his cups, and I was not at all certain of what to expect. Certainly he'd not been in very good spirits when we had parted, but he seemed tonight to have rallied himself. "Evening, Gwen," he said amiably as he descended the stairs, making minute adjustments to his cuffs.

He was not rigged out as Milburn this evening, nor was he truly garbed as himself. He was in black, with a white evening shirt, and a modest, although elegantly tied, cravat. His hair fell straight across his forehead and his eyes were, well, completely unreadable. His only concession to dandyism, in fact, was the violent green of his waistcoat. He bowed over my gloved hand. "You are looking very lovely this evening," he said, as his gaze held mine. And then he straightened and turned away to pull on his own gloves.

Thérèse drifted down the stairs, just then, a vision in sea-green tulle, *trés décolleté,* in a cloud of dark curls and scent. She winked at me as Cambourne turned to make his bows. In the carriage, the two of them made light conversation as I gazed out the window and worried.

It was apparent from the blaze of light and crush of carriages as we pulled up at my parents' house, that this was no small, intimate dinner.

"Milburn," my mother said, in cool tones, when he had made his bow. "How nice to see you." And then she turned away to exclaim fulsomely over another new arrival.

His brow was raised as he turned to me. "I seem to have fallen considerably in your mama's estimation," he whispered to me.

"She believes you really *are* Milburn," I whispered back. "I have disappointed her no end by accepting you." And then we were separated as he was borne away by some cronies of Milburn's. I circulated through the rooms, greeting friends and acquaintances and accepting proper introductions to those I'd not met before. I could not help but wonder what these same people would think of me later that evening. But that, I reminded myself firmly, was of no account to me.

I laughed politely, if somewhat absently, at Sir Reginald Blatcheley's witticisms, even though I had heard all of them numerous times before. I waved to Myrtia, who was deep in conversation with James, and noticed Milburn in the corner with Cambourne's friend Atherton. Milburn, I noted, had garbed himself quite similarly to Cambourne this evening. For the first time in a long time, I understood how easy it was for them to switch places at will, particularly at social events where one's conversation with any one person was limited. The Lord Lieutenant from Hildcote told me quite a lengthy tale about a fox that escaped its pursuers and ended up under the bed in the Harleys' second-best chamber. The Dowager Lady Grenham was deep into a digression on her bunions and their seasonal changes when we were summoned in to supper.

Mama had outdone herself. There were at least forty at table, and I will not bore you with the minutiae of the seating arrangements, except to tell you that I was between the Viscount Spenborough on my left, and old Lord Benjamin on my right. The real Cambourne was across the table from me, and Milburn was two down on my left. Cambourne was between Thérèse and the lovely, but very fresh out of the schoolroom, Miss Venetia Lawson.

Milburn said to Cambourne, across the table, "Are you well, brother? You are looking just slightly, oh, I don't know, not up to snuff this evening."

Cambourne sipped his wine. "D'you think, Cambourne? Rothwell thinks me a genius. Verdigris and black," he drawled. "Told me so earlier."

"I agree that you are most splendid indeed, sir," ventured Venetia Lawson.

Cambourne inclined his head. "Thank you, Miss Lawson, but do, please, call me Milburn, or Lord Bertie, if you prefer. But as it happens," he said, languidly, "I must confess that of late, I can no longer find gentlemen's apparel of consuming interest."

"Never say so!" said Spenborough, looking up from his soup for the first time.

"Still look like a demmed man-milliner if y'ask me!" bellowed Lord Benjamin.

"I feel that having done my time, to quote Rothwell, as a visionary, leading my peers forth, I am ready for a rest," said Cambourne, his eyes on Milburn. "And my wife has convinced me to turn my attention in other directions."

"I have?" I whispered.

"Yes, darling," Cambourne replied. "Enclosure Acts, if you recall."

"Yes, now that you mention it, I do." I narrowed my eyes at him. *What were they getting up to? How did he know about that?*

"And the decisions," Cambourne said, shooting me an amused look. "What to wear, which fobs, jewelry, quizzing glasses, canes, etcetera—it was simply becoming too fatiguing."

"Fatiguing for you or the valet?" Spenborough asked his soup bowl.

"Oh, for me," replied Cambourne, those blue eyes as guileless as could be. "I was the one making the decisions, you understand. My wife has convinced me that all of the emphasis on remaining an arbiter of fashion was taxing me overly. My health, you must know, is delicate."

"My—ah, *your* health is delicate, brother?" Milburn asked him in incredulous tones.

"Oh, yes, vastly." Cambourne threw him a limpid glance. "I have been thinking about taking myself away to take the waters at Bath."

Milburn spluttered into his serviette. "Have you, Milburn?" he asked.

Cambourne nodded, and sighed. "I am not certain I am up to the rigors of the Season this year. And, too, I have quite a bit of legislation on Enclosures with which to familiarize myself."

"Good idea, young fellow," suggested the Dowager Lady Grenham, whose hearing—which she professed gave her a great deal of trouble—always became remarkably acute at any discussion of ill health.

"Enclosure Acts! How fascinating," ventured Miss Lawson, bravely undertaking the task of getting the conversation started up again.

Cambourne nodded. "Thank you, Miss Lawson. Ask me anytime, and I shall be glad to undertake educating you on them." He slanted a sly look at Milburn. "But I also have several new hobbies at the moment."

"Oh, *do* tell, Milburn," murmured Milburn. "You are a veritable font of surprises this evening!"

"Well, of course, there is the gardening," replied Cambourne limpidly. "I have always been fascinated by it, but previously was deterred by the thought of the dirt under my fingernails. And I am no longer bothered by the . . . feminine aspect of it, you see."

"Oh, I do, indeed," Milburn assured him with a raised brow. "And one almost hates to ask, but is there more?"

"Only the tatting, really," replied Cambourne. "Lord Bertie's Frivolities, I am calling the products."

It was awfully hard not to laugh. I choked on my wine. I wasn't sure what they were up to, but it *was* amusing.

"Tatting? Lord Bertie's Frivolities?" Milburn almost shrieked. He really had been remarkably calm up to this point.

Thérèse raised a brow at Cambourne. "This lace, it is for your old acolytes to wear, perhaps, Cousin Ber-tee? Since you are such of the visionary?"

I had to look down to hide my laugh.

"I am not yet that expert," Cambourne told her. "For now I am confining myself to doilies."

That, finally, was apparently too much for poor Milburn. "I do not tat!" he cried.

"Well we ain't talking about you, are we, Cambourne?" Spenborough observed.

Just then, my father shouted down the table at Milburn. "Hey! Cambourne! Almeria wants to know what chance you think Preston's motion stands now."

"Preston's motion," echoed Milburn. "That would be Preston's motion on, er . . ."

My father frowned. "You said it was worthless, as I recall. He did say it was worthless, did he not, Almeria?"

"Yes, Axton. Worthless," she replied.

"Oh, right. Well, I said it was worthless because it had no, er, *worth* that I could discern," Milburn said.

"I agree," Spenborough said, around a mouthful of food. "Its lack of control over imports is altogether misguided."

"Imports?" asked Milburn. "Refresh my memory if you will."

"Corn, brother," replied Cambourne through gritted teeth.

"Preston's motion, Cambourne," I told Milburn. "He wants to change the price at which the high duty ceases, according to the Act of 1804. Right now it stands at sixty-three shillings." I *had* done my reading. Cambourne smiled at me, and that warmth licked over me.

A gleam came into Milburn's eyes that I could not like. "Oh, yes, right. Corn Laws," he said, leaning back in his chair, as footmen served the next remove. "Actually, I've quite given those up," he said airily. "Don't look for me in Parliament again. Took an age, but now it's as though I've seen the light in recent months: dashed waste of time all these years, as it turns out, time when I could have been pursuing my real interests."

"Was it, Cambourne?" Cambourne said, as he paused in lifting his glass.

My father's fork clattered to his plate. "Given them up, you say! Almeria did say you'd gone off a bit with this new stance—thought you was in danger of becoming a Whig—but given them up, altogether!"

"I believe what my brother meant with his new stance," Cambourne said, toying with his wineglass, "is that these laws were written with the assumption that every man was dependent upon the land for subsistence. Cambourne—forward-thinking fellow that he is—believes industry will increasingly supplant agriculture, and that it is a foolish man who believes the world he lives in will never change around him. And an even more foolish man who does not prepare for that change."

"Dashed pack of nonsense," my father said. "Right, Almeria? Dashed pack of nonsense?"

"Well, perhaps I did care about that at one point," said Milburn languidly. "But I came to understand that I was turning into quite the dry old stick. Really, I'd become the most dashed, deadly old bore. And at the moment I'm far too busy with *my* new interests to have much time or interest to spare on fusty old Corn Laws."

Apparently two could play at Cambourne's game.

"I didn't think you a bore, brother," Cambourne said.

"Oh, you might not have, but many did, brother, many did." Milburn nodded earnestly. "Why, people were practically running when they saw me approach, I had become so very tedious on the topic."

"You have the new interests, then, also, Cambourne?" Thérèse asked Milburn. "I think this is quite the, how you say, coincidence, is it not?"

"Yes, do tell, brother," said Cambourne, taking a long drink of his wine. "I suspect we are all agog to hear how you have reformed your dull ways."

"Well?" inquired Spenborough. "Don't leave us in suspense, Cambourne."

Milburn nodded. "First, there is the smuggling," he said.

"Smuggling, brother?" Cambourne inquired.

"Smuggling?" my mother echoed, in faint tones.

"I don't actually cross the channel myself," Milburn allowed. "It wouldn't be seemly, given my . . . position and titles, etcetera. But overseeing things takes up a good deal of my time."

"I can see that it would," Cambourne replied.

"And there is a second new interest, I think?" Thérèse prompted.

"Yes, cousin, there is. Although I am quite proud of the fact that I am the first Earl of Cambourne really, well, *ever,* to be engaged in trade," Milburn said, and my mother gasped aloud in horror, "the second is more of a hobby, you understand, in accordance with my own *personal* interests than it is a business venture, although it did spin off quite naturally *from* the smuggling."

"What is it?" my mother practically shrieked.

Milburn raised his voice. "The import and distribution of lewd drawings!"

Cambourne choked at this. "Do I," he asked, when he had finished, "get any type of discount on merchandise as I am family?" he asked.

Milburn laughed. "Touché, brother," he said.

"I've an *entirely* new respect for you, Cambourne," Spenborough said to Milburn.

At this new information from Milburn, my mother had looked doubtful for just a moment, but then, I saw her elbow my father in the ribs. "Ouch," he screamed, as she gave him a meaningful look. "Oh, er, yes, right." He stood. "Ah, Cambourne," he said, looking at Milburn. "Could I have just a quick word in the, er, other room? About, ah, Preston's motion."

Right, I thought, one last quick try at blackmail: Bed my daughter or we reveal that your father's been attempting to commit treason. How nice to have concerned parents!

"Now?" asked Milburn.

"Now?" my father asked my mother. She glared at him. "Er, yes, now," he said, looking again at Milburn, who cast me a glance as he rose. Cambourne looked as if he, too, were about to rise.

"Now," Myrtia mouthed at me.

"Milburn," I said to Cambourne. "Could I have a word with you also?" I raised my voice. "Somewhere private."

My father and Milburn left the room.

My mother stood. "Milburn!" she said to Cambourne.

"Please excuse us," Cambourne said as he came round the table to me and rested his hand on the curve of my waist. I felt it there, warm and reassuring as we walked out. It was only his measured pace that kept me from breaking into a run, so agitated was I to be clear of all the eyes fixed upon us.

"But Milburn, Gwen!" Mother called. "You cannot leave *now*."

"Oh, but we can," I said, not looking back and continuing on my way.

"No, no," she cried, almost trotting behind us. "I believe your father and *Cambourne* shall have an important announcement to make when they return. Although I am not altogether certain I can recover from his being in trade . . ."

I was pulling Cambourne up a flight of stairs and into the second-floor drawing room where it was private and I knew there would be a fire. "I suspect you'll manage," I told her.

"It is imperative, Gwen, that you be there for the announcement," Mother tried again.

"Good-bye, Mother," I said, as we stepped into the room and I closed the door in her face.

She knocked.

"Go away," I called. "You are neglecting your guests." And we waited in silence until we heard her retreat. I had preceded Cambourne into the room, and now I turned to face him.

"I know about the blackmail," I said.

"I figured that much," he replied. "And Bertie told me."

"Why didn't you just tell me, Cambourne? All those times I asked? I would have kept the secret about your father."

He smiled down at me. "Forgive me, Gwen. There is no good way to tell the woman you have always longed for that you were forced to marry her by her odious scheming parents, in order to save your father's hide. It doesn't seem like much of a way to start a marriage. And besides, would you have believed me, that I married you because I wanted to, if I had simply told you at the beginning?"

I hesitated. "I don't know," I admitted. "But I disagree now. I think it is an excellent way to start a marriage. But, Cambourne, what is to stop my parents now?"

"Well," he said, carefully, "I suppose it all depends on what happens next. It's perfectly possible that by the time we leave this room they will have lost their desire to reveal anything, anyway."

I nodded. "Now," I said, without preamble.

And he did not pretend to misunderstand. He smiled. "Here?"

I nodded.

"There will be hell to pay," he said. "In the eyes of the world, you will be married to your smuggling, pornography importing, brother-in-law, who married you under false pretenses, with a traitor for a father, and idiot for a mother, and a gardening, lace-tatting dandy for a brother."

"I know," I said. "You will be married to a formerly spineless, but now managing female, with a blackmailing idiot for a father, and a blackmailing gorgon for a mother."

"I know," he said.

"You have no plan to save our reputations?" I said.

"No," he said. "Not a one."

"And you are willing to take that chance?" I said. "That the names of Cambourne and Winfell might be smudged for the foreseeable future?"

"Absolutely," he said. "And you, Gwen, you are falling in with your mother's plans for you far better than she ever could have hoped. And when they eventually unravel who is who, she'll know it."

"Yes," I agreed. "I know that. Although," I said, advancing a step on him, "there is some hope that all is ruined in her eyes by the fact that you are now a disgrace to your own name."

He smiled that long, slow smile that always seemed to make something warm happen in my midriff. "This," he said, leaning back against the door, and not taking his gaze from mine, "is not how it should be."

"I don't care," I said.

He began to unwind his neckcloth, his mesmerizing eyes still not leaving mine. "Particularly the first time," he said, as he dropped the white square on the floor.

"I know that, too," I said. "I still don't care."

He laughed then, and held out his arms. "Come, Gwen," he said, and buried his face in my hair as he held me against him. "It's been a long wait."

I wanted to breathe him in, rub my face against his jacket, to run my fingers through the silky hair falling over his brow, but I was aware that we did not have much time. I was also, to be honest, extremely impatient. "Now, Harry," I said, again.

"You have to give a fellow a chance to figure out where he's headed, Gwen."

"You know where you're headed," I said.

He laughed again. "You are truly not like any virgin I've ever met," he said, still into my hair. "I shudder to imagine what you will be like when you've had a little experience." But then he pulled me against him, hard, like I wanted, and kissed me, extremely thoroughly, his tongue moving over my lips until I parted them for him.

I reached up and put my arms around his neck, pulling him nearer still. "I read the letters," I said against his mouth.

He lifted his head and looked down at me. "I love you, Gwen," he said, very quietly. "I loved you at the beginning and I have loved you more each day. I'll give up what I need to in order to have you—as long as you are willing to live in disgrace with me."

"Oh, Harry, that's absolutely the nicest thing anyone has ever said to me."

He smiled, slowly, at me. "At least, since *I married you because I was being blackmailed to do so?*"

"Yes." I looked up at him. "And I would *love* to live in disgrace with you."

The next few moments passed extremely pleasurably, and then, I said, "Did you have your stewards and your secretary set out to make it awful for Milburn?"

He nodded. "I'm afraid so. Really awful. No one could have stuck it out."

"I thought so. Is someone truly digging up St. Dunstan's? Bertie told me a hair-raising tale about some antiquarian, dead bore, Oxford cove, as he put it."

"Of course," he said, as his dimple appeared. "Fascinating project." And then he kissed me again.

"Mathilde!" I said, when he had finished.

"Mathilde," he said, slowly, lifting his head. "Milburn and I have been bringing money to Toulouse."

"Why?" I asked. "What is there? Other than women eager to show travelers their fathers' barns, that is, and what does it have to do with Mathilde?"

"Well, the why is that we've been blackmailed into doing so. A small group of Frenchmen who are more sympathetic to the Royalist cause than Boney's is what is there, and the Crown is eager to assist their mission with funds and supplies. But getting them there is not an easy piece of business, and not one that people are lining up to undertake. Before our return journeys, we pick up information from them about the planned defenses of certain cities. When Milburn did not return, this time, there was some concern at Whitehall, fanned by some of your nearest and dearest, that he had disappeared with both the money and the information."

To tell the truth, I already understood the gist of what they had been doing, and with his body pressed up against me in such a delightfully scandalous manner, I was not all that interested in hearing the particulars. In the future, absolutely, but not at this moment. There *was* that one thing, though. "Mathilde?" I reminded him.

"Her father is in Toulouse. He is one of the War Office contacts there, and she has been assisting us for some time. She was helping me try to learn—outside of Whitehall channels, since we were not sure who inside them was involved in the blackmail—what had become of Milburn, and then recently, to destroy evidence of what my father was attempting to do. Between us, we managed to divert the funds, and now if anyone tries to say anything, it's nothing but an empty accusation. Which, to be honest, I doubt even your parents would dare make against the Duke of Winfell. She is not averse to some, ah, entertainment, so I asked her to make a few, shall we say, extra demands of Milburn."

"So you were not lovers?" I asked.

"No, Gwen," he said, gently. "We were. I'm sorry. But not since I married you."

"Oh Harry, I love you," I said, throwing myself against him with gusto.

"Are you the same person who told me that gently bred females don't have baser instincts?" he asked, kissing me, and simultaneously struggling with his jacket.

"As I recall, you told me I wasn't gently bred," I reminded him.

"That explains it, then," he said.

"It must." I was trying to help him pull the tight sleeves off.

"I'm so glad," he said, as his arms came free and he pulled me closer, deepening his kiss, with a rhythm that made me writhe against him. We rocked back against the door and his hands came up; he rubbed my breast none too gently, and I could feel the nipple harden in his hand. I clutched at his shoulders and would have cried out, but he said, "Ssshh," and again covered my mouth with his.

"Someday," he said, against my lips, as his hands slid under my gown, and up my legs to my buttocks, cupping me, pulling me nearer, "we will be private. Completely unclothed. In a bed. And this will be long, and slow, and I will kiss and memorize and then kiss again, every inch of you, and we can make all the noise in the world." He gently bit my earlobe.

"I don't care about any of that," I whispered back, mirroring his motion, and sliding my hands down over his buttocks.

He groaned.

"Sssshh." This time it was me cautioning him, and he laughed.

"I must have lost my sanity," he whispered, hoarsely, "to even consider doing this here."

I was terrified he would stop. "Don't stop," I panted, and he turned us around so that my back was against the door. He leaned his forehead against mine, his hands again cupping my breasts, rubbing the nipples through the fabric of my gown. I squirmed, shamelessly, wanting more contact.

"I'm not stopping," he said. Then he took my hands by the wrists and held them over my head against the door, as he bent to kiss the hollow in my throat, his lips continuing toward my breasts.

"Let go, Harry," I managed to say. "I want to touch you, too."

"No," he said, transferring my captive wrists to one hand, while the other dipped below my bodice. I gasped and let my head go limp against the door. My eyes drifted closed. "Act like a biddable virgin for a change."

"Please," I said, in a strangled-sounding gasp as he pushed my bodice down with his free hand and his lips found the nipple, kissing it. "Now."

"So much for the biddable virgin," he said, his breath feathering hot across my skin. "Gwen, the first time, you have to be ready."

"I'm ready, Harry, I've been ready for months." Which was no lie. My body was not my own. It was entirely his, waiting for whatever he chose to do to it next. Heat was pooling like fire, my legs were trembling, my stomach was turning over with longing. "Please, I'm begging."

He pressed his body tightly against mine and rocked his hips into me. I whimpered as he pressed against all the right places. "Not standing up, Gwen," he whispered, his voice almost a groan, as he released my hands, reached behind me and turned the key in the lock. "Last chance," he said, "to flee."

"Too late," I said, as I began boldly tugging at his breeches. "I'm compromising you completely. I don't do things by half measures."

In reply he pulled me onto the floor on top of him, behind the blue sofa. "Have your way with me, then," he said as he pushed my gown up over my waist and tore his breeches down. He rolled us so that he was on top, but hesitated at the last, his breathing labored. I moved against him, desperately trying to feel more of his skin against me. His breath was as shuddering as mine, and we were as damp from his sweat as my own. I could feel the thundering of his heart, and knew he was holding back because he was afraid of hurting me. And so, I did something I would never have dreamed of until that very moment. I reached down, put my hand between us, and guided him up against me.

"Oh God!" he shuddered and then groaned, and swore under his breath, before saying, "Forgive me, Gwen." And then with one sharp thrust slid inside me. I gasped. "God almighty," he said, in a voice I hardly recognized. I could not tell if it was a curse or a prayer, and then he stilled. He looked almost as though he was in pain.

"Harry?" I whispered.

"Yes?" He closed his eyes.

"Are you all right?"

He laughed harshly. "Yes," he said. "I am. But that is what I am supposed to ask you."

"It didn't hurt!" I said, in surprise.

"Really?" he said, cautiously sliding himself out a little way.

"No," I grabbed at him and he slid back in. I gasped at the sweetness of the sensation. "It didn't hurt," I said again.

"Stop talking, Gwen," he said, pulling back and sliding in again, this time with more force.

I gasped again. "Oh! But shouldn't it have hurt?"

"Are you complaining?"

I shook my head. "Do it again, so I can make sure. I'm not supposed to like this, I've heard. But, oh! I like it."

"You're going to like it, Gwen," he said into my ear as

he did another one of those heavenly slides. "But you're going to have to wait to find out how much, because I want to talk now." He had stopped moving and was holding himself very still.

I was desperate for him to move again. "Harry, please," I panted, running my hands over the hard smooth muscles of his back and buttocks and pushing up against him. "Please."

"No, Gwen," he said. "Not until I've said a few things."

"Say them fast," I begged, unable to keep myself completely still.

"I love you," he said. "I have loved you for a long time. Likely always have, but was resigned to the fact you would marry my brother even though I believed you to be ill-suited—"

I moved slightly under him.

"Oh God!" He closed his eyes and I could see a shudder pass through him as he held himself, rigid over me. "—but when your father switched the names and pulled the blackmail card—stop that!" He pushed farther into me, pushing my hips into the floor to still them; I tilted myself up toward him and his voice broke. "—I saw my opportunity and took it, never mind the consequences."

"Harry," I panted. "Not to be rude, but you can tell me this after."

He pulled back just the slightest bit, and then slowly slid back. "Am I boring you?"

"Ah," I gasped. "No. Are you done talking?"

He laughed, a strangled sort of sound, as he slid out and then in again. "I haven't decided," he said. I had no shame, though. I moaned and moved beneath him, having figured out that my moving must feel as good to him as his moving did to me. I ran my hands over the muscles of his back and shoulders and . . . down, and pushed myself up against him.

"I think," he said, "that I've forgot what I was going to say."

Which was what I'd been waiting to hear. I arched against him, in an effort to keep as much of our bodies as close as possible. He lowered himself over me with a groan that sounded as though it had been wrenched from him, and plunged wildly into me. The sweet pleasure that rose, the increasing sense of tension was stronger than before. His hair brushed my face as he murmured into my ear. His lips brushed mine as he buried himself again and again, and now with every stroke, a little cry broke from my lips. I was helpless to stop my body rising to meet him.

He moved differently then, and honestly, I no longer cared about anything except the tension that rose unbearably until my body convulsed around him. I dug my nails into his shoulders to pull him closer, whimpering, and mindless with the sensation.

Fortunately—on account of the forty-some people belowstairs—he caught my scream with his lips as he plunged again. I could tell by the noise he made that he was finding the same release. I rose to meet him, hoping to give him even half the pleasure he had given me, and think I may have succeeded, by the way he collapsed over me, his body damp with sweat, and his breathing harsh. After a few moments, in which neither of us spoke, he rolled onto his side, pulling me against him.

"Jesus!" he said, when he finally spoke.

I tucked my head under his chin. He kissed my hair, and then collapsed back against the carpet. And there, on my mother's drawing room floor, with my gown rucked up around my waist, and my reputation no doubt in tatters, I knew I had never been happier.

"I have never experienced anything like that. Ever," he said, holding me close against him.

"It's me," I told him, with, I admit, a flash of pride. "I am clearly some kind of vixen."

"I don't doubt it," he murmured. "I hope you don't end up killing me."

I inhaled against his chest. "I hope not, too," I said, and then sighed, thinking that I would have been content to remain here, with him, tangled in our half-discarded clothing, sated and sleepy, for quite some time. Possibly forever. "Harry?" I said.

"Yes, my love?" he asked, sounding as sleepy as I was beginning to feel.

"Can we redecorate your house?"

He laughed. "Yes."

I rubbed my face against his shoulder. "I suppose we have to go back down."

"Already? Is it too much to ask that I be allowed a moment of peace after deflowering my wife?"

"Consider yourself fortunate that I did not require hours of gentling and sweet-talking."

"I should say not," he said. "I've never before been attacked so voraciously by a female!"

"I had to compromise you quickly, before you had time to think of all the reasons not to let me."

"I'd already thought of them, Gwen. I let you anyway," he murmured into my hair.

"God, I love you," I said, and he pulled me more tightly against him.

"Mmm," he said. "How much?"

"Are you really going to make me tell you the specifics?" I asked, lifting my head and looking down at him.

"Absolutely," he said.

"More than I'd ever imagined possible," I told him, lowering my head to his chest and listening to the rhythm of his heart. "More than life itself, and then even more than that. But, Harry?" I said, suddenly nervous, and he lifted his head to give me a questioning look before once again subsiding against the carpet. "I have woefully few accomplishments, I must warn you. Nothing out of the ordinary wifely way."

He kissed me lingeringly. "You bring me heaven, Gwen."

"But is that enough for you?" I said. "No more mistresses, Harry, not a one!"

"There is no question of that," he said, and kissed me in a way that made me believe him. "It will be pathetic, slavish devotion from here on. And you will find more accomplishments down the years. I have no doubt you'll be writing my speeches before long."

"I have changed quite a bit," I said. "If you'll pardon my lack of modesty. I think it started when someone said to me that we all find ourselves at some point in an unfortunate situation not of our own making and that it was up to me to decide how I wanted to go on from there. And actually, now that you mention it, writing your speeches doesn't sound bad."

He smiled. "You should never have listened to me. Goodness knows I could not have made worse decisions about *my* unfortunate situation not of my own making. And you're not writing my speeches. Actually," he said, after a moment. "I don't think it was so much a matter of changing as it was of letting yourself discover that there is more to you than you knew. This frighteningly managing part of you has always been there. It's just been buried under many layers of dutiful daughter."

"Are you frightened of me, Cambourne? I vow, you are falling in my estimation already!"

He kissed me. "Give me another two minutes and I think I can raise myself in your esteem. And also," he said, kissing me again, more deeply, "prove to you that I'm not frightened of you in the least."

"I suppose it's only fair to give you the opportunity to try," I allowed. "But Cambourne? What are we going to do? What about my parents?"

"Well," he said. "We could scare the life out of them by going down—it will be obvious what we've been up to—and announcing that we have decided that we do not suit, after all."

"Very tempting," I said. "But do you have another suggestion?"

"Possibly," he said, and then he was silent for a moment. "James and I have cooked up a plan that should save us from the worst of the scandal."

I raised a brow at him.

"He has managed to get Bertie some type of commendation for extraordinary valor. He is of the impression that all we need do is spread the word that we had switched places in order to protect the integrity of the secret missions. Omit the blackmail and Bertie will be a hero. People will still talk, of course, but not much or for long."

"Let them," I said.

"I simply can't believe," he said, after a moment, "that

not only did I risk my own life over saving the family name, but sent Bertie to do the same. Small wonder he hates me."

"He doesn't hate you, Cambourne," I said. "And, do you know, I really do think he will be happy with Thérèse. You don't think that my parents put her up to waylaying Bertie, though, do you?" I asked. "It seems awfully fortuitous that he went missing and you just *had* to step in."

"I think," he said slowly, as if he were thinking about it, "that if they did, she'll never tell. I've wondered, too, but, no, overall I'm inclined to think that it was just fortuitous. Although I don't really care." He kissed me.

"Me either," I sighed. "But, Harry?"

"My lovemaking does not seem to have emptied your mind, Gwen," he said. "Do I need to do it again?"

"Yes," I said. "You do."

"I will," he promised. "But first tell me what you are wondering about."

"If it were my parents blackmailing you, why did they bother calling you away from the wedding breakfast? They already knew that you weren't really Milburn."

"Only to further confuse things, I'd guess. Of course it was a great joke on me. There I was, pretending to be Milburn and marrying you so that whoever was looking for him would think he was here in London, publicly getting married, and the only people who cared were your parents, and they knew the truth."

I sighed with contentment and rested my cheek on his chest again. "Do you suppose they will keep quiet now that they have what they want?"

"I would imagine," he replied, after a moment. "Now

that you're part of the family, it won't reflect well on them if my father is known to be a traitor."

"What would you say if I told you that I am in possession of some rather . . . delicate information that I suspect my parents would just as soon keep to themselves?" I asked him.

"God." He laughed. "I think I'd say that the apple falls frighteningly close to the tree."

"I'm serious, Harry," I said. "Is the Earl of Cambourne above engaging in some blackmail of his own?"

"Absolutely not," he replied, against my lips, "if it gets him what he wants. What did you have in mind, my love?"

"Well, I've been thinking," I said. "Do you not think that my mother and Violetta have a rather *close* relationship? Some might even say, unnaturally close."

He was silent for a moment, and then said, "Do you know, love, I think that's something I just as soon *not* think about again."

"I agree completely," I said. "But in case you were inclined to threaten to, shall we say, put about something to that effect, I do know where some compromising and highly scandalous paintings are to be found."

"Gwen, my love?" he murmured, sleepily.

"Yes, Harry?"

"Is either your mother or Violetta partially or entirely unclothed in these pictures?"

"Yes, actually—"

"Say no more," he said. "Gwen, I do not ever want to see those paintings. Ever."

"All right," I agreed. "Why not go back to telling me how much you adore me?"

"Because," he said, "mere words seem inadequate to convey how I feel about you. The very fact that I still am in a state of abject devotion to you *after* what you have just told me should be proof enough of that."

"You could show me," I suggested, moving against him. "I believe your two minutes are past up."

And he did. Until my toes curled.